BOOMERWORLD

By

Robert Q. Apple III

This is a work of fiction. Names, characters, businesses, places, events and incidents are either the products of the author's imagination or used in a fictitious manner. Any resemblance to actual persons, living or dead, or actual events is purely coincidental.

Many of the facts, figures, analogies, observations, and descriptions contained herein were culled from extensive Internet research about the Baby Boom, using many different search engines, blogs, unsourced and unsolicited emails, and anonymous pdfs and PowerPoint compilations.

Kafka Press, First Edition, September 2021

ISBN: 978-1-7378358-0-6

Email: RobertApple1952@yahoo.com

Cover Art: Logo (TypeStyler). Photo compilation (iStock): Wind Blown Face © George Peters and Vibrant Tie Dye © Strathroy. Chapter graphics (iStock).

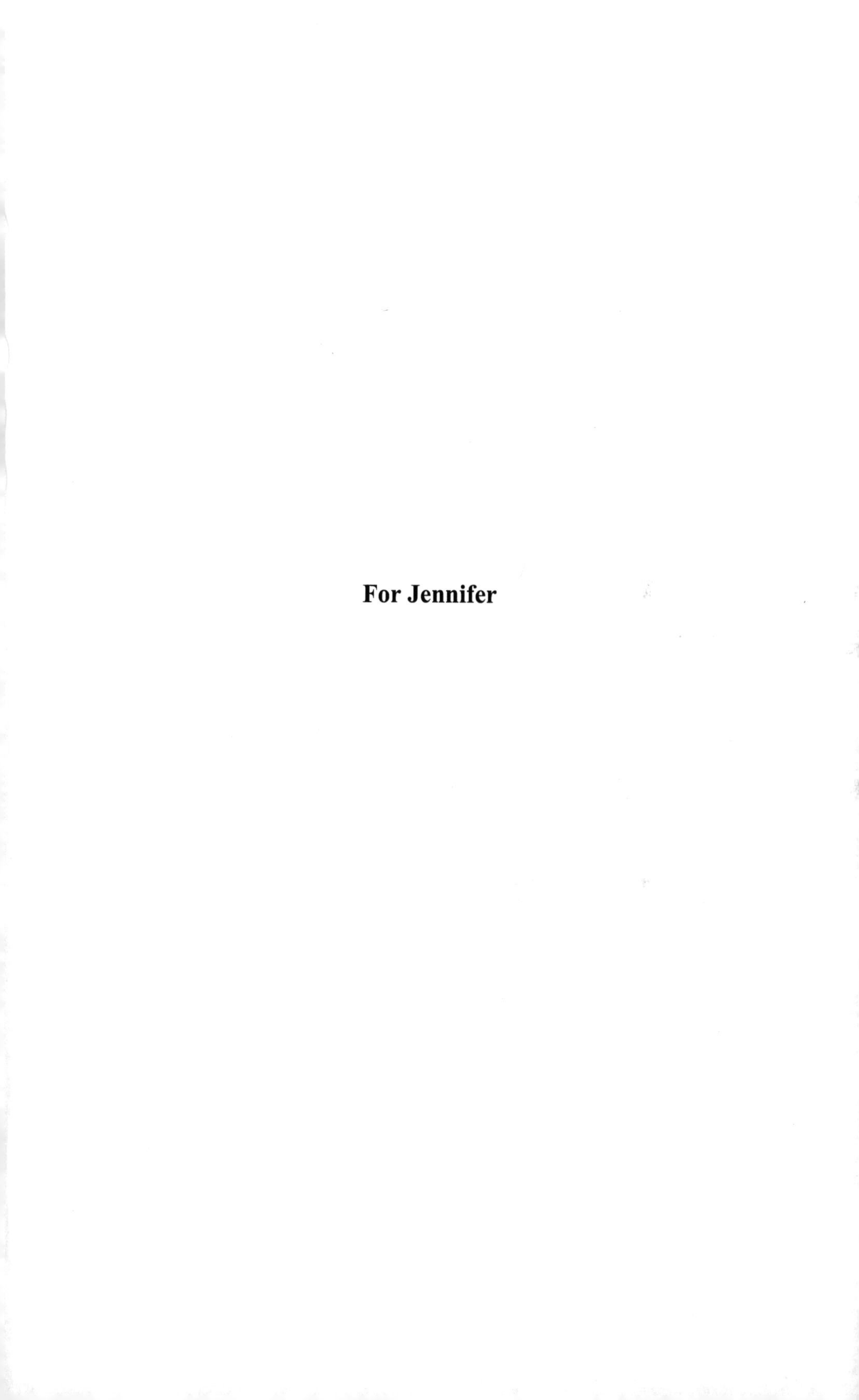

For Jennifer

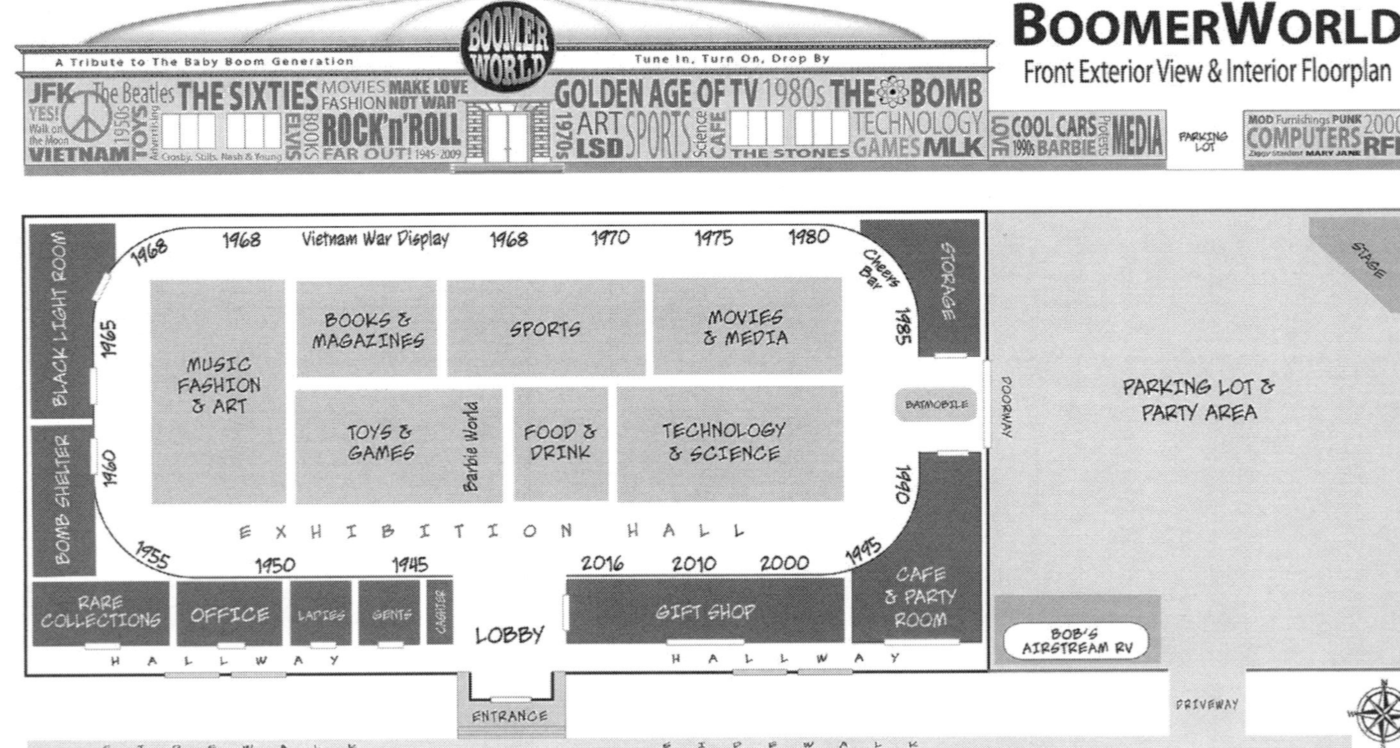
BoomerWorld
Front Exterior View & Interior Floorplan
A Tribute to The Baby Boom Generation
BOOMER WORLD
Tune In, Turn On, Drop By
JFK The Beatles THE SIXTIES MOVIES MAKE LOVE FASHION NOT WAR ROCK'n'ROLL FAR OUT! 1945-2009
YES! Walk on the Moon VIETNAM 1950s TOYS Advertising Crosby, Stills, Nash & Young ELVIS BOOKS
GOLDEN AGE OF TV 1980s THE BOMB 1970s ART LSD SPORTS Science CAFE THE STONES TECHNOLOGY GAMES MLK
LOVE COOL CARS 1990s BARBIE Protests MEDIA
PARKING LOT
MOD Furnishings PUNK 2000s COMPUTERS Ziggy Stardust MARY JANE RFK
BLACK LIGHT ROOM
BOMB SHELTER
1968
1968
Vietnam War Display
1968
1970
1975
1980
Cheers Bar
1985
STORAGE
1965
1960
MUSIC FASHION & ART
BOOKS & MAGAZINES
SPORTS
MOVIES & MEDIA
TOYS & GAMES
Barbie World
FOOD & DRINK
TECHNOLOGY & SCIENCE
BATMOBILE
DOORWAY
1990
EXHIBITION HALL
1955
1950
1945
2016
2010
2000
1995
RARE COLLECTIONS
OFFICE
LADIES
GENTS
CASHIER
LOBBY
GIFT SHOP
CAFE & PARTY ROOM
HALLWAY
HALLWAY
ENTRANCE
SIDEWALK
SIDEWALK
STAGE
PARKING LOT & PARTY AREA
BOB'S AIRSTREAM RV
DRIVEWAY

Author's Note

WARNING: This is not one of those classy 'book club' novels filled with dazzling lyrical descriptions and hypersensitive characters that will move you to spontaneous weeping and literary orgasm.

Nor is it anything like the two excellent retrospectives on the Baby Boom Generation: *The Life and Times of the Thunderbolt Kid* by Bill Bryson and *The Baby Boom* by P.J. O'Rourke. Or even that brilliant, but "contemptible document"[1]: *The Boomer Bible* by R.F. Laird.

This book is more like that candy bar floating in the pool at Bushwood Country Club in *Caddyshack*—a little nutty but something to chew on.

But enough with the lame analogies. Let's rock!

---

[1] *Eliot Naughton, (Cambridge, MA), First Preface, The Boomer Bible (New York, Workman Publishing 1991), vii*

2019

1

Monday, October 26, 2019
11:15 a.m.

"(I Can't Get No) Satisfaction"

I'm not going to sugarcoat it… I'm going batshit crazy…

No, I'm not some whack job wearing a tin foil hat with a matching tie and pocket square. And I'm not suffering from dementia with a drool cup strapped to my chin and a name tag pinned to my shirt. I'm just a typical middle-aged American schmuck, knockin' on Heaven's Door, and wondering what the hell happened to my life, my country and this mad, mad, mad, mad world.

It seems like just yesterday I was starting my life journey down the yellow brick road—just a boy on a bike with his head in the clouds. Young, confident and full of hope, I glided along on my shiny blue Schwinn Super Deluxe Sting-Ray. Colorful plastic streamers trailed from my handlebars. Playing cards, held in place by clothes pins, flapped rhythmically against the steel spokes. I felt invincible, ready to grab the proverbial brass ring and leave my indelible mark on the universe.

Yes, I was dreamin' big. And why not? Back in 1952, I was lucky to be born in the richest country on earth at the perfect moment in time.[2] I arrived on the scene in the early years of the Baby Boom, which blossomed in the aftermath of World War II when America was an unstoppable economic force, destined to be the world's super power.

I grew up in a brand new, four-bedroom, two-bath, ranch-style tract home in a safe, predominantly "white-bread" middle-class suburban community in sunny California with a caring family, a dog and cat, and two hamsters named Chester and Mildred.

Yeah, I had it all. But now, over sixty years later, things have changed.

Big time.

Somehow that quaint golden lane has morphed into the L.A. freeway at rush hour and most, if not all, of my childhood dreams lie rusting on the side of the road. Like that vile "knockout game" played by heartless young punks on the streets of our big cities, I feel like I've been cosmically sucker-punched on every existential level.

Physically, I'm slowly falling apart, but I keep chugging along. I imagine myself as a classic cherry-red 1965 Mustang convertible with black leather bucket seats and a stick shift knob made of polished oak. But if truth be told, I'm more like an abandoned AMC Gremlin with a missing back bumper, duck-taped windows and a million miles on the odometer.

It's been a bumpy ride.

I've already survived a bout with "The Big C," knee and hip replacements, carpal tunnel and cataract operations, and penile reduction surgery. Okay, maybe I lied about that last one, but at least I'm still on the road, leaking fluids and lurching along on bald tires toward a dark, dead end.

Emotionally, I'm a borderline basket case. Deeply depressed after losing the love of my life twenty years ago, I've battled back to being

---

[2] *It is rumored that three wisemen tried to bring me gifts on the night of my birth, but got lost in the Hollywood Hills.*

functional and somewhat happy. But there are still those moments, perhaps prompted by a song, a photo or a comment, when I'm suddenly flooded with memories of our time together—the good and the bad. Inevitably, those recollections degenerate into a deep depression, and I find myself heartbroken and alone, staring into the abyss.

And to put it bluntly: the view sucks.

Spiritually, my search for enlightenment and inner peace has been a total bust. I've tried many religions: Christianity, Judaism, Buddhism, Transcendental Meditation, Jediism, Pastafarianism (better known as Church of the Flying Spaghetti Monster, which is good for the soul but bad for the waistline), and Frisbeetarianism (ask the late, great George Carlin). I even joined Heaven's Gate, the American UFO cult that all committed suicide in 1997. Luckily, I had the wrong pair of Nike tennis shoes and was not allowed to board the spaceship trailing the Hale-Bopp comet with the rest of the crew.

I've also walked on hot coals, eaten peyote buttons and spent a few days in an Indian sweat lodge; that is, until I got seriously dehydrated and the paramedics had to be called when I saw Carlos Castaneda soaring above me on a broomstick.

At this point, my last viable option for spiritual awakening is celebrity worship—conveniently available on countless cable TV networks and grocery newstands everywhere. Now, whenever I feel the need to fill the metaphysical void in my soul, I just grab one of those trashy lifestyle magazines and contemplate Kim Kardashian's kaboose.

Problem solved. Nirvana achieved.

And career-wise, well, it's been worse than finding a dump in the C-Suite. After graduating from college, I spent the next twenty years in advertising, mastering the fine art of bullshit. Since 2004, I've run BoomerWorld—a quirky museum in Venice Beach, California, dedicated to the Baby Boom. Alas, instead of becoming a rich and powerful titan of the business world, I've turned into a washed-up Willie Loman, clutching a set of steak knives and muttering to myself. After almost fifty years of busting my ass, I should be enjoying a comfortable retirement. You know, play a little bocce ball, sip pinot grigio in the shade and take some long naps. Instead, I got a prostrate exam by the Fickle Finger of Fate and the prognosis is bleak. You see, I have to close the doors of BoomerWorld in seven days and, if the two big weekend events aren't a total financial success, I'm facing bankruptcy. But more about that later…

By now you're probably asking yourself: Who is this loser and why won't he just shut up? Well, my name is Bob Apple. People around town affectionately refer to me as "Boomer Bob" or just "That Weird Old Fart."

At least I'm still on somebody's radar.

As you can probably tell, I'm a rather verbose, opinionated, cranky old geezer who's schlepping more emotional baggage than Woody Allen's doorman. I'm just trying to make it to the finish line of life with a modicum of grace and dignity, but even that seems to be getting harder everyday.

If you need some kind of visual for what I look like, just think of the gifted actor Paul Giamatti—but without the rugged good looks.

The fact is, I'm remarkably unremarkable.

Befitting my role as the eccentric owner of BoomerWorld, one of the most kitschy attractions in L.A., I dress the part. Basically, I wear two "costumes," as I prefer to call them. On warm days, I usually opt for the laid-back beach look. You know, a tie-dye or Madras shirt, cargo shorts, Crocs and Ray Bans—á la The Dude. But since it's late October and there's a chill in the air, today I'm decked out in another outfit that would make Wavy Gravy envious: casual dress shirt with rolled up sleeves, crazy psychedelic tie, baggy corduroy trousers with red suspenders, and topsiders with no socks. Cheap drugstore reading glasses dangle around my neck on a colorful macramé cord. I'm also sporting a two-day-old beard, a thinning wad of gray-tinged brown hair, and pale blue, bloodshot eyes.

With respect to my demented diatribes and spontaneous rants, let's get something straight right from the get-go: I'm a card-carrying member of that exclusive club called the Baby Boom Generation.

Actually, it's really not all that exclusive since there are seventy-five million of us.

Regardless, we still think we're special, can say and do whatever we want, and oh yeah, we're entitled to a cushy lifestyle until we're six feet under. Any half-baked sociologist will tell you Boomers are the most pampered, self-obsessed collection of serial whiners the world has ever known. Hence, we bitch and moan constantly.[3]

Bottom line: Thanks to a pure accident of birth and timing, my generation was anointed by the Gods to lead mankind out of the ashes of World War II and into a new golden age of enlightenment, progress and peace.

And how's that working out for ya?

"Reelin' In The Years"

If you've never heard of BoomerWorld, you're not alone. It certainly doesn't have the fame and panache of other big Southern California attractions like Disneyland and Universal Studios Hollywood. Nor is it quite as obscure as the Bunny Museum, East Jesus, the Museum of Selfies, or the L.A. Coroner's Gift Shop.

Situated in the heart of Venice Beach, one block off the Ocean Front Walk between Speedway and Pacific avenues, BoomerWorld occupies a large one-story, art deco building which was originally a roller rink built in the 1950s. Over the years, it also housed a furniture store, weekend flea market and a series of other failed retail enterprises. It was a half-empty warehouse when I walked through the front door

---

[3] *Other sociologists dispute this slanderous allegation, claiming Millenials and Centennials are far more annoying, entitled and self-absorbed than Boomers. Just saying...*

back in 2002. The moment I saw the huge oval hardwood floor and 20-foot walls I knew it was the ideal space to set up the museum.

Venice Beach is famous for its murals. I wanted the BoomerWorld exterior graphics to be eye-catching so I covered the front of the main building and adjacent parking lot wall with a series of compelling graphics and teaser words about what awaits within. In the early years, passersby stopped and gawked at the vibrant facade; however, as my funds have dwindled for updates and repairs, the original vibrant graphics are now faded and lackluster.

As you enter the facility through tall double glass doors, there are hallways on either side of the large lobby leading to the café/private party room, office, bathrooms and gift shop. Unfortunately, the interior is looking a little shabby too. The walls could use some fresh paint. The carpets are thread-bare and frayed in places. In the early years, the hardwood floors were routinely buffed into a high sheen on a weekly basis. Now, they are dull and dusty since the cleaning crew only comes once a month.

After passing through the foyer and by the ticket counter, you enter the heart of BoomerWorld—a cavernous exhibition hall packed with historical graphics and electronic displays, artifacts and memorabilia, classic products and collectibles. Along with the dramatic lighting and surround sound system, it blows every Boomer's mind.

The first thing you see at the entrance is a large sepia-toned photograph from 1949 featuring a gigantic baby nursery in a New York City hospital with row after row of newborn infants in bassinettes, as proud fathers peer at them through glass windows. The photo caption below it reads:

From 1946 to 1964, more than seventy-five million Americans were born during an era of unparalleled post-war prosperity. They are universally known as the "Baby Boom Generation."

With the explosion of technology as well as traumatic economic, social and political changes, "Boomers" have lived through the most intense and dynamic cultural period in world history.

This is their story...

The most spectacular visual in the pavilion is the massive, floor-to-ceiling historical photo collage, which wraps clockwise around the entire inside periphery of the building. It sets the mood and theme for the entire museum. Featuring color and black-and-white photographs, interspersed with captions, quotes, dates and headlines, it is a twenty-foot tall chronological timeline from August 1945 through January 2016—representing the seventy-plus-year life span of the Boomer generation.

The first photo, to the immediate left of the entry, shows the mushroom cloud over Hiroshima, signifying the end of World War II. It is followed by hundreds of other images and historical notations until it reaches the last photo, just to the right of the entrance, featuring Donald Trump being sworn in as the 45th President of the United States.

D'oh!

To give BoomerWorld a more interactive "time machine" quality, there are furnishings corresponding to the wall's graphic timeline. For instance, along the 1950s section, you can plop down in a Barcalounger "Floating Comfort" Chair and watch *The Honeymooners* on a vintage B&W television. Or, in the 1970s area, you can lay on a waterbed (aka "A Pleasure Pit") and stare at a *Jaws* or Farrah Fawcett poster.

Or not.

Scattered throughout the exhibition, there are hundreds of

freestanding graphics and hanging posters to remind and educate visitors about the events, people and places that influenced the generation. Plus, you'll find elaborate displays of Boomer toys, games, fashions, technology, advertising, consumer products, sports, books, magazines, music items, clothing, food and drinks, and more. From Tinker Toys, Lincoln Logs and Erector Sets to Groucho glasses, Pet Rocks, Brownie cameras and avocado-colored kitchen appliances, you'll marvel at the quantity and quality of thousands of Boomer items.

To enhance the overall experience, I installed a sound track consisting of loops of classic rock and pop songs interspersed with famous audio outtakes from historic Boomer moments: Those announcements to warn students of a pending nuclear missile attack and to "duck and cover" under their desks during shelter drills. Neil Armstrong saying "That's one small step for man, one giant leap for mankind." The classic Woodstock announcement about "the bad brown acid floating around," etc.

The combination of the visuals, memorabilia and soundtrack creates an impressive spectacle—but sadly, after fifteen years, I'm down to my final days running this operation. Serious financial problems, the termination of my building lease and a severe case of "Boomer Burnout" are forcing me to throw in the towel.

"Purple Haze"

Maybe that's why I'm comfortably numb right now, sitting in the infamous Black Light Room in the back corner of BoomerWorld—a place of legendary debauchery that would make Billy Idol blush.

Just off the main exhibition floor behind the 1960s section, you enter a dark, surreal room through a doorway of hanging beads. The space is about fifteen feet wide and fifty feet long, with tracks of UV flourescent tube lights across the ceiling. The walls are covered with classic black light posters, adorned with vibrant iridescent inks and 3-D flocking, which were all the rage during the psychedelic fashion scene of the late 60s. The glowing images include everything from rock stars and exotic animals to eye-popping geometric patterns and fantasy art that have a mind-bending, surrealistic pillow kind of look and vibe.

Bean bag chairs in primary colors and large cushions are piled along the walls atop a thick shag carpet—beckoning you to plop down and space out amid the visual splender. A rare, eight-foot tall lava lamp swirls in a far corner beside a glass case featuring an impressive collection of head shop paraphernalia: Zig Zag papers, ornate roach clips and water pipes, including one of the prized keepsakes from my college days: a two-foot tall bamboo bong that Ken Kesey actually used in the summer of 1973.

The Black Light Room has its own Marantz stereo system with a working turntable. Beside it is a bin filled with vinyl albums from the psychedelic-era that guests can play themselves. In fact, I'm currently listening to a scratchy, deep cut from *Electric Ladyland* by The Jimi Hendrix Experience. Cued up next: *The Wall* by Pink Floyd.

To add to the ambience of this phantasmagorical setting, smoke wafts up from a joint dangling from my fingers. I haven't been stoned in years, but today I'm making an exception.

Last week, I rented out BoomerWorld to a famous LA rock star so he could host a private party for his Boomer parents who were celebrating their 50th wedding anniversary. After his parents and their geriatric friends shuffled out of the building, the rocker and his entourage retired to the Black Light Room for some serious R&R. The next day when I was cleaning, I found a small baggie of medicinal marijuana, which must have fallen out of someone's pocket. It was ominously labeled: Zimbabwean Snap-neck. I patiently waited for an anxious call from the weed's owner, who surely needed it to treat a paper cut, hang nail or "blisters on me fingers." But the call never came. I thought it was only fitting that the final week of BoomerWorld should be christened with a celebratory toke.

Holy smoke! That African bud really packs a punch! No wonder over the last 400,000 years, Zimbabwe's greatest achievement was a few primitive cave drawings—and, of course, killer kush.

Feeling like an extra in *Reefer Madness*, I sat there for more than two hours, completely unable to function. My IQ had dropped at least ten points and I had an insatiable craving for Cheetos.

Man, how things have changed when it comes to weed… The average lid (ounce) of grass consumed by Boomers in the '60s and '70s looked like a deconstructed bird's nest, consisting mostly of twigs, seeds, bugs, dry "shake" and God only knows what else. The Mexicans down in Oaxaca were laughing their asses off knowing we would gladly shell out $20 for an ounce of that crap. After smoking half a bag, you felt "thick as a brick" and had to nurse a dull headache for hours. If you were lucky enough to actually get your hands on any Acapulco Gold, Maui Wowie or Thai Stick, you were everyone's best friend.

Now, the genetically engineered marijuana is so potent it should be classifed as a psychedelic. It's THC on steroids. We used to smoke whatever we could get our hands on, but now you can even pick the kind of high you're looking for. Apparently, there are two main pure or hybrid varieties of cannabis: Sativa, which delivers a cerebral, energetic high; and Indica, for a sedated body buzz. With names like Green Crack, Purple Urkle, Trainwreck, Death Star, Strawberry Cough, Donkey Dick, Love Lettuce, Purple Monkey Balls, Cat Piss, Super Silver Sour Diesel Haze, Crouching Tiger Hidden Alien and, for us geezers, Cataract Kush—you better choose carefully because either your head will spontaneously combust or you'll never get off the couch.

Even as little kids, Boomers were already experimenting with how to get high. Before drugs, we would go out on the grass *(the kind you mow not smoke)* and spin around about a dozen times, get dizzy and fall down. It produced almost the same basic effect as a hit of Alaskan Thunderfuck—and it was free! With no paranoia!

Luckily, I have my best friend and constant companion, Walter, laying beside me on the rug. With black, brown and white fur and a friendly personality, the ten-year-old basset hound keeps me grounded and relatively sane. Although he generally keeps a low profile *(pun intended),* he's prone to howl for no reason at all. Sometimes I howl along with him. Walter spends most of his time snoring, which he does laying on his back with all four feet pointing straight up in the air. Truly a sight to behold!

Anyway, where was I?

Oh yeah. Well, after another hour of mild hallucinations enhanced by some tasty vinyl tracks from Cream and Vanilla Fudge, I finally emerged from the Black Light Room. Standing in the northwest corner of BoomerWorld's main exhibition area, it took me a few seconds to adjust to my surroundings, like when you leave a movie matinee and walk outside into the jarring light of day. Since the museum was closed, the overhead lighting, backlit displays and TVs were all turned off. The only ambient light came from the opaque glass ceiling dome—so the transition back into the real world wasn't too harsh.

I was moving slowly, but there was work to do. Vaguely remembering I had two meetings scheduled in the afternoon, I pulled out the small spiral notebook I kept in my back pants pocket to look at my notes:

3:30 PM – Courtney Collins re: receptionist job
4:30 PM – Elizabeth Frost from the bank

Unlike virtually everyone else on Earth, I don't have a smartphone. I'm a technotard, preferring to use a notepad and pen to keep track of my daily calendar, shopping lists and reminders about all the things I should do, but probably won't.

I own an ancient flip phone that only has two functions: making and receiving calls. That's why they call it a "phone." I like the simplicity of it and always feel like Captain Kirk when I snap it open and say, "Uhura. Put on something sexy and meet me in my quarters."

Let's get real: smartphones are dumb. After all, why would anyone want to put all their personal information, financial records, schedules, cherished photos and videos on a small electronic device that can easily fall out of your pocket and into the toilet at any time? And do you really need instantaneous texting, email and an Internet connection to be successful and feel relevant? What's so damn urgent anyway? Afraid you're going to miss the next horrific beheading LIVE from some Middle Eastern shit-hole, details about the latest marital spat between Jay-Z and Beyonce, or some cute little puppie eating peanut butter? Face it, most of cyberspace is a wasteland. There are millions of websites for shopaholics, gamblers, news junkies, lonely hearts and sexual perverts. Billions of blogs written by morons and political hacks. Trillions of gigabytes of useless and often inaccurate information.

"I fear the day that technology will surpass our human interaction.
The world will have a generation of idiots."
– Albert Einstein

I've always thought that life is a precious, fleeting gift—not something to be squandered away by playing mindless cyber games involving worms or angry birds. Instead of giving yourself a daily digital lobotomy, perhaps you should unplug your Bluetooth and exit the information highway to smell the roses and contemplate the beauty of life. Don't worry. All that cyber crap will still be there when you return. Plus, with all the buttons, screens, files and a million apps, smartphones are just too damn complicated for my feeble mind. The only thing I like about them are the maps, since I'm always getting lost. But I'm not gonna trust some virtual, disembodied chick named Siri for directions. I have no idea where that name came from, but I do know Siris was the Mesopotamian patron demon of beer, which may explain a few things.

And what's all this chatter about "the cloud?" Sounds ominous… Clouds are usually dark and foreboding—unless of course, you're laying on a grassy hillside, staring up into the bright blue sky and you happen to see a white, fluffy cloud in the shape of a poodle or Buick. Remember, clouds rain on you; if your smartphone gets wet you won't be able to download your latest Facebook message and your pathetic social life will suddenly end and you'll become a lost soul wandering the Earth in search of a new, waterproof smartphone with an extra large screen and...

Man, I'm not shittin' you. That Zimbabwean weed is sick!

2:30 p.m.

"I Heard It Through The Grapevine"

Since my next appointment was an hour away, I took a stroll around the BoomerWorld exhibition floor. I was feelin' down, knowing the doors would be permanently closed in less than a week. As I passed by the toy section, I noticed one of my precious Rock'em Sock'em Robots had fallen off the top of a display case and had a broken leg. I scooped it up and headed to the front office to repair it.

Passing through the lobby, I unlocked the front doors so my afternoon guests could come in. I also made sure the poster on the front sidewalk was still prominently displayed in hopes of selling more tickets for the final two days and the big events on the coming weekend:

FINAL TWO DAYS!

Saturday, October 31 & Sunday, November 1

Museum Open

10:00am-5:00pm

Adults: $15 • Seniors: $12 • Ages 12-18: $8 • Kids Free

Halloween Costume Party

Wear your favorite Boomer costume!

Saturday, 7:00pm-11:00pm
Appetizers, Full Bars, DJ and Dancing
Prizes for Best Costume & Hula Hoop Contest
$40 per person (400 tickets only)

Dinner & Live Concert

Featuring "The Hey Judes" - a Beatles Tribute Band

Sunday, 7:00-11:00pm
Auction, Wine Tastings, Full Bars,
Buffet Dinner and Dancing
$75 per person (350 tickets only)

For weeks, I've promoted the last days of BoomerWorld. This will be the first time I've allowed such large public parties here, always fearful of possible damage and theft. Now, I couldn't care less.

Since I can't afford to place any expensive print ads or run a TV campaign to support the events, I'm relying on guerrilla marketing to stretch every dollar. I paid some hotshot computer geek to set-up an online ticket page and handle all the social media. I also hired a service to post flyers all over Venice Beach, Santa Monica and Marina Del Rey, and forced one of my employees to walk around town with a sandwich board to promote the final weekend. So far, ticket sales are lagging. However, in the next few days, I'm counting on generating some big exposure via scheduled interviews with the local newspaper and a classic rock radio station.

In the meantime, I need to hire a new receptionist for the final weekend. I placed a small classified ad online, hoping to get a mature, dependable individual who required virtually no supervision. Instead, I got a high school kid named Courtney. She was the only one to respond to the ad and, unbeknownst to her, I was going to hire her no matter what. She promised to come by right after classes ended.

3:30 p.m.

"Brown Eyed Girl"

I was applying some glue to the fractured leg of my Rock'em Sock'em Robot when I saw a new Maserati convertible pull into the green parking zone near the front door.

Courtney, a pretty, perky high school senior with a blonde ponytail and tight designer jeans, bounded out of the car with a Starbucks coffee and ran up the front steps. I walked out into the lobby to greet her.

"I'm Courtney," she chirped with way too much enthusiasm.

"Of course you are! And I'm Bob Apple at your service," I said, using my best Sean Connery voice and bowing with great fanfare.

Courtney flushed at my dramatic welcome.

By the way, that's a shtick I've been using for years. Early on, I realized I was going to have to be a flamboyant, outlandish pitchman for BoomerWorld. As part of my on-going act, I always speak in a loud, commanding voice like a vaudeville barker. Stealing Professor Irwin Corey's act, I pontificate to anyone within earshot about the impressive history of the Baby Boom, spewing little known factoids and historical tidbits from its rich cultural archives, hoping to drum up more ticket sales and buzz.

Moments later, Courtney was sitting across from me in my office.

"It's an honor to meet you, my dear," I said and handed her my circular, tie-dye colored business card with a peace sign on one side and my contact info on the other. She studied it for a moment and then placed it under her coffee cup, thinking it was a coaster.

Hmmm...

She leaned forward to study my colorful tie. "That's a cool tie, Mr. Apple."

"Thank you.

"It's an original Jerry Garcia design."

"Jerry who?"

"You know, The Grateful Dead."

A puzzled look crossed Courtney's face. "Grateful Dead? I don't get it."

I shrugged. "I guess you had to have been there."

"Where?"

"Never mind."

Next, she spotted my wristwatch. "Wow! Is that an original Mickey Mouse watch?"

"Yes," I replied, extending my arm to give her a closer look. "It was a gift from my first true love, Annette Funicello."

"Annette who?"

I wanted to launch into a long lecture about the original cast members of The Mickey Mouse Club, but I'd just be wasting my breath.

"Did you bring a resume?"

"Sure! I've got it right here."

Courtney dug around in her enormous purse. Finally, she pulled out a single folded page, partially smeared with lipstick, and handed it to me.

Her resume was thinner than Twiggy.

"I see you have a great deal of babysitting experience," I said, trying to be positive.

"I love kids—just as long as they're not mine," she giggled.

"I also see that you volunteer at the Food Bank. That's impressive!"

"Yes, after I crashed my father's Mercedes, I told him I wanted to 'give back' to poor people. You know, to make things right. But I only did it once, because it was sooooo depressing."

Stroking the stubble on my chin, I asked, "Tell me, Courtney. Why do you want to work here?"

"Well, after I lost my third iPhone, my father said I'd have to pay for the next one." She shrugged and let out a long sigh. "Can you believe it? He's so mean!"

"What does your father do for a living?"

"Oh, he's a producer over at Sony Pictures."

"And your mother?"

"A few months ago, she ran off to St. Barts with Rafael, her pool boy from Costa Rica. We Skype all the time. Do you know what she misses the most?"

"You!" I said with a reassuring smile.

She raised her coffee cup. "No, silly. Starbucks!"

I put her resume down on my desk, solemnly folded my hands together and looked into her big brown, vacuous eyes. "Although you don't have any substantial experience in the business world, I see great potential in you, Courtney."

She smiled skeptically. "You do?"

Not really, but I'm desperate.

"Of course! Tell me, how are your grades?"

She tossed her ponytail back and proudly announced, "I'm in the top half of my high school class. I plan to attend an online college next year. I want to become an astronomer."

"Impressive."

She looked a little bumfuzzled. "Or is it astrologer?"

"I think you probably meant the latter."

Courtney looked around the office. "What ladder?"

Note to Self: Make sure Courtney knows how to count before showing her how to open the cash register.

After a quick tour around the museum, I showed Courtney the reception area/ticket counter in the lobby where she would work. Exhibiting great patience, I taught her how to answer the phone, the proper way to greet guests, how to make change for any cash transactions and the basics of the Will Call ticket system. I also explained the job would be only for the final two days of BoomerWorld, Saturday and Sunday, and she would be paid minimum wage.

"How much is that? Like $50 an hour or something?"

"More like $12," I said, and quickly added, "but you'll make hundreds of dollars, plus a bonus if you do well."

Her eyes glazed over as she tried to do the math in her pretty little head.

"It's going to be a life-changing experience for you, Courtney," I said, trying to spin it. "Just think: You're going to gain valuable work experience that you can add to your already impressive resume. And on Saturday you get to dress up in a Halloween costume for our big party. It'll be fun!"

Courtney thought long and hard. "Maybe I'll come as Lady Gaga!"

I cleared my throat. "Actually, in keeping with the BoomerWorld theme, you should probably pick a costume from the hallmark Boomer years. Consider Wilma Flintstone or Gladys Kravitz."

The blank expression on her face was so priceless I couldn't resist. "Hey, how about 'That Girl'?"

"What girl?"

Fuhgeddaboutit... I didn't have the time or the crayons to explain it to her.

I handed her a BoomerWorld brochure, which was filled with photos and copy about the museum. "Read this for some more ideas and do a little research online about the Baby Boom Generation."

With a panicked look on her face, she asked, "Is there going to be a quiz?"

I winked. "Multiple choice only. No essays."

Courtney swallowed hard.

"Relax, I'm kidding! Just remember to be here on Saturday morning at 9:00 a.m. sharp for a staff meeting and you'll meet the rest of the team. Until then, mind your Ps and Qs."

"What's that?"

"I have no idea. They never told us," I said with a straight face.

As usual, Courtney looked confused, but I was starting to like her. Sweet kid.

I stood and shook her limp little hand.

"Congratulations, Courtney! You're now an official ambassador for BoomerWorld. Live it! Love it!"

4:00 p.m.

"Dreams"

After parting company with the charming Courtney, I retired to the lobby to do a little light reading while I waited for my next visitor: Elizabeth Frost, an executive from the bank that owns the building.

The hallways and lobby of Boomerworld feature an eclectic mix of memorbilia. The walls are covered with vintage movie posters from *The Longest Day, Cool Hand Luke, Mary Poppins* and *Midnight Cowboy*, among others. There is kitschy stuff like a huge aluminum white Christmas tree with a spinning electric color wheel circa 1965, a Huffy Radio Flyer bike, a row of antique superhero pinball machines featuring Superman, The Hulk and The Green Hornet, and display cases filled with a mix of Boomer goodies like pea shooters, Tiddlywinks, wooden pick-up sticks, a dribble glass, hand buzzer, paper dolls, Sea Monkeys, a slide rule, a few Wacky Packs and an ancient *TV Guide*. You can even take a selfie next to full-size wax figures of Muhammad Ali, The Lone Ranger and Tonto, Alfred Hitchcock and other luminaries.

Years ago, we were fortunate to have Trigger, Roy Rogers' famous stuffed horse, on consignment. Displayed in the front lobby, Trigger reared up on his hind legs. It was really cool—that is, until some crazy Boomer tried to climb up onto the saddle, fell off and fractured his leg. That was the first major insurance claim against my BoomerWorld policy. The second claim featured a stoned visitor who bounced around on a pogo stick before crashing into a glass display case, severing an artery.

Thanks, guys.

I walked over to one of the most popular props in the lobby: a replica of Archie Bunker's classic arm chair from the TV show *All in the Family*. I bought it on eBay from some guy in Iowa who found it in his mother's basement. It came with a great backstory: Originally, the

TV show's set designer purchased Archie's chair for only eight bucks from a local Goodwill thrift store. After eight seasons on the air, Norman Lear thought the show would be cancelled so he donated both Archie's and Edith's chairs to the Smithsonian. When the show was renewed at the last minute, Mr. Lear had to spend thousands of dollars to replicate the chairs.

While Walter stretched out on the floor, I lifted up the tattered, brown tweed seat cushion to reveal several dog-eared *MAD Magazines*. After selecting one of my favorite issues with Alfred E. Newman on the cover dressed as a hippie, I plopped down into the easy chair and flipped through the vintage periodical. Unable to resist the temptation, I yelled out, "Hey, Meathead! Get me a beer!" I started to read a hysterical parody of *Mission Impossible*. Yawning, I fell asleep and had a strange, terrifying dream…

Under a bright blue sky, I stood inside a large circle outlined in chalk on a grassy field along Venice Beach.

A short, mysterious man faced me about a hundred yards away. In his left hand, he held a long metallic spear-like object with red fins. Like an Olympic javelin thrower, he hurled it toward me. I tracked its trajectory as it arched high into the sky until it disappeared into the harsh glare of the sun. There was a loud swoosh of air as the object soared down from the heavens and embedded itself into the grass a few feet away from me.

I studied the lethal projectile protruding from the turf. It looked exactly like one of those 1950s lawn darts on display in the toy section at BoomerWorld. However, instead of being only a foot long, this surreal specimen was as tall as I was.

As I pulled the giant projectile out of the turf, I noticed that the super sharp tip could easily skewer a large animal. Or a human!

I spun around just in time to see the man launch another deadly dart into the air. Frantically, I ran to my right to elude the airborne missile, which almost hit me in the head.

Glaring back at the man, I wondered who he was and why was he trying to kill me. I figured that the best way to avoid certain death would be to turn and run, keeping a watchful eye on the sky.

Another dart[4] slammed into the ground to my immediate left. Stumbling backwards, I almost lost my footing.

Looking up into the sky, I tried to avoid another scary projectile, but I tripped and tumbled onto my back. Laying spread eagle on the turf, I watched helplessly as the giant lawn dart streaked downward directly towards my heaving chest.

Frozen with fear, I prepared myself for its lethal impact ...

"I Saw Her Standing There"

"Hey! Wake up!"

I abruptly opened my eyes to see an elegantly dressed, middle-aged woman towering over me. With the light to her back, she was outlined with a lustrous glow that accented her hair and full figure.

"Well… I can see you're hard at work," she said.

Rubbing the sleep from my eyes, I mumbled, "I must have dozed off for a minute."

Elizabeth Frost stepped back to let the glare of the overhead lights in the lobby hit me in the face. Wearing a dark blue suit with a white blouse, she was about five-foot-eight with long legs and shoulder-length brunette hair tinged with wisps of gray.

I had never met Ms. Frost in person. We had spoken a few times on the phone, where she projected a businesslike, no-nonsense

---

[4] *In the original game, people would throw the Lawn Darts at circles across large swaths of grass to score points; however, those dangerous projectiles were eventually banned in the U.S. after several deaths and serious injuries.*

demeanor. Initially, I tried to loosen her up with a few of my best banker jokes. No such luck. She gave off a cold, distant vibe.

Squinting, I said, "Running such a large operation is truly exhausting."

Folding her arms across her chest, she replied, "I'll bet."

As I straightened myself up in the chair, the *Mad Magazine* slipped from my lap onto the floor. She watched as I stood up and tossed it back under the seat cushion.

I extended my hand. "You must be Elizabeth Frost. Nice to finally meet you."

Tentatively, she shook my hand, eyeing me from top to bottom. "So—you're the infamous Bob Apple."

"Famous perhaps, but certainly not infamous," I smiled as I straightened my tie.

"Years ago, I read about you in People Magazine."

"Yes, that publication is a true beacon of journalistic integrity!" I declared, slipping into my huckster persona.

"I believe it referred to you as 'The P.T. Barnum of the Baby Boom Generation.' I never forgot that."

I shoved my hands into my pant pockets and puffed out my chest. "Well, it certainly was a very flattering profile, but—"

"Flattering?" she asked, her eyebrow arching up like Morticia Addams.

Her remark caught me a little off guard. That article along with the scores of others that ran in local and national newspapers and magazines had been universally positive. The new museum had been hailed as a "the quintessential Boomer time capsule," attracting thousands of Boomers who sought to revel in their colorful history.

"Tell me, P.T.—"

"You can call me Bob."

"Well, I like 'P.T.' It suits you better," she said stone-faced.

She was absolutely right. I am a shameless promoter.

"Fine. Can I call you Liz?"

"I prefer Elizabeth."

Realizing that it was smarter not to push the river, I relented. But in my head, she was gonna be Liz.

Gesturing down at Walter, who was snoring loudly at my feet, I said, "And this is Walter. As you can see, he's the ultimate watchdog, forever on the alert to protect BoomerWorld's exquisite collection of historic baubles from would-be thieves and scalawags. After all, we don't want to invite a major heist."

Liz looked down at Walter. "I seriously doubt that the *Ocean's Eleven* crew is plotting to steal your cache of old *Mad Magazines*."

"Au contraire!" I bloviated. "The magazines under the cushion are just for my personal reading enjoyment. The pristine, museum-quality collection of comic books are displayed in the main BoomerWorld exhibit hall in a special glass case, where each issue is protected in an acid-free plastic sleeve."

She wasn't impressed.

"Perhaps you'd like to thumb-through an original issue of R. Crumb's *Zap Comix*. I'll bet you're a big fan of the whole Keep on Truckin' hippie thing."

She looked around dismissively. "Frankly, I find this whole thing to be a little bizarre."

I was genuinely perplexed. "How so?"

"Well, you've crammed the most precious memories and belongings of an entire generation into a condemned roller rink."

"Crammed? This heralded venue is over 25,000 square feet. And Boomers love it!"

She slowly exhaled like she was dealing with a petulant child. "Yes, I know how big it is. After all, my bank owns the building."

"Have you been here before?"

"No," she replied matter-of-factly.

I gestured toward the main exhibition hall. "That magnificent pavilion is filled with the greatest collection of Baby Boom heirlooms mankind has ever seen. Would you like a private tour?"

"I'll pass."

Elizabeth Frost came across as a real "Ice Queen." However, given my precarious financial situation, I needed to warm her up. And fast!

I smiled, "Come on. You're a Boomer too, right?"

"Sorry. I don't discuss my age with anyone."

With great theatrical flair, I pulled a crumpled envelope (stamped PAST DUE INVOICE) from my pocket and placed it against my forehead, reminiscent of Johnny Carson's 'Carnac The Magnificent.' I closed my eyes and divined, "You were born in—1960. Correct?"

She blanched, "Like Groucho Marx said, 'I refuse to join any club that would have me as a member.'"

"Sorry, you're automatically in! Besides, the Baby Boom isn't a club," I said, spreading my arms in a grandiose gesture. "It's a glorious global community!"

"Come on. This is all about making a buck, isn't it?"

"Absolutely not! BoomerWorld is a great labor of love, not a crass commercial venture. But as you know, I do have many expenses to cover."

Liz held up a bulky case folder. "Perhaps we should review your file now."

I was dreading the discussion, but I maintained my phony upbeat attitude. Gesturing down the west hallway, I said, "Great idea! Let's adjourn to my office."

Soon, we were face-to-face across my desk in the cluttered, dusty room. The walls were covered in old film and TV posters, and all kinds of Boomer memorabilia and tchotchkes covered every surface: an egg of Silly Putty, a small fleet of Hot Wheels, Chattering Teeth, wax lips, and a couple of truly creepy Troll Dolls with green and pink hair.

In an attempt to bring some levity to the situation, I pushed a tin of Play-Doh across the desk. "Would you like to sculpt something? Then, we can dry it in one of the Easy-Bake ovens out in the exhibition hall."

Slowly tapping her sharpened pencil against the file spread across her lap, she asked, "Are you capable of being serious for even one minute?"

I did my best Humphrey Bogart impression. "I'm just getting started, sweetheart."

Shaking her head in mock disgust, Liz stared down at her notes. "As you know, I'm here today to review a few things related to the building lease. First, there is the matter of the past due rent for September and October. At $5,000 per month, you currently owe the bank $10,000. When can we expect payment?"

When I signed a new ten-year lease back in 2008, I was much more solvent. BoomerWorld was still a relatively popular attraction and generated a modest profit—in stark contrast to the current state of affairs.

I picked up a Magic 8 Ball and gave it a shake. "Perhaps we should ask the great spirits?"

She was not amused so I didn't offer to break out my Ouija Board too.

Nervously, I reached over for the Play-Doh, popped the top and dug out a handful of soft dough. "I should be able to pay that back rent by early next week."

"Yes, I saw the poster outside promoting those two big parties. They should be very lucrative for you."

Yeah, right. If I'm able to squeeze every cent of profit out of both those events, I'll be lucky to pay off most of my big debts—but I'll still be teetering on the precipice of bankruptcy.

"Ticket sales have been slow, but over the next few days I hope to see a big surge." I reached into my desk drawer, pulled out a ticket for the Halloween party and slid it across the desk. "Here ya go. My treat."

"No thanks."

"Come on. You could dress up as *Barbarella!"*

"You know, most women would regard that comment as sexist and rude."

"But you're not like 'most women.' I can tell. You're unique, confident and adventurous!" I knew I was pushing it, but sensed that she was slowly warming up to my bombastic ravings. "Imagine: a banker in a buckskin bikini. Now that would be a sight to behold!"

"Stop digging, P.T. You've already hit rock bottom," Liz said, dismissing my feeble flirtation.

She returned to her notes. "Secondly, you promised to supply us with a copy of the BoomerWorld insurance policy as specified in our lease agreement. Where is it?"

This was exactly what I was dreading.

The insurance issue is a real problem for me. The fact is, I don't have any business insurance. My policy was cancelled two years ago due to a bogus lawsuit: An unemployed attorney claimed to have sprained her ankle when she walked into one of the standing displays in the exhibition hall and fell on her fat ass. After making a huge scene, she threatened to sue me for her "pain and suffering." It was an obvious case of legal extortion, but I still offered to pay for any medical bills, plus $2,000 to settle it on the spot. She laughed in my face and then hobbled out the door in a wake of contrived tears. The very next day, I was slapped with a $50,000 boilerplate personal injury lawsuit. She threatened to file complaints with the City of Los Angeles and the Better Business Bureau, if I didn't pay up fast. I referred it to my insurance company, but after a background check revealed the plaintiff had a long record of filing fraudulent lawsuits, they refused to negotiate with her. To make matters worse, I was behind in my monthly insurance payments and my liability policy was abruptly cancelled. The "She Demon" made my life a living hell until I eventually paid her $10,000, depleting all my cash assets. Unfortunately, after being cancelled twice by other insurance companies, getting replacement coverage at a fair price was virtually impossible.

I smiled tightly, rolling the Play-Doh on my desk. I couldn't tell her the truth because it would jeopardize the last big BoomerWorld weekend, but I didn't want to outright lie either.

I had to buy some time.

"I think my insurance agent is over in Hawaii on a vacation. He gets back on Sunday so I'll get it to you early next week."

"Sorry P.T., that's not good enough. You now have the added liability of hosting hundreds of people at those weekend events, many of whom will probably be drunk, stoned or both."

"What do you expect?" I asked with a hearty laugh. "They're Boomers!"

"Exactly."

"Hey, no worries," I stammered, "I'll get it to you soon."

"No later than this Wednesday."

"Anything else?" I asked as I began to mold the Play-Doh with both hands.

"Yes. As you know, the lease ends on November 30. The building has been sold to a developer who plans to tear it down immediately to build a hotel. We will apply your security deposit to the last month's rent, but you need to remove everything by then."

Dealing with BoomerWorld's massive inventory was a daunting and unpleasant task. All the most rare and expensive items—the cars, major collections, and one-of-a-kind artifacts—were on loan from wealthy benefactors and would have to be returned. Originally, I hoped to find a major museum or wealthy collector to purchase the rest of the items, but it never panned out. After the Smithstonian blew me off, I contacted a few other museums and galleries, but there was no interest. Lastly, I sent letters to a few of those huge retirement communities like The Villages in Florida, Sun City and that new mega-development, Silver Shores in Arizona—thinking an exhibit of Boomer items would appeal to their clientele. But alas, I never heard back from any of them… Now, I'd have to hold a "going out of business" sale and then dump the excess items on eBay. With my luck, I'll spend the rest of my life waiting in line at the post office to mail an original Chatty Cathy doll to some crazy shut-in in Topeka.

I noticed that Liz was watching me as I finished molding my work of art.

"What's that supposed to be?" she asked, staring down at the fat ring-shaped blob of Play Dough.

"That, my lady, is Homer Simpson's donut."

"You know, your little act of sub-referencing everything back to some obscure Baby Boom trivia is wearing very thin, P.T." Liz narrowed her gaze. "Let's stick with business."

"Sorry. For the last fifteen years, I've been constantly promoting BoomerWorld. I guess it's just second nature."

I tried to hand her the fake donut. "Here. Have a little bite. Tastes just like chicken."

A small smile crossed her lips.

I was slowly winning her over!

Her cellphone rang, torpedoing the moment.

"Excuse me. I need to take this."

She looked around my office in a detached manner as she listened to the caller. With her expressive blue eyes and full lips, she reminded me of another Elizabeth—Elizabeth Taylor.

Suddenly, she stiffened and said, "I'll be there as soon as I can. Thank you."

After an awkward silence, I asked, "Is everything okay?"

She stood and sighed deeply. "That was the St. Luke's emergency room. My father just fell again and banged his head. I have to go."

"I'm so sorry," I said, walking around to her side of the desk. "Is he going to be okay?"

"Probably not. He's dying."

"Please, let me drive you there."

She hesitated.

I put my hand on her shoulder, but she gently pulled away.

Holding the file tight against her chest, she said, "No. I'm fine. Really." Turning away, I saw a single tear run down her cheek, which was quickly wiped away. "We'll talk in the next few days."

As she walked briskly out of my office, I thought: *The "Ice Queen" was starting to melt.*

5:15 p.m.

"Hot Fun in the Summertime"

Walter and I usually take a walk twice a day. In the morning, we stroll along Venice Beach for about an hour, looking for beach glass and picking up garbage. And then in the late afternoon, we usually head over to the Westminster Off-Leash Dog Park, which is open every day and just a few blocks away from BoomerWorld.

With a name like Westminster, you conjure up an image of the famous annual televised dog show with thoroughbreds prancing about—or perhaps the quaint English countryside where the Royal Family walk their Welsh Corgis and Scottish Terriers through a lush, rolling green landscape with sculpted gardens and stately old oaks.

Well, think again.

This dog park features a large, shabby fenced-in area of dirt and wood chips with all the basic amenities you'd expect in a place designed for compulsive butt-sniffing and defecation: handy waste-bag stations, pooper scoopers beside steaming garbage cans, as well as some odoriferous homeless people. To spiff up the joint, there are some sickly-looking palm trees, cement picnic tables and benches, a water fountain and lots of colorful but confusing signs about the hours, parking guidelines and hypothetical "rules."

Depending on what time Walter and I show up, the park is usually populated with pooches of every breed, size, shape and temperament. From rescued pit bulls, rottweilers and chihauhaus to groomed bichons, cocker spaniels and schnauzers, it's a diverse bunch.

Supposedly, there is a three-dog limit per owner, but there are plenty of inconsiderate douche bags who drop off a carload of unruly beasts and then split for a day at the beach.

Besides the illegally parked cars and occasional vicious dogfights, there are also plenty of rude owners who don't pick up their dog's poop. Over the years, I've chastised a few owners who didn't follow the rules. But that changed after a tatted-up Hispanic gang member with an aggressive Mastiff the size of a Humvee threatened to strangle me with his chain-link leash.

Now, I maintain a much lower profile.

I avoid the park during the hot, dusty summer days when Venice Beach attracts thousands of tourists and a few scummy locals. But like most dog parks, you also meet all kinds of interesting and weird people who love their pets: wannabe screenwriters, lonely housewives, senior citizens, and kids with puppies. It can be a fun place to hang during the off times, particularly in the fall and winter months.

Anyway, Walter wagged his tail the moment he spotted a few of his furry friends frolicking about in the dog run. After we entered through the gate, I released Walter from his leash and he shuffled out into the fray, cruising for some excellent doggy action. When they aren't chasing tennis balls, peeing and pooping, many of the canines blissfully hump one other. Since Walter lost his precious gonads as a puppy, he never got to realize his full potential as a thoroughbred stud, but he still enjoys the occasional dry hump on a complacent bitch—or some guy's pant leg.

I sat down on a bench near the front and surveyed the scene of usual suspects. While Walter tried to unsuccessfully mount "Darlene The Dachshund," I was surrounded by a pack of drooling dogs who knew I carried small treats in my pocket.

After Walter pinched a loaf in the center of the run, I uttered his namesake's classic sign-off: "And that's the way it is." Then I walked out to collect the crap in a plastic bag. With the sleight-of-hand of a gifted magician, I plucked up the poop, quickly turned the bag inside out, knotted it and dropped it into a trash can—while holding my breath for the obvious reason.

Mission accomplished, Walter and I headed west towards Booker's Beach Bar, a popular hangout over on the boardwalk.

6:15 p.m.

"Walk On The Wild Side"

Venice Beach has always been one of the most fascinating beach communities in the country. Its history is as crazy and colorful as its geography, wacky locals and street performers.

Back in 1904, a world traveler and eccentric developer named Abbot Kinney won the land in a coin toss. He dreamed of turning this patch of Southern California wetlands into a cultural center for music and art. It was originally called "Venice of America." He began to build a stunning series of canals that eventually stretched for 16 miles, and even imported gondolas and gondoliers from Venice, Italy. Unfortunately, the project didn't receive widespread support and was a financial failure. In a stroke of marketing genius, Kinney quickly switched gears and instead created a popular ocean-side resort and amusement park. He built Venetian-style businesses along the canals, a large amusement pier, a breakwater to protect it from the surging Pacific Ocean, and a 2.5-mile miniature steam railroad that encircled the Grand Lagoon—promoting it as the "Coney Island of the Pacific." Trolley service from downtown Los Angeles and nearby Santa Monica brought in the masses in search of a classic California beach scene, amusements, and freak shows.

Over the years, many ongoing issues like stagnant water, mosquito infestations, flooding and sewage overflows plagued the Venice canal system. Eventually, the waterways were reduced to a pristine 1.5 miles that are now lined with manicured gardens and multimillion-dollar homes.

From the earliest days of motion pictures, Venice Beach has also been a haven for movie making. Buster Keaton, Harold Lloyd, Carol Lombard, Cary Grant, Orson Welles and Charlton Heston all worked here. Many of the *Keystone Cops, Our Gang* comedies, and Roger Corman horror flicks were filmed on locations in and around the boardwalk. Boomers will remember other classics shot here like *Grease, They Shoot Horses, Don't They?, Harry and Tonto, Mother, Jugs and Speed, Down and Out in Beverly Hills, The Doors, L.A. Story, White Men Can't Jump*, and God only knows how many underground and porno films.

Once a home to Beat Generation poets and artists, Venice Beach is now L.A.'s number one tourist destination, visited by more than 5 million people each year. Whether it's the area's classic art deco buildings, murals and neon sculptures, vibrant energy or the international and multi-cultural people watching, Venice Beach is truly unique with a laid-back yet crazy vibe.

Where else can you find this strange mix of entertaining and certified crackpots along the boardwalk: fortunetellers, fire eaters, Mexican skull vendors, snake charmers, skate dancers, unicyclists and scrap-wood painters—not to mention that dog accepting dollar bills in his thong, a lady with a birdcage on her head and stilt-wearing Treeman—an "amphibious celestial being" who hides in hedges to surprise unwitting passersby.

And those are the normal, well-adjusted folks.

Then there are the street musicians, wannabe rappers and out-of-tune garage bands hustling their CDs, and the improvisational jam sessions of the Venice Beach Drum Circle, where Rastafarians from around the globe gather to beat their drums and congas while others dance and chant.

You can get a surfing lesson, shoot hoops with some serious "street-ballers," play volleyball, handball or mini-tennis as well as practice gymnastics, fish off the pier, jog along the beach or on the footpaths that weave through the entire town. Maybe rent a bike or hang out at the skate park; a 16,000-square-foot facility where pros and posers intermingle along its rolling contours. Or get pumped-up at Muscle Beach—an area bulging with gyms and fitness studios, including Gold's Gym, where Arnold Schwarzenegger and other legendary bodybuilders bench-pressed their way to fame and fortune in the 70s.

After visiting one of the many marijuana shops, you'll probably want some munchies, too. There are ice cream shops, pizza by the slice, corn dogs, food trucks of every variety and exotic libations to quench any thirst. Grab a blanket and picnic in the park or on the beach where the sand is ideal for creating sculptures and sandcastles.

If you want to shop or just loiter, check out the poster stands, T-shirt and specialty boutiques, and the aquarium. Walk a few blocks inland to Abbot Kinney Boulevard, heralded by *GQ Magazine* as "The Coolest Block in America," for its restaurants and bars, clothing shops, art galleries and more. Years ago, the neighborhood was plagued with drugs and gang violence, but given the influx of some Hollywood heavies and high-tech start-ups, the median home price is now $2 million.

Depending on your mood, a stroll through Venice Beach can be a fun experience, but you'll also encounter plenty of trash, uninspired graffiti, massive homeless camps, human waste, passed-out drug addicts and other sketchy people. Regardless, there's rarely a dull moment.

As Walter and I sauntered along in the cool late October air, we passed a young group of skateboarders huddled on the grass. Pungent, highly potent marijuana smoke rose above them like the mushroom cloud over the Bikini Islands. I distinctly heard one of the young rascals call me a "geezer," which was greeted by some laughter among his stoner friends. It was nothing to get upset about, but I did loudly retort, "Get a job, whippersnapper!"

One kid yelled back, "Okay, Boomer!"

That got a big laugh.

"Dock Of The Bay"

Eventually, we arrived at Booker's Beach Bar, which sits on a busy corner in the heart of Venice Beach. The forty-foot-long bar fronts on the boardwalk and then wraps down a side street, providing an open and welcome watering hole to the throngs of thirsty patrons. It's well known for its micro-brewed beers, burgers, fish tacos, ceviche, chips and guacamole.

Surfboards, old nautical antiques and quaint historic photos of the beach scene cover the ceiling and walls. Besides the bar stools, people can sit at small tables along the sidewalk to watch the endless parade of tourists, locals out for fresh air and street performers who will do practically anything to make money.

Almost every day, Walter and I spend some quality time there with the owner, Booker Salerno, a retired N.Y.P.D. cop and his obese cat, Big Al.

I've known Booker for about twelve years, ever since he arrived in town from The Big Apple. He's quite a character with his chrome dome, thick New York accent and feisty political views. Dressed in his usual Hawaiian shirt, khaki pants and tinted aviator glasses, Booker looks and behaves like he's on an extended vacation. And technically, he is. After a long career working as a beat cop and later as a patrol sergeant, he needed a healthy change of scenery. Armed with his pension and a decent wad of savings, he headed for the sunny shores of the Pacific Ocean and never looked back. "Retired cop buys bar" is one of the oldest clichés, but that's exactly what Booker did.

We met one late afternoon at BoomerWorld. It had been an uneventful day and I was doing my closing rounds prior to locking up, checking to make sure everyone had left and there was no theft, breakage or other surprises. As I approached the 9/11 Memorial near the end of the giant mural, I heard some muffled sobbing. I saw a big, fair-skinned black guy with his head in his hands, sitting on one of the couches in front of a twisted metal sculpture where people can contemplate that horrible day.

The 9/11 tribute is one of the most compelling exhibits in the museum. On consignment from a famous New York artist, the twenty-foot tall statue consists of a jagged, charred metal girder from one of the fallen WTC buildings, protruding upward from a large block of clear Lucite. Like that mysterious monolith from *2001: A Space Odyssey*, it has a powerful presence, but there was no mystery about its origins. Disturbing photos from that fateful day cover the mural directly behind the imposing sculpture: the planes striking the buildings, panicked souls leaping to their deaths, the heroism of the first responders, the smoldering aftermath and clean up.

The poor guy was distraught, so I left him alone and wandered around the facility for another fifteen minutes, dusting off exhibits—which is an endless task. As I circled back, he stood and tried to compose himself.

"Excuse me for intruding, sir, but it's closing time," I said softly.

He looked at his watch with misty eyes. "I'm sorry. Didn't know it was so late."

"No sweat… Are you okay?"

"Yeah," he said, still looking a little unsteady.

He struck me as a sensitive guy who obviously had a strong personal connection to 9/11.

"Looks like you could use a drink."

He nodded. "Sounds good."

"Great, let's go. My treat."

We introduced ourselves and I put the leash on Walter. As we exited the museum, I asked, "Do you know that place, Bottoms Up, over on Abbot Kinney? They've got a decent Happy Hour."

Booker replied, "Sure. I know every bar in town."

I was curious. "So—when you're not hanging out in funky museums, you like gin joints?"

"Actually, it was more like business research. Had to check out the competition before I opened my own bar."

"That's great! Where is it?"

"Signed the lease two weeks ago for that old dive around the corner on the Boardwalk. I'm just starting to remodel it. It'll be open in a couple months, but it's already stocked with plenty of booze—so I'm buying."

As they say: That was "the beginning of a beautiful friendship."

During that long night of drinking, I learned a lot about Booker. After the light talk getting to know each other, he told me he broke down in BoomerWorld remembering his experience on 9/11. Working out of the 7th Precinct on the Lower East Side, he saw the whole tragic scene unfold and lost numerous close friends. Like many of his co-workers, he became depressed and disillusioned, and was put on temporary disability. Over the next twenty-four months, he worked a desk job over in a Brooklyn precinct near where his parents lived, while he got some much-needed counseling to deal with his anger and frustration. Finally, Booker pulled the pin after twenty-five years on the force and came West in search of a new life beyond the ghostly shadows of the World Trade Center. It was tough to leave New York, his family and fellow cops—but it was time.

Smart, street wise and likable, Booker was the product of a mixed marriage and unique upbringing. His father, Marco, an Italian N.Y.F.D. captain, met and fell in love with his mother, Winnie, a beautiful and vibrant immigrant from Jamaica who ran a restaurant in Flatbush. Married in the late '50s, they endured racial prejudice and social exclusion from both sides of the ethnic divide, but taught Booker the values of hard work, respect for authority and tolerance. Following in his father's footsteps, he brought a positive perspective to a tough, demanding job—until the Twin Towers came down.

Booker's two biggest passions are politics and women. When he isn't watching cable news, listening to talk radio or offering pithy insights about the world at large, he's trying to get laid. He had already been married and divorced three times before he arrived in California. Now, he claims he's looking for "soon-to-be ex-wife number four."

And he doesn't have to look far, given the constant flow of women into his bar.

When Booker spots a potential date, he usually sends over a round of free drinks. If he gets a nice "thank you" smile, he drifts over and turns on the charm. Since he spends most mornings at the gym, he's in good shape for his age and lures lovely ladies upstairs to his swingin' bachelor pad above the bar he calls "The Love Lair."

Early in our friendship, he dragged me along on some blind dates; however, I was uncomfortable with the whole thing and begged off. After a few drinks, sometimes he'll regale me with tales of his latest sexual exploits, but I only half-listen. Still, he has a heart of gold and is my best friend.

Booker hangs out at the far end of his bar surrounded by everything he needs and cares about: a laptop, a fan to blow his constant cigar smoke out the back door, a small flat screen TV, and of course, Big Al.

Famous for his gargantuan girth and epic farting, Big Al is a thirty-pound Maine Coon cat and a living legend around Venice Beach. He spends most of the day sleeping on top of the bar. Every few hours or so, Big Al rises and ambles slowly down the long counter to relieve the boredom. He routinely knocks over drinks and snags food off the plates of appalled diners.

One time, an inebriated dolt made the mistake of knocking the huge cat off the bar as he sashayed by. Bad move. A split second later, Big Al leapt out of the shadows and attached himself to the feckless fool's face like that creature in *Aliens*. Eventually, Booker was able to pry Al's claws out from the back of the guy's head before he was smothered to death by the cat's enormous furry belly. Luckily, the man was too drunk to remember the disturbing incident.

Big Al is actually quite a loveable animal. In fact, Walter and Al get along great, sleeping and playing together. Sometimes, Booker and I walk our pets along the oceanfront. With Big Al leading the charge—heads turn, jaws drop, and traffic stops as the boys stake out their territory. Then, we usually return to the bar for some welcome refreshments. Both Walter and Al lap up a bowl of tap beer while Booker and I usually open a good bottle of wine.

"Greetings, earthlings!" I bellowed as Walter and I entered the bar, easing once again into my verbose BoomerWorld alter ego.

During the long warm days of summer, Booker's is usually packed, but since it was a Monday night in late fall, the place was practically deserted, except for a few diehards enjoying Happy Hour and watching *Monday Night Football* on the screens above the bar.

As we made our way to the back corner where Booker was glued to the tube, I noticed a tabletop version of my poster (promoting BoomerWorld's final weekend events) prominently displayed in the center of the bar. Several of my friends around town, who own restaurants and retail shops, were helping me sell tickets.

I asked Booker, "So how goes the battle, my friend?"

Without moving his eyes away from the news broadcast, he observed, "Man, this country is going to Hell in a hand basket."

"Tell me something I don't know."

Holding a freshly lit Cuban cigar in one hand and a beer in the other, Booker shook his head in utter disgust. "I'm telling ya, between the self-serving boobs in Washington and all those freeloaders who expect unlimited government subsidies, we're a heartbeat away from fiscal collapse! The gross incompetence of our nation's leadership is breathtaking… When did we transition from "we the people" to "screw the people?"

"Take a chill pill, bro!" I said, but Booker was on a tear.

"And what happened to our basic values? Our culture? Our borders? Our language? Did you know that they now print the official California voter guide in seven different languages? It's insane!"

A couple of customers farther down the bar shot us disapproving looks.

"Come on, you can't let that shit get under your skin," I said, trying to calm him down. But secretly, I wished Soupy Sales was still around to throw cream pies into the faces of virtually every politician and news anchor in America.

Booker raged on. “And don’t even get me started on the media! Those bastards have destroyed this country. They don’t just report the news—they pick and choose the facts and then manipulate them to fit their own agendas!”

Trying to lighten the mood, I said. “Yeah. Whatever happened to those great journalists that we grew up with like Edward R. Murrow, Huntley & Brinkley, and Howard Beale?”

Booker took a deep breath and then a long pull on his beer. He looked down at Walter who was lying next to Big Al on the floor. “Our pets have more common sense than most politicians, plus they can lick their own junk, which can come in handy.”

I sat down beside him. “We should all be so lucky—and limber.”

“You should have been here an hour ago. Big Al coughed up a hairball the size of Rhode Island.”

“Nice visual.”

“How was your day?” asked Booker.

“You know, the regular. Helped a little old lady cross the street, rescued a stranded kitty cat from a tree and collected some money for UNICEF.”

Booker finished his beer. “Want a glass of wine, Bob?”

“Absolutely.”

Booker gestured over to his bartender, a shapely brunette, and said, “Open a bottle of that fabulous Hardman Vineyards Cab and bring us two glasses.”

I inquired, “I’m almost afraid to ask, but have you sold any more tickets for BoomerWorld’s weekend events?”

A big grin crossed Booker’s face. He leaned over the bar, reached down for a small metal cash box and opened it. “So far, we’ve sold 25 tickets for the Halloween Party and another 20 for the Sunday night gala. That’s a total of $2,375! Not too shabby, huh?”

He handed me a stack of cash, checks and the receipts.

“I really appreciate it,” I said with sincere gratitude. “As you know,

I need every dime."

Pouring us each a glass of wine, Booker replied, "No problema."

"You da man!" I said. "You're coming both nights, right?"

"Wouldn't miss them for the world!"

"I'll put you on the comp list. And I assume you'll be bringing a date so I'll add a 'plus one' for each night."

"Better make it a 'plus two' because the gal I'm currently wooing has a twin sister."

I raised my glass to him. "Oh, you dirty dog!"

As Booker turned back to the TV, my cellphone rang. It was the first good news I've had in a long time…

A few years ago, I was at a charity fundraiser in Beverly Hills at the home of an old ad client of mine when I met the owner of the famous Batmobile from the 1960s TV show. He was a great guy and a fellow Boomer. We hit it off. I took him for a private tour of BoomerWorld and we ended up spending the entire day together. We drove my classic VW van up the coast and had lunch in Malibu. He had such a good time, he promised to let me display the Batmobile at BoomerWorld sometime—if the dates could be worked out. When I never heard back from him I assumed he just forgot about it. But he was true to his word!

Over the phone, he said his prized possession was scheduled to be a featured attraction at an auto show up in Santa Barbara the next week; however, I could display the Batmobile at BoomerWorld this very weekend. There was only one catch: I had to supply a 24-hour bonded and insured security firm to keep a watchful eye on it. Knowing the Batmobile's presence could have a dramatic impact on ticket sales, I enthusiastically agreed to his terms. He confirmed his travel team would deliver the legendary vehicle on Friday at five p.m. and would pick it up the following Monday at nine a.m. I thanked him profusely and hung up.

"Hallelujah! I yelled. "That's the guy I told you about who owns the Batmobile. He's going to let me display it at BoomerWorld this weekend."

"Do you think I can borrow it to take the twins for a spin? It may help me close the deal."

"Sorry. The owner said, 'you can look—but not touch.'"

"Still, that's great news, Bob! Now you really have something to promote during the final days."

For once, the Gods were smiling on me.

I savored the moment. After a few glasses of wine, I said goodbye and hit the road with Walter in tow.

7:30 p.m.

"Stand By Me"

Walking back to BoomerWorld, we dropped by a few of the other local businesses that were selling tickets for me. Sales were slow and I only picked up about $500; however, I did spread the word about the imminent arrival of the Batmobile, which everyone agreed would juice sales.

After making sure the museum was secured for the night, I retired to my humble home. After my wife's passing in 2002, I sold our old house, which we had mortgaged to the max to pay for her outrageous medical expenses. Fortunately, a client friend traded me his thirty-four-foot long 1990 Airstream Excella 1000 trailer to settle an outstanding invoice. At the time, it was parked at an exclusive RV community up in Malibu that was a popular enclave for some of Hollywood's most interesting characters. For the next few years, I mourned, took long walks on the beach and made plans for BoomerWorld. After the mobile park lease ran out, I moved the Airstream into a corner of the museum parking lot behind a tall wall on the east side of the building. To give it a more inviting atmosphere, I added some awnings, laid down

Astroturf across the front along with some potted plants and lawn chairs—all surrounded by a white picket fence posted with a sign reading: Private Residence. It wasn't much, but it was home. And a short commute to work.

Entering the trailer, I turned on the TV and found an old movie station. As Walter crashed in his bed in the corner, I sat down at the built-in booth dinette. As much as I hated doing any kind of accounting, I needed to drill down on my finances. Stacks of correspondence, unpaid invoices and legal documents covered the table. I started to flip through all the paperwork. It was a sad state of affairs.

I poured myself two fingers of Scotch. Like they say: *Alcohol won't solve your problems, but then again, neither will milk.*

BoomerWorld was never about making money. It was conceived, nourished and brought to fruition based upon a sacred promise I made to Amy, my late wife. But it still has to be run as a business. I'd invested everything into this mad enterprise, including liquidating my IRA to pay for many of the Boomer artifacts and collectibles, the exterior and interior graphics, TVs, computers, programming and wiring, licensing and consignment fees, etc.

Throughout my long career in advertising, I always had an accountant handle the books. I was an idea man and a presenter, not a bean counter. But now I was on my own and my pedestrian accounting skills left a lot to be desired. Barely able to balance my own checkbook, I kept track of BoomerWorld's entire profit and loss statement on a single sheet of paper.

Originally, my attorney brother-in-law had strongly recommended that the museum be set up as a corporation or LLC, but as usual, I let it slide. Now, I'm personally liable for its pathetic economic condition and any claims. Besides owing the two months of back rent, I had amassed major credit card debt that kept growing and oozing like *The Blob*.

Throughout my entire professional life, I've been a rather foolish and reckless businessman, but at least I was an honorable one. I fully intend to pay my bills and live up to my promises, no matter what. I always thought declaring bankruptcy was unethical and a cowardly cop-out. In early 2000, during the big dot-com bust, my ad agency got screwed by several clients. Regardless, I still honored all my financial commitments to every production and media company.

I took a hearty swig of my drink and began to crunch the numbers, including all the expenses for the last big weekend, plus current debt versus the projected profit margin:

Accrued Debt:	
Back Rent	$10,000
Credit Card Debt	$18,000
	($28,000)
Upcoming Expenses:	
Advertising, Website, Social Media, Ticket Printing	$ 4,000
Employees	$ 4,000
Catering, Waiters, Bartenders, Parking Attendants	$20,000
Tables/Chairs/Porta-Potties	$ 2,000
Entertainment (DJ & Band)	$ 5,000
Cleaning Services	$ 1,000
Security Guards	$ 3,000
Utilities	$ 1,000
Misc.	$ 1,000
	($41,000)
Projected Sales/Profits:	
Regular Weekend Tickets	$ 5,000
Halloween Party Tickets	$16,000
Sunday Night Party Tickets	$26,250
Auction Proceeds & Bars	$12,000
Gift Shop Sales	$12,000
	$71,250
Projected Profit	**$ 2,250**

As I stared down at the balance sheet, I knew I was in big trouble. Even if I was lucky enough to sell out both weekend events, turn the bars into cash gushers and sell everything in the gift shop, I'd barely have enough dough left over to promote the "going-out-of-business" sale before slipping out of town as a pack of bloodthirsty creditors chased me down like Dr. Richard Kimble.

I rummaged through a pile of legal documents and found a copy of my cancelled liability insurance policy. As Ms. Frost from the bank pointed out, the terms of my building lease required I have comprehensive insurance coverage at all times. Plus, I'm sure the gentleman who owns the Batmobile also assumed I had bulletproof insurance. Unfortunately, to get just a two-day "event" policy, with special indemnification for alcohol sales, would cost thousands of dollars and must be paid up front. Since I'm broke and need every penny of the advanced ticket sales for the down payment on the catering services and other mandatory expenses, I just couldn't afford it. Up until now, I had avoided the whole issue, but The Ice Queen expected to see proof of insurance by Wednesday and she was not going to let it slip through the cracks.

Then I got an idea... An idea I was very uncomfortable with—but I had no choice.

I flipped through my trusty Rolodex and found the telephone number for my old friend, Pete "Pipes" Pendergast. Pete was a voice-over talent who earned his nickname for the husky, authoritative drawl that had graced thousands of radio and TV commercials.

I gave him a call. After one ring, I got his voice mail. "Hello, this is Pete. Start talking."

Pacing around my trailer, I began to speak. "Hey, Pete! It's Bob... I'm calling because I'm in a real bind and need your help… I'm finally closing BoomerWorld, but first I've got to get through this upcoming weekend. My business liability insurance got cancelled a while back and now the bank that owns the building wants confirmation that the policy is still valid or they'll shut me down. I'm broke, can't afford to pay for insurance and don't have any other options. I feel like such a jerk for even asking, but do you think you could pose as my insurance broker over the phone?... It's a standard liability policy. I'll mail you a copy tomorrow so you have the details. The bank's rep is named Elizabeth Frost. There's a good chance that she might not even call, but if she does, I know you can schmooze her."

Fighting back the guilt, I added, "Listen, if you don't want to do this, I'll completely understand. But if you agree, I owe you big time! Thanks Pete, and call me if you have any questions."

I hung up, walked to the back of the trailer and sat down on the bed. As I massaged my throbbing temples, I struggled to rationalize how I could ask my friend for such a despicable favor. I've always tried to be an honorable person and this was an all-time low. Grasping for any excuse, I told myself those earlier lawsuits were flukes—that BoomerWorld was a safe place and the likelihood of an accident was minimal.

I really didn't need a stinkin' insurance policy, right?

Anyway, I knew my old buddy Pete would come through for me, but I still had to lie to Liz about it. Suddenly, I felt nauseous.

I barely made it to the bathroom.

10:00 p.m.

"Ready For Love"

Throughout the evening, I drank heavily and reflected on the last fifteen years...

After Amy died, I founded BoomerWorld on a shoestring—with my fingers crossed. Unfortunately, my financial projections were too optimistic and it was destined to be a break-even venture at best. The first five years, from 2003-2008, were decent and the business was in the black. For a while, I was the new shining thing. Then the big recession hit and I was able to renegotiate the new ten-year lease for a fraction of the original cost. At the time, I thought the cash flow would improve, but attendance eroded and my deteriorating finances became an omnipresent issue. Every penny I earned was pumped back into the business. To make ends meet, I took my Social Security at age 62, dropped my health insurance and lived a quiet, frugal life. Except for my routine beach walks and trips to Booker's, I worked in the museum every day and hunkered down in my Airstream at night. I still put on the show and worked my ass off to make ends meet. But as BoomerWorld slowly devolved into a stagnant and irrelevant attraction, I became increasingly disillusioned, bitter and alone.

Over the years, a few women showed an interest in me. However, since BoomerWorld was a tribute to my ex-wife, I felt like I was cheating on her and always found an excuse to avoid any romantic entanglements.

And sex? Well, that's another pathetic story…

I did have a brief, purely physical fling about ten years ago, which I didn't initiate… Frequently, I park my VW van out in front of the museum in a yellow zone and forget about it. One day, after my windshield was buried under a pile of parking tickets, I confronted the meter maid. A curvaceous, energetic woman about half my age, she was also a sex addict with a domination fetish. We cut a deal. Instead of writing me up, she would drop in unexpectedly, lock the door to my office, slap handcuffs on me, and well—"light my fire." These intense, purely physical sessions would only last about ten minutes, and as often as twice a day. After two highly erotic weeks, she was abruptly transferred to another precinct for some unknown reason.

And I never saw "Lovely Rita" again.

By midnight, I was totally wasted—emotionally and physically… I took another swig of scotch, wallowing in self-indulgent melancholy.

Besides the financial anvil hanging over my head, I was genuinely lonely. Booker and Walter were great friends, but there was a hole in my heart. In six short days, I would begin the transition to a new phase in my life and I wanted a woman to share it with. In my pitiful state, I told myself that when the final curtain comes crashing down, it would be nice to be crushed with someone I loved. But the odds were against it.

I was hardly a great catch: old, broke, and more than a little crazy.

2

Tuesday, October 27
6:45 a.m.

"House of the Rising Sun"

I woke up with a vicious hangover. Between the marijuana, booze and a few sleeping pills, my frontal lobe was throbbing like Robert Plant's crotch.

Over the last few months, the stress of dealing with the imminent closure of BoomerWorld had taken a toll on my confidence and general psyche. Virtually every night, I stumbled home from Booker's place to my trailer, and promptly passed out. It had become a very unhealthy routine. And I wasn't sleeping well either.

You've probably heard that saying: "the hour of the wolf." You know, that restless period of half-delusional sleep in the wee hours of the morning where everything is exaggerated into full-blown paranoia. Well, I just don't have a lone wolf, I've got an entire pack. The beasts of pending financial ruin claw and gnaw into my dreams, tearing at what's left of my fragile ego and self-confidence. I toss and turn, stressing over stupid details out of my control, rehashing a lifetime of mistakes and worrying about the future. That is, until the angel Ambien whispers in my ear.

It took an extra-large dose of sleeping pills to knock me out after I left that voice mail for my friend, Pete. It was sleazy and wrong. I desperately wanted to call him back, apologize and call the whole thing off, but I couldn't do it. Instead, I wanted to escape reality. I kept hitting the snooze bar on my alarm clock like a lab rat with a raging crack cocaine addiction.

Eventually, I stumbled into the tiny bathroom and looked in the mirror. Some loser with sunken eyes, crazy hair and a skid-row beard stared at me.

Yeah, death warmed over.

After a long, hot shower to burn out the remaining toxins, I shaved, swallowed some aspirin and put on fresh clothes. Still moving slowly, I ambled over to my favorite coffee shop—Jitters Java Hut. While Walter chomped on an almond biscotti, I gulped down a cup of joe fortified with a triple shot of espresso, aptly named "The Nuclear Option." Soon, the color returned to my face and I started to feel normal again.

As I stared out at the ocean, storm clouds were slowly building. Intermittent rain showers were predicted for the next few days. Since both of my upcoming weekend parties were being held in the outside parking area, I desperately needed perfect weather. Luckily, the forecast promised clear and warmer days ahead.

10:00 a.m.

"Won't Get Fooled Again"

An old contact of mine at the *Times* had set up an interview for a feature story about the final days of BoomerWorld. A reporter named Clark something (sorry, I'm really bad with names) was scheduled for a special BoomerWorld tour and interview. A photographer, a nice kid with a bow tie, tagged along too. It was a great opportunity for me to promote the weekend events to a wide audience throughout Southern California.

In an effort to make BoomerWorld look its best, I turned on all the lights, TVs, sound system, etc. Despite nursing a dull headache, I unleashed my full-blown Boomer persona as I ferried the boys through the sprawling pavilion. Like a demented history teacher, I bombarded them with facts and figures about the economic, social and cultural events that shaped the Baby Boom. I spouted esoteric trivia about the most influential people, places and things, ranted about the era's politics, and even recited song lyrics, colloquialisms and one-liners—the minutiae of a generation. I laughed, I cried, I danced. I must admit, it was one of my best performances. While I prattled on, the photographer snapped photos of yours truly and the exhibits with his fancy digital camera.

When we sat down in my office to complete the interview, the old red rotary phone on my desk rang. "Excuse me, gentlemen, it's the 'hot line' to the President."

Clark and the photographer both laughed as I picked up the receiver.

"Hello, you've reached the international headquarters for BoomerWorld." I winked at my guests. "This is General Jack D. Ripper. How can I help you?"

The voice on the other end said, "My name is Monica Cummings. I'm the personal assistant to Stuart Whitehead, the senior U.S. Senator from California."

I put my hand over the mouthpiece and whispered, "I was close. It's Senator Whitehead's personal assistant."

The boys looked impressed.

Ms. Cummings continued, "The Senator would like to attend the Sunday night party at BoomerWorld."

"I didn't know the Senator was a fan."

"He's a proud Boomer, born in 1947."

I didn't know much about Whitehead, except that he was one of those unsavory politicians who went to Washington as a young man and ended up staying for a thousand years. With his white hair and big shit-eating grin, Whitehead was the epitome of everything that's wrong with American politics. I recalled the time when he got caught cheating on his taxes and, instead of going to jail, he somehow became chairman of the Senate Committee on Finance. Or when he voted for Obamacare, but made sure he and all his elitist cronies were exempt from it so they could keep their cushy Congressional healthcare plans.

Only in America!

"Senator Whitehead told me that he has always wanted to visit your museum."

"Really? You know, BoomerWorld has been open for fifteen years."

"Yes, he's just been very busy doing the People's work."

I wanted to say something cynical, but I held my tongue. After all, the Senator's presence at the party could spur ticket sales too, just like the Batmobile.

Ms. Cummings said, "There will be a total of four guests. Do you think you can accommodate us?"

What? They expected me to comp them? At $75 a ticket, that's $300! I needed every cent to stay afloat.

This was so typical of the powerful, rich and famous who think they're somehow entitled to free access, free food and drinks. Isn't it ironic that politicians, the Hollywood elite and billionaires can never find their wallets? "Gee, I'd like to pay for that bottle of Cristal Champagne, but I left my billfold out in the Lamborghini."

I guess I was supposed to be awestruck by the Senator's generous offer to attend my little soirée. Well, forget it! I couldn't afford to give away tickets—but I didn't want to offend them either.

"You know, I only have a handful of tickets left. Of course, I'd like to comp your tickets, but all proceeds benefit a private charity."

Yeah, the 'Save My Sorry Ass' charity!

There was a long pause. Finally, she said, "I guess we can pay."

“Great! Your tickets will be waiting at ‘Will Call.’ That’ll be $300. And I’ll look forward to personally welcoming all of you.” I smirked at the newspaper guys and added, “You know, we still have some tickets left for our big Halloween costume party on Saturday night. The Senator can dress up like his favorite Boomer character and—”

She cut me off. “I really don’t think the distinguished Senator is going to dress up like ‘The Fonz’.”

Actually, I was thinking of “Diamond Joe” Quimby.

I pressed on, trying to playfully bait her. “Are you sure? There will be all kinds of cool Boomer-era activities, including a Hula Hoop contest. I’ll bet the Senator is a natural.”

“Trust me, that’s one film clip that will never make the eleven o’clock news.”

“Alrighty then! We’ll see you on Sunday night, Ms. Cummings. Thanks so much for calling.”

I hung up.

With his pen at the ready, Clark quickly asked, “So Senator Whitehead will be attending the party?”

“Looks like it.”

“Would you mind if I mentioned that in the article?”

“Sure, but please don’t make it the main focus. I want Sunday night to be a final tribute to BoomerWorld, not an impromptu political rally.”

11:30 a.m.

“Magic Carpet Ride”

As I escorted the guys from the *Times* out of the building, Clark suggested that I pose for a photo under the imposing BoomerWorld logo above the front door. Hamming it up, I sat on the top step and assumed the *Dobie Gillis* ‘Thinker’ pose while the photographer snapped a few shots. As the guys were leaving, Elizabeth Frost approached on the sidewalk.

"Hello, Ms. Frost," I said. "It's nice to see you again."

She smiled wearily. "Sorry about leaving so abruptly yesterday."

"No problem. How's your father doing?"

"Better, but he's still at St. Luke's," she sighed. "I doubt he's ever going to leave."

"I'm so sorry… Is there anything I can do to help?"

"As a matter of fact, I'd like to take you up on your offer to drive me to the hospital. My car is in the shop."

I was happily surprised she chose me over an Uber. "Absolutely!"

I locked the front door, leaving Walter inside to hold down the fort.

"How'd you get here?" I asked.

"I really needed some fresh air so I walked from my condo near the Canals."

"That's a pretty long trek. You should sit down… Come! My chariot awaits!"

I led her over to my classic 1967 VW van. Sporting a custom paint job with swirling psychedelic images of rainbows, sunbursts, peace signs and BoomerWorld logos mixed with slogans like "All You Need Is Love" and "Flower Powered"—the exterior of the mini-bus was a mesmerizing kaleidoscope of iconic hippie graphics.

Proudly, I said, "Behold! The BoomerMobile!"

"Surely, you can't be serious."

Wow! She walked right into that famous *Naked Gun* set-up line. I couldn't resist. "I am… and don't call me Shirley!"

Liz didn't budge. "This van looks like somebody's idea of a bad acid trip."

"It's a travelling billboard for BoomerWorld! I've driven this exquisite machine for years and enjoyed every minute!" I said, trying to forget the numerous times it had broken down or caught fire.

I opened the passenger side door for her. "Check out the interior. It's like stepping back into the Sixties."

Reluctantly, she climbed in and sat down. Glancing at the colorful love beads hanging from the rearview mirror and the purple shag carpet, she commented, “All you need is a mattress, a bong and a bag of weed.”

I slipped in behind the horizontal steering wheel. “I’ve got that covered, too! When BoomerWorld is open, I always park this van right near the entrance to give our visitors a preview of coming attractions. I open the side doors of the bus and set up an entire display with burning incense, rock music, a water pipe and a big baggie filled with oregano. I can’t tell you how many times those bags of fake weed have been stolen.”

“What a surprise,” Liz said as she slipped on a pair of sunglasses to deal with the vibrant clash of colors. “Do you know where St. Luke’s Hospital is?”

“Yeah, Santa Monica.”

As we drove around the corner, she noticed the eight-track player under the dashboard. “Don’t tell me that thing actually works?”

“Like a charm!”

I grabbed a shoebox filled with tapes from under the seat and handed it to her. “Here. Pick one and we’ll cue it up.”

Liz flipped through the box and pulled out the *Rumours* tape by Fleetwood Mac. “I love this album. Used to listen to it all the time in college.”

I shoved the cassette into the player. “An excellent choice!”

As the tape hissed to life, we listened to “Gold Dust Woman,” driving along Pacific Avenue. After a while, I said, “Tell me more about your father.”

She stared out the window at the passing landscape. “I really don’t want to talk about Fred.”

I did a double take. “Wait a minute! Your father is Fred Frost? As in ‘Fastball’ Frost, the famous Major League pitcher?”

Liz did not avert her eyes. After a long moment, she exhaled, “Yes, that’s him.”

"Frosty is a legend!" I blurted out. "He was my hero when I was a kid."

"Good for you."

Looking bored, she turned her attention back to the box of eight-track tapes.

"What a stud! He pitched for five different franchises over his incredible career."

Liz remained silent… Realizing she was a little put off by my fawning comments, I asked, "Do I detect some friction between you and your father?"

She looked at me and said, "If you want to know the truth, my father is a pathetic, self-obsessed, old drunk."

A palpable tension filled the van.

Forever the showman, I tried to lighten the mood. "But he still made it to the Hall of Fame, right?"

"Yes, the one for assholes," she said with a note of exasperation. "Look, can we please just change the subject?"

"Sure," I said, turning the van right onto Santa Monica Blvd. We drove in silence for a while until we pulled up to a stoplight.

"By the way, do you have a copy of the BoomerWorld insurance policy we discussed?" she asked.

"Darn! I left it back in my office."

"I need it by tomorrow. Okay?"

"You got it." I exhaled slowly, relieved I had bought more time. But I knew she would probably put me on "double, secret probation" if I didn't deliver the papers soon.

After a short drive, we rolled up to the front doors under St. Luke's Hospital's porte-cochére.

"If it's okay with you, I'd really like to meet your father."

She sighed, "Okay, but don't get your hopes up. He's nobody's hero."

After pulling the van into a short-term parking spot, I climbed out and went around to open Liz's door, but she beat me to it.

"Chivalry is dead, P.T.," she said, stepping out on her own.

"Having good manners will never go out of style!" I declared.

We started to walk up to the front entrance when I remembered something.

"Just a sec," I said. I ran back and slid open the van's side door. I slipped on my L.A. Dodgers cap and gave her a big smile. "If I'm going to meet your father, I'd better look like a real fan."

"Whatever."

"You know, I was at that World Series game back in 1974 when Frosty came in as a reliever and pitched three perfect innings against the A's. It was a great moment in baseball lore."

"And then he went out and got drunk, fell down a flight of stairs and broke his wrist, which ended his career permanently," Liz said with disgust.

"Well, at least he went out on top!"

"Actually, his teammates found Fred at the *bottom* of that staircase—passed out cold. The Dodgers ended up losing the Series. He let them down just like he always did with everyone."

Yikes! I didn't want to get between Liz and her father, but I still had to meet one of baseball's greatest players.

"Let's go," I said, grabbing a small stack of promotional flyers for BoomerWorld, which were covered with splashy graphics, photos of the exhibits, and a blurb about the upcoming weekend events. "I can do a little marketing while I escort you to your father's bedside."

Noon

"Sympathy for The Devil"

Liz and I walked through the spacious hospital lobby and took the elevator to the fifth floor. As she led the way, I passed out flyers to every ambulatory adult in sight.

"You never stop, do you?"

"Can't afford to!" I replied, littering a waiting area with more handbills. "The show must go on!"

We walked down a long, sterile hallway, passing many patient's rooms and busy nurse's stations.

"My father's room is right up here," Liz said, as we approached a private room at the end of the corridor. At that moment, a silver-haired physician studying a medical chart, emerged from inside. Looking up, he said, "Oh, Ms. Frost. Nice to see you again."

"Hello, Dr. Lollar," replied Liz and gestured at me, "This is Bob Apple, a business associate of mine."

As he shook my hand, he gave me the once over. With longish, graying hair sprouting out from beneath my baseball cap, cartoony tie and funky clothes, I looked more like the crazy cousin from Cleveland than a "business associate."

Steeling herself for possible bad news, she tightly clasped her hands together and made direct eye contact with the doctor. "How's he doing today?"

The doctor gave me another suspicious look and turned to Liz.

"May I speak freely?"

"Go ahead."

Dr. Lollar closed the chart and said, "He's got so many things wrong with him, it's tough to nail it down: major liver disease, kidney and prostate issues, diabetes. The list is long and getting longer... Most patients in his state are so weak and depressed they can't get out of bed, but Fred is in there flirting with the nurse. Despite all his problems, he still has the heart of a lion—and apparently, the libido of one too."

Liz nodded. "You know, when he fell at home yesterday he was trying to get to the liquor cabinet."

The doctor said, "He's lucky he didn't break his hip or worse."

"He's been drunk for years... What's the prognosis?"

Lollar sighed and gave her a solemn look. "I'm ordering more blood tests and an CT scan for tomorrow. We'll know more after that… Despite all he's going through, your father is one tough old bird. He probably still has a few fastballs left up his sleeve."

The door to Fred's room burst open. A flustered, female nurse emerged, trying to hide a naughty little smile.

"And a few rockets in his pocket," I added.

As Liz shook her head, the Doc and I shared a knowing smile.

"Please let me know when those test results are ready," she said.

I handed the doctor a flyer. "Listen, if you want to cheer up any of your patients, send them over to BoomerWorld this weekend."

As Dr. Lollar studied the handbill, I pitched the program, "You would also enjoy many of our exhibits! We have a lab coat worn by *Marcus Welby*, a medical tricorder used by 'Bones' McCoy on *Star Trek* and everyone's favorite: an original *Dr. Kildare* 'Thumpy–The Heartbeat' Stethoscope."

"Well, who can resist seeing an original 'Thumpy'?" replied the physician as he tucked the flyer into his pocket. "Maybe my wife and I can stop by."

He nodded goodbye and then ambled down the hallway toward the nurse's station.

"Are you sure you still want to meet Fred?" Liz asked pensively. "As you now know, he's very ill and has some dementia."

"Come on, let's go cheer him up!" I said, gently placing my hand on her back while reaching for the door.

This time she didn't flinch.

"Centerfield"

Sitting upright in his hospital bed, Fred "Fastball" Frost stared out the window, lost in his thoughts. I was struck by how much "Frosty" had physically deteriorated. When he played ball, he had been a big, lanky man, maybe six-foot-four with huge hands. During his playing years, Frosty exuded total confidence both on and off the mound. When he wasn't in the ballpark, he did commercials for Wheaties and Coca-Cola, until his carousing and legendary bar room brawling undermined his polished Madison Avenue image. After he retired, he worked briefly as a color commentator for televised MLB games throughout the 1980s. Then, he just faded away. Now, he was a shell of his former self, but he still had a commanding presence and those piercing cobalt blue eyes that intimidated batters for two decades.

"Well, hello, Lizzy," Fred mumbled in his trademark Texas drawl as we approached his bed, which was strewn with the newspaper sports section.

"It's Elizabeth, remember?" she said as she swept up the paper, placing it on the bedside table.

"Whatever you say, Lizzy," Fred replied, winking at me. "Who's your friend?"

"This is Bob Apple. He's a client of the bank."

Tipping my hat, I said, "I'm a big fan, Mr. Frost."

We shook hands. Fred's grip was clammy and weak.

"Hey, you can call me Fred or Frosty or just 'Asshole', which is the endearing name Lizzy prefers," he said with a smirk.

She rolled her eyes and walked off.

Glancing at my baseball cap, he asked, "So you're a Dodger's fan?"

"Absolutely! I was born and raised here in LaLaLand. In fact, as I was just telling your charming daughter, I was at that historic World Series game when you pitched for the Dodgers against the A's."

Fred smiled humbly. "The reporters covering the sports beat always talked about how relaxed and cool I was on the mound, but I was petrified when I came into that game."

"No wonder! It was the top of the seventh inning and the Dodgers were clinging to a one-run lead. There were no outs, the bases were loaded, and Reggie Jackson was at the plate. But you struck him out and the next eight batters too!"

"For a fleeting moment, I had lightning in a bottle," Fred shrugged. "I just got lucky."

"Lucky? You fired three pitches over a hundred miles an hour in that game!"

"Actually, earlier that season, Nolan Ryan was the first pitcher ever to be officially clocked at over a hundred miles an hour. He was awesome."

"Yeah, but you were pitching in the frickin' World Series!"

"It's nice to know that someone remembers."

"Are you kidding? I followed your entire career! You played twenty-one years in 'The Bigs'—starting with the Red Sox in 1953. Later, you suited up with the Pirates, Orioles and Tigers before finishing with the L.A. Dodgers. Unbelievable!"

Liz sat in the corner flipping through a magazine. "What is it about boys and balls?"

"Isn't it obvious?" I asked with a straight face.

Fred chuckled and looked over at Liz. "You just missed the doctor."

"We bumped into him in the hallway," she replied. "He filled me in."

Fred shook his head. "That guy is always so damn serious."

"Your condition *is* serious, Fred."

"Don't worry. You won't have to put up with me for much longer, Lizzy." Fred sighed heavily. "God is slowly turning off the lights in the ol' ballpark."

Without looking up, she said, "Oh, don't be so melodramatic."

There was a long, painful pause in the conversation. I felt like a fly on the wall—a very uncomfortable fly.

Clearly, Fred and Liz had a very strained relationship that had evolved over many years. Based upon his wild, headline-grabbing antics off the field, I guessed she was angry over being abandoned as a child while he pursued his baseball career and other testosterone-fueled activities, including many adulterous affairs. Meanwhile, Fred was forever trying to get back into her good graces. And now, as he stood on death's doorstep, weak and vulnerable, she had become the reluctant parent and caregiver, which added even more tension to their fragile relationship.

Fred grimaced in pain as he tried to hoist himself higher up on the bed. I reached out to help him, but he waved me off.

"I'm fine, Bob," he said, exhaling slowly to control the discomfort. "You know, you're probably the last real fan I've got."

"I doubt that. If word got out that you were here, I'm sure throngs of baseball fans would flock to your door to pay homage to one of the great players of all time."

"I don't want any publicity. Except for a few memorabilia shows over the last few decades where I signed a bunch of balls, T-shirts and hats, I've managed to lead a quiet life."

"Don't forget about the two DUIs and the fist fight at that country club bar, which made national headlines a few years ago," Liz interjected, still staring down at her magazine.

Fred looked over at me and shrugged. "Some drunk Yankee fan got in my face and I had to straighten him out."

She added. "You were drunk, too. And that little escapade cost you the last penny of your savings."

"Then I got sick and hit rock bottom," Fred said. "But my little girl came to the rescue and took me in."

"And I've been regretting it ever since," she said under her breath.

"Do you and Lizzy work together?"

Grateful for a shift in the conversation, I said, "Yes. I'm one of her favorite clients!" I handed Fred a flyer. "BoomerWorld is my tribute to the Baby Boom Generation, but after fifteen years, I'm closing the doors after this weekend."

Fred studied the handbill. "Technically, since I was born in 1935, I think I'm a member of the so-called 'Silent Majority.'"

"Silent?" asked Liz. "You never seem to shut up."

Fred chuckled. “That’s my girl!”

“I’ve read all about your generation,” I said. “You were wedged in there between ‘The Greatest Generation’ and us Boomers. Luckily, you missed most of the Depression and were too young for the horrors of WW2 or the Korean War. Generally, your compatriots were considered hardworking and conventional. They didn’t protest, issue any demented manifestos or try to change the world. In essence, the exact opposite of my generation.”

“I identified a lot more with you hedonistic Boomers,” Fred said, coughing a little. “I had a rather hard time keeping a low profile.”

“Of course! You were famous! Flamboyant! A shooting star!”

“Geez. You can really lay it on thick!” Fred hung his head. “The fact is, I was a selfish prick who was swept up in the insanity of the Sixties and Seventies. It was all about *me*. I put my own needs and desires before my responsibilities as a husband and father.”

He turned to Liz and, in a sincere tone, said, “And I deeply regret it.”

She looked away unable to cope with her father’s spontaneous, heartfelt confession. Once again, I felt like I was intruding on a sensitive family moment.

“Listen, Fred. If you feel up to it, I’ll give you a VIP tour of BoomerWorld any time.”

Fred forced a smile and shook his head. “Thanks, but I’m never leaving this place.”

Liz put down the magazine and walked over to his bed. “Don’t be so negative. Tomorrow’s test results could be good news.”

Wearily, Fred said. “Nah… it’s the bottom of the ninth and the stands are empty.”

After a pregnant pause that lasted longer than an “In-A-Gadda-Da-Vida” drum solo, I switched gears again. “You know, I have your rookie card on display at BoomerWorld. Had it since I was a kid. It’s pretty dog-eared, but still a classic.”

“I appreciate you trying to cheer me up, Bob. That old card will probably be worth more when I'm dead."

I glanced over at Liz. Detecting a slight softening in her irritable attitude toward her father, I took off the baseball cap and handed it to Fred. "Well, at least try this on for size."

Fred slipped it on. It fit perfectly. Once again, he was the legendary "Fastball" Frost. With a mischievous sparkle in his watery blue eyes, he said, "You know, before I die, I only want two simple things."

"What?"

"A cold beer and a hand job."

"Oh, my God!" Liz gasped and quickly turned away.

For a fleeting moment, Fred's pale cheeks flushed with excitement. "Despite being so sick, the doc says my heart is still strong. I can handle it. It's a dying man's last wish."

"Well, it sounds good!" I said, imagining me and Booker dragging Fred into a local massage parlor like a scene from *Weekend at Bernie's*.

"Please! Don't encourage him."

Realizing that it was time to go, I shook Fred's hand again. "It was a pleasure to meet you, sir."

"Come by any time, Bob," Fred said. "But don't wait too long because… well, you know."

"Keep the hat! It looks a lot better on you," I said, turning toward the door.

Fred called out, "And don't forget that beer!"

Liz accompanied me out into the hallway. "Sorry about Fred. He's on drugs, you know."

"Are you kidding? That was the thrill of a lifetime!"

"I'm glad you think so."

I gave her a serious look. "It's bad, isn't it?"

"Seems to be getting worse every day."

Recalling the final, painful days I spent with my wife, I just nodded.

After yet another long, awkward silence, she said, "Well, I'd better go back inside. As you can see, Fred is still a handful."

"Thanks again for letting me tag along."

"And thanks for the lift."

2:30 p.m.

"Born in The U.S.A."

After running some small errands around town, I returned to BoomerWorld to find three guys peeking through the glass panels on the front doors.

"Can I help you, gentlemen?"

The men turned to face me. Sporting loud golf attire and sunburns, they appeared to be in their late sixties.

The short stocky guy with a weird bowl haircut said, "Oh, hello there. We just stopped by to check out the place."

Looking up at the big BoomerWorld logo above the entrance, the thin dude with a shock of curly gray hair said, "The graphics are very compelling."

The fat, bald dude chimed in. "It's 'poifect'!"

I smiled, barely able to control laughing out loud. These guys were right out of central casting. I immediately named them Moe, Larry and Curly.

Larry asked, "Do you work for BoomerWorld?"

"Yes! I'm Bob Apple, the owner. Nice to meet you."

We all shook hands.

Each guy stated his real name, but of course, I wasn't listening. They would always be *The Three Stooges* to me.

Blinded by their plaid polyester pants and garish pink and lime-green shirts, I slipped on my sunglasses. "You guys look like you play golf."

"How'd you guess?" asked Curly.

Moe chimed in. "We're here on a golfing vacation from Chicago. Hitting all the top courses. We heard about your museum and decided to stop by."

"We're all Boomers!" said Curly.

"And we already bought tickets online for your Halloween Party," said Larry, the guy with the weird hair.

"Well, thanks for your support, fellas." Remembering that I left all the lights on inside during the tour with the newspaper guys, I said. "Come on, I'll let you take a quick look inside."

I unlocked the front door and held it open for my guests. The men walked through the foyer to the main exhibit hall. They seemed awestruck by all the interior graphics. In addition to the giant wraparound wall mural, there were many more graphics hanging from the ceiling beams as well as tall, freestanding displays scattered throughout the large open space.

"Wow!" said Moe.

"Ditto that!" replied Curly.

Larry said, "You must have spent an enormous amount of time securing the usage rights for all these images."

"It was a daunting task, but I was lucky. My brother-in-law is a retired intellectual property attorney. Many of the photos are government owned or are in the public domain like the ones of the U.S. presidents, various wars and the space program; however, we had to negotiate with the owners of the copyrighted images. Generally, everyone agreed to contribute once they learned that BoomerWorld was an educational retrospective. And then I hired a graphic designer to help me put it all together."

Staring at a tall display in the center of the hall that featured side-by-side photos of Howdy Doody and Ho Chi Minh, Larry asked, "Were those two images randomly placed together or are you trying to make a point?"

Moe and Curly considered the display too.

Curly blurted out, "Hey, it's Howdy Doody. I loved that guy!"

"Buffalo Bob was a God," added Moe solemnly.

While Moe and Curly clearly belonged in the "Peanut Gallery," it was obvious that Larry was the intellectual of the bunch.

Turning to Larry, I asked, "What do *you* think?"

"Well, I may be over analyzing it, but by juxtaposing a funny marionette that American kids loved with the leader of the Viet Cong, I think you're trying to say that our generation went through a dramatic transition from childhood innocence to the harsh realities of the real world."

I smiled. That was exactly what I was trying to convey, but very few people actually make the connection.

"Heavy," said Curly.

Moe said, "Only a university professor could sum it up so precisely."

Larry sheepishly acknowledged, "Yes, I taught humanities at Yale before I retired."

"He may be brilliant, but his putting sucks," said Moe, like having a good short game was more important than a keen intellect.

"Can't chip worth a damn either," said Curly, playing pocket pool.

Looking at Moe and Curly, I asked, "So, what did you guys do for a living?"

"I worked for the IRS," Moe replied.

Curly said "And I ran a plumbing business!"

"You'd still be in the slammer if I had audited your books," said Moe, poking Curly in the ribs with his elbow.

"What books?" said Curly.

They all laughed on cue. It was obviously an old joke between them. Still, I wondered why these guys would even hang out together. I asked, "Can you guess what photos are on the other side of that display?"

"Captain Kangaroo!" Moe blurted out.

"With Mr. Green Jeans!" exclaimed Curly.

Luckily, this wasn't an I.Q. test.

"Actually, it's the Partridge Family and the Manson Family," I said.

Larry nodded. "Another brilliant dichotomy."

His friends looked a little confused.

I noticed that Moe was checking out all the televisions scattered throughout the arena. "What's with all the different TVs, Bob?"

"That's one of my proudest technical achievements. I hired a multimedia firm to put it all together. There are over twenty TVs all networked together via a sophisticated computer system. Each screen has its own special programming, which relates to the historical or cultural section where they're positioned."

I pointed at the vintage TV set at the corner of the Hiroshima photo, "For instance, that unit plays a half-hour loop of old news footage depicting the final days of World War II, the devastation, the post-war celebrations, America transitioning from a war-time economy to an industrial giant, etc. As you walk around the pavilion, these televisions will take you back through every phase of your lives. You'll see hundreds of major political and social events, sports events, classic TV shows, commercials, and more.

"For an extra five bucks, you can rent one of our hand-held digital media players. You just click on the TV screen number and the sound will automatically stream into your headphones. You can pull up a chair and watch TV for hours."

Larry observed, "TV is the ideal medium for us Boomers. It defines us. After all, we were all suckled on the Boob Tube."

"Suckling boobs?" asked Curly. "Well, sign me up!"

"Me too!" said Moe.

I was starting to like these knuckleheads. Sweeping my hand across the room, I said, "You can spend a whole day in here and not see everything. BoomerWorld will be an intense experience for you. The smallest item, news clip or song can trigger a flood of memories to come rushing back."

Moe said, "Your brochure mentioned that there's an exact replica of the Cheers Bar here somewhere."

"Yup. It's way back there," I said, pointing to the northeastern corner of the exhibition hall. "Tell you what. I'd love to buy you guys a round of drinks at the party on Saturday night."

Curly blurted out, "Right on!"

"Can you guess what costumes we'll be wearing?" asked Moe.

"Surprise me!"

"We're coming as *The Three Amigos!* Remember the movie?"

"Loved it!"

"And our wives are all dressing up like *Charlie's Angels*," said Curly.

The visual of their geriatric counterparts packed into spandex jumpsuits was a disturbing thought.

Larry asked, "So what is the most valuable artifact in your collection?"

I pondered the question. "Well, there are many really unique items from the Fifties through the Eighties. Rare products, toys, clothing, book and magazine collections, classic cars and sports memorabilia. It's not really the monetary value of any single item. Rather, it's the sum total of all the displays and artifacts. The comprehensive collection is priceless!"

"Given the sentimental value, it may seem priceless to us," observed Larry. "But I'm sorry to say, younger generations would probably call most of it 'worthless'."

I shrugged. "You're absolutely right."

I pointed over towards the toy exhibit. "I know that you guys probably can't relate, but we also have one of the biggest Barbie Doll collections in the world."

"Remind me to skip that section," said Moe as the other guys nodded in solemn agreement.

"Remember Poindexter? That guy really creeped me out," Curly said.

"I believe that he was the original, archetypal nerd," said Larry.

"I got the worst spanking of my life after I twisted the head off one of my sister's Ken dolls," Moe added. "But it was worth it."

We all laughed.

Curly said, "We're sorry to hear this is the final weekend for BoomerWorld."

"Yeah, it's a real bummer," said Moe.

"But there is some good news. For this final weekend, we're featuring a very special item that should turn every head in the place," I teased. "I'll give you a hint: it's worth over four million bucks."

They all looked at me like I was about to open Door Number Three on *Let's Make A Deal.*

"The original Batmobile!"

"Holy Hollywood, Batman!" exclaimed Curly. "That's the coolest car on the planet."

"I had a model of the Batmobile when I was a kid. Kept it right next to my bed," Moe said proudly.

"The owner is a fellow Boomer," I said. "He knows how special that car is to our entire generation."

"It's only fitting that you drive off into the sunset behind the wheel of the Batmobile, Bob," said Larry. It was a nice thought, but given my fiscal situation, driving over a cliff in my old VW van was more realistic.

Moe checked his watch. "Hey guys, if we're going to make that last tee time before the rain starts again, we should get going."

Larry asked, "Do you play golf, Bob?"

"Yeah, maybe you can join us," added Moe.

"No, I quit back during the Carter Administration. Got a hole-in-one and retired on the spot. It's always better to go out on top."

"I got a hole-in-one once," said Curly with a huge grin.

"Miniature golf doesn't count, numbskull!" said Moe, playfully slapping Curly on the side of the head.

"I enjoyed talking with you, fellas. Here's a gift for the road." I dug into my pocket and removed three round, red candies and dropped them into the guy's outstretched hands.

"It's an Atomic Fireball!" said Larry.

Moe marveled, "I haven't seen one of these in fifty years."

Impulsively, Curly popped the fireball into his mouth. "I love these things."

Moe said, "I'll bet you twenty bucks you can't keep it your mouth until it's completely dissolved."

"Soitenly," said Curly, but his shaved head was already starting to glow like Three Mile Island.

We bid farewell, promising to meet up on Saturday night at the Halloween party.

As they walked over to their rental car, I could have sworn that I heard Curly mutter, "Nyuk, nyuk, nyuk"—right before his head exploded.

"People Are Strange"

Like a jar of Jelly Belly "Belly Flops," Boomers come in all shapes, sizes and colors, philosophical and religious types, rich and poor, cool and nerdy.

There are countless Baby Boom clichés and stereotypes, and I've shamefully exploited every last one to promote BoomerWorld. Of course, most of those profiles are exaggerations, rising to near mythic proportions, thanks in large part to the craziness of the 1960s. In truth, the vast majority of Boomers are reasonably sane, successful in their careeers and lives, and pay their taxes (reluctantly); however, there is some truth to the notion that many are as useless as a pack of Sylvania Blue Dot Flashbulbs.

Take the aging Hippie—please.

In January 1967, the famous "Human Be-In" was held in Golden Gate Park in San Francisco, which came to symbolize the dawn of a new counterculture. The great "Gathering of Tribes" included Timothy Leary—"The Pied Piper of LSD"—beat poets, religious and political activists, and local rock bands. The Hippie Movement ushered in The

Psychedelic Era, with its promises of greater unity, social, artistic, and political awareness, and "higher" consciousness.

Eight months later, when George Harrison came to Haight Ashbury to experience "all these groovy kinds of gypsy people" who were having "spiritual awakenings," he quickly realized this new culture was infested with a bunch of drugged-out "bums." The legendary musician was so disillusioned, he abruptly left town, stopped taking LSD and turned to meditation.

Nevertheless, in our unrestrained, self-obsessed pursuit of nirvana and just having a good time (*all the time*), millions of Boomers "turned on, tuned in and dropped out." Our mantras were: "Make love not war" and "live in the moment." We jumped aboard the "Crazy Train" of sex, drugs and rock'n'roll, and promptly careened over the nearest precipice. Many of us never recovered. For some, Woodstock—"3 Days of Peace & Music"—was the seminal event in the hippie saga. For others, it was the ugly and violent Altamont Free Festival, where the Hell's Angels stabbed a guy to death right in front of the stage where The Stones were performing.

No wonder our generation is so schizophrenic, conflicted and downright depressed at times.

Anyway, by the end of 1969, after Tiny Tim had strummed his ukulele and sang "Tiptoe Through the Tulips" in his falsetto voice for the millionth time, the counterculture movement was fading faster than a blotter of Orange Sunshine on a hot VW dashboard.

Today, many of those old hippie burn-outs still cling to their liberal, utopian fantasies. You see them everywhere: driving beat-up Subarus plastered with Bernie and COEXIST bumper stickers, protesting on freeway overpasses, and using their EBT cards at Costco. You imagine they have some Boone's Farm Strawberry Hill Wine chillin' in the fridge and boxes of Screaming Yellow Zonkers in the cupboard. However, it's more likely they exist on Kirkland Beer, Domino's Pizza, and stool softeners. With their crazy political conspiracy theories, these tie-dyed ne'er-do-wells still consider themselves to be valiant social justice warriors, but they can be pretty hypocritical. Back in the day, they proclaimed their universal love and respect for all "living things"—yet they had no problem ridiculing Hare Krishnas, "Jesus Freaks" and anyone else who disagreed with them.

Personally, I subscribe to the old adage: "If you're not a liberal at twenty-five, you have no heart, but if you're not a conservative at thirty-five you have no brain." It took me a long time to figure out that a lot of the social commentary and revisionist history I had been fed as a college student was bullshit. Like a character from Doonesbury, I clung to those idealistic notions until the real world bludgeoned me into being a cynical iconoclast.

Of course, every generation gets a rude awakening at some point. Our parents were shocked when Charles Van Doren was exposed as a fraud on the hit quiz show *Twenty-One*. Boomers were nonplussed when social activist Jerry Rubin of The Chicago Seven became a stockbroker. Or when Anton LaVey became a "born again Christian." (Not really, but he did die in a Catholic hospital.) What's next? Ted Nugent becomes a vegan? Al Sharpton actually pays his taxes? Louis Farrakhan converts to Judaism? Mike Lindell accidentally suffocates under a 'My Pillow'? Michael Moore stops being an insufferable ass?

No doubt, the Baby Boom has produced many accomplished (and often inspirational) individuals: Stephen Hawking, Tim Berners-Lee, Steve Wozniak and Steve Jobs, Bill Gates, Dr. Ben Carson, Sally Ride, Pat Tillman, Michael Jordan, Steven Spielberg and Oprah Winfrey, among others. But at the same time, our generation has also spawned the greatest collection of serial killers in history: Ted Bundy, David Berkowitz, Richard "The Night Stalker" Ramirez, Jeffrey Dahmer, Edmond Kemper, Aileen Wuarnos, Wayne Williams, Kenneth Bianchi, Charles Ng and Dennis "The BK Killer" Rader.[5]

With Boomers, it's always one extreme to the other.

---

[5] *Most people assume Charles Manson was a Boomer because he was so closely associated with hippie culture; however, he was actually a member of the preceding Silent Generation, which is ironic since he had such a big mouth.*

4:30 p.m.

"One Bourbon, One Scotch, One Beer"

Walter and I headed out for a long stroll down the beach. I especially enjoy walking along the shore in the cooler fall and winter months when there are fewer tourists. By and large, the locals are nice, smiling and waving as they walk or jog by. And Walter bumps into plenty of his canine friends.

As we rambled along, from the breakwater down to the pier and back again, my thoughts shifted to the future…

After the coming weekend, which will probably be followed by the biggest clearance sale of Boomer items ever, I hoped to have enough dough to buy a decent truck to tow my trailer to some distant place where I could start a new life. For months, I tried to devise a plan of action with a specific destination, but for some reason, I just couldn't stay focused on it. The idea was intoxicating, but down deep I knew that until I put BoomerWorld in my rearview mirror, I was never going to sort things out.

When Walter and I arrived at Booker's place, a light rain was falling. As we approached Booker's perch at the end of the bar, I could tell he was feelin' no pain. His daily ritual consisted of power-drinking coffee all day before switching to craft beer during cocktail hour. Later, he'll usually whip up some margaritas and sample some wine with dinner—before swan diving into a pool of expensive bourbon. He could put it away like Foster Brooks, but never seemed to get drunk. He was fond of quoting Rodney Dangerfield: "I drink too much. The last time I gave a urine sample, it had an olive in it."

"Can I buy you a drink," Booker asked.

"No thanks. I overdid it last night."

"Well, how about a Bloody Mary? Hair of the dog!"

"A soda water with lime will be fine."

As the bartender handed me my drink, Booker checked out a wide angle shot of a gorgeous gal with perfect posture and great gams on his small TV. "Where does FOX find all those news babes?"

"I think they're secretly bred on 'The Island of Dr. Ailes'."

"Road trip!"

"Road?"

"Okay, we'll charter a boat!"

We watched the newscast for a while. In this age of non-stop political insanity, division and resistance, intersectionality and identity politics, I tried to avoid hot-button partisan issues. Everyone has an opinion about the sad state of our current affairs—and everyone thinks they're right.

"I could agree with you, but we'd both be wrong."

Maybe that's why I like museums. Everything is past tense—factual, documented, and frozen in time. Whenever I think about American politics the first image that springs to mind is the severed head of the Statue of Liberty jutting up from the beach at the end of *Planet of the Apes*. For me, it's the perfect metaphor to sum up how Boomers have handled the levers of government, the economy and culture over the last fifty years. Frankly, we blew it—and it started at the top.

The talking heads on TV were discussing the next crop of presidential candidates. One commentator asked the age-old question about likability: "Which candidate would you rather have a beer with?"

Booker looked at me. "Tell me, Bob. Of all the previous Boomer presidential candidates, who would you like to hang out with?"

I took the bait, knowing I was probably going to alienate everyone within earshot, but frankly I didn't give a damn. I'm an "Equal Opportunity Offender."

Abandoning the soda water, I bellowed, "Bring me a scotch! This is gonna take a while."

Channeling Dennis Miller, I launched into a major rant. "That question is more loaded than Charlie Sheen in a Bangkok strip club, but here goes… We've elected four Boomer presidents: Bill Clinton,

George W. Bush, Barack Obama and Donald Trump. They all had different personalities and agendas, but knew the secret for success was to keep it simple and over promise: “It’s the economy, stupid,” “Compassionate Conservatism,” “Yes we can” and “Make America Great Again.” Face it, we’re suckers for superficiality and easy answers. In essence, if “Mikey likes it!”—it must be good.

“Let’s start with ‘Slick Willie.’ William Jefferson Clinton was born in 1946 at the very genesis of the Baby Boom. Over the course of two presidential elections, he faced three impressive “Greatest Generation” candidates. In 1992, Clinton squared off against George H.W. Bush, who possessed the best resume ever (*sorry, Hillary*), and Ross Perot, a fiery, independent Texas businessman, who was lampooned as a ‘hand grenade with a crew cut.’ After Perot siphoned off nineteen percent of conservative voters, Clinton easily beat Bush—depriving him of a second term. Boomers finally had one of their own in The Big Chair. Then in 1996, Clinton easily vanquished both Perot and old Bob Dole, an affable WW2 hero who referred to himself in the third person and spent his golden years hocking penis pills.

"Despite attending Yale and Oxford, Clinton (aka “Bubba”) came across as a good ‘ol boy who enjoyed playing the sax, lying about smoking dope and his countless sexual escapades. The biggest problem with having a beer with Bubba was sooner or later the evening was going to go downhill faster than Fat Bastard on a Hobie Super Surfer Skateboard. Once Bubba got a good buzz on, it was only a matter of time before the next ‘Bimbo Eruption.’ One minute you’re swigging a Budweiser in the Oval Office, and the next, Bubba has his pants around his ankles, waiting for a hot intern to deliver a pizza. Plus, you always had to worry about Hillary barging into the room right when Bubba broke out the cigars. Forget the blue dress, rumor has it that when he finally left office, they had to power wash the place to get all the stains out.”

“Gross, but true,” observed Booker. “Clinton’s true legacy wasn’t a booming economy or welfare reform, it was elementary kids learning about oral sex and that Presidents lie. Talk about ‘crying in your beer.’”

The bartender delivered my drink. "Next, we have George W. Bush versus Al Gore in 2000 and then John Kerry in 2004—all bona fide, blue-blood Boomers. Unlike most of our generation who were either lower or middle-class, these scions of wealthy and politically well-connected families weren't just born with silver spoons in their mouths—they all arrived choking on an entire place setting.

"Although the media painted Gore and Kerry as intellectually superior to the bumbling Bush, (including rumors that he wrote his autobiography with finger paint)—somehow 'Dubya' won both elections, including that farce down in Florida. As privileged Ivy League elitists, all three were mediocre students who enlisted in the military during the Vietnam War. While Bush joined the Texas Air National Guard and spent most of his time falling off a barstool outside of Houston, Gore and Kerry actually went to Southeast Asia.

"Gore worked as an Army photojournalist, mostly shooting 'meet'n'greets' in the rear with the gear. During his presidential campaign, Gore came off as stiff and arrogant, which probably turned off many beer drinkers, particularly in his home state. And after his movie *An Inconvenient Truth*, which made *The Hellstrom Chronicles* actually look plausible, most sane people would rather share a melting iceberg with a starving polar bear than sit through another movie by the pompous, self-ordained 'High Priest of Global Warming'."

Booker said, "Yeah, that self-serving hypocrite sold Current, his cable television network for something like $100 million to Qatar, the owner of Al Jazeera and supporter of Islamic terrorism. Apparently, Gore needs all that dirty oil money to subsidize his gigantic carbon footprint."

I said, "Meanwhile, Kerry collected so many citations and medals (including a few of dubious merit) as a Swift Boat commander in Vietnam, he made Audie Murphy look like a member of Code Pink. One would think that voters would prefer to have a beer with such a decorated veteran, but Bush won that election too. Given his effete persona, Kerry didn't seem comfortable tipping back a brewski and laughing at a dirty joke. Instead, that windbag would rather open an expensive bottle of Château Lafite Rothschild while pontificating about the nuances of wind surfing, cycling wear or investment strategies for his wife's multibillion-dollar ketchup inheritance. And based upon Kerry's tenure as Obama's bungling Secretary of State, where his crack negotiation skills were on display for all to see, we should all be forever grateful that Lurch was never elected President. He couldn't find the prize in a box of Cracker Jacks."

Booker laughed. "Yeah, he's dumber than Dan Quayle at a spelling bee."

"Rimshot!" I yelled and sipped my drink. "And then there's George W. Bush. He seemed like a regular guy to hang with and he'd probably even give you a funny nickname like 'Turd Blossom,' but he needed an extra helping of 'strategery' to run the country into the ground. Sure, as an ex-college fraternity president, Bush was capable of planning a toga party, but had no idea how to pay for it or how to clean up the huge mess afterward—kinda like the Iraq War. During his first campaign, he promised 'no nation-building.' And what did we get? Trillions of dollars more in national debt, botched wars and futile, half-assed nation-building projects in both Iraq and Afghanistan."

Booker said, "Thanks to 'The Surge' during Bush's second term, Iraq was eventually stabilized, but that whole Neo-Con wet dream of bringing democracy to the Middle East was a Texas-sized historical blunder, despite the incredible sacrifices of our military. Of course, the world is a better place without Saddam Hussein, but at what price?"

"And having some beer with Dubya wouldn't be a picnic either," I said. "While you pounded back some potent longnecks, George, a reformed alcoholic, would abstain while psyching himself up for an intense workout. Next thing you know, he talks you into 'a little bike ride' around his ranch in Crawford, Texas. After you huff 'n'puff about twenty miles out into the hot, dusty desert, Dubya remembers there's a Rangers' game coming on TV. He and his Secret Service detail ditch you out there with the tumbleweeds and rattlesnakes. Your body is never found."

I noticed a small crowd was tuning into my rant. I turned to Booker and said, "Bring me another shot, bro. I'll need it to finish this wretched tirade."

As Booker reached for the bottle of Glenfiddich, I ramped it up.

"Next, we come to Barack Hussein Obama, aka 'The Emperor'—his words not mine. Born in the last years of the Baby Boom, he squared off against another honorable war hero, John McCain, in 2008. While Obama was learning to parse words in a Muslim elementary school in Jakarta, McCain's Navy jet was shot down over North Vietnam. McCain fractured both arms and a leg when he ejected. Then, after nearly being drowned in a lake, he was dragged to shore by a bloodthirsty mob, where he was bayoneted and bludgeoned. From 1967-1973, when most Boomers were tossing around Frisbees at rock concerts, McCain was being tortured, starved and mercilessly beaten in the Hanoi Hilton. And when he was offered an early release from captivity, he rebuked his captors and stayed with his fellow prisoners."

"Brass balls!" said Booker.

"A political moderate, Senator McCain had much more experience than Obama, the smooth-talking former community organizer from Chicago, but he got stomped worse than Gordon Gekko at an Occupy Wall Street protest. Who would want to have a beer with a cranky, crippled old war vet like McCain when you could shoot a few hoops and then enjoy some home-brewed honey ale with 'The Annointed One'?"

I could hear some angry muttering among the liberals in the crowd, but forged ahead anyway.

"A gifted teleprompter reader, Obama spent more time running against Bush than McCain. Obama was just too cool. Standing at the podium, with his jutting jaw, head tilted back and eyes gazing upward at the Heavens, Obama looked like he was doing a Vulcan mind-meld with God himself. As the fawning media applauded his every move and rarely pointed out any of his foibles, Obama even picked up a Nobel Peace Prize for *not* being Bush. However, after his first term, many Americans were chanting: 'Yes we can'—replace him."

Booker chimed in. "Mitt Romney was just too damn timid for the blood sport of presidential politics. And having a beer with such a devout Mormon wasn't gonna happen. You'd be lucky to get a nice glass of chocolate milk or, if 'Pierre Delecto' was feeling a little frisky, maybe a caffeine-free Diet Coke. Boring!"

I said, "Forget the beer analogy for a second. Plenty of stoners relished the idea of chilling with Obama—the undisputed bong master of 'The Choom Gang.' Very few people know that Obama had his own black light room down in the bowels of the White House, which probably explains where he was on the night of the Benghazi attack... Face it, getting baked with the most powerful man in the world would be totally da Bomb."

Booker laughed. "Hey, Barry, don't bogart that joint!"

"Electing our first black President was historic. It was a very proud day for our nation. With Democratic party majorities in both houses of Congress, Obama had unprecedented power and the opportunity to do some truly great things. And when he pledged to 'fundamentally transform' America he wasn't just blowing smoke with his old high school buddies."

Booker said, "When he wasn't playing golf or using his handy selfie stick, Barry ran an imperial presidency. Like he once said, 'That's the good thing about being president. I can do whatever I want.' And he was right!"

The eavesdropping crowd was growing restless.

"When the history books are written, Obama's failures will be quietly swept under the rug: the weakest post-recession recovery ever, the dual catastrophes of Obamacare and the failed stimulus plan, a bevy of growth-killing regulations, doubling the National Debt to almost twenty trillion dollars with virtually nothing to show for it, a major deterioration in race relations, the IRS and VA scandals ('not even a smidgen of corruption'), the phony 'red line' in Syria and basically handing the country over to the Russians, the 'Fast & Furious' arms debacle, abandoning Iraq and the destabilization of Libya which led to the rise of ISIS and displacement of millions of refugees into Europe, the flawed nuclear Iranian arms deal and the cash ransom payments to the mullahs who are still chanting "Death to America!" It's quite a legacy."

"Regardless, Obama will always be remembered for looking great in a suit," said Booker.

I continued, "And you can be assured that his mega million-dollar, multi-volume autobiography will portray him as a brilliant globalist who valiantly tried to save the planet, but was thwarted by racists, conservative talk radio scoundrels, FOX News, and those annoying Lilliputians in the Tea Party."

"Hey, go easy on the brother!" Booker laughed, which got a few claps from the crowd. "One may not agree with his politics, but he did hold the first ever presidential 'beer summit' between that cop and professor."

"*That* was probably his greatest achievement."

Booker told the bartender to mix up a couple of free pitchers of margaritas for the crowd. "What about the last Presidential election? Donald Trump versus Hillary Clinton. They're both Boomers. Does the old beer analogy still apply?"

I shook my head in disgust. "My God, that election was a clusterfuck of epic proportions! The Blowhard versus The Bitch."

"You're not going to have a brewski with Trump, that's for sure," said Booker. "He's been a teetotaler his entire life."

"Trump hasn't had time to drink! He's been too busy being the biggest huckster in the history of mankind. He's slapped his name on more products and ventures than you can shake a Trump Steak at: buildings, golf courses, a failed university; casinos, suits, shirts, ties, wallets, watches, eyewear, and cufflinks; wine, water, energy and coffee drinks; a board game, books and magazines; furniture and home accessories; shampoo, body wash, moisturizers, shower caps, towels, pet collars and leashes, and more. For the right price, he'd license his name on a shit sandwich."

"Hey, don't forget Trump Vodka," said Booker, pointing at a tall, thin, dusty bottle adorned with a golden 'T' on the top shelf of the back bar. It had been sitting up there for years and had never been opened.

"Trump may be a petty, thin-skinned, narcissistic, egomaniacal, 'short-fingered Vulgarian,' as the smug Gotham media elites love to call him, but the guy sure knows how to grab the spotlight," I said. "During that long and ugly Republican primary slog in 2015-2016, Trump generated millions of dollars in free media coverage for himself. Any one of the other seventeen candidates probably would have been a safer, saner choice. Yet despite his numerous bankruptcies, failed marriages, hidden tax returns, bogus military deferments during the Vietnam War, his boorish sexual behavior and lewd comments about women, sophomoric taunts of 'Little Marco' and 'Lyin' Ted'—Trump managed to slime his way to the finish line and win the nomination with his horrendous orange comb-over still intact. He's the Tony Clifton of American politics."

"What about Hillary?" asked Booker. "I don't think anybody would want to have a drink with her. Just ask the Secret Service."

"If she wasn't married to Bill Clinton, she'd just be another blob in a blue pants suit. An honest evaluation of Hillary's record shows that she's not burdened by actual achievement."

Booker said, "I think Carly Fiorina had the best line of the primary campaign. After Hillary boasted she had successfully flown over a million miles as Secretary of State, Carly said, 'Flying is an activity, not an accomplishment.'"

"Yeah, Hillary lied about everything: the endless scandals, health questions, her illegal and hacked email server, the 33,000 missing emails, the Benghazi fiasco, her 'pay-for-play' deals as Secretary of State that benefitted the dubious Clinton Foundation, and on and on and on. And yet, she still thinks she was, and is, entitled to be President. Go figure."

I sipped my drink. "Her coronation was virtually guaranteed, especially after the DNC screwed Bernie Sanders. With his quixotic demands for free healthcare, free college, a tax-free living wage and free Ben & Jerry's 'Chunky Monkey' for everyone on the planet, that crazy Commie codger pushed the party so far to the left it may never recover. Millions of entitlement-sucking voters who embrace subsidized self-reliance could 'Feel The Bern' for an endless flow of free stuff. However, the ultra-rich liberals who run the Democratic Party didn't like the notion of a ninety percent income tax rate. They're all for 'income equality' as long as it doesn't come out of their wallets. Consequently, they made sure Bernie sat out the rest of the campaign in his new waterfront crib on Lake Champlain where he could yell at kids: 'Get the hell off my beach, you little bastards!'"

Booker nodded, "And then came the big election of 2016…"

"It was the ultimate Celebrity Death Match! Hillary had more money, over a billion bucks, political connections up the yin-yang, and the mainstream media and Hollywood in her pocket along with an autographed copy of Saul Alinsky's *Rules for Radicals*. Plus, she had the massive support of blacks, Latinos, feminists, government workers, union members and environmentalists. Even the great Obama campaigned for her. But while Hillary ran a lousy campaign, Trump aimed his messaging at the forgotten Americans who were totally fed up with the Washington swamp and out-of-control 'political correctness.' He tapped into their angst with his relentless Twitter attacks and pushed back against the 'fake news' media. He strutted around his giant rallies like Il Duce, pounding the nationalistic themes of 'America First' and 'Make America Great Again.' No one, not even Trump himself, actually believed he could actually beat Hillary… The world was shocked."

Booker said, "Man, can you imagine the vibe around Hillary on election night? I heard she just kept shrieking 'I'm melting! I'm melting!'"

"That 'basket of deplorables' was a lot bigger than anyone knew."

Booker shook his head. "Without a doubt, it was the weirdest presidential election ever."

"And now, after the biggest upset in presidential history, we have Trump at the helm of the USS Titanic and there are more icebergs out there than anyone can count. Who knows what the volatile future holds, but the nastiness, anger and outrage on both sides of the political divide have reached new lows. The Left still can't accept the election results and will resist The Donald on anything and everything—regardless of his many prudent policies. But he just makes things worse by taking politics too personally, going on petty tirades, and patting himself on the back constantly."

I finished my drink. "Remember when the Clintons were renting out Lincoln's Bedroom in the White House to all their rich donor friends? Well, Trump could easily flip out at any moment and turn The White House into a timeshare. I can see it now! The place gets repainted gold and a giant Trump logo hangs over the front door… But you know what scares me the most? If Kim Jung Un and Trump ever get into a nuclear war over who has the best haircut."

I plopped down onto a bar stool, exhausted from my looney lecture.

"Wow!" said Booker, looking a little incredulous. "Clinton, Bush, Obama, Trump, and all the Baby Boom contenders—you trashed every one of them."

"Yeah, it's a big clown car. Just because our last four presidents are Boomers doesn't mean they get a pass. There could have been much better candidates over the years. After all, the bar was set pretty high by the star of *Bedtime for Bonzo*."

"Tragically, Senator Bluto Blutarsky never had a chance to run."

"And what about Cheech and Chong? Even Bevis and Butthead could have been a winning ticket."

"I would have voted for Max Headroom!" said Booker.

"The best and brightest of our generation sat on the sidelines. They didn't want their private lives, finances, and any past or present peccadilloes put under the public microscope. Nowadays, if you want to be President, or serve in Congress, you have to be a masochist, a raving megalomaniac or a complete idiot."

"Or all of the above!" laughed Booker. "So—in the final analysis, of all the Boomer presidential contenders who would *you* want to have a beer with?"

"Well, that's a no-brainer… Pat Paulsen, of course."

"Turn, Turn, Turn"

Booker turned off the TV. "Anyway, what's the latest with you?"

"It's been a very bizarre day."

I filled him in about the newspaper interview and that Senator Whitehead and his entourage planned to attend the Sunday night event.

"Actually, the Senator wanted free tickets, but I made sure they're paying the full freight."

"Excellent!"

"But the highlight of the day was meeting Fred Frost."

"No way! 'Fastball Frost'? The myth, the man, the legend in the flesh?"

"Yeah, he's the father of my banker. Nice guy… Unfortunately, he's dying.

"Say it ain't so, Joe," said Booker. "You know, he came in here many years ago. I sat with him for a few hours while he ran up a big tab. He was very entertaining. Told some great stories. When he wasn't talkin' baseball, he was flirting with a cougar down at the end of the bar. They ended up leaving together."

I chuckled. "Sounds like Fred. He's still an old horn dog."

Remembering Fred's last wish, I asked, "Who's that hot redhead who comes in here occasionally?"

Booker smiled. "Desiree, the working girl?"

"Yeah."

Booker let loose with a hearty laugh. "Don't tell me you finally want to get laid?"

"Not for me. For Fred."

I told Booker about Fred's last request. "As baseball fans, it's the least we can do."

After consulting the address book on his laptop, Booker wrote down Desiree's telephone number on the inside flap of one of his bar matchbooks and palmed it to me along with a roguish smile. "Mention my name for a good discount."

"Thanks."

Booker gestured at the small private patio behind him. "Want to play a quick game of chess?"

"Nah. My political rant gave me a headache. The booze didn't help much either. I should go home."

Over the years, we've engaged in some intense chess matches. As a kid growing up in New York City, Booker's father used to take him to Washington Square Park on weekends to learn the nuances of the game. He's a damn good chess player. I only accept his challenges after his umpteenth cocktail and he still whips me virtually every time.

Tired of getting my ass kicked, I started showing up with some classic board games of my own, lifted from the display cases at BoomerWorld: Chutes and Ladders, Clue, Game of Life, Yahtzee, Sorry, Battleship, Mouse Trap, Operation, and Monopoly. Booker and I would sit on the back patio and get blitzed on shots of tequila while we rolled the dice, shuffled the cards and reveled in the great games of yesteryear.

One evening, I showed up with Candy Land, but Booker told me in no uncertain terms that he would never play that game, claiming that he'd be a laughingstock if any of his old buddies on the N.Y.P.D. ever got wind of it.

I narrowed my gaze and called him out. "Well, I think you're afraid I'll get to the Candy Castle before you!"

Booker reached behind the bar and removed his old nightstick from his early days as a patrolman in the Bowery. As he slapped the scarred weapon against his open palm, he said menacingly, "Keep it up, son, and you could disappear in the Peppermint Forest—forever."

Finally, I reluctantly agreed to play a quick game of chess. Of course, I got crushed like Wile E. Coyote.

3

Wednesday • October 28
7:30 a.m.

"Good Vibrations"

For the first time in days, I rolled out of the sack with a slightly improved outlook on life and only half a hangover. With the Batmobile arriving in a few days, some much-needed media exposure on tap and ticket sales on the rise, the prospects for a successful weekend were looking up.

I had a big day planned and needed an early start. Knowing the article about BoomerWorld would be in the morning edition of the *Times*, I woke Walter from a deep canine snore fest and quickly fed him. As we strolled down to Jitters Java Hut, a light drizzle dropped from an ominous gray sky.

I picked up a newspaper and started to thumb through the various sections. I was pleased to see my article was featured above the fold on the front page of the Lifestyle section. There was a photo of yours truly standing in the center of the pavilion surrounded by various Boomer collections and graphics. The headline read:

The Final Days of BoomerWorld
Baby Boom Museum to Close

The article had a very positive spin. It chronicled the history of the venue, described many of the exhibits, and detailed all the planned weekend events—including mentions about the Batmobile and Senator Whitehead. Here are a few of my favorite excerpts:

"For the past fifteen years, BoomerWorld has been a sleepy venue in the seaside town of Venice Beach, but an important one. It is a unique time capsule packed with thousands of artifacts and historical references that capture the scope and spirit of the Baby Boom Generation. But now, its days are numbered.

"... Half-historian and half-huckster, Bob Apple is the founder and poster boy for BoomerWorld. Constantly in motion and using his sharp wit and encyclopedic memory, the animated and entertaining host bombards you with facts, trivia and opinions about the events, personalities, social and cultural contributions that shaped one of the most fascinating generations in American history.

"... Apple seems to know every facet of the colorful Boomer saga. Strolling around the expansive BoomerWorld pavilion, which is housed in a former art deco roller-skating rink built in the 1950s, Apple recites speeches and quotes from notable Boomer politicos, spouts little-known stories about his generation's most famous inventors, scientists and celebrities, and even sings vintage TV commercial jingles verbatim as well as a few choice classic rock lyrics. Like they said back in the 1960s: 'It's far out, man!'"

I could have kissed that reporter! Even though I came across as a self-absorbed fruitcake—you can't buy that kind of publicity. Given my advertising background, I knew that article would really jumpstart ticket sales.

After grabbing some more coffee, Walter and I went straight back to the office. I was elated to see the online ticket site had processed over a hundred requests for tickets. Knowing I would also collect $1,200 that day from a local high school coming to tour BoomerWorld on a special field trip, I now had enough money to cover the down payment for the caterer, who would be arriving soon to go over the final details for the weekend events.

"Paint It Black"

In preparation for the arrival of the students at 11:00 a.m., I walked through the pavilion to make sure all the display cases were locked and the surveillance camera system was on and working properly.

Over the years, I've hosted many student tours at BoomerWorld, which provided much-needed funds to keep the joint afloat. By and large, most of those high school field trips went smoothly; however, I also dreaded dealing with those teenage morons who chose to engage in theft, vandalism or graffiti. In the wake of those unpleasant incidents, I had to hassle with embarrassed teachers and belligerent parents. And in the worst cases, the cops were summoned. Over time, I wised up and agreed to only host the schools with the most well-behaved students and parents who can easily pay for any damages. *(Milking "white privilege" for all its worth.)*

After surviving The Great Depression and WW2, our parents wanted life to be easier for us Boomers. Still, we were genuinely afraid of them. They would not spare the rod if we did not follow the rules and got into trouble. Getting sent to the Principal's office was nothing compared to the fate that waited back at home. "Just wait until your father gets home!" was a familiar refrain that gave us cold sweats. If you screwed up, getting a good spanking was routine. Belts, rulers, hairbrushes, ping pong paddles, switches or an open hand were used with brutal efficiency. And any parent could mete out discipline to any kid without fear of a lawsuit or recrimination.

Ahh, the good old days of corporal punishment!

Apparently, all those beatings had an indelible impact on us, because when Boomers became parents, spankings became a thing of the past. Instead, we created 'timeouts,' which consisted of horrendous punishments like sitting in a corner, taking away PlayStations or Pokemon, or the denial of gummy bears for a fortnight.

The horror! The horror!

9:00 a.m.

"Chain of Fools"

Speaking of entitled young'uns, Mick and Mona, my two part-time employees were vaping on the front steps of the museum before starting their workday. I opened the door and let the happy, slobbering Walter out to greet them.

"Yo, Boomer Bob! It's the big boss with the secret sauce! What up?" said Mick, a twenty-five-year-old slacker who looked like Jeff Spicoli, but with half the I.Q. Perpetually stoned *("It's medicinal, man."),* Mick was my official go-fer. When he wasn't running the parking lot, he wore an old-fashioned sandwich board around town to promote BoomerWorld.

"So how are my favorite employees?"

"We're your *only* employees," replied Mona, rubbing Walter behind the ears.

"And that's what makes you sooooo special!"

"You hear that, Mona?" asked Mick. "I'm special."

"Yeah, special needs," she snarked.

Mick started to play air guitar. "Hey, check out this tasty riff," he said as he shredded on his invisible axe like Nigel Tufnel. "Pretty gnarly, huh?"

"Luckily, we can't hear a thing," mused Mona.

"It rocks, mama!" Mick said, giving Mona a suggestive wink. "Hey, wanna come to my next concert?"

"I'd rather set myself on fire."

When he wasn't working at BoomerWorld, Mick was an aspiring rock star, fronting a pathetic punk band. Once, he invited me to one of his gigs at some rundown, artsy warehouse in Long Beach. The concert was god-awful. As his three bandmates flailed away, Mick gyrated behind a microphone, hitting ear-splitting power chords on his guitar and singing like he was being water-boarded. At some point, Mick decided to dive into the mosh pit. Unfortunately, there were only a handful of fans in attendance and he landed flat on the floor, breaking his collarbone. I had to drive him to the emergency room.

It was a long night.

Over time, Mick and I developed a weird, father-son relationship, which consisted mostly of ridiculing each other in a light-hearted way. Whenever I tried to educate Mick about the history of the Baby Boom, he responded like a bored child. He was Dennis The Menace to my Mr. Wilson. A typical conversation went like this:

"Today, let's learn about Boomer economics," I'd say.

"Just what I need: More worthless information."

"Did you know that back in 1960, a McDonald's hamburger cost fifteen cents, a first-class stamp was four cents and minimum wage was only a dollar an hour?"

"Wait a minute! Isn't that what you're paying me?" asked Mick.

I pointed my old bony finger at him and scowled in jest, "Careful! You're cruisin' for a bruisin'!"

"Bring it on, gramps! Right after your nap."

Mona was a real character, too. Dressed in black from head to toe, with long raven hair and purple lipstick, she was going through a Goth phase. Cynical and aloof, Mona had a wicked sense of humor. She was always making flip comments like, "You know, there would be a lot more parking spaces over on Abbot Kinney Boulevard if someone released the plague." One time I was complaining about poor cash flow and she suggested, "Why don't you just burn this place down. My uncle, 'Vinnie The Torch,' is hooked up with The Mob. I think he's offering a half-off sale this week."

Actually, that wasn't a bad idea, but then I remembered I didn't have any insurance.

Given her charming ways, I put Mona in charge of the gift shop. She loved to make outrageous comments to customers who were perusing the many Boomer items for sale. One day, I got a complaint from an elderly customer who claimed she was about to buy a DVD collection of *The Patty Duke Show* until Mona chimed in. "Do you remember the theme song, ma'am? You know, that a hot dog would make Patty lose control? Well, I prefer a big, fat bratwurst—if you catch my drift." The woman was appalled at the sexual innuendo, but I was laughing too hard to fire her.

Despite Mona's lethal sarcasm and Mick's chronic tardiness, they were actually good employees, except for the time I caught them in the Black Light Room doing the naughty. After their brief affair, the ex-lovers traded more barbs than *The Bickersons*. To be honest, I was sad these were their final days at BoomerWorld. Soon, they would be cast out into the pool of the unemployed. As I opened the front door to let us all in, I inquired, "So, have you guys given any thought about finding new jobs?"

Mick said, "I'm gonna focus on the band. Toe Jam has a couple of righteous paydays lined up."

I said, "Toe Jam? I thought your band was called Rug Burn."

Mick's band was constantly changing its name, thinking it was more important than actually practicing their music.

"It was, but we're developing a new jammin' sound. So now we're called Toe Jam. Get it?"

"Gross!" said Mona. "How could you name your band after that disgusting crap that gets trapped between your toes?"

"What? You got a better idea?"

"Sure. Something that captures the true essence of the band."

"Like what?"

"How about: Fingernails on a Chalkboard."

Mick scowled.

"By the way, when's your world tour, Mick?" she asked drolly. "No need to put it off any longer."

"Don't piss on my parade, Mona. Besides, what are you gonna do?"

"Actually, I'm thinking of joining the Marines. I hear they're looking for a few good trannies."

Mick freaked. "What the—!"

Shaking her head in disgust, she replied, "It's just a joke, Mick. Geez, buy a clue!"

This was typical banter for them. Annoying at times yet always worthy of a good laugh. But it was time to break up the lovefest and get to work.

Turning to Mick, I announced, "The parking lot is now officially closed. We need to prep it for the two big weekend parties. I want the entire area cleaned and pressure washed. Completely spotless! The catering company will start delivering the tables, chairs, bars, area rugs, tents, etc. on Friday morning."

I wasn't sure Mick heard a word I was saying. I asked, "Want to take some notes?"

"Nah, I've got a photographic memory."

Mona burst out laughing. "Too bad it's permanently overexposed."

Brushing off her barb before Mick could fire back, I continued, "Also, clear a space near the side entrance into the museum for the Batmobile."

Mick leapt to his feet. "The Batmobile is coming here?"

"Finally, I'm impressed," Mona said.

I quickly filled them in on the details and got back to business.

"Mick, you need to spend a couple hours today wearing the

sandwich board along the Boardwalk to promote the weekend events. There'd better be a line waiting to get into the museum on Saturday morning."

"News flash! No one cares about the Baby Boom," scoffed Mick. "If people want to learn about prehistoric times, they can visit the La Brea Tar Pits."

He was right. Sometimes wishful thinking clouds my better judgement.

"Besides I hate wearing that thing. It makes me look like a dork and it weighs a ton too."

Mona couldn't resist. "Oh, come on, Mick! Women love a man in uniform."

"Shut up, Mona!" Turning to me he pleaded, "Why can't I get one of those giant, super lightweight Styrofoam fingers?"

"Hey, I'll give you the finger anytime you want," I said.

Mick shrugged.

Lastly, I reminded him to make sure his bandmates came to the staff meeting at nine o'clock on Saturday morning. Besides Mona, Mick and Courtney, I needed three more bodies to help out with all the various weekend activities.

The last time I hired the band to do some menial work around the museum, I smelled the pungent scent of weed drifting over the side fence into the parking lot. I strolled over to surreptitiously eavesdrop on their conversation. I could hear the sound of bubbling water as they took turns doing bong rips. Typically, they were discussing deep philosophical matters…

"The name's Bong. James Bong."

Laughter…

"You know, when I get stoned, I start to think about life… Sometimes it just doesn't make much sense."

"I hear ya, bro … Like why do people park in driveways and drive on parkways?"

"Yeah, well, why is a 'fat chance' the same as a 'slim chance'?"

More sounds from the gurgling water pipe…

"Can you actually die in your living room?"

"And what happens if you get scared-half to death—twice?"

"That's pretty heavy… But tell me this: Why is pizza round, gets cut into triangles and comes in a square box?"

"That's like cosmic geometry—or some shit."

Remind me to miss their next Mensa meeting.

Quietly backing away, I asked myself: Is there another word for "synonym"?

Lastly, I gave Mona her marching orders. "Today, you'll need to deal with the media players during the student field trip. Make sure they're properly signed out and returned. Then you can open the gift shop for some last-minute sales before they leave. I'll be there to watch out for any attempted 'five finger discounts.' And tomorrow, do a complete inventory of all the BoomerWorld items in the gift shop and storeroom. This Saturday and Sunday, we're blowing out whatever swag is left: every coffee cup, T-shirt and postcard must go!"

She nodded.

"Also, on Saturday, you'll need to split your time between the gift shop and the box office. I hired a young gal named Courtney to handle ticket sales over the weekend, but she'll probably need some help."

"Is she hot?" Mick inquired.

"She's still in high school and definitely jailbait. So please keep it professional."

"I'll try, boss, but chicks dig me. I'm a total babe magnet."

"And Annie got her gun," Mona sighed. Turning back to me, she asked, "You want me to work two jobs at the same time? Will I be getting a raise?"

"No!" I snapped. "BoomerWorld is sinking fast and everyone needs to put in the extra effort to keep it afloat for the next few days. So—get happy and get busy, my little droogies!"

I clapped my hands. "Chop! Chop!!"

Mona frowned again. She always had an annoyed look on her face.

I asked, "Do you ever smile?"

"Only behind your back and when Mick farts."

"How sweet," I said. "Enough chatter! Get to work!"

9:30 a.m.

"Spill the Wine"

By the time the owner of Carla's Catering Company arrived to meet with me, it was pouring outside. As I let her in the front door, I noticed a lone man standing under a tree across the street. He looked vaguely familiar, but I couldn't place him. Short and wiry, he wore a camouflage boonie hat, drab green army jacket and aviator sunglasses. His hands were shoved into his pockets as water dripped off the rumpled brim of his hat. It looked like he was staring right at me, but I couldn't tell for sure.

Maybe it was Boo Radley.

I closed the door and escorted Carla to my office. I've hired her many times for all kinds of catered events at the museum and, despite her wacky, wise-cracking persona, she always did a good job at a fair price.

Carla is a tall, forty-something bleached blonde with a take-charge personality. I call her "The Catering Commandant" because when she's working an event, she always wears a black designer jumpsuit and high-tech headset to supervise her small army of waiters and bartenders. Needless to say, she runs a very tight ship.

For the next hour, Carla and I reviewed all the final details for both the Halloween and Sunday night parties. From the seating arrangements, types of food and booze, placement of the bars and porta potties to the staffing of cooks, waiters and parking attendants—we discussed every possible option. As usual, our conversation was spiced up with Carla's non-stop barrage of bad jokes. The woman is always spouting off-color humor she's overheard at one of her recently-catered corporate events, private parties and weddings.

"Hey, do you know the difference between erotic and kinky?" Carla asked.

"No, but I'm sure you're going to tell me."

"Erotic is using a feather. Kinky is using the whole chicken!"

"Please make sure *that* chicken doesn't end up in the buffet on Sunday night."

Once all the decisions were made, Carla calculated the costs. After I pleaded poverty *(as usual)*, she agreed to charge me a flat fee of twenty-thousand dollars for both events, plus we agreed to split the proceeds from the bars, which was exactly what I had projected. I gave her a down payment check and told her not to cash it until the next day, because I needed to juggle some deposits first.

11:00 a.m.

"Smells Like Teen Spirit"

Like a small herd of banana slugs, four bright yellow school buses slowly pulled up in front of BoomerWorld, just as the rain subsided and ribbons of sunshine sliced down through the overcast sky.

Two hundred students from a high school in Brentwood poured out onto the sidewalk as numerous other cars arrived with the teachers and chaperoning parents.

I cinched up my tie du jour, a colorful hand-painted masterpiece with images from *Yellow Submarine*, adjusted my funky suspenders (which were covered with old political pins and buttons) and ran my fingers through my gray, shaggy mane to look somewhat presentable.

Standing on the landing in front of the entrance to address the crowd, I spread my arms like Ed Sullivan to greet the throngs below me and proclaimed, "Good morning, everyone! Welcome to BoomerWorld—a magnificent tribute to the most fabulous, fascinating and frustrating generation mankind has ever known: the Baby Boom! I'm Bob Apple, the proprietor and your humble servant."

I bowed graciously and glanced over at a couple of the nearby teachers who had visited several times over the years. They smiled, knowing I was launching into my typical psychobabble Boomer rap.

"To give you a precise chronological history of the events and personalities that shaped the Boomer Generation, I suggest that when you enter the main exhibition hall, turn left and walk clockwise around the periphery, following the timeline on the wall. You'll see many exhibits and artifacts that relate to each specific period. Also, in the center area, there are many more displays and collections not to be missed! To enhance the overall experience, there are fifty hand-held digital media players available, which provide audio feeds linked to all the TVs scattered throughout the pavilion. These devices can be shared with your fellow students and are available at the ticket office inside. And the gift shop will be open during the last half hour of your visit, which is packed with all kinds of keepsakes and goodies."

As I rambled on, I noticed most of the kids weren't paying any attention to my canned speech. Instead, they scanned their smartphones checking for their latest texts, social media feeds, thumbnail news reports and celebrity gossip. Several kids slipped to the back of the crowd and then quietly snuck off into the neighborhood, undoubtedly planning to regroup over on the beach to party. They didn't give a shit about BoomerWorld and I couldn't really blame them. After all, from their point of view, spending hours in a museum dedicated to their grandparents was a waste of their precious youth. My generation and all it represented was nothing more than an annoying anachronism. The field trip was just a good excuse to get out of school for the day.

Nevertheless, I continued. "This is the last week this unique venue will be open to the public. Sadly, after fifteen years, BoomerWorld is shutting its doors." I paused, looking for some small acknowledgment from the crowd that such a great cultural institution was closing down…

No one cared.

"Over the years, I have been fortunate to host many student field trips and you are the last, privileged group to visit. I sincerely hope you will enjoy your time here. Just remember that this is a museum—so please act accordingly."

It's always wise to remind today's youth that there are boundaries of behavior, especially when at least half of them are either stoned or planning to be.

Recognizing boredom was starting to set in with the audience, I quickly concluded my remarks. "Anyway, have fun, learn a little, and don't forget to tell your parents there are still tickets left for this weekend's final two evening events. Thank you."

I opened the doors, and everyone began to file in. One of the teachers, whose name I can never remember, handed me an envelope stuffed with the $1,200 in cash and checks to cover the reduced admission fees for the entire group. I thanked her and then stashed it in the safe in my office.

After I stuffed my pockets with some goodies to pass out to the little ingrates: Root Beer Barrels, Squirrel Nut Zippers and Bit-O-Honeys, I wandered out into the exhibition hall to interact with the students. Since this would be the last field trip to BoomerWorld, I wanted the next few hours to be an intellectually-stimulating and positive experience for the students—and me. However, based upon past experience, it was destined to be more irritating than a concert by *Alvin and The Chipmunks*.

"Start Me Up"

Just inside the pavilion entrance, a few students were contemplating a section of the tall wall mural that featured a photo collage of some of the iconic images of post-World War II, the Korean War and the advent of the Atomic Age, along with some accompanying captions and newspaper headlines.

A nerdy, nervous student who bore a striking resemblance to Napoleon Dynamite approached me. "Can I, ahh, ask you a question?"

"Heck, yes!"

"In our American history class, we were taught that Boomers are the most spoiled, narcissistic generation the world has ever seen. Do you, ahh, agree?"

This sounded like the typical crackpot crap today's students are fed on a daily basis by the legions of incompetent, woke bureaucrats who run the Department of Education and the National Education Association; however, in this case, I actually agreed.

"No one wants to admit their peer group is composed of a bunch of privileged, self-absorbed sybarites, but well, the historical facts speak for themselves… After thousands of brutal years when mankind had to struggle for basic survival, Boomers were blessed with an incredibly rich bounty of opportunities, freedoms and unprecedented material wealth."

Staring up at a B&W photo of Dwight D. Eisenhower being sworn in as the thirty-fourth President of the United States, I continued. "The parents of the Baby Boom were rightly dubbed 'The Greatest Generation' for many reasons. They were smart, tough and gritty, and never gave up. After suffering through many trials and tribulations like the Great Depression and The Dust Bowl years, these exceptional role models somehow sucked it up and saved the world from the unspeakable evils of Adolf Hitler and the Nazis, Italian Fascists and the ruthless Japanese Empire—all before lunch. And then they thwarted the communistic hordes from taking over Samsung—oops, I mean—

South Korea."

He didn't get my joke.

"Anyway, in the wake of our parents' hard-earned achievements, my illustrious generation was handed the world on a silver platter, complete with a full bar, a Godzilla-size vat of fresh shrimp and a dessert cart taller than the Empire State Building. And what did we do with such an incredible inheritance? You got it: 'Foodfight!' Like that scene from Animal House, we've made a huge mess of things in the world and it won't be cleaned up anytime soon, if ever."

I pointed at the famous Eisenhower quote on the mural:

"A people that values its privileges
above its principles soon loses both."

"When I was designing this timeline, I added that quote because it says so much about Boomers. In many ways, we placed our own desires and privileges above the traditional philosophies and principles of our forefathers. Our parents sacrificed everything to give us better lives and the brightest possible future. Instead of being grateful, we shit in their hats. Self-gratification became the holy grail of the 'Me Generation' and we clung to it like the "Orb" in Woody Allen's *Sleeper*.

"Growing up in an era of cataclysmic social change, Boomers reveled in uninhibited drug and sex experimentation, social revolution and counter culturalism. We questioned and attacked organized religion, traditional family values, political institutions and confronted authority *('The Man')*, burned draft cards and the occasional bra."[6]

"Wanting to change the world for what we thought was the better, we shirked our responsibilities while focusing mostly on our own

---

[6] *One of the great myths about the "Women's Lib" movement included reports of giant bonfires of burning bras to protest the West's commercialized culture of superficial beauty, in which women were judged on their looks, not their intellect and inner beauty. "Going braless" was meant to empower women, but to the chagrin of horny guys everywhere, most of the fires were small, and ultimately, a real letdown—in more ways than one.*

personal passions. Yeah, we thought we knew it all and were often impulsive, vain and careless in our behaviors. It was always our way or the highway. The consequences of our free-spirited hedonism were increases in alcohol and drug addiction, suicide, abortion, laissez-faire child rearing, divorce and broken families."

Napoleon was a little taken aback. "Gosh! I thought you'd only talk about how great Boomers are!"

"Despite being a bunch of self-obsessed, pot-smoking, free-loving, opinionated, unstable, solipsistic brats—Boomers have many talents and fine qualities. Generally, we are competitive, resourceful, independent, self-assured, and have a strong work ethic. As risk-takers, problem solvers, inventors and 'midnight-tokers,' we've made notable contributions at home and abroad. Evolving from yippies and yuppies to she-shedders and man-cave dwellers, Boomers are the most generous generation in history—funding thousands of charities and global initiatives to cure diseases, feed the poor, and improving the lives of millions of people in the developing world by greatly reducing poverty. We've championed the advancement of civil rights, racial and gender equality, and the environment. Produced brilliant literature, art and music. Pioneered major scientific and medical breakthroughs. Extended life expectancy. Created amazing technological inventions that have fueled the ever-expanding world economy like the personal computer, smartphones, Internet, and of course, the beer helmet."

After I literally patted myself on the back, I plucked a red, white and blue Eisenhower presidential campaign button off my suspenders and handed it to Napoleon. The classic memento proclaimed: "I Like Ike."

"Please accept this small memento from today's field trip."

As the kid stared blankly at the old button, I added, "Ike was the Supreme Allied Commander in Europe during WW2 and responsible for leading the massive 'D-Day' attack on Nazi-occupied France that changed the course of history."

"D-Day? Is that kinda like Black Friday?"

I was beginning to think he and Courtney were related.

Years ago, I thought those classic Jay Leno "man-on-the-street" interviews were funny. You know, when he would ask young people simple questions about history, politics and geography—and it was painfully obvious they didn't have a clue. Now, I find such encounters to be sad and depressing.

I decided to throw out a few funky facts that would get Napoleon's attention. "You know, Ike was a workaholic. To keeping going, he smoked four packs of cigarettes and drank up to twenty cups of coffee every day."

"Dang!"

"Luckily, Ike never had to wait in line at Starbucks for his caffeine fix or we might have lost the war."

"That would've been bad, right?"

"You think?"

"Hitler was a frickin' sicko, but he did have a pretty cool moustache." Napoleon said with great authority. "If he'd won the war, he probably would've banned all the cool stuff like tether ball, nunchucks and chapstick, and ahh, moon boots and tater tots."

"Tater tots?"

"Oh yeah. They're delicious!"

I patted him on the back. "You know, I think you'd be a great history teacher."

"Really?"

"Absolutely. You have an excellent grip on the facts and are an inspiring speaker."

Based upon the weird expression on his face, I couldn't tell if Napoleon was surprised, grateful or hopelessly mental. But alas, it was time for me to go because I was due back on the mother ship.

"Blowin' In The Wind"

I walked along the great mural toward the 1960s section, passing by a primo 1957 Chevrolet Bel Air two-door convertible with a powder blue paint job, big tail fins and oodles of chrome.

God, I wish I owned that beautiful machine.

Like the other classic cars scattered throughout the exhibition hall, the enormous Barbie Doll exhibit, and many other exceptional Boomer-era collections, the most expensive artifacts were on loan from wealthy benefactors around the country. Those valuable items gave BoomerWorld credibility and panache. My heart was heavy knowing these amazing gems of yesteryear would have to be returned to their rightful owners as soon as the museum shut down.

Pausing at the edge of the Music, Fashion & Art section, I noticed it was still one of the most popular areas with the students. From the blues and rock'n'roll to the Motown Sound, music played such a pivotal role throughout the Baby Boom years, influencing the greater culture and forging our generational identity. The high school kids studied the consigned array of rare, autographed items: guitars from legendary musicians like Eric Clapton and Jimmy Page, Andy Warhol lithographs, and vintage rock concert posters from Fillmore East & West and CBGB, plus some outrageous stage outfits worn by the likes of Elton John, David Bowie and Prince. As the kids flipped through bins filled with old vinyl R&B and rock albums, highlights from *American Bandstand, Shindig* and *Soul Train* played on a few strategically placed TVs.

A vintage yellow Ford pickup truck was perched on a bed of white sand on the edge of the exhibit. It was a dead ringer for the cover art from The Beach Boys' *Surfin' Safari* album in 1962. For those who took a closer look through the front window, they could see a well-used Fender guitar and a notepad scrawled with a mock-up of Brian Wilson's handwritten lyrics for "409" laying on the seat.

When I originally staged BoomerWorld, I scattered other subtle, often humorous mini-displays throughout the exhibits, rewarding those curious visitors who looked a little closer. Crazy things like an autographed photo of Mr. Ed, a reel-to-reel tape labeled "18.5 Minute Gap" (White House: June 20, 1972), and nude Ken and Midge (Barbie's best friend) dolls shagging in the shadows behind the Barbie Pool House exhibit.

Another display was The Bomb Shelter: an exact replica of a fortified bunker designed to protect a typical American "nuclear" family from an imminent Russian missile attack. A solid four-inch-thick lead door adorned with an official black and yellow 'FALLOUT SHELTER' sign was built into the mural wall right at the transition from the 1950s to the 1960s. The inside room featured cement cinder-block walls with a ventilation pump, bunk beds, shelves packed with a large supply of jarred, canned and dehydrated food, large containers of water and a portable gas stove. There were also medical supplies, flashlights, batteries and candles, as well as books and board games to fight the inevitable boredom. A kitchen table, covered with a cheerful red-and-white checkered table cloth, was the focal point. A battery-powered radio and Kearny Fallout Meter to measure radiation levels were bolted to the tabletop.

Early Boomers were both fascinated and terrified at the prospect of a nuclear holocaust. Forget about hiding under your school desk. Everyone knew the only way to survive was to get into a bomb shelter fast and hunker down. The people who had shelters were either envied or hated by their paranoid neighbors. If/when the nukes began to rain down, the bomb shelter owner would be faced with a host of moral dilemmas...

Like a scene from *The Twilight Zone*, there would be a frantic knock on the door! Peering through the peep hole, you see half the neighborhood standing outside, terrified and doomed to a horrible fate. Knowing there were barely enough supplies to save your own family, ugly decisions would have to be made. You might survive, but the guilt would haunt you forever.

When I was about ten years old, I visited my friend's family bomb shelter. One of the first things to catch my eye was a shotgun and a box of shells on a top shelf above the food shelves. My friend said his father put it there in case some desperate neighbors, driven insane by radiation sickness, tried to break in. I doubt it ever occurred to him the gun could be used in another way—such as, God forbid, if things became unbearable and hopeless *inside* the shelter.

To add a little levity to the depressing display, I created a soundtrack loop with air-raid sirens and the sounds of distant explosions mixed in over Randy Newman's great song "Political Science." For those taking a closer look, they could see a small sculpture sitting on a shelf between some cartons of dehydrated milk: Dr. Strangelove's black leather glove clutching a flask of pure grain alcohol.

As I wandered into the 1960s section, the largest display area by far, there was a replica of the 1961 Lincoln Continental convertible that played such a prominent role in the assassination of John F. Kennedy. Every older Boomer knows exactly where they were on that fateful day in 1963 when the "Dawn of Camelot" was snuffed out. It is forever seared into our memories, because it was the first in a series of existential wake-up calls, forcing us to acknowledge that the world was not as idyllic as originally advertised. Essentially, the assassination of JFK was the beginning of the end of innocence for the Baby Boom. Since the end of WW2, we had lived in a bubble of surreal naiveté—and it was about to burst.

The only bright spots during the early 1960s were John Glenn's first orbit of the earth, the successful handling of the Cuban Missile Crisis, Dr. Martin Luther King's "I have a dream" speech, the passage of the Civil Rights Act, the founding of the Peace Corps, the World's Fair in NYC, and the arrival of The Beatles. But those positive developments were tempered by the Bay of Pigs disaster, the USSR's detonation of its Tsar Bomba 50-megaton hydrogen bomb, and the building of the Berlin Wall.

Lost in my thoughts, I walked deeper into the heart of the 1960s exhibits. These hallmark years always attracted the younger crowd, because even they knew it was one of the most transformative decades in world history. From the shocking assassinations and escalation of the Vietnam War to the on-going Cold War and omnipresent threat of nuclear obliteration, my generation was defined by the confusion and chaos during those years—especially 1968.

We never quite recovered from that traumatic year, which was sandwiched between two other turbulent years. In 1967, we witnessed the Six-Day War in the Middle East, China joining the thermo-nuclear club, explosive race riots across America, the Summer of Love, Acid Rock, the first heart transplant and Super Bowl. And in 1969, along came the My Lai Massacre and cover-up, escalating anti-war protests, the Charles Manson murders, Richard M. Nixon sworn in as President, the Walk on the Moon, ARPA (Internet) going online, Chappaquiddick, Woodstock, and the beginning of The Beatles breakup.

Yes, 1968 was perfectly positioned to be the ultimate shit storm. Given its tremendous impact on the pysche of the Baby Boom, I dedicated half of the back wall on the northeastern side of the pavillion to that tumultuous time. A ten-foot-tall "1968" metallic sculpture, covered in psychedelic graffitti, hung on the mural wall surrounded by huge photos and headlines capturing that crazy, colorful and extremely violent year.

Beginning with the bloody Tet Offensive in January, where an average of a thousand U.S. soldiers died each month in the jungles of Southeast Asia, we witnessed a twelve-month parade of death and destruction. Beyond the horrific war footage, political assassinations took center stage. In April, a sniper murdered civil rights leader Martin Luther King, Jr. in Memphis, which spawned destructive race riots across the country. In June, after winning the California Democratic presidential primary, Senator Robert F. Kennedy was shot in the head at point-blank range in Los Angeles. Their back-to-back deaths left us with a profound despair, believing both men would have had a major impact on American politics for decades to come.

Next, on the heels of Russia's invasion of Czechoslovakia, came the helter-skelter, anti-Vietnam war protests and police beatings in the streets of Chicago during the Democratic National Convention. The Black Power movement gained momentum and outraged white America when two African-American sprinters at the Olympics in Mexico City bowed their heads and raised their fists at the awards ceremony. Feminists protested at the Miss America pageant. The Weathermen conducted scores of bombings and arson attacks. Movies became more violent and sexually explicit. The foreboding Apollo Eight transmissions from space kept us on the edge of our seats. As the mysterious Zodiac Killer began to stalk his initial victims in California, Boomers became increasingly cynical about the world and our future.

The 1970s were like a bad sequel to the previous decade. The madness and mayhem continued with the Kent State shootings, airline hijackings, the terrorist attack at the Munich Olympics, the Watergate scandal, raging inflation, the fall of Saigon, the Three Mile Island meltdown, oil embargos and long gas lines, the Son of Sam murders, the Jonestown massacre, the Iranian hostage crisis, and the earthquake in China that killed a mere 240,000 people. Even Elvis Presley croaked.

In 1978, the announcement that the first test-tube baby had been born was met with a shrug, since many Boomers were so disillusioned about life in general that the idea of bringing laboratory-created children into such a mixed-up, dangerous world was downright depressing.

One of the best things to come out of those years were the classic muscle cars. Scattered throughout the BoomerWorld exhibition hall were several candy-colored road rockets that would make any gearhead drool: a 1966 Pontiac GTO, 1969 Corvette Stingray, 1973 Firebird Trans Am and a replica of the 1968 Ford Mustang GT Fastback that Steve McQueen drove in the great car chase scene in the movie, *Bullitt*—all on consignment from their generous owners. Those badass, gas-guzzling Detroit behemoths reminded visitors that despite a burgeoning oil crisis in the 1970s, when the price for a gallon of gas doubled from 30 cents to a whopping 60 cents, there was no substitute for good old-fashioned American power and speed. Guys dreamed of getting behind the wheel of one of those cool cars, but first we had to learn how to drive…

One of the high school rites of passage was Driver's Education. In California, we were forced to watch gruesome movies, like *Red Asphalt,* to scare us about the dangers of drinking and driving. Every student had to take the course to graduate, but the actual driving part was optional. For four consecutive Saturdays, a coach or wood shop teacher would take three students out for boring day-long drives in crappy Oldsmobiles. The nervous teacher sat in the front passenger's seat with his foot on the special emergency brake and would tell us where to drive. We would take turns behind the wheel—once in the morning and once in the afternoon. It was like the Ninth Circle of Hell. You'd sit there for hours waiting for your turn, surrounded by a bunch of smelly geeks and freaks. Little did we know, it was all part of a master plan to prepare us to deal with the DMV.

I spotted two pimply-faced nerds ogling a bitchin' 1970 Plymouth Hemi Barracuda. They were actually wearing name tags: Tristan and Jules. With names like that they were probably bullied every day at school. If I ever had a son, I'd give him a strong name like Thor or Ragnar.

It may not be PC nowadays, but when I was a kid, if you had a girlie-man name you were destined to get shit-hammered, "pantsed" and sat on the water fountain on a regular basis:

"Hey, what's your name?"

"Ahhh... René."

"René? What the fuck?! Are you French or something?"

"No, but—"

"Well, my name is Ragnar. I'm named after the King of the

Vikings… Here, Flóki. Hold my battle axe while I give this dork a swirly."

And then came the 1980s. Watching the ridiculous big-hair glam metal bands like Motley Crue, Poison and Twisted Sister was a brief, weird interlude before the next round of horrors like the AIDS plague, the shocking assassination of John Lennon, the Mount St. Helens eruption, the bombing of the U.S. Embassy in Beirut, the Chernobyl nuclear accident, the Challenger Space Shuttle explosion, the downing of Pan Am 103 over Lockerbie, the Exxon Valdez spill, and the Chinese protestors massacred in Tiananmen Square. We did get a little closure with the opening of the Vietnam War Memorial and the tearing down of the Berlin Wall. But that was ruined when someone handed you a home mortgage with a nightmarish eighteen-percent interest rate or a fuckin' Rubik's Cube.

"I Put A Spell On You"

Strolling near the Sports and Movies & Media sections in the heart of the exhibition hall, I handed out candy to anyone who asked a semi-intelligent question or made an insightful observation, which was rare.

Predictably, the Sports venue was packed with guys ogling the collectibles on consignment, like the mint-condition trading cards for every major-league sport, posters and team pennants, uniforms and gear: A Willie Mays game-used glove surrounded by autographed baseballs from Yogi Berra, Roger Maris, Reggie Jackson and other greats; and the famous "Holy Roller/Immaculate Deception" football the Oakland Raiders shamefully fumbled, kicked and batted into the end zone for a last-second, game-saving touchdown against the San Diego Chargers in 1978.

On the TVs, there were clips of legendary sports events: "The Shot

Heard Around the World" when the New York Giants' Bobby Thompson hit a home run in the bottom of the ninth to beat the Brooklyn Dodgers for a trip to the World Series in the first-ever nationally televised baseball game. Muhammad Ali (originally Cassius Clay, aka "The Louisville Lip") knocking out the intimidating Sonny Liston with the "Phantom Punch." The "Miracle on Ice" hockey game when the U.S. beat the Soviet Union at the 1980 Winter Olympics.

Lots of the schoolgirls clustered in the Movies & Media section. They pointed and giggled at the walls covered with ancient movie posters and black-and-white promotional headshots of A-list and obscure movie and television stars from the 1950s-1980s. Eavesdropping on their conversations, it was clear they recognized only a handful of the legendary actors. Compared to the rather anemic collection of Hollywood greats today, (with the notable exception of that extraordinary thespian, Ron Burgundy), Boomers were entertained and enchanted by an endless parade of legendary leading men and sirens of the silver screen who hailed from The Greatest Generation: Humphrey Bogart, Lauren Bacall, Marlon Brando, Rita Hayworth, Richard Burton, Sean Connery, Joan Crawford, James Dean, Bette Davis, Judy Garland, Burt Lancaster, Audrey Hepburn, Charlton Heston, Grace Kelly, Sophia Loren, Robert Mitchum, Marilyn Monroe, Paul Newman, Sidney Poitier, George C. Scott, James Stewart, Rock Hudson, John Wayne and Orson Welles—just to mention a few. What a cast! Even the second and third tier actors were impressive.

Now don't get me wrong, I like some of the actors working today, but the celebrated Hollywood royalty of yesteryear, who were discovered, nurtured and often exploited by the old studio system, seemed larger than life. They played heroes and villains, cowboys, cops and crooks, cads and femme fatales—all timeless stars to be idolized and emulated. Maybe it's because they loomed above us like gods on giant movie screens—their expressive faces laughing and crying, whispering and screaming, and always uttering the coolest one-liners.

"Going to the movies" was always a thrilling and much anticipated event that lasted for hours and discussed for days. No ratings were necessary because movies were responsibly produced so viewers of all ages and types could enjoy the experience. These days, most movies are filled with grotesque violence, a healthy dose of "wash your mouth out with soap" profanity, blatant sex scenes and full-frontal nudity, labeled with a multi-tiered MPAA ratings system, and often require earplugs, blindfolds and barf bags.

The old movie houses were opulent cinematic cathedrals where fans came to worship their favorite stars and escape reality. From their huge backlit marquees and soaring ceilings supported by ornately painted columns to the lush carpeting and dimly lit alcoves, movie theater architecture ranged from art deco to classic Roman to kitschy Egyptian.

Those regal movie palaces were always packed on Friday and Saturday nights, and for the weekend matinees that sometimes featured two movies for the price of one. The lines were long at the ticket booth and the snack bar. If you were one of the lucky last patrons to actually get past the red velvet ropes, you usually could only find a seat in the first row. But you didn't care. You were ready to be transported to a mythical place and time. It was a stimulating, multi-sensory experience that began when the massive curtain slowly parted like the Red Sea in *The Ten Commandments*, unveiling a newsreel or cartoon before the main feature. The scent of fresh buttered popcorn filled your nostrils. Boxes of Jujubes, Good & Plenty and Milk Duds were ripped open and devoured. Huge sugared sodas were slurped, dropped and accidentally kicked over. As the audience sat spellbound in the darkness, the floor became a sticky mess of soft drink cups, candy wrappers and popcorn bags.

In the early 1960s, Cinerama made its debut in specially constructed theaters around the world. The ultra-widescreen process used three different projectors to cast images onto a large curved screen that wrapped over 140 degrees around the audience. It was a stunning departure from traditional flat screens, but the production costs limited the number of movies. In addition to such classics as *2001: A Space Odyssey* and *The Greatest Story Ever Told*, the best usage of the new medium was the sweeping epic, *How the West Was Won*. No one will ever forget sitting in the middle of the buffalo stampede as the thunderous surround sound shook your fillings loose.

Tragically, most of those classic cinemas are long gone. Nowadays, with the exception of a few IMAX theaters, your only option is the local Cineplex: a nondescript warehouse where twenty flicks play at the same time in shoebox-size rooms. Instead of polite, young ushers with flashlights directing you to your seat, you've got to be wary of psychopaths with automatic weapons and body armor, as well as a cast of rude patrons.

With affordable high-definition TVs and theater-quality sound systems available in the comfort of one's own living room, it's no surprise that fewer and fewer people are going to the movies these days. After all, who wants to be sitting behind some obese, flatulent, loudmouthed jerk that wants to share his opinion about every nuance of the film just because he took some obscure film class in junior college?

"Hey, shove that Costco-size bucket of buttered popcorn into your pie hole and shut up! We're trying to watch Pauly Shore save the world!"

With the exception of some independent films, the big releases today have replaced thought-provoking plotlines and witty dialog with an avalanche of mind-numbing computer animations, special effects and graphics. Sure, it's always fun to see a virtual Tyrannosaurus Rex chase down and rip apart a teenage hussy in a skimpy bikini or watch a gigantic meteor crash into Earth—creating a nuclear fireball that causes mutations, earthquakes and tsunamis that wash away civilization, leaving only flesh-eating zombies to reclaim the planet! But I do miss the occasional insightful conversation.

Beneath another BoomerWorld monitor, playing a long loop of vintage TV and movie trailers, the kids pawed through racks of movie posters and peered into display cases filled with original props from the biggest flicks spanning the Baby Boom's golden years. From real memorabilia like a helmet from *Ben Hur*, an M-16 from *Apocalypse Now* and a TV remote control from *Being There* to a few gag props like a glass beaker filled with green slime from *Ghostbusters* and a cucumber wrapped in aluminum foil from *Spinal Tap*. The closer you look the more you see.

The most popular prop of all was a replica of the giant acrylic penis sculpture from *A Clockwork Orange*. Some of the girls straddled the rocking phallus and took salacious selfies. I realized just how much I was going to miss these student field trips—and how years from now, those girls would regret sending out such lewd photos of themselves into cyberspace, where they will live forever.

"I Got You, Babe"

I walked over to one of the smaller exhibits and a favorite of mine: a collection of print and broadcast advertising from the early Boomer days.

Posted on several free-standing panels and spread out in long display cases were some of the most politically incorrect magazine and newspaper ads ever created. Celebrities, politicians, doctors and even Santa gleefully hocking Camel, Pall Mall, Lucky Strikes and Chesterfield cigarettes. Babies swigging soft drinks. And obedient housewives dreaming of kitchen appliances, washers and dryers, and vacuum cleaners under the tree on Christmas morning.

Throughout the 1950s and 1960s, Madison Avenue churned out a bounty of blatantly racist and misogynistic ad campaigns that would give Don Draper a bad hair day. Women were kept in their place with incredibly sexist headlines like: "Show her it's a man's world" (Van Heusen), "Successful marriages begin in the kitchen" (Pyrex), "The harder a wife works, the cuter she looks" (Kellogg's), "Don't worry dear, you didn't burn the beer" (Schlitz), and even that age old quandary, "Is it always illegal TO KILL A WOMAN?" (Pitney Bowes).

Ah yes, the grand old days, when men were men and women climaxed at the sight of a new Frigidaire.

Back then, everyone read more. Newspapers and magazines played a major role in people's lives and were chock-full of ads. Of course, many of those ads were tongue-in-cheek teasers, but they captured the intensely chauvinistic mood of the country at the time. Millions of marketing dollars were spent to correct ghastly problems that plagued women like "dishpan hands," insufficient bust lines, "the heartbreak of psoriasis," and a national obsession with feminine hygiene.

Apparently, a refreshing Lysol douche always did the trick!

American housewives were bombarded with ads for both methamphetamines (to keep them thin, attractive and energetic) as well as benzodiazepines (to address their unacceptable mood swings. "Mother's Little Helpers" (Valium and Librium) helped women get through their busy days of domestic bliss: doing loads of laundry, house cleaning, grocery shopping, watching soaps on TV, ironing, rolling their hair onto curlers the size of oil drums, and waiting breathlessly for their husbands to come home from work.

Even pouting Boomer babies offered sage advice to their forlorn mothers: "Before you scold me, Mom… maybe you'd better light up a Marlboro."

"Help!"

In 1964, when I was twelve years old, the British Rock Invasion hit the U.S. mainland like Hurricane Katrina. The Beatles' performances on *The Ed Sullivan Show* transformed our generation. We were completely consumed with "Beatlemania." Almost overnight, the coolest kids had "pegged" pants, Beatle Boots with loud heel-taps and mop top haircuts. I begged my mother to buy me a pair of skintight jeans, but she adamantly refused, because she thought I'd look like one of those "hoods" in *West Side Story*. It took weeks of groveling and extra chores before she finally bought me a pair of jeans at J.C. Penney. I still looked like a hopeless dweeb with PF Flyers and a crew cut with "Beatle bangs," but at least it was a start.

Short of a surprise nuclear attack by the Russkies, the worst thing that could happen was when your TV went on the blink. A mesmerizing pattern of zigzag lines would suddenly appear on the screen right before your favorite show was about to start. You had to frantically adjust the "rabbit ears" or crawl up on the roof to rearrange the antenna. This disaster occurred about twice a year and was always cause for sheer panic and endless hand-wringing.

Wearily, my father would open up the back of the TV and begin rummaging around, looking for a broken vacuum tube or capacitor. This was always an adventure because my dad was a salesman and couldn't fix anything. Inevitably, he would yank out half the tubes and we would drive to the drug or grocery store to find the tube tester machine. After a painstaking process of elimination, we would eventually identify the burned-out bulbs and try to find replacements, which were usually missing inside the cabinet below. Returning home, my father tried to remember where to plug in the new tubes. This rarely worked so we had to call the equally incompetent TV repairman, who showed up a week later with bourbon on his breath and a bad attitude. Half the time, he would haul the broken TV to the shop where it would gather dust for weeks, waiting for parts. In the interim, I missed precious episodes of *The Man from U.N.C.L.E., Secret Agent, The Avengers* and *The Prisoner*.

One of the greatest days of my life was when my father won a new RCA color TV in a sales contest. As usual, we were excited about the annual Thanksgiving Day airing of *The Wizard of Oz* with host Danny

Kaye. We were shocked when Dorothy opened the front door of her house after it crashed down in The Land of Oz, and the screen morphed from dull B&W to eye-popping color. We had no idea that half the classic movie was actually in color.

It was a revelation!

In the early days of television, the greatest movies of all time were only broadcast on special occasions. *The Ten Commandments* and *Ben Hur* were always featured around Easter while *The Miracle on 34th Street* and *It's a Wonderful Life* were Christmas favorites.

When I was in 4th grade, all of my friends were into the original B&W horror flicks like *Frankenstein, Dracula, The Mummy,* and *The Wolf Man.* A rare showing of *The Bride of Frankenstein* was scheduled for Sunday afternoon and we could hardly wait. Unfortunately for me, my teacher informed my mother on the preceding Friday that I was lagging far behind on learning my multiplication tables. I was supposed to have mastered all the math through the six-times tables; however, as a borderline cretin, I was still counting on my fingers, staring off into space and picking my nose. My parents informed me that unless I mastered all the multiplication tables through nine-times, I would not be allowed to watch the movie. It was all or nothing.

With the pressure on, I buckled down and spent the weekend using flash cards to memorize the arithmetic. As the clock ticked down to air time, I was half way through the nines—almost done. I begged my parents to let me watch the movie, but they did not relent. I freaked out and threw a terrible tantrum. The next day, everyone at school talked about the movie and ridiculed me for not watching it—but I had the last laugh. For the next few weeks, I was the smartest kid in the class, being the first to raise my hand to answer every math question perfectly. That experience taught me a very valuable life lesson:

Math sucks.

“Eight Miles High”

Boomers have witnessed the most rapid, mind-blowing surge in scientific and technological advancements in the history of mankind. For that reason, I dedicated a large portion of BoomerWorld’s center section to Technology & Science. Packed with some of the greatest gizmos, gadgets, thingamajigs and doohickeys, it’s one of the most popular exhibits with visitors of all ages. I watched as the teenagers swarmed through the section like it was a technology yard sale, pointing and snickering at the primitive View-Masters, Super 8 movie cameras and projectors, vinyl record changers, reel-to-reel tape machines, transistor radios, Walkmans, and giant “ghetto-blasters.”

At the heart of the display was a Bendix G-15 computer, another gem on consignment from a wealthy benefactor in Silicon Valley. Hailed as the “first personal computer,” this 1956 behemoth weighed over 950 pounds, stood 5 feet tall and 3 feet wide, and had a base cost of $50,000, which computes to about $500,000 in today’s dollars. Stuffed with a huge magnetic memory drum, 450 vacuum tubes and diodes, and a spiffy metal cabinet—it has less speed and functionality than one of today’s freebie pocket calculators.

Using the old Bendix as an historical benchmark, I arranged other important tech relics in chronological order to show how our communication devices evolved over the last fifty years: Mimeograph and ditto machines > IBM Selectric typewriter > fax machine > shoe-size Motorola mobile phone > IBM PC > Apple Macintosh computer > iPod > iPhone > iPad, etc. I thought it was a pretty cool presentation, but the high school kids weren’t impressed, laughing at the clunky, old devices. I couldn’t really blame them since they were born and raised in the digital age where everything is sleek, lightweight and colorful.

Technology was the touchstone of my generation. For instance, on Christmas Eve in 1968, the Apollo 8 astronauts snapped a photo of Earth from behind the arid surface of the moon. Our planet was a vibrant blue and white orb, teeming with life. We were the youngest generation ever to see Earth photographed from outer space. For some, it symbolized hope and the incredible natural beauty of our world. For others, it changed the way we thought of mankind's relative importance on the grand existential spectrum. There was our dinky planet, floating in an endless black universe—reminding us that our world was nothing more than a microscopic speck among billions of stars, a blip on the space-time continuum, detritus on the sole of God's shoe.

Heavy...

"Money For Nothing"

A serious, young brunette with a pageboy haircut and trendy red designer eyeglasses approached me. "Excuse me, sir. You're the curator of BoomerWorld, right?"

"Yes. How can I help you?"

"My teacher said we have to write a paper about the Baby Boom. I was thinking that television had a big impact on—"

"We have a winner!" I yelled, hoping to attract a crowd to my brilliant, forthcoming oration. Not surprisingly, it fell on deaf ears since the other kids in the vicinity were too busy playing with their smartphones and talking amongst themselves.

"You are absolutely right, my dear! In my humble but erudite opinion, television had the biggest impact on the psyche of the Boomer generation, because it shaped our view of the world from the time we were toddlers, through 'The Wonder Years' and into adulthood.

"From the earliest days of fuzzy black-and-white broadcasts, which started at 6:00 a.m. with some local yahoo doing weather and farm reports and ended at midnight after playing the national anthem and some poem about God, we watched on a daily basis—hypnotized and enthralled, even by the test pattern. Excessive TV viewing became the Baby Boom's first real addiction, and now seventy years later, we're still hooked.

"As kids, we used to sit inches away from our ancient Magnavox TV, staring at the small, flickering B&W screen and listening to the snap, crackle and pop of the frayed sound system. We were enchanted by talking dummies like Charlie McCarthy, Jerry Mahoney and Knucklehead Smiff. Cute little hand puppets like Rootie Kazootie, Lamb Chop, Topo Gigo, *Captain Kangeroo's* Mr. Moose and Bunny Rabbit reassured us that the world was a safe, magical and happy place. There were heroic dogs named *Lassie* and *Rin Tin Tin*, and later, wisecracking animals like *Mr. Ed*, and Arnold Ziffle on *Green Acres.*

"In those early years, television portrayed a very idealistic view of white America. Programs like *The Adventures of Ozzie and Harriet, Father Knows Best* and *The Donna Reed Show* featured perfect middle-class families dealing with the most mundane problems. When Mrs. Cleaver on *Leave it to Beaver* would ask, "Wally, what's gotten into The Beaver?" she wasn't worried that her son was getting strung out on stolen prescription drugs from Ward's medicine cabinet, contemplating a name change to Caitlyn or bullying some classmate on social media. The Beaver was more concerned about getting a bad haircut, being harassed for having freckles or trying to avoid Lumpy Rutherford."

The young student was actually taking notes, which inspired me.

"Family life centered around our television sets. There was programming for every demographic: Families ate Jiffy Pop from metallic bags (which we all knew was "as much fun to make as it is to eat") and Swanson TV Dinners on tray stands as they religiously watched *Walt Disney's Wonderful World of Color, Candid Camera, My Favorite Martian, Gilligan's Island* and *Laugh-In*. Guys loved primetime Westerns like *Gunsmoke, Rawhide, Have Gun Will Travel, Bat Masterson, Branded, Wagon Train, Wanted: Dead or Alive,* and *The Rifleman* as well as other manly classics like *Sea Hunt, Dragnet, Adam-12, The Rat Patrol,* and *The Untouchables*. Gals were devoted to the daytime soap operas such as *The Guiding Light, As the World*

Turns and *General Hospital*, and at night to *Petticoat Junction, Laverne and Shirley and The Carol Burnet Show. Wonder Woman, The Bionic Woman, Bewitched* and *I Dream of Jeannie* were the first shows that portrayed men as a bunch of bungling idiots who had to be saved by powerful women with secret powers.

"With the exception of *Amos and Andy* and minor supporting roles like Rochester on *The Jack Benny Show* or Hop Sing on *Bonanza*, minorities were grossly underrepresented on TV—that is, until the Seventies when comedies like *Sanford and Son, The Jeffersons, What's Happening, The Cosby Show* and *Good Times* were 'dyn-o-mite!' in prime time."

Initially, my parents tried to restrict our TV viewing to a few hours per week, but they became addicted to "The Idiot Box" too—watching their favorite variety shows and late evening soaps like *Ben Casey* and *Peyton Place*, which were the precursors to *Dallas, Dynasty,* and *Falcon Crest.*

Taking breaks from the doldrums of homework, my siblings and I would casually drift into the kitchen to get a snack and then sneak glances at the more adult shows like *Perry Mason, 77 Sunset Strip,* or *I-Spy*. Our parents would tell us to go back to our rooms and study, but we still hung around like gawking bystanders at a crash scene. Eventually, they grew tired of constantly reprimanding us and threw in the towel. Soon, we were all sitting on the couch together.

"In the early days of TV, shows were sponsored by major advertisers. The symbiosis between TV programming and commercial products created long-term brand loyalties, which remain strong after so many decades. The clever use of sex and humor made their messaging memorable: "Take it off. Take it all off." (Noxema); "That's a spicy meatball!" and "I can't believe I ate the *whole* thing!" (Alka-Seltzer); and "Where's the beef?" (Wendy's). We ate it up—literally.

"Back in those halcyon times, there were no VCRs, DVRs, TiVo, or any other fancy, streaming devices and services to deliver your favorite programs on demand. You had to see every precious TV episode right when it aired or it was gone forever—that is, until the networks discovered 'reruns.' The next day at school, all your friends would be talking about certain shows and the latest commercials. If you hadn't seen them too, you felt like a total loser."

I paused to see if anyone had tuned into my rant, but the girl was the only one.

"Television transported my generation from childhood innocence to the real world. And it all seemed to happen so fast. One moment we're watching *Kukla, Fran and Ollie* in our jammies in front of a B&W television set—and next, we're watching young G.I.s getting slaughtered in the jungles of Southeast Asia in living color. As young Boomer soldiers burned villages and tried to kill the enemy, who kept popping up out of holes in the ground like an insane 'whack-a-mole' game, *Gomer Pyle, U.S.M.C.* didn't seem so funny after all.

"When the civil rights movement exploded, the nightly newscasts were filled with footage of blacks being beaten by police in the South. We didn't understand. How could nice cops like Andy Griffith and Barney Fife be so mean and cruel? And when it was revealed that *The Monkees* didn't even play their own instruments (at least in the beginning)—the last vestiges of our innocence were wiped away faster than the sweat from Richard Nixon's brow during the 1960 Presidential Debate."

I shook my head and sighed. "Yes, TV became our window on the world. We were shocked, confused and disillusioned. In essence, *The Mike Douglas Show* got replaced by *Jerry Springer*. Not even a nose-twitching witch or blinking genie could rescue us from cold, hard reality."

By the look on the girl's face, she had no idea who or what I was talking about.

Sometimes I delve too deeply into Boomer esoterica, which usually leaves younger people scratching their heads in bewilderment.

In the current vast wasteland of television, we're exposed to hundreds of cable channels and networks featuring every possible movie, mini-series, sports event, rerun, serial crime report, and shopping venue. Most young people have the attention spans of gnats and don't read much. They want their information and news (fake and/or real) distilled to simple headlines or punchlines delivered by late night TV comedians. With the exception of a few reliable sources, journalism is dead. Newspapers are vanishing and electronic media is the new norm. Most of the talking heads on the alphabet TV news networks and cable channels are nitwits who spout their opinions like they're facts. There should be a laugh track under every newscast.

Plus, the majority of the agenda-driven news cycles aren't exactly uplifting. Seems like every day, some suicide bomber blows up hundreds of innocents in a crowded marketplace or a psycho with a gun opens fire on a concert, church, business or school. Random acts of terrorism, endless wars, genocide, human trafficking, mass murders, homelessness, crazy dictators trying to get nukes, drug overdoses, forced migrations, endless ethnic and racial conflicts are shoved in our faces 24/7. Gratuitous, ultra-graphic violence across every media has escalated to the point where we're all getting numb to it. Nothing shocks us anymore.

It's depressing and getting worse. Hey, no worries: Just have a toke, microwave some Pepperoni Hot Pockets and cue up some warm and fuzzy video games like Call of Duty or Manhunt.

The inquisitive gal lowered her note pad. "You know, my generation has grown up with 'reality television.'

"Yeah, sorry about that."

In the beginning, shows like *Survivor* and *American Idol* offered some decent entertainment value; however, with so much airtime to fill, the public's diminished IQ and a thirst for the most sensational content, we have been subjected to cringe-worthy series like *Jersey Shore, The Osbournes, My Big Fat Obnoxious Fiancé, I Survived a Japanese Game Show, Here Comes Honey Boo Boo, Growing Up Gotti, Bridalplasty, Date My Mom, Who's Your Daddy, 16 and Pregnant, Cheaters, Sex Box, Orgasm Wars, Born in the Wild, Brat*

Camp, The Biggest Loser, and *My 600 Pound Life.*

I asked her, "Speaking of reality TV, have you seen *The Real Housewives of Chappaqua*?"

"Is it just like all those other stupid Housewives shows?"

"Of course! It follows Hillary Clinton and her merry band of Chardonnay-swilling girlfriends in search of Bill's hidden mistresses stashed around the quaint New York town. In the first episode, as Bill cowers in the cellar, Hillary finds "The Energizer" (the ex-president's voluptuous, longtime paramour) under their bed, holding a plate of chocolate chip cookies she made for the Secret Service guards. Viewer discretion is advised."

I glanced at my *Bozo The Clown* wrist watch. It was after 2:00 p.m. The field trip would end soon and I still had to make the rounds.

Quickly, I summed up. "There are lots of clips from those old TV shows online. Watch them and you'll get a better idea about the early influences that shaped the Boomer mentality and why we're all a little nuts."

I handed her a pack of Blackjack gum. "Good luck on that paper."

"While My Guitar Gently Weeps"

I walked the final stretch around the inside of the exhibition hall, staring up at the giant wall mural. By the time the 1990s rolled around, most Boomers had decent jobs, young families, and owned houses. Somehow, we had become our parents and were now the dreaded "Establishment"—the very thing many of us despised.

To highlight the final years of the 20th Century, I used deep space photography from the Hubble Telescope as the background, which was overlaid with pictures and headlines from Operation Desert Storm, the collapse of the Soviet Union and the official end of the Cold War, the first case of Mad Cow disease, the Rodney King riots, Waco, the

Oklahoma City bombing, the cloning of sheep that led to the mapping of the human genome, the O.J. Simpson trial, the capture of the Unabomber, and the Columbine High School massacre. Plus, who could forget Bill Clinton's sexual exploits, subsequent impeachment, and the well-timed introduction of Viagra—a bitter pill for trophy wives everywhere.

The final section of the mural, highlighting 2000-2016, had been updated twice since I launched BoomerWorld. It features images from the U.S. Cole bombing, Enron scandal, the 2000 presidential election controversy, the second Iraq invasion and its subsequent civil war horrors, Hurricane Katrina, the collapse of the housing market, Barack Obama's presidential victories, the horrific Sandy Hook slaughter, the emergence of the FAANG tech behemoths (Facebook, Apple, Amazon, Netflix and Google), the rise of ISIS and mass migrations from the Middle East to Europe, and finally, the surprise election of 'The Donald.' Luckily, the mural ended there, because I didn't have the funds, space or desire to do any more updates.

"My Generation"

About twenty students were hanging around the 9/11 display, waiting to board the buses back to school. The tall metal sculpture always attracted a crowd. For Millennials, it was a transforming event just like the JFK assassination was for Boomers; however, these iGens, born after the turn of the century, were rug rats on that terrible day. For them, 9/11 is more of a historical footnote than a visceral gut punch.

As I meandered through the crowd, several students approached me. "You certainly have a fine enterprise here, Mr. Apple," said the leader of the pack.

It was Eddie Haskell incarnate. "May I ask you a couple questions, sir?"

Trying to score points with his teacher, who was lingering nearby, I could tell Eddie was a typical "askhole." You know, one of those annoying people who asks for your opinion for the sake of making conversation, and then says or does their own thing anyway. But I didn't care. Any interaction was welcome.

"Fire away!"

"Tell us, what are the biggest differences between Boomers and our generation?"

Relishing my last performance in front of a group of impressionable young minds, I wanted to deliver a short speech worthy of that great cartoon rooster orator from *Looney Tunes*, Foghorn Leghorn. Slipping my thumbs beneath the suspenders holding up my baggy corduroy pants, I puffed out my chest and began, "I say, I say, the differences are enormous, my young friend! Boomers were lucky to have even survived childhood. Most of our mothers drank martinis and puffed on cigarettes throughout their pregnancies. Unlike today's C-sections, that are planned around a mother's schedule, natural childbirth was the norm and many of us were yanked into this world with a pair of cold forceps.

"Our cribs were lethal, with deadly design flaws and painted with toxic lead-based paints, plus our bedding and clothes were flammable. And there were no 'childproof' medicine bottles or cabinet locks to stop us from crawling under the sink to drink all those tasty disinfectants and household poisons.

"In addition, we were totally oblivious to dangerous situations: Soaring ten feet off the ground on rickety swing sets. Falling off 'Monkey Bars' and "Jungle Gyms' onto concrete playgrounds. Leaping off rope swings into unknown waters. Bouncing on pogo sticks along busy streets. Hitchhiking and playing Mumblety-peg with knives and screwdrivers.

"Every car trip was a potential disaster. There were no seat belts, car seats or air bags. Instead, we piled into the back of a pick-up truck or big, boxy, solid-metal automobile for a free-for-all: fighting with each other, crawling over the seats, hanging out the windows.

"It's no wonder we were manic and often out-of-control. From candy cigarettes, bubble gum cigars and Pixie Sticks to sugar-frosted cereals and gallons of Cokes and Kool-Aid, we were jacked up on sugar and caffeine—all day, every day. Forget your low-fat and gluten-free foods. We scarfed down gross quantities of fatty foods: bacon, butter, hot dogs, cupcakes, marshmallow spreads on peanut butter sandwiches, ice cream. But most of us never got fat because we burned it all off—running around, riding our bikes and skateboards, and playing outside for hours on end—not sitting on our flabby fannies playing video games and trolling the Internet.

"Candy was one of our major food groups: Mars Bars, Goobers, Charleston Chews, Pop Rocks, Bazooka Bubble Gum, Zagnut Bars and SweeTarts were consumed in mass quantities. But we were also forced to eat plenty of other disgusting food like Spam sandwiches, Jello molds stuffed with carrot shavings and weird fruit, and tuna noodle 'Sorry Charlie Casseroles' *(with the potato chip crust, of course!)*

"We lived in mortal fear of contracting polio and ending up in a dreaded 'Iron Lung.' Our annual visits to the doctor and dentist also scared the hell out of us! If you needed an annual vaccination or a shot of Novocain to fix a cavity, you were terrified. Instead of those fancy, new hi-tech disposable syringes with needles as thin as a human hair, we were stabbed with big stainless-steel needles the size of railroad spikes, which were boiled again and again before they were used on the next screaming patient.

"We weren't allowed to swim for one full hour after eating, but we routinely climbed and fell out of trees, got plenty of scrapes and cuts, broken bones and lost teeth, and got our hands cut open by soda can tabs. Gashes were treated with a few butterfly bandages and a healthy dousing of Mercurochrome, which contained trace amounts of poisonous mercury and stained the skin with a hideous reddish-brown color that lasted for days.

"Bullies made us eat worms, mud pies, dirt clods and tasty

'boogers.' Rock wars, Daisy BB gun battles and Wham-O slingshot skirmishes were commonplace. Trying to set each other on fire was always in vogue. Tossing lit matches onto the hair and clothes of your friends was a fun and frenetic activity. The more sophisticated arsonists could disassemble a wooden clothespin and rebuilt it into a lethal 'Match Gun'—capable of shooting a lighted matchstick up to twenty feet away.

"Hoping that we would become famous scientists, our parents gave us dangerous chemistry sets outfitted with alcohol lamps, sodium cyanide, and acids; "Atomic" energy labs packed with radioactive uranium ore; and even glassblowing kits with blow torches. We built weird, dangerous stuff in the garage that blew-up or caught fire, like mini-bombs crafted from bundled firecrackers and cherry bombs, and go-carts that plummeted down hills with no brakes, crashing into parked cars and fences. And if you were maimed, disfigured or killed, there were no lawsuits. And no one went to the hospital unless you had a compound fracture or were at death's door."

By now, given my raised voice and professorial tone, most of the kids in the area were clustered around me, listening to my little lecture. "Most of the time, boys and girls were separated. Girls went to ballet classes, played the piano, helped their mothers around the house, were Campfire Girls and Girl Scouts. Boys joined the Cub and Boy Scouts, and played all kinds of sports, except soccer of course, because no one ever heard of it. Tryouts for swim teams and Little League baseball were always stressful. Not everyone made the cut and disappointment was the name of the game. One of the great embarrassments was being the last person picked for a team, *if* you got picked at all. Nowadays, everyone makes the team and gets a big round of applause just for showing up.

'Hey, you're not a loser. You're just the last winner! Everybody gets a trophy!'

"Instead of streaming the latest Marvel or DC superhero flick, we had all kinds of weekly chores to do around the house: getting all our laundry together, cleaning our room, picking up all the dog shit in the yard with a shovel, dragging out the trash, cutting and trimming the grass, pulling weeds, raking leaves, watering the plants, washing the car, and more—all for an allowance of maybe fifty cents a week.

"And if you were a boy, there was a good chance you had a newspaper route. That meant getting up before 6:00 a.m. every day to pick-up the papers, wrap them with rubber bands and then deliver them to your customers along your route on your bike. Once a month, you had to collect the monies owed by your clients. Some customers refused to open their doors or pretended they weren't home when you came by to collect. These deadbeats were often the recipients of acts of revenge—or as Boomers liked to call it: "karmic payback." They found flaming bags of dog poop on their porch or their front yard covered in toilet paper. And we routinely harassed them with crank telephone calls, doorbell ringing and ditching.

"We actually looked forward to the first day of school each year. We got to wear new clothes and shoes. Toted fresh school supplies, including new pencils and pens, pads of paper, and three-ring binders with colorful vertical tabs for each subject. We were expected to say the Pledge of Allegiance every day, learn math, science, history and geography, and spell 'Mississippi" in two seconds flat. And if you screwed up, you had to repeat grades. And believe it or not, administrators and teachers were allowed to beat us with rulers and paddles in front of the class—and our parents fully supported them."

The teacher gave me a sly wink.

"Every kid was forced to take a daily P.E. class. In the early 60s, President Kennedy implemented the 'U.S. Physical Fitness Program' that reguired students to do sit-ups, push ups, jumping jacks, stretching exercises, run the mile and climb ropes in the gym that were higher than Jack's Beanstalk. You were graded on your performance, and if you passed, you were given a special Fitness Award patch."

In retrospect, I think the government was getting boys ready for boot camp before they were shipped over to Vietnam.

"In high school, you had to change into a gross outfit consisting of a thick, two-sided shirt and God-awful shorts for your daily one-hour workouts. By the end of the week, those damp clothes reeked of sweat and snot, and were occasionally stained with blood. If you forgot to take the clothes home to be washed at the end of the week, you started Mondays smelling worse than a beached whale.

"After ten to fifteen minutes of warm-ups and calesthentics, we engaged in all kinds of sports. But on rainy days, we were forced to play deadly games of Dodge Ball. The sadistic coaches sat on the bleachers in the claustrophobic gym, laughing as the older, stronger boys mercilessly pulverized the weaker ones. Kids were viciously blindsided in the face and smacked in the groin. Geeks got knocked out. Eyeglasses were shattered. Big, red, round welts swelled up on torsos, arms and legs. It was a brutal gauntlet, but you quickly learned the art of survival. And if you lived to be a junior or senior, then it was your turn to prey on the newbies as the coaches cheered you on like young gladiators."

It was a rush!

"By the way, if you flunked P.E. you didn't get a diploma. And there were NO expensive presents for kindergarden, elementary, middle or high school graduations. If you didn't get decent grades and pass, you faced beatings, 'groundings' and/or additional chores on the homefront. And your parents had to sign every one of your report cards, which were returned to your homeroom teacher."

Many Boomers went on to become master forgers.

"Of course, family life was much different than it is today. In the summer, we were completely unsupervised—running wild from dawn to dusk in our Keds and Converse sneakers. We played outdoor games like Kick the Can, Hide and Seek ("Tag! You're it!"), Red Light/Green Light, Capture the Flag, and stick ball, plus we invented many games ourselves. Predictions and fortunes were revealed with our origami Cootie Catchers. 'Playing Doctor' in some kid's basement or in the woods was surely a precursor to the coming Sexual Revolution.

"At night, our parents stood on the porch and rang a bell, whistled, yodeled or yelled your name to come home for dinner or to go to bed. Each night, we sat down together at the table to eat a relatively healthy, multi-course meal—and we had to clean our plates (even if it meant sitting there for hours), because 'people were starving in China.'"

I studied the kid's faces. I wasn't sure anything I was saying was even registering. I wrapped it up. "If you lived in the suburbs or America's heartland, life was generally safe and innocent. Our idea of 'gangs' consisted of the Jets and Sharks dancing on a Broadway stage. There were no scary gangbangers, guns, rampant drug dealing or drive-by shootings. Race issues meant who ran the fastest. The worst thing you could catch was 'cooties.' Mistakes were 'do overs.' And the ultimate weapon was not a Glock or AR-15, it was a harmless water balloon."

"How enlightening!" Eddie said smugly, still keeping up his brown-nosing act in front of the teacher. "Baby Boomers have definitely lived through some interesting times, Mr. Apple. But what do you think about our generation?"

After snapping my suspenders to wake up the crowd, I raised my hands in a salute to BoomerWorld. "Luckily for you, three new generations have sprung from our fertile loins! Oh, how Boomers loved to fornicate! Of course, most of your parents hail from 'Generation X,' also known as the 'Baby Busters' and the 'MTV Generation.' Next came 'Generation Y,' or the so-called 'Echo Boomers' or 'Millennials.' And finally, you folks, who were born after 1995 have been christened 'Centennials,' 'the Selfie Generation,' 'iGens,' and 'Gen Zers.' I paused and scratched my head. "Looks like we've finally run out of alphabet names. Your kids will probably be known as 'Generation Z 2.0.'"

A few chuckles rose from the restless crowd.

"While my generation was transfixed by television, the Internet has dominated your lives since birth, connecting everyone with everything—the good, the bad, and the ugly. You have a supercomputer right in your pocket. The entire history of the world, instantaneous news and entertainment, social networking and e-commerce are just a click away. Want to purchase a used Russian submarine, charcoal toothpaste, exotic reptiles, candle holders crafted from Himalayan salt rock, an ugly Christmas sweater or a nice pair of hemp slacks? Just Google it. Tired of watching cute animal videos, playing Fortnite, or checking your Twitter feed? You can scan the Dark Web to watch a hilarious snuff video, pledge allegiance to ISIS, buy a human being, score drugs or banned weapons. It's all right there at your lightning-quick fingertips."

I paused and then offered some gratuitous adult advice. "But do us all a favor… As you cruise down the information highway at a million miles per hour, please remember to never text while you drive. Tomorrow it'll be okay because you won't be driving at all. Artificial intelligence will be doing all the work so you can spend more time forwarding revenge porn and being constantly entertained."

Deaf ears.

Still, I prattled on. "Your generation can 'data mine' information in a matter of seconds. When we were your age, researching *anything* took hours. You were lucky if your family owned a set of World Books or the Encyclopedia Britannica. For everything else, you had to go to the library, search through the card files to locate a book or periodical, and then try to locate it among rows and rows of shelves. Half the time, the book or magazine you needed was either checked out or stolen. And don't even get me started on road maps and directions!"

Eddie smirked. "Yeah, you Boomers had it so hard. My old man said he had to hike through a shag carpet to just change the TV channel."

A few of his friends cracked up.

"But you forgot to mention that it was 'uphill both ways,'" I added.

I didn't want to gaslight them, but if young people pulled their heads out of their smartphones and laptops for a minute, perhaps they'd see the dangers of living constantly in the great digital desert.

Technology is a tool—not a way of life. As they feed their online addictions, it's no surprise that ADHD among youngsters is on the rise. Even if they did stop for a few seconds to "smell the roses" (the actual plants, not the computer-generated versions), they'd feel compelled to take a photo and text it to all their friends. Of course, there is a trade-off. There always is. They have completely surrendered their privacy. Every email, text, Tweet, movement, Internet search is stored in the great Cloud. Nevertheless, you'll need a Jaws of Life to pry those smartphones from their "cold dead hands."

"Take the Money and Run"

In a last gasp of phony inquisitiveness, Eddie asked, "And what about the future, sir?"

With all the sincerity of Wink Martindale, I boldly pronounced, "Let me be absolutely clear: *You guys are screwed!"*

The expressions on the student's faces morphed from amused smirks to concerned frowns.

"I wish I could say the future was bright, but you face some enormous problems: First, despite your digital dreams, you are stuck with us Boomers. And we've only just begun to make your lives miserable."

Eddie stepped forward. "What do you mean?"

"When the Boomers took control of the country, things were in great shape. There were no world wars, plagues, pestilence or major financial crises to deal with. America was Numero Uno, the economy was fundamentally strong and the National Debt was low. But over the last forty to fifty years we've made a complete mess of things. We've borrowed outrageous sums to fund our enormous entitlement programs, endless wars and other crazy ventures. The fact is, Boomers have never really been very smart when it comes to money.

Despite all the opportunities we've had, fifty percent of Boomers have no savings."

I noticed the crowd had swelled to about thirty kids who were actually paying attention to my demented discourse.

"The biggest single threat to your future is the out-of-control National Debt and long term under-funded liabilities."

I pointed up to the live streaming feed from the U.S. National Debt Clock mounted on the mural wall. "When I installed that debt clock back at the year 2003, the tab was less than $7 trillion. Thanks to our gross financial incompetence and constantly raising the Debt ceiling, we've buried you under a staggering debt of over $22 trillion. That's a 300% increase in just fifteen years… Do you have any idea how much money that is?"

A sea of blank stares greeted me.

"The sheer numbers are mind boggling. Think about it… A billion is one thousand million and a trillion is one thousand billion, right? If you stacked one trillion one-dollar bills it would rise up almost 68,000 miles high. The moon is about 240,000 miles from Earth. You could stack those bills to the moon and back—over three times. And it goes up almost $4 billion a day!"

The crowd looked dazed and confused, but one kid did manage to blurt out, "That's some serious scratch!"

It's a shame so many young people no longer believe in The American Dream. Since birth, they have only known an unprecedented level of prosperity yet they still feel oppressed by the evils of capitalism and think the whole system is rigged against them. Shockingly, many of these kids believe socialism is a more viable economic system than capitalism. They have been given so much, but expect even more: The Green New Deal, free college, free healthcare, a guaranteed living wage— even a better ending to *The Game of Thrones*.

Yeah! Unicorns and rainbows for all!

However, as the National Debt continues to grow, the economic landscape will get much bleaker. Our out-of-control spending is unsustainable and will lead to the country's ruination. Younger generations will have a lower standard of living, fewer life options and opportunities, and will probably have to learn to speak Chinese to serve their new master: #weloveXi

Over the decades, many of the worst government pork programs have been exposed; however, the pinheads in Congress, who couldn't pass muster in *F-Troop*, continue to piss away valuable taxpayer dollars on asinine projects like a soccer field for detainees at Gitmo and luxury gym memberships for federal bureaucrats. Do we really need to fund research on the gambling habits of primates, the effects of Swedish massages on rabbits, if cocaine makes Japanese quail engage in sexually risky behavior, synchronized swimming for sea monkeys and everyone's all-time favorite: analyzing mudskipper fish on treadmills? And don't forget about the Arts! Productions like *Zombie in Love, Stoner Symphony,* and *RoosevElvis* (a "hallucinatory" road trip featuring Theodore Roosevelt and Elvis Presley) as well as film festivals featuring decapitated heads, public urination and sexual depravity are certainly worth the investment. It's only money, right?

A $~~billion~~ trillion here, a $~~billion~~ trillion there...

"And it's only going to get worse, my friends. There are over three-hundred thirty million U.S. citizens and seventy-five million are Boomers. Everyday, another 10,000 of us retire. We want our Social Security and Medicare, for which we paid taxes over our lifetimes—even though there are plenty of people collecting big checks who have contributed absolutely nothing. For the next thirty years, we'll be clogging up the healthcare system, filling the hospital emergency rooms and demanding expensive medical procedures. And guess who's going to pay for it all? Well, don't expect Boomers to pick up the check. Our earning days are over. Looks like your generation is going to be on the hook for the whole enchilada. You're stuck with the bill for a meal you never got."

The student's faces betrayed their angst.

"Given the rapidly expanding cost of entitlements and the hundreds of billions of dollars in annual interest payments on the National Debt, there's no money left for anything else. Even if you snatched every penny from the super rich one-percenters and made everyone pay ninety-five percent in personal income taxes, you'll never be able to support the current system, let alone pay down the Debt. No one in power has the cajones to even broach the subject. It's Kyrptonite for politicians."

Nothing to see here, folks. Just move along.

"And don't forget that after the Boomers are dead and gone, you'll have to bankroll those massive welfare programs for another eighty-two million Gen Xers and then eighty-three million Millennials! It's like an endless trailer for *Night of the Living Dead.* Your generation is probably looking at apocalyptic economic depressions and world wars… In the past, America lamented the two absolutes in life: death and taxes—but now, there's shipping and handling too!"

I felt bad about my unvarnished candor. My young audience looked despondent… These kids have many good qualities and could make the world a better place, but thanks to the Debt and other monumental screw-ups, their options are limited. They aren't to blame. Boomers are. Even worse, we've done a lousy job of educating them. While many other countries have much higher academic standards and test results, most of our kids have poor reading, writing and comprehension skills, and are grossly ignorant about history, civics, geo-politics, math and science.

Mr. Wizard would be appalled!

In many cases, schools are little more than warehouses where illiterate students are just shuffled through the system and then shoved out into the marketplace with no life skills or basic knowledge. To compound matters, we have allowed them to rack up obscene college loan debt for worthless degrees while fostering unreal expectations for high-paying jobs, automatic salary increases and promotions. Most students today can't balance a checkbook or identify the three branches of government, but they know the top-trending micro-celebrities on Instagram, YouTube and TikTok—and think that getting "bottle service" at some sleazy dance club du jour is the pinnacle of cool.

What did we expect? After excessive pampering during childhood and doping up many of these kids with Ritalin, Adderall, opioids and anti-depressants, no wonder they want to escape the ugly realities of life, dashing to their cry closets or living in our basements. They have been traumatized by the threats of terrorism, endless wars, horrific school shootings and the often exaggerated dangers of climate change, which leaves them feeling helpless and victimized. Safe within their digital cocoons, young people escape into a fantasy world by binge-watching TV, playing video games, trolling the Web and downloading the latest creepy emojis. And thanks to globalization, young adults throughout the world are just as narcissistic and mesmerized with tech and social media.

It's a sad commentary, but I wanted to give them a ray of hope.

"I know it all sounds dire, but there is a simple solution to deal with all the older generations. It's sustainable, organic, and eco-friendly too!"

A hush fell over the crowd as I paused for dramatic effect… "Two words: *Soylent Green*."

None of the kids seemed to know what I was talking about.

"Just do a little research."

I passed out the rest of my disgusting sugar treats and blasted out of there like Evel Knievel.

For the last half hour of the student field trip, I helped Mona in the gift shop. Eventually, the students boarded the buses and drove off into the L.A. haze.

Another brick in the wall…

4:15 p.m.

"Welcome to the Jungle"

The museum was completely quiet except for a strange, distant metallic clicking sound emanating from the back wall in the 1960s section. I went to investigate…

After cutting through the Toys and Sports areas, I emerged directly behind the Vietnam War exhibit on the north wall—one of the best displays at BoomerWorld. Its centerpiece is an old, scarred UH-ID Huey helicopter that I purchased at a military auction. To get it to fit as tightly as possible against the back wall, the tail boom and rear propeller were removed. Several authentic-looking mannequins are outfitted in Army garb: a pilot, a door gunner perched behind a thirty-caliber machine gun in the open side door, along with a medic and two infantrymen loading a wounded soldier into the chopper. Lush plastic jungle foliage surrounds the entire scene, giving the display a very realistic look.

To convey that the grisly war was brought into our homes on a nightly basis, vintage living room furniture faced the exhibit, including an old TV set positioned right below the front of the copter.

A man sat on a couch facing the display, watching the silent newsreel footage of the war on the TV. As I approached him, I could see the source of that clicking sound. He was slowly opening and closing an old metallic Zippo lighter.

I circled around the couch to get his attention. Although I could only see the left side of his face, I recognized him as the man standing in the rain across the street earlier in the day. He was still wearing the camouflaged boonie hat and green Army jacket.

Treading lightly, I asked, "May I help you, sir?"

He didn't move, his eyes still locked on the TV set. An unlit cigarette dangled from his lips.

Again, he opened his lighter, paused and then snapped it shut. I stood there wondering if he was deaf or perhaps was just too absorbed in the TV footage.

The man looked to be about seventy years old. He was a small guy, maybe five-five and 150 pounds, with a strong, wiry physique and intense eyes.

As I stepped closer, he finally saw me. “Sorry, I didn’t see you there.” Pointing at his left ear, he added, “Plus, my hearing is bad.”

“No problem.”

“I came in about half an hour ago. The front door was unlocked and no one seemed to be here so I started to wander around. When I came across this exhibit, I just sat down and—”

“Hey, I’m glad you’re here.” Gesturing at the cigarette, I added, “But there’s no smoking inside.”

The man shrugged and removed it from his mouth. “Oh, yeah… I don’t smoke anymore. Gave it up years ago.” He put the cigarette in his breast coat pocket and patted it. “As a former nicotine addict, just knowing it’s there gives me a certain satisfaction.”

Next, he opened and closed the lighter again. Realizing that I was watching him, he said, “Oh, that’s another old habit too.”

There was an awkward moment between us. Finally, he said, “I read in the paper today that Senator Whitehead will be attending your big party on Sunday night. Is that true?”

“Looks like it. Why?”

“I grew up with him.”

“Really?”

He seemed to drift off for a moment, alone in his thoughts. “It’s… a long story.”

I was genuinely curious about this man. I knew that we had met before, but I couldn’t remember when or where. I sat down on the couch. “Please tell me.”

He shrugged, keeping his eyes on the display. “Stu, that was his nickname, and I were like brothers from childhood all the way through high school. His family was filthy rich, but I was poor. My father abandoned my mom and me when I was a baby. She worked as a maid and we were barely making it… Anyway, Stu and I graduated in 1965 and were both accepted to USC, but he got kicked out after the first semester for bad grades and too much partying. Meanwhile, I had to pay my own way through college. Since I only had a small scholarship as a member of the wrestling team, I had to temporarily drop out to earn enough money to stay afloat. At the time, the war in 'Nam was really ramping up and we both got our draft notices, telling us to report for our physicals. His rich daddy paid off some doctor and Stu showed up with a phony medical report about having chronic asthma and a bad back. Complete bullshit, but he got a medical deferment and promptly re-enrolled at USC. Since I had no medical excuses or connections with the local draft board, I was classified as 1-A and was told to report to Ft. Ord for basic training."

I was about to bellow, "Good morning, Vietnam!" but it would have been disrespectful and out of place—so I kept my mouth shut.

The man's gaze narrowed. "The illustrious senator managed to weasel out of his duty to serve his country, but I got fucked."

"What happened?"

"I got shipped to 'Nam in 1966 as part of the Army's 1st Infantry Division, 173rd Airborne Brigade. Our base was built right on top of the massive underground Viet Cong tunnel complex at Cú Chi."

I was fascinated by the legend of Cú Chi. Built over 25 years, dating back to the 1940s when the French tried to colonize the country, it had more than 200 miles of tunnels spread out under a large rural area. The Viet Cong used the subterranean system to store supplies, manufacture weapons and launch attacks. It was an underground city with command centers, hospitals, schools, kitchens and sleeping quarters for thousands of soldiers and support staff. Some people lived underground for years and virtually everyone contracted malaria. The U.S. tried everything to flush out the enemy, pumping in gas, water, and even hot tar—but the enemy endured. Earlier that year, General William Westmoreland commenced a B-52 carpet-bombing campaign that turned the surrounding jungle into a moonscape, but a lot of those tunnels survived, were repaired and even expanded. Over the years, it is estimated that more than forty thousand Vietnamese died trying to protect the incredible tunnel complex. Eventually, the U.S. brass created special squads of "tunnel rats" for underground search and destroy missions.

I said, "It's a tourist park now."

He scoffed at the notion. "When I was there it was a fuckin' hellhole. Literally."

Once again, he flipped open his lighter, paused, and then snapped it shut.

"So… were you a 'tunnel rat'?"

Without responding, the man pointed over at the display. To the right of the helicopter, hidden back in the fake shrubbery, you could barely see the mannequin head of a Viet Cong poking up out of a camouflaged hatch in the ground. It was another of those subtle things I added to displays to reward those who closely scrutinized the exhibits.

"I saw that Cong immediately as I was passing by. Nice touch," he said with a sly smile.

"Very few people see it."

"Old reflex, I guess… I developed a sixth sense for knowing where the enemy was lurking. It saved my life many times."

Most veterans preferred not to talk about their war experiences and I didn't want to pry; however, I said, "I've read about Cú Chi, but I've never met anyone who actually fought in the tunnels."

With a furrowed brow, he just stared down at the lighter and didn't say a word. He seemed to be deciding if he should reveal anything about the horrors of his past. Finally, he sighed and began to speak…

"When I arrived in-country, the Cú Chi tunnel complex was still a royal pain in the ass for the U.S. I didn't know anything about tunnel warfare until one day when my platoon was out on patrol. A Cong tossed a grenade at us and disappeared down one of those holes. The blast killed one of our guys and left two others with some ugly wounds.

After a chopper hauled away the dead and wounded, our C.O., some gung-ho First Lieutenant from West Point who eventually got fragged, asked for a volunteer to go down after the guy who ambushed us. As the smallest dude in the unit, all eyes fell on me. Of course, I was scared shitless, but I didn't want to look like a pussy—so I reluctantly stepped up.

"After stripping off all my gear except my pants, knife and boots, I was handed a .45 caliber handgun and flashlight. The platoon sergeant tied a long rope around my ankle. When I asked what it was for, he said that if I didn't come back out within ten minutes, they would drag me out 'dead or alive.' As I dropped down into the hole past the camouflaged wooden trapdoor, he warned, 'Watch out for booby traps.'

"I was in a near panic as I looked into the tunnel. It was the scariest thing I'd ever seen—barely three feet wide, lined with tree roots and sticky red clay. The walls seemed to be sweating and the humidity was off the charts. Slowly, I started to make my way into the black hole, with the gun in my left hand and the flashlight in my right... Of course, I had heard the stories about all the horrible things that infested those tunnels: poisonous centipedes, giant spiders, fire ants, bats and huge rats. Charlie also devised some very clever booby traps to stop any GI stupid enough to try to invade their underground sanctuaries. Scorpions in boxes with hidden trip wires, spiked mud balls, bear snares, and crossbow traps with arrows covered with feces. There were also deadly explosives like gunpowder-filled coconuts, land mines and grenades stashed under dead bodies... Anyway, I crawled deeper and deeper into the tunnel, frantically looking for any pressure plates, trip wires or cubby holes where the enemy could be hiding.

"Eventually, I saw something thrashing around in an intersection of tunnels about fifteen feet in front of me. As I got closer, I saw a six-foot long Cobra tethered to a stake in the ground. That fuckin' Cong placed it there to cover his rear. If I wanted to go after him, I'd have to kill the snake. It was royally pissed off 'cause the tether had cut deep into its body and it was bleeding badly. It kept striking at me with its long white fangs exposed. After three or four near misses, it paused to regain its strength. I pulled a Ka-Bar knife from my belt sheath and stabbed the viper squarely in the head. Its body violently contorted and writhed in the mud, tearing itself loose from the stake. Soon, it was flopping and twisting all around me, spraying its blood everywhere—but I kept its head pinned to the ground until it bled out."

"Holy shit!" I blurted out. I couldn't imagine the sheer terror of being face-to-face with a deadly serpent in a damp, claustrophobic underground chamber while enemies lurked nearby.

As I slowly regained my composure, I noticed the profile of the man's face was like stone, seemingly detached from the awful memory. He spoke robotically like he was reading the phone book. "… It seemed like an eternity since I had entered the tunnel, but since I hadn't felt a tug on the rope around my ankle, I figured I still had some time left. At the forked intersection, I had to make a decision about which way to go. The tunnel to the left sloped downward and I could hear dripping water in the distance. Instead, I chose the right fork and crawled deeper into the blackness. Rounding a corner, I saw a pool of sunlight beneath another open trap door. Suddenly, there was an explosion above ground, dislodging dirt and dust near the top of the tunnel. I thought it was going to cave in on me, but it held. A man's bare feet dangled down into the crawlspace. I crept forward with my semi-automatic handgun aimed in front of me. A Cong dressed in black clothes and holding an AK-47, slipped down onto the landing. When he saw my flashlight, he froze. He couldn't hide his utter shock at seeing a grunt covered in mud and blood aiming a .45 caliber gun at him from just a few feet away. With my heart pounding, I pulled the trigger. The gunshot was deafening and my left eardrum ruptured. My head was ringing in pain and the smell of sulfur from the gunpowder was overwhelming. After puking a couple times, I managed to crawl over his corpse and into the light of day."

I was dumbfounded at the man's incredible bravery under such chilling circumstances. And he wasn't even finished.

"As I tried to adjust my eyes to the harsh outside light, I heard the screams and yells of my comrades nearby. And then I looked up to see an M-16 pointing right at my head. The Sergeant, a battle-hardened vet with three tours under his belt, calmly said, 'The next time you pop up out of one of these fuckin' holes you better be whistling 'Dixie' or you'll get your head blown off.'"

He shifted on the couch and once again slowly opened and closed the lighter. "Well, after that, I was the platoon's official tunnel rat. Over the next six months, I became a savage. A killing machine… I made many runs, playing a deadly game of hide and seek with a lethal and fearless enemy. I saw and did some terrible things down in those damp, dark crawlspaces that will haunt me forever."

"It all ended in January 1967 during Operation Cedar Falls. My mentor, an Aussie we called 'Frankie the Ferret,' and I were part of a special reconnaissance team sent into a tunnel complex outside the village of Bên Súc—a hotbed of Cong activity. Frankie was a veteran of the early Cú Chi tunnel raids and knew every trick in the book for evading booby traps and killing the enemy at close quarters as quietly as possible. Frankie was special, invincible. You know, one of those guys who was impervious to all the death and mayhem around him… I'd seen plenty of other experienced guys crack up under the pressure of being down in 'The Black Echo'—as we called the tunnels. We'd drag them out, crying and screaming in terror, but Frankie always emerged, calm and collected.

"One day, Frankie and I went down two different holes to search for the enemy and to plant some explosive devices. After an hour or so, I emerged from the tunnel, but Frankie was still down there somewhere. I went back down twice to search for him, but came up empty. He just seemed to vanish… Later that night, we found his head on a spike near our base. His cigarette lighter was shoved in his mouth."

He stared at the silent, flickering TV. "I never went into a tunnel again."

I looked down at the lighter in the man's hand. "Is that it?"

He slowly nodded.

Looking more closely, I saw an engraving on the front: a cartoony rat holding a gun and flashlight, surrounded by some Latin words that read: "Non gratum anus rodentum."

"What does that saying mean?"

He exhaled. "Not worth a rat's ass."

We sat there for a while, lost in our own thoughts. The man's bravery and daring exploits were incomprehensible to me.

I felt like a worthless wimp.

"Did you serve?" he asked, catching me a little off guard.

"Uhh… no. I was in the draft lottery in 1971. My number was 297. I got lucky."

No kidding. Like many young Boomers who faced the draft during the waning years of the Vietnam War, getting a high number was a blessing. Sheer fate determined whether you would be forced into the military and sent into the shit—or allowed to enjoy a carefree life at home or college.

Growing up, I always thought I'd be a soldier one day. Throughout my childhood, I used to play Army with my buddies. Toting toy rifles and BB-guns, we'd plan attacks and ambushes, and fight hand-to-hand with rubber knives in mock war games. Most of our fathers had served in WW2 or Korea, and we fully expected to fight for our country one day, too. All of us had stories about acts of military heroism, like my crazy uncle who claimed he killed an SS Nazi Colonel with his bare hands during The Battle of the Bulge—and kept his Luger as a souvenir. In addition, there were all kinds of war movies at the theaters and on TV every weekend to fuel our macho fantasies. Hollywood stars like Audie Murphy, John Wayne and Steve McQueen were cinematic role models for our impressionable young generation. They were the great heroes who vanquished the evil forces of totalitarianism and saved the world.

From 1962 to 1967, I religiously watched *Combat* every Tuesday night. It was a way to bond with my father and revel in the glorified version of war. Like Sgt. Saunders and his band of brothers, I always imagined a routine day on the battlefield would consist of killing a dozen nefarious Nazis, hiking across the picturesque French countryside, chatting with the friendly locals—and eventually, spending the night at a quaint farmhouse, dining on French bread, cheese and wine before a possible roll-in-the-hay with a farmer's daughter named Monique.

Instead, Vietnam came along and bitch-slapped us back to reality. With its hot, steamy jungles filled with venomous snakes and hungry leeches, punji stick pits and an endless supply of sneaky Ninja-like guerilla warriors who never stopped trying to kill you—the Vietnam War didn't match our pre-conceived, highly-romanticized notions of combat. Besides the bullshit political reasons behind the war, watching the carnage unfold every night on television scared the crap out of us.

As I sat there watching the man play with his lighter, I felt even smaller. Here was a guy who risked everything while I was a feckless student, feeling put out for being required to carry my draft card in my wallet. I had been opposed to the Vietnam War, but still had respect for the men and women who served. Like most brain-washed college students, my anger was directed at the politicians and the evil "military industrial complex" that prospered from all the death and destruction. Dogmatic and cloaked in my Leftist delusions, I was convinced my world view was sacrosanct back then. For me, every issue was black and white.

My parents were both highly patriotic WW2 veterans who supported the war in Vietnam. My father barely survived a terrible training accident at Ft. Bragg right before his battalion shipped out to the South Pacific. He spent a year in the hospital while the rest of his comrades were slaughtered by the Japanese. For over thirty years, he carried the physical scars as well as the guilt that he was the lone survivor among his fellow soldiers. My mother also served in the Women's Army Corps (WACs) as a recruitment officer. Needless to say, we had many arguments about the Vietnam war and my draft status. Finally, they flatly stated that if I was drafted and refused to serve, I would be disowned. Fate would have to be the final arbiter.

In late 1971, despite the political tension between us, my father took me to an Oakland Raiders' game. He worked for a big corporation and had two tickets for each home game to entertain clients. When it was time for the national anthem before the start of the game, everyone stood—except for me. With my long hair and Mao Tse-tung's "Little Red Book" tucked into my pocket, I just sat there, head down and staring at the concrete floor, trying to convince myself I was protesting on principle… I remember the darkness. The sun was blocked out by the fans standing around me. It was amazing that those testy Raiders fans didn't beat the shit out of me for being so disrespectful to the flag. I would have deserved it. But (irony of ironies) since I was wearing my fathers' old Army field jacket from WW2, maybe they thought I was a disgruntled, damaged former soldier… My father just looked down at me. There was disappointment in his eyes, but he never said a word. In retrospect, it's my biggest regret.

I tried to steer the conversation back to the man's relationship with the Senator. "So, when was the last time you saw Whitehead?"

"It's been about fifty years… When I got back to the States, I wanted to rekindle our relationship even though I was still pretty disgusted about how he lied to get out of going to 'Nam. Not to mention all the shit I had to go through 'cause I didn't have his money and connections… Anyway, I went to his fraternity house at USC one Friday night. As usual, there was a big party going on. I made the mistake of wearing my uniform and one of Stu's drunken buddies got in my face, asking me if I was a 'baby killer.' I punched that jerk in the mouth and we got into a big fight. I expected my old friend to back me up. Instead, he told me to leave… We haven't had any contact since."

"He sounds like a real ass. But you came here today to confirm that he'll be at the Sunday night party. Why?"

The man seemed uncomfortable with the question. Avoiding eye contact, he said, "I'm… I'm really not sure."

His nebulous comment didn't really put my mind at ease—so I persisted. "Are you going to punch Senator Whitehead in the mouth too?"

A weird little smirk flickered across the left side of his face. "No. You don't have to worry about that."

Actually, I wouldn't mind watching him rearrange the Senator's smarmy Chiclet smile. In fact, I'd like to punch him myself, but only after his check for the tickets was safely deposited into my bank account.

The man stood and said, "Anyway, I'd like to buy a ticket for that party." Reaching for his wallet, he turned to directly face me for the first time. Looking like the menacing Sgt. Barnes from the movie *Platoon*, he had a long, jagged scar on the right side of his face, running from just below his eye to the corner of his mouth. I assumed he got the gruesome wound while fighting in the tunnels, but didn't have the nerve to ask him about it.

The last seven complimentary tickets to the Sunday night gala were stashed in my wallet. I had already handed out all the other comps to special friends and colleagues around town. Without hesitation, I pulled out two tickets and handed them to him. "Here you go and there's no charge. Your service to our country is truly inspirational. Bring your wife, too."

When the man flinched at the mention of his wife, I realized my faux pas. He handed the extra ticket back to me. "Thanks, but I only need one."

"I didn't catch your name," I said, extending my hand.

"Just call me Matt."

That's one name I'll never forget: "Matt–The Tunnel Rat.'"

"Well, I'd better be going," he said.

"I'll walk you out."

As we circled back to the front foyer, I asked, "Do you live here in town?"

Matt shook his head. "No. I used to live in Inglewood, but not anymore."

I could tell that he was tired of talking and anxious to leave.

"I enjoyed meeting you, Matt. I'll look forward to seeing you on Sunday."

We shook hands and he walked out the front door.

I'm always in awe of the veterans that I meet. Regardless of where they served, whether they were drafted or enlisted, were injured or emerged from the battlefield unscathed—they are generally humble, good people. As a former peacenik who never put on the uniform, I'm self-conscious being in the presence of vets, especially those who have been to war. They faced death on a battlefield: the primordial rite of passage to reach true manhood.

Matt's detached recitation of his horrendous war experiences was both powerful and unsettling. He seemed like a very decent guy, yet his vague comments about Senator Whitehead were a little ominous. I still wasn't sure if he wanted to reconnect with his old friend to forgive and forget, or just throttle him.

More troubling to me was the uneasy feeling that Matt and I had met before. I have a decent memory, yet I still couldn't place him—and it was really bugging me.

4:45 p.m.

"Under the Boardwalk"

I retired to my office to check my email and voice messages. Both weekend events could still possibly sell out, but only if I kept the pressure on. I also called to confirm my appearance the next morning on a local classic rock radio station.

There was still the matter of the insurance policy for

BoomerWorld. Elizabeth Frost had insisted I deliver the policy to her today. Up until yesterday, she was just an annoying banker who was always hassling me about my precarious financial situation. But now, after spending time with her and her father, I was starting to develop an affection for her.

Dreading the idea of deceiving her about the policy, I decided to do the cowardly thing and punt. I left the insurance paperwork on my desk, put Walter on the leash, locked the front door and scurried off for a long walk on the beach.

It was a glorious late autumn day. The rain had passed and the sun hung like a shimmering golden disco ball over the Pacific Ocean. As we headed north towards the Santa Monica Pier, warm wisps of wind rolled in with the briny waves. Sailboats and packs of surfers bobbed off shore. Empty teal-colored lifeguard stations and small groups of people were scattered along the wide swath of sandy beach. Seagulls pecked at abandoned food scraps and dogs chased sticks into the water.

Walter and I walked behind three young women who were engaged in an animated conversation about some new Netflix series. Luckily, I couldn't hear all the sordid details, but I did get an eyeful of the tattoos that graced their nubile backsides.

I'm not a "dirty old man" but I felt like Tyrone F. Horneigh from Laugh-In, fingering some Walnettos in my coat pocket.

When did our society become obsessed with body art? And I use the word "art" very loosely… When I was a kid, the only tattoos I ever saw were those little black anchors on the forearms of Popeye during Saturday morning cartoons. On trips from The Burbs into the Big City, you might spot a tatted-up Marine, longshoreman, ex-con or scary-looking biker at a taco stand. These were badass hombres who led hard lives and never watched The Mary Tyler Moore Show—even once. But these days it seems like everyone has a tattoo. I can understand a woman may want a small butterfly or rose on her ankle or maybe even some exotic image to tantalize a lover, discreetly hidden under her clothes. However, if you put a full-length leg tattoo of a demonic serpent crawling out of the eye socket of a flaming human skull wrapped in barbed wire, you should probably get your head examined—that is, if it isn't already adorned with Maori tribal inkings. Choosing to cover your body with disturbing tattoos of Tweety Bird copulating with The Prince of Darkness may get you a guest shot on Dr. Phil, but years later (or maybe the very next day) you might regret it: "What the hell was I thinking?"

Whoever invents a cheap, painless tattoo removal system is gonna be a billionaire!

One of those young gals had a new tramp stamp centered right above her hip-hugging jeans. It was a colorful design, featuring a dolphin leaping over a setting sun above a deep blue sea. It was vibrant and definitely eye-catching. Of course, in forty years when her skin starts to sag, and those inks fade and lose their luster, that dolphin is going to look like Flipper on his deathbed.

Most Boomers are afraid of tattoos because getting one hurts and we don't like needles. When we wanted attention, we opted for safer, painless options like flamboyant clothing or crazy hairstyles.

Remember: The best thing about a mullet is that you can always cut it off.

5:45 p.m.

"You've Lost That Lovin' Feelin"

Walter and I walked up the coast for a while until I saw the lights on the pier's big Ferris Wheel and rollercoaster glowing in the twilight. Eventually, we turned around and headed to our favorite watering hole.

It was dark when we finally arrived at Booker's Beach Bar. Every Wednesday evening from four to seven p.m., seniors can buy well drinks for two dollars each. A regular group of geezers who call themselves "The Dead Peckers Society" always congregates to imbibe, complain about their medical maladies and wives, tell dirty jokes and plan charity events. Given their namesake, there were always plenty of good jokes.

The group's flamboyant leader, a verbose rascal with rosy cheeks and silver hair named Harry, spewed more one-liners than Henny Youngman. He was holding court as we entered.

"Hey, guys, did you hear about that new wonder drug called Gingko Viagra?" Harry asked his blurry-eyed friends. "It helps you remember what the fuck you're doing."

His geriatric audience erupted into raucous laughter. Another round of drinks was ordered as several other old timers tried to remember raunchy jokes.

To guarantee no drunken "Dead Pecker" got in trouble with the law, Booker insisted they all surrender their car keys before the libations began to flow. The keys were safely stored in a jar next to a cash register behind the bar. And no one left in their car unless they passed a breath analyzer test, administered by the old cop himself.

As I wandered along the bar, Big Al was stretched out on the counter right in front of the draft beer taps. The enormous feline slowly rose and dropped to the floor to welcome Walter. A waitress filled a saucer with some fresh beer and the boys eagerly lapped it up.

As usual, Booker was watching cable news on his small TV and his blood was boiling. "Check out this moron, Bob!" Booker exclaimed, pointing at the TV. "He's some administrator from University of California promoting the latest PC insanity on our college campuses."

On the screen, a smug-looking bureaucrat droned on. "We're encouraging our faculty and students to eliminate certain offensive phrases from their vocabularies like 'America is the land of opportunity,' 'I believe the most qualified person should get the job,' and 'Everyone can succeed in this society, if they work hard enough.'"

Leaping to his feet, Booker blurted out, "*Offensive*? That's what

America is all about!"

I patted him on the shoulder. "Take it easy, buddy."

The administrator observed. "Those types of hurtful clichés are what we call 'micro-aggressions.' They make some students very uncomfortable and upset."

Booker was incredulous. "What a steaming load of crapola!"

The TV moderator observed, "Back in the '60s, University of California was famous for advocating free speech. Now, this sounds like the administration is trying to control speech."

"Insensitive statements like 'America is a melting pot' are racially, ethnically and politically demeaning," said the U.C. spokesperson.

"But it's a historical fact," the moderator countered. "For over 300 years, America has been a beacon of hope and opportunity for immigrants from all over the world. We've welcomed and assimilated millions of people, representing every race, religion and nationality."

"Diversity should be celebrated on our college campuses."

The moderator responded, "But many college administrations, faculties and liberal student groups are increasingly intolerant of any views that don't match the progressive agendas. For instance, the concept of 'American Exceptionalism' is ridiculed and under attack."

"And it should be," the administrator smirked. "In the great global community, America isn't special. We're just another nation at the table—equal to every other country."

"Jesus! This guy is dumber than a urinal puck!" said Booker, downing a Margarita in one gulp.

"Time to check your blood pressure," I said.

The administrator added, "We need 'safe spaces' where students can shelter themselves from dissenting opinions about politics, religion and race."

Totally frustrated, Booker asked, "Can things get any more absurd? What about the First Amendment? Don't kids go to college to be exposed to all kinds of ideas and then make their own choices?"

Next, the university administrator started babbling about the value of "trigger warnings" in the classroom, where professors warn students about potentially distressing material before it's introduced.

"Wait until those super-sensitive college nimrods get out there into the real world!" Booker exclaimed. "'Trigger warnings'? Are you kiddin' me?! Back when I was a patrolman with the N.Y.P.D., a trigger warning was when some asshole shoved a 9mm handgun in your face and yelled, 'Give me your money or I'll blow your brains out!'"

"Sit down, Booker," I said, gently pushing him onto his stool. "You've really got to stop watching TV news. You're going to have a coronary."

"I know, but I care, man."

A big roar of laughter erupted farther down the bar where the Dead Peckers were ramping up the revelry. Old Harry threw down the gauntlet to his comrades. "Okay, gents, I've got a proposition. I'll buy a drink for whoever comes up with the best name for a pecker. Let the games begin!"[7]

The guys all cracked up and started shouting out names.

"Russell, The Love Muscle!"

"I like Caesar The Pleaser!"

"Baron von Schlongerweiss!"

"No! Vlad—The Impaler!"

Harry needed to write down the numerous salacious submissions, which were coming fast and furious. He asked the bartender if he could borrow a Sharpie and the small white board next to the cash register.

"I got one! Kaptain Kielbasa!"

"The Lap Lizard!"

Another old fart shouted, "He Who Must Be Obeyed!"

As Harry quickly scrawled the names on the board, Booker and I watched as the inebriated group became even more rowdy.

One guy said, "I vote for The Chief of Staff!"

"No, The Dicktator!"

"How about El Presidente?!"

---

[7] *When the narrative needs a little pizazz, you can never go wrong with dick jokes!*

I whispered to Booker, "Sounds like an election year."

More names were hurled at Harry.

"The Purple-Headed Yogurt Thrower!" some old bald guy yelled.

"That's gross! I prefer The Zipper Ripper!"

"No! Mount Vesuvius!"

"Mr. Goodbar!"

A guy in the back yelled, "My Hard Drive!"

The guy sitting beside him opined, "I think you mean Your Floppy Disc!"

Luckily, the bar was mostly empty, except for two attractive women sitting at a side table, quietly sharing a bottle of wine. They seemed mildly amused at the older men and their schoolyard banter, chuckling among themselves as the names kept popping up.

Bad pun. Sorry...

Harry noticed the women and said. "Hey ladies, do you have any suggestions?"

The bar went silent. One of the women, who wore a wedding ring, shyly suggested, "Woody." The other gal, who had the vibe of a party girl, said in a smoky voice, "You can never go wrong with—Easy Rider."

The guys roared with laughter.

"Somebody buy them another drink!" chortled Harry as he added the names to the list.

The oldest geezer in the group raised his hand and proudly stated, "My wife calls mine The Thrill Drill."

"Right," said a skeptical Harry. "But I'll bet it's more like 'The Hanging Chad'."

Finally, the white board was filled with lewd names. Harry turned to Booker and said, "I think our gracious host should be the final judge... What's the best name, Booker?"

Booker walked over to the group. "Okay, gentlemen. The final round of drinks is on me. But then it's time for all you old peckers to go home and take your medicine."

The guys saluted their thanks and yelled out their drink orders as Booker studied all the names on the white board. After some careful deliberation, he announced, “Sorry, but I think you missed the best name of all.”

A hush fell over the crowd as Booker paused for dramatic effect. “And the winner is—‘Shaft! Can you dig it?’”

Everyone in the place burst out laughing and clapping.

Booker ambled over to the women’s table, picked up their check and ripped it in half. “Sorry, ladies. I want to apologize for that rude display of male immaturity. Those gentlemen come here every Wednesday evening to blow off a little steam. I hope you weren’t offended.”

While the married gal smiled demurely, her sultry friend said coyly, “It’s okay. I know *I* can dig it.”

Booker flashed his killer smile. “Another bottle of wine on the house, perhaps?”

Before they could respond, he looked over at the bartender, snapped his fingers and pointed at the table. “Mind if I sit down for a minute?”

Well, I could see where that was going. Once again, Booker was on the prowl.

For the next half hour, I sat at the end of the bar by myself, watching the Dead Peckers polish off their drinks as the festivities slowly came to a conclusion. A few cabs and Uber drivers waited patiently out front to ferry the boys home. One old timer thought he was sober enough to get behind the wheel and demanded his keys, but the bartender told him Captain Hazelwood of the Exxon Valdez had a better chance to be a designated driver.

Since Booker was still preoccupied with the women, Walter and I slipped out the back of the bar and headed home.

4

Thursday • October 29
6:00 a.m.

"Life in the Fast Lane"

Walter and I rose early to get a jump on the day. Since I had to get to the radio station by eight o'clock for my on-air interview at The Growl 104.5 FM, I needed to leave Venice Beach before seven a.m. because of heavy morning traffic. I barely had enough time for a short walk and a cup of coffee before we hit the road.

I drove along Lincoln Boulevard until I got on the Santa Monica Freeway heading east. Sitting in the passenger seat, Walter stuck his head out the window, his big ears flapping in the wind. Traffic was moving at a decent pace right up to the Harbor Freeway maze near the Convention Center when it came to a grinding halt. As my old VW van idled irritably in the blocked slow lane, I checked my watch. I needed to be at the studio in a half hour and was running late. Predictably, my blood pressure began to rise faster than an Anthony Weiner selfie on Snapchat.

I tuned into The Growl, the classic rock radio station, to see if the morning drive team was hyping my pending interview. As usual, "The

Mike and Ike Show" was in full swing. After the classic Stones' song "Satisfaction" ended, Mike said, "I've heard that song a thousand times and it never gets old."

His partner Ike observed, "You know, that incredible eight-note guitar riff has a great back story. In 1965, Keith Richard woke up in the middle of the night in his hotel room in Clearwater, Florida, with the melody in his head. He recorded it on a cassette recorder and then fell back asleep. The next morning, he listened to it. There was about two minutes of acoustic guitar and the mumbled words "I can't get no satisfaction," followed by forty minutes of snoring."

Laughing, Mike added, "No doubt, it was inspiration from a bottle."

"Pure genius, baby!"

"Speaking of classics, in the next hour we have a special guest and old friend of ours—Bob Apple, the owner and curator of BoomerWorld in Venice Beach."

"Yeah, after fifteen years, Boomer Bob is closing his venue, but he's got some great things planned for this final weekend and he'll tell us all about it. But if he's stuck over on I-10, he may be a little late. According to the CHP, some yahoo in a pick-up truck dropped a chalupa and rear-ended a Tesla. Traffic is really backing up."

As I inched along the freeway, I reflected on my long-term relationship with Mike and Ike. They both had interesting backgrounds in the music business. Michael Johns, an Englishman, came to America as a roadie with Black Sabbath in the early '70s before he segued into the radio business. Isaac Brown was a sought-after studio bass player and part time DJ in Detroit for years. In 1986, they met backstage at the Whiskey A Go-Go during a Guns 'N Roses show. There was an immediate chemistry between them that evolved into a thirty-year on-air partnership as the morning drive team at The Growl. I met them when my old ad agency was buying radio commercials to promote car dealerships in Southern California. Over the years, we became good friends.

After about twenty minutes of stop-and-go anxiety, I was able to slip off the freeway and drive along side streets to the radio station in the historic core of old downtown Los Angeles. I parked in the lot next to their building and rode the elevator up to the studio, arriving fifteen minutes late.

When The Growl first went on the air back in the late '60s, the area was a haven for prostitution, gang-related drug dealing, grindhouses and porn theaters—an appropriate backdrop for the station's hard, edgy rock music. Over the last few decades, the legendary Old Banking District had enjoyed a renaissance, becoming a hip destination with trendy restaurants, retail, renovated movie palaces and art galleries.

Unlike most of the other major L.A. radio stations owned by Wall Street conglomerates, The Growl still had the homey feel of an old-time station à la *WKRP in Cincinnati*. Nestled on the second floor of an old brick building, its narrow hallway walls were covered with classic gold albums from great L.A. rock bands like The Doors, Van Halen and The Eagles, autographed electric guitars and drumsticks, and faded photos of the station's DJs mugging with rock stars.

Walter and I were ushered into the cramped on-air studio by a young female intern with green-and-purple-streaked hair, a torn Clash T-shirt and a metallic tongue stud.

Her parents must be so proud.

"White Rabbit" was playing on-air as my old friends greeted us.

"Yo! There he is! Our main man!" said Ike, a black guy with short salt-n-pepper hair, reading glasses and big friendly smile.

Walter immediately flipped over on his back so he could get a quick tummy rub from the guys.

"Sorry I'm late. Got stuck in that freeway traffic jam you warned about."

"No worries. It's great to see you, Bob," replied Mike. The pasty-faced Englishman looked like Ben Franklin, except for the Sex Pistols' T-shirt and leather sandals with tire treads.

We all man-hugged briefly and I sat down across from my hosts.

“Thanks for having me. I really need to promote my weekend events. It’s the final act in a long fifteen-year play.”

As the Jefferson Airplane song played in the background, I showed them the flyers for both events and filled them in on the details. Right before the song ended, Mike positioned the guest microphone in front of me and held up a set of headphones. “Want to put on the cans?”

I shook my head.

After giving me a warm introduction to their radio audience, we chatted about BoomerWorld in general terms and pushed the ticket sales angle.

Mike said, “Ike and I have known Bob for a long time. We used to do live remotes at some of his car dealership clients back when he was in the ad biz.”

“Yeah, I worked on ‘the dark side’ for many years.”

“Compared to now, those were wild‘n’crazy days,” Ike said. “Hundreds of people would show up at those events. We gave away prizes and tons of candy.”

He was referring to boxes of ‘Mike and Ike’ fruit-flavored candies that have been around since 1940. Given their same namesake, those candies became a natural promo item for their morning show. For almost thirty years, they slapped station logo decals on the boxes and passed them out to their adoring fans at every rock concert, street fair, community appearance and commercial event.

I avoided the dish of colorful ‘Mike and Ike’ candies in the center of the table because the last time I gnawed on one of those tangy chews, I ripped out a filling.

Mike turned to me and said, "Hey, why don't you tell our listeners that great story about how you landed the big Japanese car account."

"Yeah! That's a hoot!" Ike chimed in.

"Sure. Back in the mid-Eighties, some Japanese businessmen bought a bunch of failing dealerships throughout the greater L.A. area to create a new chain of showrooms for their imported cars and trucks. Initially, sales sucked because they had to compete against the big U.S. brands like Chevrolet, Ford and Dodge/Chrysler.

"At the time, 'Hap' McCoy owned McCoy Motors, the biggest GMC auto group in the West. Every weekend he bombarded radio, TV and newspapers with his wild sales promotions involving animals, midgets, free BBQs, special drawings and giveaways. He starred in all his radio and TV commercials and everyone in Southern California knew him well. He was a stocky guy with a big mustache and slicked-back red hair. He wore jeans and always sported a huge belt buckle featuring a car logo. Depending on what brand he was promoting—Chevy, Buick, Pontiac, or whatever—that belt buckle always got lots of exposure."

Mike said, "He was one feisty, relentless pitchman: always promising the lowest prices, biggest selection and plenty of freebies to grab the attention of car buyers."

"McCoy definitely had a stranglehold on the local car market," Ike said.

"Well, my ad agency got invited to pitch the advertising account for the new Japanese dealerships. Like we used to say in the ad biz, it was a real 'gang bang' with about twenty agencies competing for some big ad dollars. Somehow, we made it to the final round, presenting to two Japanese executives in our office conference room over on Wilshire. It was the classic 'dog and pony show.' After my Creative Director and Media Supervisor presented their strategies and plans, I gave an impassioned speech about how we could outsmart McCoy—

using guerrilla marketing tactics, head-to-head price comparisons and plenty of giveaways. I was working myself up into a frenzy, shouting we would 'kill the competition' with a relentless barrage of clever, wacky ads. Suddenly, the door snapped open and there stood Hap McCoy, looking very angry.

"Of course, it wasn't the *real McCoy*, so to speak, but the Japanese guys didn't know it. I had actually discovered this look-alike actor while casting another TV commercial a few weeks earlier. We dressed him up just like the famous car dealer and rehearsed a shtick that was sure to grab the attention of our potential clients.

"What the—!?" I snarled. "No one invited you here, McCoy."

"I wanted to tell these Jap interlopers that the only way they'll ever get a foothold in L.A. is over my dead body.'"

"Too late!" I said. "I was just telling them that we're going to destroy your business. Your days of ruling the Southern California car market will be over soon!"

McCoy sneered, "Oh yeah? Those are fightin' words!"

"He stepped forward and threw a wild haymaker at me. I ducked and punched him in the stomach, buckling him over. Then, I kneed the fake McCoy in the side, which sent him crashing to the floor. I began to strangle him with both hands. The Japanese guys couldn't believe their eyes! They stumbled out of their chairs and backed up against the wall. I looked up at the startled executives and said, 'I promised to kill the competition and I meant it!' I tightened my grip around McCoy's neck and soon the car dealer was dead—or at least, looked like it.

"I stood, stepped over the body and looked the executives in the eyes. 'That's how we roll at Apple Advertising. We always win for our clients—no matter what!' The businessmen were both stunned and horrified by the seemingly violent event. Then, after a moment, I turned to my colleagues and we all started to laugh. I bent over, cupped hands with the actor and pulled him to his feet… Realizing it was just an elaborate hoax, the Japanese guys slowly began to laugh, too.

"I calmly asked, 'So do we get your business?'"

They anxiously nodded at each other. The senior executive turned serious and in broken English he said, 'Your presentation was quite creative, Mr. Apple. Yes. I think you will work hard for us and destroy the competition. Congratulations!' We all bowed and shook hands."

"I love that story!" said Ike.

Mike laughed. "A little showmanship can go a long way."

During the next half hour, we had a long conversation about the importance of music to the Baby Boom Generation. Mike and Ike did a splendid job of referencing songs and groups to various historical events. I was sure the audience was eating it up.

Approaching the top of the hour, we wrapped.

"Listen, folks," said Ike, "you gotta go visit BoomerWorld before it's too late. It's fabulous! The museum will be open for the last time this Saturday and Sunday from ten to five!"

"And order your tickets today for the big Halloween Party on Saturday night and the Sunday Night Gala," added Mike. "Tickets are available online but going fast!"

I chimed in. "Yeah, come on down! Seeing the Batmobile up close and personal is worth the price of admission alone!"

As Steppenwolf's "Born To Be Wild" was cued up by the engineer, I thanked my hosts for their support and offered to comp them and their wives for the Sunday night party, but they had a previous commitment to host a rock concert to benefit the homeless. There were more man hugs, tummy rubs for Walter and promises to get together in the coming weeks.

Soon, I was back on the Santa Monica freeway driving home to Venice Beach. The Growl played a trio of songs from the Allman Brothers' *Eat a Peach* album. I sang along as Walter howled in the seat beside me.

11:30 a.m.

"Can't You Hear Me Knockin'"

Knowing I needed to have extra security to guard the Batmobile, I made some phone calls searching for a fully bonded firm at the cheapest price. Since I had limited funds, I settled on Dudley Security, a small outfit out of Van Nuys. They promised to have one guard on duty at all times—from Friday evening until Monday morning. It was an expensive investment, but I had no choice. Bottom line: the Batmobile was probably a bigger draw for attendance than BoomerWorld itself and I had to make sure it was safe.

I also got a call from my sister, Sarah, who invited me to her home up in Malibu the next day. She knew how busy I was, but insisted I come because she had something "very important" to tell me and it couldn't wait.

Sarah's a fairly well-known psychiatrist who lives with her partner, Julie Smith, a successful dentist. Relentlessly positive and life-affirming, she also doesn't take "no" for an answer. She's a true force of nature. I agreed to show up around one o'clock.

"Doctor My Eyes"

Around midday, a man about my age knocked on my office door. He was a harried pediatrician on his lunch break. Dressed in a white doctor's smock, he had a couple brightly colored leis dangling around his neck, featuring super-hero figurines, plastic animals and other weird trinkets that would fascinate children. Under his arm, he carried a large box wrapped in a black trash bag. He quickly introduced himself, saying he had something to show me. I invited him in and he unwrapped the package. It was a pristine Giant Blue & Gray Battle Set.

I was intimately familiar with this incredible play set. Santa had brought me one on Christmas morning in 1961 when I was nine years old. Thanks to a big ad campaign on TV, every boy in America wanted the set. It had 330 pieces, including dozens of Union and Confederate soldiers, horses, tents, cannons, ambulance wagons, a metal Southern mansion, and cool accessories like a record with sound effects and a paint set. It was only available at Montgomery Ward and cost a whopping $11.99, which was big money back in those days. The Blue & Gray Battle Set was a favorite among toy collectors. I had a few miscellaneous pieces on display in the Toy section out in the main pavilion, but to discover an unblemished box in perfect condition was very unusual.

The doctor told me a sad story… The same year I had one of the best Christmases of my childhood, this guy had suffered a terrible loss. Like me, he had asked Santa to bring him a Battle Set. He had been a good boy and fully expected to find it under the tree, but his father was killed in a freak auto accident the day before Christmas. The family was devastated. His mother fell apart and Santa never came. After the funeral, the poor kid searched his big house from top to bottom, never finding Santa's secret stash of presents. Then he realized that the gifts had probably been in the trunk of his father's car, which was consumed in the deadly flames. Heartbroken, he pushed any more thoughts about that horrible holiday out of his head. His widowed mother remained in the family home for the rest of her life until she passed away three months ago. It took the doctor weeks to clean out the house to get it ready to be sold. Up in the attic, he found a secret cubbyhole hidden behind an old couch that hadn't been moved in sixty years. Inside, he found the Battle Set and some other unwrapped gifts from Santa… He cried for days.

I was very moved by his story and asked him why he had brought the Battle Set to me. The doctor replied he did not want it because it was too painful a reminder of what happened so long ago. Further, he had brought his two children to BoomerWorld a couple times to teach them about the life and times of his generation. With tears in his eyes, he said, "I really love this place."

Well, that was about the nicest, heartfelt thing I ever heard about my little museum.

"It's a wonderful gesture, Doc, but you should sell it on eBay. You could get at least $1,000."

He shook his head. "No. I want you to have it. Other Boomers will see it and remember."

"But I can't afford to pay you a fair price."

"I don't want any money. Who knows? Maybe it will bring you a little luck."

"I could use it."

Remembering that I still had some comp tickets left for the gala night on Sunday, I offered them to him. He respectfully declined, saying the family was holding a belated memorial service for his mother over the weekend.

He checked his wristwatch. "I have to get back to the clinic. It's nice to finally meet you."

We shook hands and he hurried out the door.

1:00 p.m.

"You Really Got Me"

Anxious to put it on display, I carried the Giant Blue & Gray Battle Set out to the Toy section in the main museum. To make room for the big box, I moved around some other artifacts in one of the large glass display cases: a Fort Apache Stockade and Alamo Playset, etc.

With great care and concentration, I set up an elaborate Civil War battle scene on a piece of green felt on the top of the case. A regiment of Confederate soldiers faced off against Union soldiers, manning a mortar and cannons beside an encampment of tents and ambulance wagons. It was impressive.

To create the right mood, I got an old Zenith Cobra-Matic Stereo Record Changer from the Technology section, plugged it in, removed the small 45 RPM record from the battle set box and cued it up. Music and sound effects from the Civil War blared as I staged a mock battle.

Lost in my own make-believe world, I yelled, "Attack!"

Deftly, I moved the Confederate soldiers forward one by one towards the Union army. Adding in my own sounds of gunshots, explosions, screams of agony and threats of revenge, I fired a small plastic cannon ball from the mortar into the ranks of gray-colored soldiers. I split off a platoon of Union soldiers to flank the enemy on the right side. I must admit, it was a brilliant tactic worthy of Ulysses S. Grant.

"Look out! They're flanking us!"

Just as I hit the button on the exploding bunker that sent Union soldiers flying into the air, I heard someone clear their throat behind me. I spun around to see Elizabeth Frost standing about ten feet away.

Embarrassed, I mumbled, "Oh… Hi. I didn't hear you come in."

I started to put the figurines away as she walked around to the front of the display case.

"New toy?"

"Yes, an ardent fan of BoomerWorld just donated this magnificent Battle Set to the collection. As you can see, it's in stellar condition!"

"How old are you anyway?" she asked, once again folding her arms across her chest like an exasperated schoolmarm.

"Old enough to know better, but not give a shit," I laughed. Gesturing down at the remaining figurines, I said, "Perhaps you'd like to play too. Knowing how much you like to be in control, I'll let you be in charge of the Union soldiers."

Liz sighed. "Get real, P.T. I came here on business—not to engage in a juvenile flashback."

"Too bad. I was going to let you win."

As I started to put the Civil War pieces away, she rolled her fingertips on the glass case.

"How's Fred?" I asked.

"Physically, he's stabilized for now; however, he's rather depressed. Not surprising, all things considered."

"Maybe he needs an old fashioned 'boy's night out.'"

"He's not going anywhere," she said emphatically.

"Maybe I'll stop by and cheer him up."

"He'd like that."

I finished putting everything away. "Are you finally ready for the grand tour?"

"No. I came by to pick up the insurance policy. I need to complete the file."

Damn! I was hoping she had forgotten about it.

Trying to play it cool, I calmly replied, "Oh yeah. I meant to drop that off at the bank. Slipped my mind."

She frowned.

I closed and locked the display case. "Come on. It's in my office."

As we were leaving the Toy section, I noticed she was staring at the collection of toy household appliances. I launched into full huckster mode. "Now, there's a blast from the past. It's the entire Suzy Homemaker line of products! Remember?"

Liz walked over to the display of household gadgets: a Super Stove and Oven, Refrigerator, Dishwasher-Sink, Budget Blender, Deluxe Grill, High Speed Mixer, Ice Cream Maker, Jet Spray Iron, Juicer, Popcorn Popper, Soda Fountain, Hair Dryer, Washing Machine, and Vacuum Cleaner. All the things a young girl back in the 1960s would need to become a clone of her mother.

"Yes, I owned all of these things," Liz said softly.

"Really? I don't know anyone who had more than one or two of these items."

"My father missed most of my childhood. He would suddenly show up on my birthday or Christmas Day and shower me with every present money could buy," she said as she moved through the exhibit. "By the way, P.T., this is not the entire Suzy Homemaker collection."

"This set is on consignment from a collector down in Georgia. She assured me that it was complete. What's missing?"

"The Taffy Puller."

"It's an outrage!" I bellowed, my voice echoing through the pavilion. "I shall put the woman's head in that little oven and set it on 'broil'!"

"For safety reasons, there's no such setting, PT."

Liz approached a Suzy Homemaker Vanity with a large, three-panel mirror where little girls could comb their hair and apply lipstick, pretending to be their mother or a movie star. "I had one of these too. That is, until I smashed all the glass one day after good old Fred promised to visit and stood me up."

Her sudden, candid confession caught me off guard. Nervously, I adjusted my Looney Tunes necktie (the day's fashion statement) and said nothing.

As we were leaving the main exhibition hall, Liz stopped to read the small plaque mounted next to the wrap-around wall mural. Pretending not to notice, I kept walking.

The plaque was a special tribute to my deceased wife. It read:

BoomerWorld
Inspired by Amy Apple (1952-2002)
A wonderful woman, wife and passionate Boomer

I paused by the Green Hornet pinball machine in the lobby to wait for her. When she rejoined me, she lightly touched my shoulder with her hand.

"I'm sorry. I didn't know your wife was the inspiration for BoomerWorld. Please forgive my earlier sarcasm."

Her genuine compassion surprised me. I felt guilty as well for originally labeling her an "Ice Queen."

Entering my office, I pointed at a chair facing my desk. "Please have a seat."

"No thanks. I spent most of the morning at the hospital and there are a few pressing things I need to get done by the end of the day. I'm taking the day off tomorrow."

"Doing anything fun?" I asked, as I rummaged around on my desk looking for the envelope with the expired insurance documents.

She sighed. "Not really. I'll spend some time with Fred in the morning and then I may take a drive."

Remembering the date with my sister, I wondered if I should invite Liz to join me. She seemed to be warming up to me a little, but if/when she discovered my nefarious actions to hide the fact that I was an uninsured, lying son-of-a-bitch—she probably wouldn't want anything to do with me.

Figuring I didn't have anything to lose, I said, "I have to go visit my sister tomorrow around noon. She's a pretty well-known shrink and big-time author. Lives up in Malibu with her girlfriend Julie. I think you'd like them. Mellow drive, nice house and ocean views. Wanna come?"

Liz pursed her lips and avoided eye contact. "Full disclosure… I know Sarah."

"Really?"

"I figured you were related. Apple is a rare last name. I didn't want to say anything about it earlier, because… well, it's embarrassing."

"What's the big deal? My entire life is an embarrassment."

Contritely, she admitted, "I read her book about relationships. Eventually, I became her patient after my last marriage fell apart a few years ago."

Reaching into her purse for a tissue, she turned away to dab away a tear. Obviously, this was another sensitive topic for her.

After a long pause, I said, "It's truly a small world, isn't it? … I don't mean to pry, but did my sister help you?"

"Yes. She was wonderful."

“That’s what everybody says about her: ‘She’s so smart and compassionate! A real saint!’ But as her younger brother, I’ve seen her evil side. Like when we were kids, I accidentally broke a neighbor’s big picture window with a slingshot and Sarah found out about it. She threatened to tell our parents unless I made her bed for an entire year. It was pure torture.”

That finally got a small chuckle out of her.

“Come with me, Liz. We both need a break. It’ll be fun.”

“It would be nice to see her again, but I don’t want to intrude.”

“Nonsense! I’m sure she’d love to see you.”

“Sometimes we’d sit and talk out in her garden or just hang out in the kitchen. One time we even made a pie together. Sarah said it would be ‘therapeutic’—and it was. Her approach was so casual and unstructured, but looking back I can see how she shaped the conversations and steered me to a better place.”

“When you were at her house, did you ever walk out to ‘The Point’?”

“No. Where’s that?”

“It’s a short trail, maybe a couple hundred yards out into the canyon. There’s a bench at the end with great views of the ocean.”

“Sounds beautiful.”

I finally found the insurance envelope under a Slinky and handed it to her. “There ya go. I wrote down the agent’s name and number inside. Just give him a call.”

Man, I felt slimy. My old buddy Pete “Pipes” Pendergast had agreed to pose as my agent. I mailed him a copy of my defunct policy and we reviewed it together. Pete was ready if she decided to call. Still, I felt terrible, asking him to lie for me, while deceiving Liz as well. But there was no way I could afford a two-day major event insurance policy.

“Thanks,” she said, slipping the envelope into her purse.

“Well? Do you want to go tomorrow?”

She smiled. “Okay.”

"Great! I'll pick you up at noon."

"In your hideous old VW van? I'd rather be seen in the Oscar Mayer Wienermobile. I'll drive instead."

"You're on!"

1:45 p.m.

"Get Ready"

I spent the rest of the afternoon cleaning out my office. Fifteen years of accumulated paperwork were stuffed into several tall file cabinets lining a wall. The contents ranged from old billing records and receipts to articles and personal letters from Boomers who wanted to share their life experiences.

Methodically, I went through each file. I saved a handful of the letters, but purged the rest. I filled every trash bag and box I could find. When I finally finished, only two file boxes remained: one filled with all the pertinent legal and consignment documents for the various BoomerWorld collections, cars, rare memorabilia, etc., and the other with recent billing, tax returns, and some personal papers.

Next, I cleaned out my desk. Leafing through all the junk in the top front drawer, I found the matchbook from Booker's Bar with the cell number for that call girl, Desiree. Since Liz said Fred was feeling better, I figured tonight was the right night to grant his "last wish."

I got Desiree on the line. She quoted me a price of five hundred dollars for her services, but when she found out we were talking about "Fastball Frost," she cut her fee in half, because she was also a Dodgers fan and revered the guy.

Money was tight, but how could I deny a dying man's last wish? We agreed to meet at St. Luke's Hospital in Santa Monica at midnight.

Mick hauled the trash out of my office to the dumpster. The office was looking quite sparse, so I left a few of my favorite TV show posters on the walls: *T.H.E. Cat, The Prisoner, The Avengers,* and a rare *1953 Commando Cody Sky Marshal of the Universe* playbill.

Since I was exhausted, I decided to take a short power nap. Normally, I would retire to the Archie Bunker chair in the lobby, but Mona was out there restocking the gift shop. Instead, I tilted back my desk chair, closed my eyes and quickly slipped away into dreamland…

"Highway to Hell"

Once again, I was standing on the same grassy field in Venice Beach, under a bright blue sky. Frantically, I scanned the horizon searching for the man with the giant lawn darts.

In the distance, I saw his silhouette backlit by the setting sun. It was hard to see clearly in the refracted light. He was only wearing camouflaged cargo pants and black boots. Again, there was something ominous and metallic in his hands.

As he started to slowly jog towards me, the landscape began to morph from an expanse of plain mowed grass into a thriving jungle habitat: huge acacia and hopea trees soared skyward, groves of bamboo, elephant grass and rice paddies sprang up across the tropical terrain— creating a lush, forbidding wilderness.

As the man drew closer, I felt exposed and vulnerable. I thought about hiding in a nearby thicket of tangled vines, but I remembered the tales of deadly booby traps, snakes and other creepy things that thrive in the vegetation of Vietnam.

I froze.

Suddenly, the man was inches from my face. To my utter shock, it was "Matt – The Tunnel Rat!"

But how could that be? This was the same man who was trying to skewer me with those giant lawn darts in my earlier dream—a dream I had before I met him at BoomerWorld. But this time, instead of carrying those pointy projectiles, he held a .45 caliber handgun in his left hand and a military angle-head flashlight in the other.

Matt's eyes were cold and black. A small smirk crossed his face, "Are you ready, Bob?"

I stepped back. "Ahhh... Ready for what?"

"You know."

He nodded down at the ground. I hadn't noticed it before but there was a hole a few feet wide, partially covered with grass. I knew at once that it was a Viet Cong tunnel.

"What?" I stammered. "You expect me to crawl down into that hole?!"

"You said you were fascinated by the Cú Chi tunnels. Remember?"

"Sure. I was intellectually curious, but I could never—"

"Come on, Bob. You can do it."

I stared down into the black hole. My latent claustrophobia began to bubble up and burn like a raw Fizzie on my tongue.

Matt gave me a long, serious look. "I'll make a deal with you... If you go down in there, I won't kill Senator Whitehead at your party on Sunday night."

WTF?! Kill the Senator? Is that what he was planning?

Before I could respond, Matt shoved the gun and flashlight into my hands. Glancing back down at the dark hole, he demanded, "Get in."

Slowly, I lowered my cowardly butt into the tight cavity, which was only about four feet deep. As my feet sank into a warm slime on the earthen floor, I turned on the flashlight and crouched down to peer into the tunnel. Bug-infested roots wrapped around the damp walls. A humid, stale scent of organic rot mixed with the distant echoes of dripping water. Sinister shapes moved in the deeper shadows as the tunnel sloped downward into the earth.

Looming above me, Matt blocked out the sunlight. It was time. I had no choice...

I swallowed hard and began to crawl into the mouth of Hell...

5:00 p.m.

"I Still Haven't Found What I'm Looking For"

I awoke with a jolt!

I was still sitting alone at the desk in my office. Looking through the door at the windows in the hallway, I could see it was getting dark outside. I could hear the muted voices of Mona and Mick out in the lobby, finishing up for the day. Still feeling spacey and freaked out from my dream, I stumbled out to say goodnight.

"Thanks, guys. Another day, another dollar."

"You mean another fifty cents," said Mona.

Knowing that Mick had spent most of the day cleaning the parking lot and dragging around the sandwich board to promote the weekend events, I said, "Go home and take a long hot shower."

Mona smirked. "Yeah, you smell worse than—"

"I'm warning you, Mona. Don't go there."

"… Hulk Hogan's jock strap."

Mick scowled.

I interjected, "Both of you, zip it! We need to support each other and be positive."

Still, Mona prodded Mick, "Does Toe Jam know how to play 'Kumbaya?"

"No, but we do an awesome version of 'Black Hearted Woman,' which I always dedicate to you."

"Good one," she said. "Don't forget to tune up your air guitar, Mick."

"And don't forget your broomstick, Mona."

Same shit. Different day.

After I confirmed their work schedules for the next day, I returned to my office to reflect on my dream about Matt. I wasn't sure if his threat to harm the Senator was real or if it was just some crazy hallucination on my part.

I was definitely stressed out on many levels. The pressure of closing down BoomerWorld, the pending big weekend events, nightmares about cash flow, lying to Liz and my uncertain future were all messing with my head. Still, there was something about Matt that had really gotten under my skin. I felt compelled to do some research on him to put my mind at ease.

I didn't know Matt's last name, but knew he had lived in nearby Inglewood. I did a quick Internet search of veteran's groups in the area and found a posting for Thursday night meetings at a Presbyterian church off West Florence Ave. It was a long shot, but perhaps someone there might know Matt and I could track him down.

I locked up the museum, put Walter out in my Airstream trailer, got into my van and headed to the church.

6:30 p.m.

"Gimme Shelter"

As usual, rush hour was a mess. Avoiding the freeway gridlock, I drove down back roads going southeast, but the traffic was still snarled. After making a few wrong turns, I found the church on a quiet side street in Inglewood. My heart sank as I pulled into the near-empty parking lot. There was only a sedan, handicapped van and a motorcycle.

According to a sign near the front door, the meeting room was in the basement at the back of the church. I circled around, walked down a ramp to a set of double doors and peered inside. It was a large, rather dingy space for social church events with a cafeteria-style kitchen, ping pong table and folding chairs stacked against the back walls. Most of the overhead fluorescent lights were turned off, except for the front section where three guys were playing cards at a small table. A coffee urn, a few cups and a package of cookies sat on a nearby countertop.

I knocked softly and entered. The men all lowered their cards and turned to greet me. The eldest gentleman slowly stood and offered his hand. “Hello, my friend. Please join us.”

As I walked over to the table, I could see they represented three generations of veterans.

The old guy looked to be in his late eighties. Tall and thin with a wisp of a mustache, he looked a lot like David Niven. He was elegantly dressed in slacks, a pressed shirt and tweed sports coat. His left sleeve was folded and pinned up.

A friendly-looking American Indian about my age sat in a wheelchair festooned with various military stickers, and small U.S. and 101st Airborne Division flags taped to the chair’s rear push handles. He had a blanket draped over his lap where his legs used to be.

The youngest member of the trio was a brooding Hispanic guy with sad, brown eyes. Staring down at his cards, he wore a U.S. Marine t-shirt under an unzipped leather jacket.

It was clear they were playing Texas Hold’em. There were four cards face up in the center of the table, waiting for the River card. Each man had short stacks of nickels, dimes and quarters in front of them. The pot held about five dollars in loose change. This was no high stakes game. It was more like an excuse to get together and talk once a week.

I cleared my throat. “Sorry to barge in on your game, gentlemen, but I’m looking for someone.”

They exchanged glances until the old guy gestured at an empty chair and said, “Please. Join us. We have an extra seat tonight. The pastor had to leave to console a member of his flock who just lost a loved one.”

“Your pastor allows gambling in the house of the Lord?”

The disabled guy roared with laughter. “Are you kiddin’ me! He’s a cold-blooded card shark. Usually cleans us all out within an hour.”

The young ex-Marine looked up with a serious look on his face. “The buy-in is ten bucks. You in?”

By joining the card game, I could probably get my questions

answered about the mysterious Matt. And since I didn't have anything else to do until my rendezvous with Desiree at the hospital, I thought—why not? Still, I hesitated. "You guys should know I'm not a vet. Never served."

No one seemed to care so I sat down and we all introduced ourselves. Of course, I immediately forgot their names.

I handed a ten-dollar bill to the double amputee. He rummaged through a leather pouch hanging on the armrest of his wheelchair and dumped a handful of coins into my hand. "Good luck."

As we played a few hands, details about their military backgrounds and lives began to slowly dribble out...

The old gentleman got his arm shot off by a sniper during the Battle of Pork Chop Hill during the Korean War in 1953. He retired twenty years ago after a career in real estate and now volunteered at a local food bank.

The disabled guy lost his legs during a mortar attack near Da Nang in 1970. Now, he worked as a limo dispatcher and manned the hotline at a suicide prevention center a couple nights a week.

The young, sullen Marine had done tours in Iraq and Afghanistan, but his injuries were hidden. He didn't directly admit it, but given his general demeanor and admitted inability to hold a regular job, I suspected he was dealing with P.T.S.D. on some level. He was soft-spoken and rather distant—and a shrewd card player.

As usual, I was embarrassed and self-conscious in the presence of men who had gone to war. I'm also lousy at playing cards. After my stake was whittled down to less than two dollars, I asked them about Matt. To my surprise, the two older guys knew him quite well.

Matt Casey had been a regular at the vet meetings for well over twenty-five years. Apparently, after he returned from Vietnam, he had a difficult time readjusting to normal life. For years, Matt drifted aimlessly around the country, doing odd jobs to support himself. When his father was dying back in Los Angeles, Matt returned home and fell in love with his nurse. She was a devout Christian and helped Matt turn his life around. Eventually, they got married and Matt worked for a large demolition company. Given his military background, he specialized in placing munitions in condemned buildings. I also learned his wife was unable to bear children, but they had a good life until about six months ago when she died after a sudden illness. Matt took it very hard. He quit his job, sold their home, never came to another vet meeting and dropped out of sight. The other vets were worried and had tried to locate him. But he was in the wind.

As the poker game stakes went higher, I went all in on a dubious hand and lost the rest of my moola to the young ex-Marine. As he scooped up the pot, he muttered something about "taking candy from babies."

Nonchalantly, I asked, "Did Matt ever make any comments about Senator Whitehead?"

The geriatric Korea vet said, "I think he mentioned something about growing up with him, but I don't remember any details."

"Matt isn't a big talker," said the Vietnam vet. "But he did tell us some stories about his exploits down in those God-forsaken tunnels. Very freaky!"

I looked across the table at the younger vet. He shrugged. "Sorry. Never met him."

Turning to the older guys, I pushed a little harder. "I've only spoken with Matt once, but he seemed a little fixated on the Senator. Apparently, there was some bad blood between them dating back to his time in the Army."

"After what he experienced in 'Nam, he should be crazier than a shithouse rat," the legless vet said, staring at his cards. "I always thought Matt was surprisingly sane and well adjusted."

The dapper Korea vet tossed some change into the pot. "His wife was his rock. When she died, he snapped on some level. Just quit everything and disappeared."

"Well, he's still in the vicinity," I said. "Does he have any other family nearby?"

"Not that I recall."

The vets finished their hand in silence.

It was a dead end. Now, I would either have to go to the cops or hire a private detective to learn more about Matt. But since I was broke, that later option was out of the question. Or I could do nothing at all... I was starting to think this was just a wild goose chase, fueled by my own paranoia.

Flashing a rare smile, the ex-Marine cut the cards. "You want to buy in again?"

"I'm done, but thanks for your time."

I stood and removed the last six comp tickets from my wallet and laid them on the table. "Here are some tickets for the final Sunday night party at BoomerWorld. Bring a friend, wife, or whoever. There'll be some good food and music. And your old friend Matt plans to be there... I'll buy all of you some drinks too."

"That's very considerate of you," replied the oldest vet as he passed around the tickets.

"I'm in," replied the wheelchair-bound vet. "My wife is always bitchin' that I never take her anywhere. This sounds like fun."

The ex-Marine studied his two tickets. "I'll bet you'll be playing some stone age rock'n'roll, right?"

"Yup. A Beatles tribute band will be putting on a live show. You might actually enjoy it."

"Maybe after a few shots." He slipped the tickets into his pocket. "After all the stories I've heard about Matt, I would like to finally meet him."

We all shook hands. "Okay. I'll see you then."

9:30 p.m.

"We Gotta Get Out of This Place"

Since I had a couple of hours to kill before I went to the hospital, I stopped at a small grocery store on the outskirts of Venice Beach to pick up a few personal items. As I wandered up and down the empty aisles, I slowly filled my shopping basket with some health food like Tang, Cheez Whiz, a TV dinner, plus some doggie treats for Walter, miscellaneous toiletries, and a chilled Heineken with a neoprene sleeve to keep the bottle cold for my rendezvous later with Desiree and Fred.

I spotted a small display of pumpkins near the front door. When I was planning the Halloween party, I seriously thought about having a big pumpkin carving contest. Bad idea. I'd have to buy all the pumpkins and it would be a huge mess with pumpkin entrails strewn about by drunken Boomers. Plus, what if someone accidently cut themselves and I got sued—again? Nope. Didn't need that headache. Still, I grabbed one pumpkin for myself.

Waiting for me at the checkout counter was a surly-looking kid who looked like he had done a face plant in a box of fishing tackle. He sported multiple eyebrow piercings, a nose ring and large ear lobe expanders, used to create those attractive "flesh tunnels"—big enough to drive a Winnebago through. In addition to some prison-quality tattoos, skull rings on his fingers and an assortment of heavy neck chains, he wore a T-shirt featuring a grotesque depiction of a Zombie Apocalypse. And he reeked of weed. No wonder the store was empty.

I'd always wondered what happened to Rosemary's Baby.

"Good evening, sir!" I said as I unloaded my basket beside the cash register.

"What's so good about it?" he snarled as he dragged a can of shaving cream across the UPC scanner.

Great. Just what I need: A cashier with an attitude.

I noticed his nametag: Dick.

Perfect.

"Well, for starters, Dick, we're both alive."

"But for how long, man?" he said, stuffing a wad of chewing tobacco under his lip. "The world is a cesspool. The ice caps are melting and the oceans are rising. Pretty soon Venice Beach will be underwater."

But there was a silver lining: All that metal he was wearing would drag him to the bottom of the sea before the rest of us.

As I reached for my wallet, his angry, judgmental eyes crawled all over me like the creepy Iguana perched on his shoulder. I could tell what he was thinking: "This worthless Boomer would make a bitchin' speed bump."

Usually, when I encounter such gloomy individuals, I tend to avoid confrontation and keep a smile pasted on my face. "Look on the bright side. If the oceans are rising, this store will be beach-front property one day. It'll be worth a fortune!"

"Money. That's all *your* generation cares about. If you had taken better care of the environment and recycled more, maybe we wouldn't be doomed."

Given his dreadful appearance and foul mood, I seriously doubted this jerk genuinely cared about the environment—or anything else for that matter. Everything about him pissed me off. "Actually, my generation has done more to protect the planet than your drug-addled brain could ever comprehend."

Dickwad seemed surprised I wasn't going to put up with his bullshit. I took a deep breath and launched into an impromptu Sgt. Joe Friday lecture. "Boomers were born and raised with recycling. There are many examples. You seem to be full of crap—so let's start with diapers."

He bristled slightly at my insult, but I just kept talking. "When we were babies our mothers swaddled us in cloth diapers, not the plastic throwaway kind. Our diapers were routinely washed and reused again and again, and then they were handed down from sibling to sibling just like the rest of our clothing. No doubt, as a little rug rat, you probably soiled thousands of those non-biodegradable, disposable diapers. The fact is: the average baby in the U.S. today uses about 3,800 plastic diapers in just two and a half years, contributing to the eighteen billion disgusting stink bombs dropped into our landfills every year."

The guy mumbled something, but I just rolled on. "We recycled everything. Milk containers, beer and soda bottles were returned, washed, sterilized and refilled. When we got thirsty, we drank from nasty garden hoses or public water fountains, not chilled plastic bottles of expensive spring water."

I pointed at the sugar-saturated energy drink he was sucking on. "You probably didn't know that over eighty percent of those containers end up in regular trash and each one takes about seven hundred years to decompose. Good job! And the next time you start to piss and moan that 'old folks' like me are polluting the planet—remember that our lifelong 'carbon footprint' is a lot smaller than yours. Nowadays everything runs on electricity, but when we were growing up, we relied on our own organic energy to get around, exercise and stay healthy. We invented 'Earth Day' for Christ's sake!

"We walked, ran and rode our bikes everywhere. There were no escalators and elevators in every business and store. No one drove us around in air-conditioned cars to health clubs so we could run on electric-powered treadmills. In the kitchen, we blended and stirred everything by hand. In the bathroom, instead of just throwing away those cheap plastic shavers, we replaced razor blades, and rationed toilet paper. We read newspapers and magazines, and then used them for art projects and packing materials, in lieu of plastic bubble wrap and Styrofoam pellets. Out in the yard, we used hand-push mowers to cut the lawn, not gas-guzzling power mowers."

I was on a roll... For a fleeting moment, I imagined Officer Bill Gannon from Dragnet was right beside me, nodding in agreement.

"At school, we refilled our fountain pens and wrapped our textbooks in brown paper bags to protect them so they could be reused year after year. And we dried our clothes outside, relying on solar and wind power, not energy-sucking electric dryers. We were lucky to have one rotary telephone with a party line, a B&W TV and radio in the house. Now you have high-definition TVs in practically every room, plus desktop and laptop computers, smart phones and pads, Alexa, electric cars, and dozens of other electrical appliances that are predominantly powered by coal-fired plants and toxic batteries."

The kid feigned complete boredom, but I had scored a few points. He finished ringing up my groceries and I handed him some cash.

Grunting, he asked, "If you're such an environmental saint, where's your recycled grocery bag?"

He had me. I could never remember to bring one of those stupid bags when I went shopping. "Just give me a paper bag. Of course, I'll recycle it later."

"It'll cost you a quarter."

"Sold!"

I was about to launch into another tirade about all the great things Boomers have done to protect the environment, but down deep I knew we could have done a better job. During our early years, we recycled and used a lot less energy—largely due to the efforts of our frugal parents. But once we took control, things went south rather quickly. Our personal excesses and sloppy policies contributed to many environmental problems: smog-filled skies, extinct species, decimated forests, overuse of chemicals and pesticides, islands of floating plastic clogging the seas and killing marine life, and all that methane gas spewing into the atmosphere everyday directly above Washington D.C. Of course, I didn't want to admit any of these screw-ups to this disagreeable young chap.

Clearly, Dick viewed my generation as a bunch of out-of-touch, reactionary Neanderthals who aren't "woke" enough to other controversial topics, like white privilege, income inequality, plastic straws and avocado toast. The fact is, Boomers were far more radical on social and political issues, but I wasn't about to waste my breath on another history lesson.

I got my change and picked up my bag of groceries. "Well, I thoroughly enjoyed our little chat. Maybe I'll swing by again in the next few years to see if the seas have risen and you've got a dock out front."

Dick just sneered at me.

As I waltzed out the front door, I yelled back, "Surf's up!"

11:30 p.m.

"Love the One You're With"

Given the late hour on a weekday night, the roads were less crowded and I got to St. Luke's Hospital in twenty minutes. I slipped on a sports coat, placed the chilled beer in a briefcase, along with a copy of the *Times*.

Security was minimal. I waved nonchalantly at a guard in the lobby who was on the phone and took the elevator up to the fifth floor. After passing the empty nurse's station, I walked to Fred's room at the end of the hall. As the nurse exited his room with a small tray of meds, I asked, "How is Mr. Frost feeling tonight?"

"He's still awake, but—"

"I'm his attorney. His niece just flew into town and will be here any moment," I lied, checking my watch with feigned seriousness. "Fred needs to sign some papers regarding his estate, before he… well, you know."

Frowning, the nurse gave me a suspicious look.

I added, "If you want, you can call his daughter Elizabeth to confirm it."

Before she could respond, another nurse poked her head out of a room down by the nurse's station. "Hey, Nancy! I could use your help here in 504."

Turning to assist her co-worker, she admonished me. "Please don't get Mr. Frost all riled up. He needs his rest."

"I can assure you he'll be in good hands for the next hour or so," I said, watching the nurse hurry down the hallway.

I thought about saying a quick "Hello" to old Fred, but decided not to sully his surprise.

At 12 o'clock sharp, the elevator doors opened and Desiree stepped out. I waved at her and she glided down the hallway like a super model walking a fashion ramp. She was wearing a sleek black coat, stiletto high heels and red lipstick.

I stood to greet her. "You look lovely tonight, Desiree. May I take your coat?"

"Of course."

She slowly unbuttoned the coat to reveal a sexy nurse's outfit: a skin-tight, super-short white dress that strained to keep her ample breasts in check. To complete the ruse, a stethoscope was draped around her neck.

Noticing my roving eyes, the gorgeous redhead said, "I borrowed this outfit from one of my girlfriends who specializes in 'role playing.' Apparently, guys go nuts for the nurse fantasy. I hope Fred likes it."

"Guaranteed!"

"As a diehard baseball fan, I've been looking forward to this trick all day. I want to make it extra special for him."

"I'm sure he'll be eternally grateful." I reached for my wallet. "Do you want me to pay you now?"

She shook her red curls. "It can wait."

I handed her the beer, which was still ice cold. "He requested this too."

"Nice! Take me out to the ball game." Sliding the stethoscope off her shoulders, she added, "Well, I should go take Fred's vitals."

"I'll be standing guard right here. Take your time."

"Oh, I will," she said, disappearing behind the door.

Over the next hour, I patiently read the newspaper, keeping watch. I heard a wide range of muffled sounds from inside the room: naughty talk, bed squeaks, sporadic grunting and laughter, etc.

Finally, Desiree emerged, looking disheveled, but in great spirits.

"How's Fred?"

"Sleeping like a baby."

"I'll bet."

As I walked Desiree to her car, she gave me a few details about their tryst. Despite his terminal state, Fred performed like a true Hall of Famer.

"Really? Three times?" I asked incredulously.

"Trust me, that old boy still has his stuff, including a wicked inside slider."

Again, I reached for my wallet, but she brushed my hand away. "Thanks, but no thanks. It was a thrill to spend a little quality time with a living legend. I'll never forget 'Fast Ball' Frost."

5

Friday • October 30
9:00 a.m.

"The Times They Are A-Changin'"

Surprisingly, Mick and Mona both arrived on time and drilled down on their respective jobs. I spent part of the morning finalizing more details with Carla regarding the catering, and drawing up a floorplan for the placement of all party furnishings in the converted parking lot.

Around ten o'clock, two large trucks, filled with the portable bars, tables and chairs, outdoor carpeting, and the stage, rolled into the parking lot. I went outside to meet with Mick and the truck crews to review my schematic and answer any questions. I reminded Mick the Batmobile would be arriving at 5:00 and a path should be cleared to the museum's large side doors where it would be stored inside.

Next, I helped Mona bring out more boxes from the storage room to the gift shop. Together, we unpacked all kinds of merchandise emblazoned with BoomerWorld logos, soon to be discarded on the dust bin of history.

Racks were filled with shirts, hats, buttons and bumper stickers. There were a few limited-edition periodicals like old *Highlights* and *Teen Beat* magazines, .45 records, sheets of Green Stamps—plus, jars of Dippity-do and tubes of Brylcreem ("a little dab'll do ya"), pouches of Jacks and multi-colored marbles, Old Maid card decks, rabbit foot key chains, foam dice for rearview mirrors, and a jar of old roller skate keys.

One of my favorites was a stash of original Hai Karate After Shave cologne, which came with a nifty set of instructions on how to fend off horny women. Years ago, I bought ten cases of it at a special auction and now there was only one case left. I confidently predicted to Mona it would all be sold during the Halloween party.

"Good. That stuff has been stinking up the shop forever!"

I held up a Hai Karate bottle, did a few quick karate chops and mugged, "Be careful how you use it."

"Give it a rest, Bob. I'm not in the mood."

"Are you ever in a good mood, Mona?"

"No. But let's check the fabulous mood ring you gave me for my Christmas bonus last year."

She held up her hand. The stone was black.

"Hmm … The black color means I'm tense, harassed and overworked," she said.

"You know, I paid a small fortune for that exquisite piece of jewelry."

"The keyword being—'small.' You can buy one online for $4.99."

"Damn! I paid twice that much!"

We packed shelves with teeth-rotting candy and other munchies like Twinkies, Ding Dongs, Ho Hos, Moon Pies, Animal Crackers, Bazooka Bubble Gum, and Pez dispensers. We filled the freezer with Drumsticks, Fudgsicles, Eskimo Pies, Otter Pops, ice cream sandwiches, and double popsicles. We were working so fast I was reminded of Lucy and Ethel in The Chocolate Factory.

Before I returned to my office, I told Mona the security guard from Dudley Security would arrive at four o'clock.

"Dudley Security? Really? Well, that certainly inspires confidence," she deadpanned. "I assume Colonel Klink wasn't available."

"What? Have you been watching *Hogan's Heroes*?"

"Yeah, yeah, yeah. I've checked out a bunch of those old shows on TV Land."

"Aren't they great?"

"No. They're totally lame, but somewhat amusing. I'm understanding Boomers a lot better now. You guys grew up in a unreal world, filled with happy, nice people."

"Yeah, it's a stark contrast to what your generation has to endure on primetime every night. All that brutality and bloodshed, painfully honest dialogue and confrontation, and those annoying GoDaddy ads."

Mona asked, "Tell me. Will the security guy's guns be fully loaded or do they have to carry a single bullet in their shirt pocket like Barney Fife?"

I howled with laughter. "I'm impressed, Mona. You're becoming quite a connoisseur of classic Boomer television."

"I wouldn't go that far, but Andy Griffith was a hunk."

"What about Matt Dillon? Napoleon Solo? Chuck Connors?"

"Who?"

"Forget it. Just keep watching and learning. Better late than never."

"Or I could just get a lobotomy," Mona said as she began to unpack another box.

Noon

"California Dreamin'"

Liz pulled up in front of the museum in a two-door BMW convertible. Walter and I met her out front.

"I hope you don't mind that I brought Walter along."

"It's fine. Just put him in the back seat."

"Are you sure? He slobbers a lot."

"More than you?"

"You're hilarious."

I loaded Walter into the car and and plopped into the passenger seat. Studying the fancy leather interior and sporty dashboard, I said, "Nice ride, but I pictured you driving something a lot more sensible, like a Prius."

"Actually, I did have one, but when Fred moved in with me a few years ago, he traded this car for rent and I sold my Prius. Later, I found out this Beamer is a lease with a whopping five-hundred-dollar-a-month payment, which Fred conveniently forgot to mention. Hence, I was stuck with Fred and this expensive car. Typical."

Not wanting to stir the bad vibes between Liz and her father, I asked, "So how is Fred?"

She steered through light traffic, heading north up Pacific Avenue towards Malibu. "I saw him this morning before I went to work. Despite being so ill, he was happier than he's been in months."

"That's great! Glad to hear it." I smiled to myself, knowing I had done a good thing for a dying man.

"But I think he's starting to hallucinate. He swore an angel with flaming red hair visited him in the middle of the night."

Yeah. An angel with 38 DD cleavage.

We drove in silence for a while. I wondered if she had checked on the status of my insurance policy. Man, I hated having that thing hanging over my head. I figured my buddy Pendergast would have told me if Liz had called. But she could have bypassed my fake intermediary and contacted the corporate office directly. If she knew the truth, she was certainly hiding it well. Or, maybe, she just put the copy of the policy in my file and didn't follow up. Since we wouldn't get back until later this afternoon, the corporate office back East would be closed; hence, the odds of avoiding the whole sordid issue were in my favor. Regardless, I vowed to confess my big lie after the party on Sunday night—and then beg for forgiveness.

Liz turned towards me and gave me serious stare. "There is one thing we need to discuss, P.T."

Oh my God! She does know!

I froze and waited. After a long pause, she said, "I found the beer bottle."

"Ahh... What beer bottle?"

"The one in the trash bin in Fred's bathroom."

Busted!

I studied her profile, waiting for a vicious scolding about fulfilling her dying father's fantasy wish. I figured I was probably already on "double secret probation" for the whole insurance sham and this would be the final blow, but she kept her eyes on the road. Totally expressionless.

Finally, a slight smile crossed her face and she said, "There's something in the glove compartment for you."

I opened it to find a baseball signed by "Fast Ball" Frost, inside a fancy clear plastic box. It was dated October 13, 1974.

"Wow!"

Liz said, "That's the last ball Fred threw in that famous World Series game. His final pitch ever... He was going to donate it to the Hall of Fame, but now he wants you to have it."

For once, I was speechless.

"Groovin'"

The trip up Highway 1 from Venice Beach to Malibu takes about forty minutes. It was a beautiful fall day with bright blue skies and a warm breeze.

I hunkered down in my seat with my baseball cap pulled down low over my old Ray Bans. Driving at the speed limit with her hands locked on the steering wheel at ten and two o'clock precisely, I studied Liz's profile. She really was a beautiful woman, with elegant features and a quiet confidence. For the first time since I had known her, she ditched her designer business suit for a loose-fitting shirt, jeans, sneakers and large pair of sunglasses. I was glad I invited her along.

We exchanged small talk until we reached Latigo Canyon Road. Since Liz had been to my sister's home many times for her therapy sessions, she knew the area and drove east up the long, windy road into the hills. We passed many spectacular multi-million dollar estates nestled amid rock outcroppings, dried brush and ravine switchbacks. The views of the Pacific Ocean and beach community below were awesome.

Eventually, we turned off the road onto a one-lane driveway a short distance above Escondido Falls. The narrow road cut back along the west side of the mountain for about a hundred yards. My sister had bought the property dirt cheap back in the early 1980s. Originally, it was a small, rundown cottage, surrounded by stoic oak trees and hiking paths along the ridge. Over the years, Sarah had upgraded the property, adding on more square footage to create a large home with an enclosed shady Japanese garden with koi ponds, fountains and secluded sitting areas—the ideal place to meet with her clients in a relaxed natural setting.

Pulling into the wraparound driveway, I could see Sarah's Range Rover and Julie's Jaguar parked in the detached garage.

As my sister swung open the massive front door, she exclaimed, "Oh my God! Is that Elizabeth Frost?"

They embraced.

With a wild mane of graying hair, Sarah was a large woman who favored billowy summer dresses, no bra or make-up, and long, smothering hugs that take away any and all pain. With her intelligent and intuitive eyes, you sense she genuinely cares about you as a spiritual being. Oprah referred to her as "The Great Earth Mother" when Sarah was on a national tour to promote her best-selling self-help book.

"You look absolutely radiant!" said Sarah. "Happy, I hope?"

Liz gave a half smile. "Hangin' in there."

Next, Sarah gave me one of her famous hugs. Then, stepped back to look at us, "So… are you a couple?"

"Actually, it's all quite professional, sis. Elizabeth's bank is the landlord for BoomerWorld. When she mentioned she knew you, I asked her to come along."

"I hope I'm not intruding."

"Of course not! You're always welcome here."

Julie Smith, Sarah's significant other, came out to greet us too. "Elizabeth! It's so nice to see you again! And Bob, you're lookin good considering all the stress you must be under."

"Thanks," I said. "Just two more days to go before BoomerWorld is past tense—dust in the wind."

Sarah grabbed my arm and pulled me inside the spacious entry. Her little shrink wheels were already spinning. "BoomerWorld has always been all about the past, right Bob? After all, it's a museum."

"Yeah, I guess so."

"Now you've got to focus on the future!" Sarah said with great gusto. "Things will fall into place and soon you'll be off on an exciting new adventure."

As Sarah and I walked by the sunken living room and into the large, country-style kitchen that overlooked the extensive courtyard garden, Julie and Liz chatted between themselves.

Sarah and Julie were polar opposities. In contrast to Sarah's flamboyant Bohemian persona, Julie was much more reserved, but with a good sense of humor. She had a thriving dental practice in the heart of Malibu, catering to many Hollywood types. An avid yoga practioner, she looked svelte in her white designer pants suit, hand-painted scarf, with short blonde hair and perfect smile.

Sarah and Julie met on an Alaskan cruise about twenty years ago. Both had recently thrown their deadbeat husbands overboard, figuratively speaking, and were more interested in a quiet lesbian fling rather than the drudgery of dating men. By the time they returned to port, they were in love. Soon thereafter, Julie sold her home in Bel Aire, moved in with Sarah and they commenced a massive remodel of their home. Along with Booker, they were the two most important people in my life.

Fester, their cat, lay in the sunlight near the French doors leading to the back yard. Sarah and Julie found him one day hunting for mice out in the garden. He was feral, abandoned or whatever. Over time, the mangy cat warmed up to them, eventually allowing a vet to treat his numerous lesions (hence his name) and other injuries sustained during a rough existence in the canyon. Unlike Big Al, Fester was very leery of ol' Walter—who wisely chose to hang out with us humans.

As the women chatted, I noticed a bottle of expensive champagne chilling in a silver ice bucket, plus a large bowl filled with big chocolate-dipped strawberries on the counter. I waited for a lull in their conversation and asked, "What's the champagne for?"

Sarah reached out for Julie's hand and they snuggled closer together. "Remember when I told you on the phone that I had something very important to tell you? Well, here it is!"

Both women raised their hands to reveal matching diamond engagement rings.

"We're getting married on New Year's Eve!" gushed Julie.

"That's fantastic!" I said amid another round of hugs.

I popped open the champagne and we all took a glass. I raised mine and made a toast. "There is only one happiness in life: To love and to be loved."

"Ohhh, how sweet," Sarah said, kissing my cheek.

We said "cheers" and took a sip.

"Thanks, Bob," said Julie. "But I was half expecting something more cynical like: 'Marriage lets you annoy one special person for the rest of your life.'"

"That's funny, but I'm trying to act mature."

As we clinked glasses again, I added, "Come to think of it—marriage is like a walk in the park... *Jurassic Park."*

The girls all burst out laughing.

"I knew he couldn't control himself" Liz said, raising her glass. "I'm lousy at toasts, but here goes: 'Love is old, love is new, love is all, love is you."

"Excellent! That's from the song "Because" on the Abbey Road album, right?" I said, sampling one of the strawberries. "You know, a Beatles tribute band called The Hey Judes are performing at the Sunday night party at BoomerWorld."

"Yes," said Julie. "Thanks for the tickets. We plan on dancing up a storm!"

"And we'll celebrate again!" I promised. Making eye contact with Liz, I asked "Would you like to come too? It's the big send off!"

"We'll see," she said, not wanting to discuss Fred's illness.

Julie swilled down the rest of her champange. "Well, I've got to get back to my office."

"Who's gonna be in the chair this afternoon?" I asked. "Bruce Willis? Jennifer Aniston? Matthew McConaughey?"

"You know I can't talk about my patients."

"Right. But you did tell me Halle Berry had a great ass."

"I was joking!"

Julie reached into another bowl on the counter and tossed me a small promotional package of dental floss. It had her contact info on one side and a quote on the other:

"Peace begins with a smile." – Mother Teresa.

"You'd better be flossing, Bob. And you're way overdue for a cleaning and check-up. Call me!" She made the call sign with her thumb and pinky.

"Thanks," I said, slipping the dental floss into my pocket.

Julie gave the girls a hug and flew out the door.

Sarah poured us another glass of champagne and we sat out on the shaded patio, eating more strawberies and chatting. After about a half-hour, Sarah checked her watch. "Ooops! I have a client coming at two o'clock for an hour session. Why don't you two walk out to The Point."

Liz said, "Sounds good."

As I went inside to grab two bottled waters, Sarah chatted privately with Liz. I decided to leave them alone for a few minutes. I bent down to pet Fester. My attempted affection was met with a cautionary hiss.

As I watched my sister and Liz through the floor-to-ceiling windows, I got the impression they were discussing Fred's situation, but couldn't hear anything. Finally, I saw a new Bentley rolling along the driveway towards the house.

Slipping outside, I told Sarah, "I think your patient just arrived."

The girls stood. It looked like Liz had been crying, but she quickly wiped away the tears.

I said, "Congrats again on the engagement, sis! We'll probably get back here before your session is over so I'll see you again on Sunday night."

Sarah squeezed Liz's hand. "I hope you'll be there too."

My sister engulfed me in another huge embrace and whispered in my ear. "Take good care of her. Trust me, she's a keeper."

And then she vanished into the house.

2:00 p.m.

"Oh, Pretty Woman"

Liz, Walter and I wove through my sister's lush, spacious garden, out the side gate and then walked out towards The Point. The dusty dirt path was narrow and level. A few years ago, a flash fire ripped up the canyon and burned away all the low shrubbery and grass, leaving patches of new growth and lots of exposed rocks. Still, the views were breathtaking and there was a light, steady sea breeze to keep us cool.

We didn't talk much on the way out. Liz seemed lost in her thoughts, perhaps reflecting on her visits with my sister years before. However, she did make some vague comments about "profound insight" and "genuine caring."

Obviously, she wasn't talking about me.

When we arrived at the end of the trail, we sat on the stone bench under a gnarled old oak that provided a little shade on the rocky hillside. Walter curled up nearby.

"Are you okay?" I asked.

"I'm fine. It's really nice to spend time with Sarah and Julie again. I think their pending marriage is wonderful."

"It's overdue. They've been together for so long," I said. "Julie is like a sister to me. I love her, but the last time I went to her fancy office, her dental hygienist gave me a deep cleaning that still hurts."

Liz wasn't interested in my petty bitchin'. Instead she said something provocative. "Sarah says you've been angry and depressed for a long time."

Oh, that's just great! Now my banker knows I'm a nut job... The last thing I wanted was a heavy conversation.

I noticed a jetliner flying high in the sky. "Look! De plane, boss, de plane!"

Liz didn't bother to look up.

Then I pointed off to the right. "You can't see it from here but Escondido Falls is right down there. Last spring, Julie and I hiked there to check out the 150-foot-tall waterfall. It was very cool. Not something you'd expect in greater L.A."

Liz wasn't falling for my avoidance tactics. "I know it's a sensitive subject, but I'd like to know about your late wife."

I exhaled. "I really don't want to discuss that now."

"Her name was Amy, right?"

I relented. "Yes."

Liz gave me a thoughtful smile, patiently waiting for the rest of the story.

"Amy and I were childhood friends. We met in junior high. Her brother and I both played baseball so I saw her often throughout our high school years, but we never dated. In 1978, I bumped into her at a party in Brentwood when she was a student at UC Davis and I was starting my career in used car sales. As the party got rowdier, she and I left and drove over to the beach where we talked, laughed and reminisced until dawn. We fell in love that night."

Trying to avoid eye contact with Liz during these intimate revelations, I watched a small lizard lying peacefully on a nearby rock. Occassionally, he would move around to catch the best rays.

"Anyway, we got married a few years later and immersed ourselves in our careers. She was an elementary school teacher. We wanted to have children but she had some gynecological issues. I wanted to adopt, but Amy was totally committed to her students. She was very passionate about her work, focusing all her energies on positively shaping their young minds." I paused for the moment to gather myself. "She was first diagnosed with a rare form of leukemia when she was in her early forties. She fought it hard and went into remission for several years. We travelled in the summers and during school holidays, but a latent weariness plagued her."

I shrugged. "She had a relapse several years later. We burned through our life savings and mortgaged our home to pay for the escalating medical bills. She needed constant care so I closed my ad agency to be at her side. We explored many different treatments and lived at the Mayo Clinic for almost three months. Finally, the doctors gave us the bad news that she had two weeks to live."

Looking out at the deep, blue Pacific Ocean, I drifted back in time...

We lay face-to-face in the moonlight.

Hours earlier, the hospice worker, an elderly Filipino woman who had helped hundreds of souls cross through death's door, gave me a knowing look and gentle hug before leaving for the night. We both knew my wife's body was rapidly shutting down. It was only a matter of hours.

"Promise me..." Amy said, her voice barely a whisper.

For over two decades, I had never refused her. And now, with the light fading from her eyes, I would say or do anything to comfort her.

"Of course. I'll do it for you."

"No. Do it for both of us," she said, using the last of her strength.

Amy shifted her gaze away and towards the full moon framed in our bedroom's dormer window. Cast in its cool embrace, she was drawn towards the soft light and began to slowly drift away.

I was losing her. I held her close. Then closer.

Her breathing became soft and shallow as the moon faded from view.

Finally, she closed her eyes and was gone.

And I wept.

"Amy passed away on November 1, 2002. She was only fifty-years old," I sighed. "She was the real inspiration behind BoomerWorld. We always joked about how cool it would be to have a museum dedicated to the life and times of our fellow Boomers. The truth is, she was a much bigger fan of the whole Baby Boom saga than I was. As she was dying, she made me promise I would make it happen... It took me almost three years to get all the elements together. It was a lot of work. But now after the last fifteen years, I'm glad I did it—even though it's ending on a sour note."

Liz turned away, pulling another tissue from her pocket.

I really needed to break away from the moment. That little lizard caught my eye again. "Hey! Have you ever petted a lizard?"

She smiled. "No. And it's not on my bucket list either."

"Oh, come on! It's fun."

She spotted the reptile and scoffed. "You'll never catch it in a million years."

"Really? Well, watch and learn."

As the lizard did a few push-ups on the warm rock, I picked up a thin, 4-foot-long stick laying next to the bench and removed Julie's dental floss container from my pocket. Pulling out a 2-foot-long strand of floss, I tied one end to the stick and made a slipknot about an inch wide on the other end. Making sure not to cast a shadow over the lizard, which would startle him, I gingerly slipped the almost-invisible noose over his head. I slowly raised the stick until the dental floss was snugly around his neck. Then I gently yanked it up and caught the reptile like a fish. Next, I grabbed the little guy and removed the noose, careful not to injure him. As Liz watched, I turned him over in the palm of my hand and began to stroke his belly.

"This is a Western Fence Lizard or 'Blue Belly.' They're completely harmless."

I continued to stroke the reptile's abdomen until it fell fast asleep. "Pretty cool, huh?"

"Amazing," replied Liz, who seemed rather captivated by the entire process.

"Here," I said, placing the small, slumbering reptile on her thigh. "Don't worry. It won't bite."

She studied its colorful skin. "It's really quite beautiful. Tell me, how long will it sleep?"

"It varies." As I reached over to pick it up, Liz flinched ever so slightly. The lizard woke and flipped over onto its feet. He looked up at us and then ran around her back.

Liz's good humor faded fast. "I think you need to get that thing off me."

"Sure thing."

I peered behind her and spotted the little guy on her lower back. As I reached to grab him, he ran up to her shoulder and paused. I shifted on the bench to face Liz. Suddenly, the little guy leapt down onto her left breast.

"Well, are you going to get it or not?" she asked.

I raised my eyebrows. "Umm, it's kinda in a—delicate place."

Looking a little nervous, she said. "I know. Just go for it."

I shot my right hand out, pinning the writhing serpent tightly to her boob. I slowly tried to tighten my grip but couldn't quite grab it. "Well, this is a little awkward."

She gave me a tight smile. "A little?"

I chuckled, "I wonder if he's familiar with Dr. King's great speech. You know, 'I've been to the mountaintop.'"

"Not funny."

I felt the lizard relax his body and was finally able to grab ahold of him. I placed him back on the rock. He quickly ran off, no doubt traumatized by the whole ordeal.

We all were.

Liz stood and rearranged her clothes. "Perhaps we should go back now."

"Are you sure? We can catch another one."

As she brushed by, she patted my shoulder. "Don't push it."

When we got back to Sarah's house, she was still busy with her patient so Liz and I quietly slipped out the garden side door.

On the drive back to Venice Beach, we talked more about our past relationships. I learned that her first husband, a world-renowned mountain climber, was her true first love; however, he was killed during a dangerous expedition on the Denali Summit in Alaska. Several years thereafter, she married an attorney friend, but dumped him when he got indicted for laundering money for a drug dealer. And finally, her third marriage lasted less than year after she caught her husband cheating with an old girlfriend. Thus, she had been single for the last three years. Between the failed marriages and dealing with her father, she admitted her lousy track record with men.

For the first time since we met, I was becoming quite fond of Liz. Getting through Fred's final days and its aftermath would surely be an emotional rollercoaster. I wanted to be there for her.

4:00 p.m.

"U Can't Touch This"

Right on schedule, the guard from Dudley Security arrived at BoomerWorld. The fat rent-a-cop lugged a Thermos of hot coffee and a giant lunch bucket up the front steps and entered the lobby. I left my office to greet him.

Easily tipping the scales at three hundred pounds, his dark blue uniform was stretched tighter than Phyllis Diller's face. Armed with a big smile and alert eyes, he reminded me of Fat Albert, which was destined to be his nickname—that is, until he introduced himself.

"I'm Tank Taylor from Dudley Security. You must be Mr. Apple."

When we shook, he crushed my hand with his massive paw.

"Tank? Now that's a name even *I* can remember," I said. "Nice to meet you."

"Yeah, my momma started calling me 'Tank' when I was five years old. As you can imagine, I was a rather large child," he said, biting into a Milky Way bar.

"Well, welcome to BoomerWorld!"

For the next hour, I gave Tank a tour of the facility, reviewing in detail what I expected from the security team for the next few days until Monday morning when the Batmobile was scheduled for departure. Tank promised to pass on all the pertinent information to his colleagues. He informed me there would be one guard on duty at all times, three shifts per day. The owner's son, Dale Dudley, would work the day shift (8am-4pm), Tank would handle the swing shift (4pm-midnight) and another guy named Gus or something would be on the graveyard shift (midnight-8am). We exchanged cell phone numbers and I handed him a set of keys to the museum.

A little after five o'clock, the large custom van that transported the Batmobile backed into the parking lot. Tank, Mick and I helped the driver and his assistant safely unload the legendary vehicle. We placed it on a special rug behind the large glass doors inside the exhibition hall. It was surrounded by velvet ropes and sturdy posts, which created a 5-foot-wide barrier around the classic car.

The driver gave us a simple rule: "No one touches the Batmobile—ever!" He also dangled the car keys. "We'll hang on to these. Don't want to tempt anyone to take it out for a spin."

I confirmed that I had discussed everything with the car's owner and pledged to take extra special care of his multi-million-dollar automotive treasure. The driver produced a clipboard containing a lot of legal paperwork. I initialed and signed numerous pages, not reading anything. I glossed over clauses pertaining to important insurance matters, praying the Batmomile would be safe and sound. I gave him a copy of the contract with Dudley Security for his file. As a courtesy, I invited the handlers to the weekend parties, but they had other plans.

Once the van left, we rearranged the tables and chairs around the parking lot in anticipation of the Halloween party the next night.

6:30 p.m.

"Somebody To Love"

Everything was ready for the weekend festivities. After Mick and Mona left and I locked everything up, I took Walter for a walk around the block. I realized how tired I was after the last few weeks preparing for BoomerWorld's denouement. Instead of swinging by Booker's Beach Bar for my usual Friday night shit-faced outing, I stayed in my Airstream and treated myself to a TV dinner.

Afterwards, I decided to carve the pumpkin I bought. I laid out an old newspaper on my small kitchen table, got out a big spoon and knife, and went to work. When I was finished, a ghastly face with a crooked smile stared back at me. I found a candle, placed it inside and lit it, and then turned off all the lights. As the creepy jack-o-lantern flickered in the darkness, I nursed a glass of Scotch and congratulated myself for winning the pumpkin-carving contest.

Ever since Liz dropped me off earlier, I found myself thinking more and more about her. It was the first time since my wife passed away that I felt a strong emotional attraction to another woman. Despite her initial frigid façade, she was an intelligent, sensitive person who had endured much adversity in her life. After years of living in a museum, self-absorbed in my own little world, I had become just another relic. I hid behind my flamboyant act of being the madcap Boomer-in-Chief; however, behind all my pontificating, ranting and raving, I felt like an abject failure—empty and alone.

Cue the violins.

9:30 p.m.

"Hello It's Me"

The phone rang. It was Pete Pendergast. He told me he had a very brief phone conversation with "Ms. Frost" yesterday and was confident she believed the insurance policy was still valid. He apologized for not calling sooner, but he was stricken with a sudden attack of kidney stones and had spent the last day at the hospital in excruciating pain. I thanked him profusely and apologized again for asking for such an unscrupulous favor. We agreed to stay in touch.

10:00 p.m.

"Bad Moon Rising"

I crashed in front of the TV. As *Goldfinger* played on a movie channel, I closed my eyes and slipped in and out of consciousness for a while… At some point I dozed off and, once again, "Matt – The Tunnel Rat" crawled into my head. And this time, he was playing with dynamite...

We were at the upcoming Sunday night party, sitting together outside in a corner, while everyone was dancing and partying.

Matt, dressed in his old army jacket and boonie hat, held a cell phone in his hand. His eyes were riveted on the Batmobile near the side entrance to the exhibition hall.

Again, I had a weird premonition that he was planning something.

"Are you looking for your old friend Senator Whitehead?"

Staring straight ahead, he said, "Yeah. Good ol' Stu."

The vibe was ominous.

Finally, I sucked it up and asked, "What are you going to do, Matt?"

"I'm going to kill him."

"But we had a deal! You said if I went down into that Viet Cong tunnel, you'd back off. Remember?"

"Things change, Bob."

For a few seconds, I couldn't focus or think... This couldn't be happening. My gut told me Matt was a fragile veteran, but a decent guy. This was too extreme, too sudden.

"Wha... What are you going to do?"

"I'm gonna blow him up. Just like all those rotten buildings I've been demolishing for years."

I took a deep breath, trying to figure out what to say or do.

"Blow him up?" I asked, on the verge of shitting myself.

Matt kept his eyes glued to the side entrance, which was only about sixty feet away. "See the Batmobile over there?"

"Yes." The classic car was surrounded by a small crowd.

He turned on the phone and the keypad lit up. "Look underneath it. See that little blinking red light?"

I strained my eyes to see past the lower legs of the partygoers. A few people shifted their stance and I could see the semi-hidden light right under the engine. "What's that?"

"Well, Bob, that's a big, beautiful bomb. Five pounds of pure C4 explosives."

My head was reeling. I didn't understand why Matt would go to such dire lengths to settle a score with his ex-best friend from fifty years ago.

I stammered, "But... but if it goes off, innocent people will die!"

"It's called 'collateral damage,'" he said casually. "Don't worry, we'll probably both be killed in the blast too. Shredded like confetti by the flying metal."

Now, I was in a state of shock.

Holding up the phone, Matt said, "This is the detonator. All I have to do is punch in a four-digit code and 'KABOOM!'"

"This is crazy, You can't—"

He cut me off. "You'll love the code, Bob. I programmed it just for you. Can you guess what it is?"

Now, I was in a total panic, but I played along. "Ahh, no... I, I give up."

He turned to me and smiled, revealing that hideous scar on the right side of his face from the war. "1-9-6-8... It's perfect, right?"

11:45 p.m.

"Werewolves of London"

My eyes snapped open. The room was spinning. I was drenched in sweat and my head throbbed. I staggered to the bathroom and splashed cold water on my face. Rummaging around in the medicine cabinet, I found some aspirin and dry-swallowed several pills.

Zombie-like, I walked out into the little living room and plopped down in my swivel chair. The Jack-o'-lantern was still flickering in the dark and the party area outside was bathed in eerie moonlight.

Although I only had met Matt once in person, for some damn reason, he was becoming an obsession. Three nightmares about him in the last four days. But why? If I hadn't met his veteran friends, I could convince myself Matt was only a figment of my imagination. The thing that haunted me the most was dreaming about Matt before I ever met him. Was he some kind of messenger from The Great Beyond? A manifestation of my latent guilt about not fighting for my country in Vietnam? Or just a symptom of all the stress and pressure I was under?

I rubbed my eyes and yawned. Once again, I came to the conclusion that there was nothing I could really do. I certainly couldn't go to the cops. They would need something concrete, like "probable cause" to get involved—not a series of insane dreams and unfounded suspicions. My only real solace was knowing his veteran friends did not believe Matt was a dangerous threat.

But I still felt uneasy.

6

Saturday • October 31
9:15 a.m.

"Under My Thumb"

My crack team of six employees gathered in my office for the staff meeting—fifteen minutes late. Generally, the group seemed listless and unenthusiastic. Knowing the importance of this weekend to my bottom line, I tried to psych-up the troops. Spreading my arms like Monty Hall, I did my best to pump some energy into the room.

"Alright! I want to thank all of you for helping me out during the last two days of BoomerWorld. We're all going to work hard, have some fun and make history!"

As I introduced everyone, I balked when I got to Mick's bandmates. Although I had met them numerous times in the past, I couldn't remember their names. "No offense, guys, but I'll be calling you Keith, Ronnie and Charlie," I said, pointing respectively at each guy. "You know, like the Stones."

They all liked the rock analogy, eagerly nodding in agreement.

I looked over at the guy I'd christened as 'Keith.' "You'll be happy to know we've got a great employee medical plan. It even includes blood transfusions."

The band looked a little confused. Without missing a beat, Mick jumped in, "Don't sweat it, bros. Most of the crazy shit Bob says relates to some obscure Boomer historical thing. You'll see."

"'Crazy shit?'" I said, giving Mick the evil eye in jest.

Turning back to the rest of the group, I said, "You'll be working long hours, until midnight both nights. But if you do a good job, in addition to your regular hourly pay, you'll also get a handsome tip. All I ask is that you do your jobs efficiently, stay focused, and be polite and responsive to our visitors. Over the years, I've worked hard to make BoomerWorld a friendly, inviting place—and I want to end on a positive note."

Next, I reviewed everyone's responsibilities: "Yours truly will be constantly roaming the entire facility and available to help out in any way. Courtney will be the greeter at the front desk and handle the tickets. Mona will manage the gift shop and assist Courtney as needed." I looked at the band. "Keith, Ronnie and Charlie will take turns working in the café, cleaning up, and doing any odd job that comes up. Since Mick has worked here for years, he'll be in charge of you guys."

Mick gave a cocky nod, digging his new management role. "Yeah, Bob may be the 'Big Enchilada,' but I'm like, ahh ... 'Enchilada Numero Dos.'"

"No, man, you're more like 'El Tostada Grande'!" said Keith, snapping a bubble of gum.

"Or 'El Super Taco Supreme' with extra cheese," said Ronnie, quite proud of himself.

"No, wait! I got it!" mugged Charlie. "Mick is—drum roll please… 'The Guacamole King'!"

Mick swaggered. "I like it!"

Clearly, the entire band was baked.

Courtney said, "I'm, like, getting hungry now."

Mona sighed deeply and dug into her purse. "I need a Xanax. Maybe two."

I tried to refocus the group on the task at hand or soon we'd be yakking about the wonders of hacky sack and sticky bud. "Based on the publicity and number of calls I've received over the past few weeks, I expect above-average attendance for the regular museum hours from ten to five. Everyone needs to be on their toes."

After I passed out bright yellow T-shirts adorned with the BoomerWorld logo and the word STAFF printed on the back, I said, "Please wear these shirts during the day shifts. When we close at five o'clock tonight, you can all take an hour break and change into whatever costumes you want to wear at the Halloween Party tonight. And for the Sunday party, please dress in your best clothes."

I handed each employee a small radio unit with a linked Bluetooth earbud and microphone, which I'd borrowed from Carla the caterer. After showing them how to operate the equipment, I said, "Now, we can all stay in touch. If you need any extra help or a customer has a problem, get on the horn fast."

"Like if there's an emergency?" Ronnie asked.

"Precisely."

Keith inquired. "So, if some old Boomer is freakin' out on LSD or having a heart attack, we should call it in, right?"

Exasperated, I said, "Yes. Yes."

Charlie pretended to make a call. "Ripley?! Are you there? I think I just saw one of those bad ass aliens crawl into an air duct on the shuttle. Copy?"

His bandmates all cracked up.

Looks like it's gonna be a long, long weekend.

I gave them a stern look. "Come on, guys, let's get serious."

They got the hint and quit goofing around. Then I carefully reviewed the schedule for the rest of the weekend and reiterated what I expected from everyone. "Okay. Any questions?"

Mona asked, "Tell us, Bob. What will you be wearing to tonight's costume party?"

"I'll be stylin' in a gold lamé Nehru jacket and a huge Afro wig."

"An Afro? That's a clear case of 'cultural appropriation.' You should be shunned and cancelled," Mona said.

"Who cares? I love Afros!"

Mick smirked, "Your regular outfits are freaky enough, boss."

"Thanks, Mick. I really appreciate that compliment."

I was going to ask everyone what they were going to wear, but I was afraid of the answers. Instead, I said, "Okay! Let's get to work!"

10:00 a.m.

"Take it Easy"

For the first time in years, I was pleasantly surprised to actually see a line of about thirty people waiting for the museum doors to open.

My VW van was parked beside the front stairs. The side doors were opened to reveal the classic Boomer artifacts within. A looped Buffalo Springfield concert from 1967 was playing on a battery-powered sound system to create the right mood.

During the first hour, I worked with Courtney to make sure she knew how to handle the ticket booth and answer customer questions. Despite my earlier concerns about her intellect and being a pampered rich kid, she proved to be competent and pleasant.

Throughout the day, I wandered around the exhibition hall talking with the visitors, offering insights and historical perspectives about the various collections. There were many more visitors than normal and I saw a lot of old faces, stopping by for the last time. They reminded me of some of the special exhibits and events held at BoomerWorld over the years. I'd made arrangements to display many famous movie items on short-term consignment: the pair of ruby slippers from *The Wizard of Oz*, Jason's hockey mask from *Friday the 13th*, Jack Nicholson's axe from *The Shining*, the bull whip from *Indiana Jones*, and more. I also staged guest appearances with some of my generation's favorite TV actors, including the stars of *Leave It To Beaver, The Brady Bunch* and

Star Trek. Since I hadn't received much positive feedback lately about BoomerWorld, I was humbled by the many kind remarks from my old guests.

My employees all performed well throughout the day, even Mick's stoned bandmates. I did see them sharing some reefer out in the parking lot behind the stage, but I let it slide.

At five o'clock, we closed the front doors and the staff all left for a break just as Carla and her catering crew arrived to set up the bars and prepare the finger foods that would be served at the Halloween party.

Later, back in my Airstream trailer, I changed into my costume and affixed a set of fuzzy antlers atop Walter's head. I also called Liz to see how she and her father were doing, but only got voicemail. I had an eerie feeling Fred may have passed away, so I called the hospital. Based on privacy rules, they would not confirm or deny Fred was even there. As I hung up, I saw Fred's autographed baseball sitting on my nightstand. I grabbed it and walked through the museum to the freestanding case in the Sports section, which featured a collection of valuable baseball memorabilia. I unlocked the display case and slid the back panel open, placing Fred's gift front and center, right beside signed baseballs by Jackie Robinson and Sandy Koufax, fellow alums on the L.A. Dodgers.

And then I said a silent prayer for him.

7:00 p.m.

"Whole Lotta Shakin' Goin' On"

Standing in the lobby wearing my awesome foot-tall Afro and long sideburns, I greeted the throngs of excited partygoers, pouring in through the front doors like the fans at a general admission Led

Zeppelin concert. Of course, the vast majority of the patrons were Boomers with a few iGens and Millennials mixed in too.

The costumes were as colorful and crazy as the Baby Boom itself. The enormous impact of television on our psyche was evident no matter where you looked. Couples came as Sonny and Cher, Mickey and Minnie Mouse, Lucy and Ricky Ricardo. There were characters from *The Flintstones, The Munsters, The Jetsons* and *The Addams Family*. Cartoon favorites like *Woody Woodpecker, Clutch Cargo, Betty Boop* and *Bugs Bunny* were all in attendance. Inspired by the movies, I spotted a *Rambo* and *Rocky, Spartacus* and *Serpico*, even a gaggle of *Apollo 13* engineers dressed in skinny ties, white short-sleeve dress shirts and horn-rim glasses. There was even a semi-nude couple from the Broadway musical *Hair*.

I strolled into the main party area in the converted parking lot. Standing next to the stage, Carla "The Catering Commandant" barked orders over her headset to her crew of waiters, waitresses and bartenders. The bars were five-deep with thirsty Boomers trying to get a buzz on. Servers passed around plates of classic finger foods: little wiener dogs, cheese cubes, and bowls of mini Snickers, Baby Ruth bars and Tootsie Rolls. The faint scent of marijuana was in the air.

The DJ—a big, gregarious character with a black top hat, red bow tie and a full goatee, who reminded me of a cross between Dr. Demento and Wolfman Jack—was up on the stage spinning vinyl records on two turntables in front of a big block of speakers.

I walked up onto the corner of the stage and looked out over the energetic, geriatric audience out on the giant dance floor. Davey Crockett coonskin caps and beehive hairdos bobbed up and down. Middle-aged gals decked out in mini-skirts and white go-go boots did The Twist and sang along. Bald guys in vintage bowling, tie-dyed, rockabilly and flouncy paisley shirts, letter sweaters and bell bottom pants in every shade and color, did The Jerk. As the DJ segued between "Twist and Shout" and "Billy Jean," an old guy tried to do a moonwalk and fell on his boney butt.

It was a weird and wild spectacle to behold.

Knowing I had to welcome the crowd, I waited until the DJ finished playing "Louie, Louie."

Grabbing the microphone, I shouted "Greetings Boomers!"

The place went crazy with hoots, hollers and whistles.

"My name is Bob Apple, the man behind the curtain here at BoomerWorld. I want to thank all of you for coming tonight! Unfortunately, after fifteen fabulous years, this is our final weekend."

Boos and jeers arose from the audience.

"I believe it was Confucius who once said: 'Life is like a roll of toilet paper. Eventually it's gonna run out.'"

A few chuckles emanated from the crowd.

"And in the end, what are you left with?" For dramatic effect, I pulled out one of those toilet paper cylinders from my pocket and held it up. "Just a crappy cardboard cylinder... 'And what is it good for?'"

Most of the crowd responded with a resounding; "Absolutely nothing!" quoting the great song "War" by Edwin Starr.

"No, my friends. It's the ideal mini-megaphone!"

I cleared my throat, held up the cylinder to my mouth and leaned into the microphone. "Attention please! Clean-up on Aisle Four!"

Yet another bad joke, but the crowd roared with laughter anyway.

"Thank you, Mr. Whipple!" I said, tossing the cylinder aside. "Anyway, let's get this party started! There will be two contests this evening. First, I'll be roaming around in search of the five best costumes. At nine o'clock sharp, the selected nominees will come up here onto the stage and everyone will vote by applause for the best costume." I held up a box. "The winner will receive this mint condition Mr. Potato Head Funny Face Kit!"

Plenty of "oohs" and "aahs" rose from the tipsy throng below me.

"But to start things off, let's have a Hula Hoop contest!"

As planned, Mick and his bandmates walked out into the center of the dancefloor with armfuls of colorful hoops.

"We need thirty volunteers to show us what they've got!"

Mostly women lunged for a hoop and began to practice. After a few minutes, I said, "Alright! When the music starts all our contestants must begin to swing those hips. But once your hoop drops, you're out! The last contestant still going—wins!"

The DJ cued up "The Hula Hoop Song" and the fun began. Many of the old Boomer broads only lasted a few seconds, as their hoops hit the floor. Soon there were only about ten gals still gyrating to the beat. As that annoying song from 1958 blared out, most of the men plugged their ears and headed for the bars. Thankfully, the DJ segued into a more popular cut: "You Should Be Dancing" by The Bee Gees. After another minute, there were only a couple of contestants left. Finally, a thin, older dame dressed as Cat Woman, was the winner. In fact, she looked like she could keep that hoop going all night.

I invited her onto the stage. "Congratulations, my dear," I said and handed her the grand prize: an original Cootie Game Set. Turning to the crowd, I added, "And all you participants can keep your hula hoops as a parting gift! Thanks again for coming tonight, folks. Have a great time, but please refrain from drinking and eating in the main museum… Now, let's party!"

As the DJ dropped "Jailhouse Rock" onto the turntable and cranked up the volume, I left the stage to work the room. I walked past The Batmobile where a large crowd was taking selfies beside the velvet ropes. Tank, the huge security guard, was looming nearby, keeping a watchful eye on the car and party goers while he sucked on a Big Gulp.

Wanting to check on Courtney and Mona, I walked through the crowd toward the lobby. Along the way, I identified five costumes I deemed exceptional: an eight-foot tall Gumby, a Snidely Whiplash, a Mr. Magoo, an Olive Oyl, and a real midget dressed as Mighty Mouse. I gave each one a BoomerWorld business card and told them to report to the DJ on the stage at nine o'clock sharp for the contest judging.

Courtney, dressed in hippie attire and flowers in her hair, proudly announced she had already collected three-hundred tickets (out of the presold four-hundred) and everything was going smoothly. I congratulated her on the Baby Boom outfit and flashed her the peace sign.

The gift shop was packed with party goers. Mona was busy running the cash register, which made my heart sing. Forever the goth nihilist, she wore her typical black attire, plus an exotic feather mask covered in silver and red sequins.

"Love your mask, Mona" I said. "Makes you look very mysterious."

"Mysterious? I'm just trying to hide my identity. God forbid, someone I know finds out I actually work here."

"Need anything?"

"Yeah, a stiff Tom Collins and foot massage."

"Hang tough," I said. "I'll come back in a little while and you can take a break."

"Gee, thanks, Bob. I guess I won't report you to OSHA after all."

"You're So Vain"

As I exited the gift shop into the front hallway, a tall guy wearing an expensive Donald Trump mask approached me. Dressed in a dark blue suit, white dress shirt and long red silk tie, his overall resemblance to the President was uncanny.

"You're the owner, right?" he said, his rubber lips moving flawlessly below his coiffed orange hair.

"Yes, Mr. President," I replied, playing along.

"Well, I just wanted to make sure that you're 'winning.'"

"Winning?"

"Yes. When I ran for office, I promised that America would win again! That we'd all be winning so damn much, we'd get tired of winning… So, are you winning, Bob?"

Winning? I was on the verge of bankruptcy!

"Actually, I'm going out of business."

“Been there, done that,” the guy sighed, staying in character. “But there’s always hope. Just look at me! I’ve had plenty of business failures, divorces and been ripped apart worse than Mr. Bill by the ‘fake news’ media. But I’ve persevered and now I’m President of the United States.”

“Yes. It’s truly unbelievable.”

As a waitress walked by with a tray of Pigs in a Blanket, The Trumpster grabbed a plateful, popping them into his mouth in rapid succession.

“I love health food!” he said, wiping off his chin with his red tie.

Egging him on, I asked, “Tell me Mr. President, what are your goals for the coming year?”

“Simple! Build the Wall, make America even greater, and play more golf.”

“More golf? Is that even possible?”

“You can never play enough golf, especially at any one of my fabulous golf resorts around the world. You know, when I get tired of running the world, I’m going to open a golf school for high-fashion models.”

“Really?”

“Yes. I’m going to start them off with the irons and then slowly work them into the woods!” He laughed like a mad man. “It’s going to be yuuuuuge!”

Remembering something, he pulled out his smartphone and quickly tapped out a message.

“Did you just Tweet, Mr. President?”

“Yup! Here, check it out,” he replied, showing me the phone. The message was another in a long series of reciprocal taunts between Trump and Rosie O’Donnell. It read: “Rosie is red. Rosie is blue. If your ass was that big, you’d be blue too!”

Snickering, he said, “My billion loyal Twitter followers will love it!”

“But I think you only have about fifty million, including all the bots.”

"Fake news!"

"Some say that constantly Tweeting isn't very 'presidential.'"

"Of course, it's 'presidential'! I'm the President and I just Tweeted."

His phone rang. "The Grand Poohbah here!... Well, hello Stormy. How's tricks?... What? You want to give me back my check for a $130,000? Sorry, honey, that boat has sailed. Besides you and the Creepy Porn Lawyer still owe me $350,000 in attorney fees for that defamation suit. You lost. I won. But I always win... Stop crying, Stormy. You know there's no crying in porn! Look on the bright side. Now, you're a famous feminist icon. You're welcome!"

He clicked off and turned back to me. "Women love me. Everyone loves me! Even the haters."

"That doesn't make any sense."

"Of course, it does. Remember, I'm the President—and an 'Extremely Stable Genius'!"

As he finished his hors d'oeuvres, he spotted a couple dressed as Boris and Natasha from *The Adventures of Rocky and Bullwinkle Show* in the crowded lobby.

"I have to go collude with those Russians," he said, waving at the couple. "Maybe we'll take a selfie together and send it to CNN. They'll freak out! Proof positive!"

Next, I dropped by the small café near the entrance to the parking area. Since Carla and her catering crews were manning the bars and passing around finger foods, I figured Mick and his bandmates could take turns making coffee for our guests in the small cafe, which was akin to running a lemonade stand.

Right up their alley.

Except for Mick and his crew, the cafe was practically empty. Clearly, our visitors were far more interested in alcohol than caffeine. I noticed they were not wearing Halloween outfits. "Where are your costumes, guys?"

"We tried to score some righteous threads from that costume shop over on Abbot Kinney when we got off work earlier," said Mick. "I wanted to come as Superman, Keith had dibs on Spiderman, and Ronnie and Charlie were gonna be Batman and Robin, in honor of having the Batmobile here. But the place was totally picked over. Go figure!"

"Well, that's what happens when you wait until the last minute," I said, sounding a little like *Father Knows Best.*

"It was a total bummer," said Keith, shaking his shaggy head in disgust. "I've always wanted to be a superhero."

Mick shrugged. "Anyway, we just decided to come as ourselves."

"Yeah, Toe Jam!" said Ronnie. "The greatest rock band in the world!"

Charlie held up a Bic lighter and fired it up. "Rock on!"

A Confederacy of Dunces.

I told Mick to go check on the parking valets out front and ordered Keith to man the café while the other guys swept the museum for any abandoned drink glasses or forgotten food plates.

As I stepped out of the cafe, I spotted Booker and his hot twin dates walking toward The Batmobile.

"Booker! My man!"

He spun around with a girl on each arm. The twenty-something identical twins wore only stiletto heels, scanty bikinis with matching Miss Universe sashes draped across their torsos. As I did a double take, Booker flashed a big smile. With his shaved head, tinted sunglasses, dark sports coat and white shirt unbuttoned down to his navel, he was a dead ringer for a black Telly Savalas. He winked at me and shoved a lollypop into his mouth. "Who loves ya, baby?"

We did a fist bump and he introduced me to the girls. Of course, I didn't catch their names because I was too busy staring at their big, ahh—sashes. Easing into my role as the great Boomer professor, I looked at the twins and asked, "Did you know the first Miss Universe Pageant was held in the year 1952?"

The twins shook their long blonde curls. Not a clue.

I asked, "Want to see a magic trick?"

The girls nodded eagerly.

"When I snap my fingers, a shiny new penny from that *very same* year, 1952, will magically appear in each of my shoes."

Before they could look down, I snapped my fingers. Then I reached down and removed both my penny loafers and showed them to the girls. Their faces lit up when they saw the bright 1952 pennies.

"Wow! How did you do that?" asked the blonde on Booker's right arm.

"Yes. Tell us! Please!!" begged the other gal.

I slipped my shoes back on and raised my hands. "You know, a master magician never divulges his secrets." I paused and gave Booker a sly smile. "But since you're with Booker, my BFF, I'll tell you the truth."

The girls hung on every word.

"Last night I placed those pennies into my shoes."

"But how did you know to use pennies dated 1952?" one of the girls asked.

"Well, that's the year I was born."

The other girl was confused. "But how did you know that we were coming as Miss Universe contestants? And that the first pageant began in 1952?"

"That my dear, is the *real* magic," I said, fanning the flames of their naïveté.

"You've got to tell us now!" she said.

"I'll make a deal with you. I'll tell Booker the secret and he can decide when to reveal it. But only if you behave!"

As the girls giggled with excitement, another big smile lit up Booker's face. I leaned in close to him to make sure the girls couldn't hear. "It was total coincidence."

"I know, brother," Booker whispered.

"Hopefully, you can tell them in the morning." Then I slipped him one of my business cards. "Use this card to get free drinks at any of the bars. Tonight, I'm buying!"

As Booker and the girls waltzed off into the main party area, I saw Moe, Larry and Curly dressed as *The Three Amigos* over at the replica Cheers Bar. Since I promised to buy them a drink when I first met them, I ambled over behind the counter.

"Gentlemen! Nice to see you again!"

"Hey, Bob!" said Moe, glancing around. "Nice party."

"Yeah, all these costumes are blowing my mind!" said Larry.

Curly asked, "So what do you think of ours, Bob?"

I eyed their fancy duds and huge sombreros. "Impressive, mis amigos!"

They all laughed and slapped each other's backs.

"So how about a round of tequila on the house?" I asked.

"Gracias!" said Moe.

I asked one of the bartenders to hand me a bottle and four glasses. The guys eagerly watched as I poured each a full shot, plus one for me.

"Cheers to BoomerWorld!" said Larry.

Curly raised his glass. "And cheers to our new buddy, Bob!"

We all took a dash of salt, sucked on a lime wedge and chugged the tequila down.

"Where are the wives?" I asked.

Moe looked over his shoulder and nodded. "They're over there."

I saw three older women talking with a fat guy in an Elvis costume near The Batmobile. They had made an attempt to dress up like *Charlie's Angels* with the big hair and sexy attire, but they looked more like *The Golden Girls* in drag.

"Looks like 'The King' is making a move on your women."

Curly blurted out, "Take my wife, please!"

"Ditto that!" said Moe. "Hey, have you seen that gal who's wearing that low-cut *Wonder Woman* outfit? Schwing!"

Larry, the serious one of the bunch, said, "We were just over in the Sports section admiring your baseball collection. I noticed you have autographed balls from some of the greatest pitchers of all time."

"Yes, but virtually all those baseballs are on consignment from a wealthy patron from New York. I only own the one from 'Fastball Frost'."

"Well, it's worth a lot more today."

"Why?"

"Didn't you hear? Frost passed away last night at a local hospital. We just heard about it on the radio on our way over here."

Damn! I guess my earlier premonition was right... Now, I was really worried about Liz. No wonder she never called me back. She was probably dealing with all kinds of unpleasant issues, like funeral arrangements, the press, crazy Dodger's fans, and God knows what else.

"Listen, guys, I've got to run."

I told the bartender to give the boys another free round of drinks. "Enjoy the party and the rest of your trip."

"Thanks, Bob. You're the best!" said Moe.

"No, thank you for all the great laughs over the years."

"What do ya mean?" asked Curly. "We just met the other day."

"Actually, I feel like I've known you my entire life."

We all shook hands and said goodbye.

As Chuck Berry belted out "Johnny B. Goode" on the sound system, the party was in full swing. The dance floor was packed. People were talking, drinking and comparing costumes. The vibe was good, but I was worried about Liz—and headed for my trailer.

"Wheel in the Sky"

Once I passed through the gate in the white picket fence that surrounded my Airstream, I went inside where it was much quieter. I took off my huge Afro, tossed it on the bed and immediately called Liz. Again, I got her voice mail. I left my condolences about her father, told her she was in my thoughts and offered to help out in any way. Hoping to see her soon, I asked her to call back.

After I hung up, I turned off all the lights inside my RV. Sitting at my little kitchen table, I watched the wild party scene outside through the side window. I felt a strong desire to go find Liz, but I couldn't leave. Besides, I didn't know where she lived, only that she had a condo somewhere near the Canals.

For the next half hour, I sat there in the dark, contemplating our relationship and hoping for a call back… I was falling for her. Maybe I was projecting, but I think she liked me too. Still, I had to be realistic. Liz had a solid career as a successful banker, probably a savings account, investments, a well-funded IRA and maybe a pension.

I had squat.

The clock was running out on BoomerWorld and I needed to figure out my next step. First, I had to vacate BoomerWorld by the end of November—four short weeks to sell my VW van, the few decent artifacts I personally owned, the display cases, TVs, furniture, etc. via a big garage sale. That alone was a massive undertaking and I wouldn't raise that much money. Plus, I had to make all the arrangements to return every item on consignment to the owners who were spread out all over the country. In some cases, like with the automotive collection, the wealthy owners would foot the bill for the transportation costs, but I was responsible for coordinating the whole operation.

In the final analysis, I'd be lucky to end up with maybe $20,000. After I bought a used truck to tow my trailer, I could probably survive a couple of months on the road. My meager Social Security check was not enough to cover all my expenses. I'd have to find some kind of job. That was another ugly dilemma. Trying to revive my ad career was never going to happen. I was a dinosaur… No, I was looking at a minimum wage gig—working as a greeter at Walmart or a cashier at some fast food joint, surrounded by a bunch of pimply-faced, burger-flipping teenagers snickering behind my back. Or maybe I'd be one of those guys who tries to wash your windshield at an intersection… Fortunately, like a lot of Boomers, I had a surefire retirement plan: Buy a lottery ticket twice a week and pray. I've never been very good with math, but I'm pretty sure the odds were in my favor.

It was time to face facts: Broke and basically unemployable, I was a washed-up gasbag—a bigger dud than Comet Kohoutek. At this rate, I'd be wandering around the mall in a bathrobe begging for spare change to buy a Cinnabon.

I really had nothing to offer Liz or anyone else.

"Walk On By"

Given my foul mood, I didn't feel like being the master of ceremonies for the Costume Contest, so I asked the DJ to handle it. A natural entertainer who loved the spotlight, he eagerly agreed.

Remembering that I promised to give Mona a break, I scurried back through the party scene and into the busy gift shop.

"Praise the Lord!" Mona muttered as she grabbed her purse and flew out the door.

Tallying up the credit card receipts and cash, my mood improved a little—until Courtney appeared in the shop. She claimed she felt sick and wanted to go home. Since most of the guests had arrived, I told her it was okay, but made her promise to be on time tomorrow, prepared to work until midnight.

When Mona returned, I went out into the lobby to man the front desk. As the partygoers streamed in and out, I thanked them for coming, steering the fresh faces towards the bars in the parking lot and the drunks toward the café for some coffee.

Around ten o'clock, I bid a fond farewell to Moe, Larry, Curly and their wives. Booker and the twins left shortly thereafter. Booker was happy and upbeat, announcing they were going back to his apartment for a nightcap and to listen to some Barry White albums.

"Oh, baby..."

Except for a few inebriated hangers-on, who were staggering around like zombies looking for a fat farm, the place was empty by closing time. Mick and his bandmates swept through the exhibit hall to make sure no one remained and all the trash was cleaned up. As usual, Carla's catering team stored away all the leftover beverages, booze and food in their portable vans and prepped the party area for the next evening's festivities. Carla collected all the cash boxes and promised to do a complete accounting of the proceeds when she got home. I trusted her implicitly. The cleaning crew arrived and began to vacuum the floors, dust off all the surfaces, and clean the bathrooms.

By midnight the entire facility was all spiffed up and everyone was gone, except for Tank, the security guard. As he gnawed on a Slim Jim, he confirmed the Batmobile had remained untouched throughout the entire evening.

Gus, an older guy with a limp who reminded me of Festus from *Gunsmoke*, arrived to handle the graveyard security shift from midnight to eight. He promised to keep a watchful eye on the entire facility, but I figured he'd be asleep in some corner as soon as I retired to my trailer for the night.

7

Sunday • November 1
12:15 a.m.

"Stairway To Heaven"

Sitting on the edge of my bed, I peeled off my shoes and massaged my aching feet. It had been a long, stressful day, but I was still wired and anxious about all the details associated with the upcoming last day of BoomerWorld. I walked into the kitchen, poured myself an adult beverage and gave Walter a snack.

The phone rang. It was Liz. Before I could even ask her how she was holding up, she asked me if she could stop by for a few minutes. "Of course," I said. "I'll meet you out front. See you shortly."

I quickly washed the dishes piled in the sink and cleaned up around the Airstream.

Lipstick on a pig.

As Walter and I waited for Liz to arrive, he watered a few shrubs along the sidewalk while I watched late revelers stagger home from nearby Halloween parties. Soon, I spotted her white BMW rolling down the street. I opened the door and helped her out. She was wearing a dark jogging outfit. To my surprise, she gave me a hug and almost melted in my arms.

I led her through the darkened museum to my trailer. As the cheap screen door snapped close behind us, she glanced around the lean, cramped quarters. "How long have you been living in this thing?"

"Eighteen fabulous years! It's not quite as spacious as The Clampett Mansion, but it's home… I hope you don't mind, but I gave the servants the night off to give us a little privacy."

She noticed a small framed poem on the wall next to the door and walked over to study it. "I haven't seen the Disiderata since my college years."

"Yeah, that poem was the rage! Horny dudes used to post them on their dorm walls to show girls how sensitive and introspective they were."

"Is that why you have it posted?"

"Actually, it's covering up a hole."

Liz peeked behind the frame, revealing a big knuckled indentation in the wall. "Talk about 'rage.' Did you do that?"

I shrugged. "I lost my cool a few years back."

She gave me that blank cop stare, waiting for an explanation.

"Believe me, I'm not a violent person. I was just going through a rough patch at the time. Besides all the financial pressures, Walter got very sick with a severe case of Leptospirosis, a bacterial infection. He must have picked it up at the dog park or along the beach somewhere. He was at the hospital for three days getting IVs and antibiotics. It was a real nightmare. The veterinarian called to say he may not make it—and I lost it."

I bent down and gave Walter an intense rub behind his long ears. "Anyway, His Majesty pulled through with flying colors. And thank God! After all, he's the real brains behind this operation!"

Satisfied with my explanation, Liz sat down on the couch.

"Want a drink?"

"Whatever you're having is fine."

I poured her a splash of Scotch and plopped into my easy chair.

She stared down into her glass. "Thanks for your calls. I really do appreciate it… I'm sorry I didn't get back to you sooner, but the last twenty-plus hours have been a real challenge."

She sipped her drink, trying to compose herself as the tears began to flow. I placed a box of tissues beside her.

"Before he died, Fred apologized for his behavior toward me over the years, saying he was sorry for being so self-obsessed and absent during the two decades he spent in baseball. Also, he expressed how grateful he was that I took him in during his final years when he became so sick."

Leaning forward, I reached out for her hand and she willingly gave it to me. "That was a very gracious thing you did after what he put you through. Most people would have slammed the door in his face and let him rot in some state-run nursing home."

"The truth is, I did it out of a mixture of guilt and an irrational need for closure between us… Trust me, I'm no angel." She took a sip of her drink and added, "Speaking of angels, one of the last things Fred talked about was that beautiful angel who visited him in the hospital on Thursday night. He said he wouldn't trade that evening for all the virgins in Paradise."

"He made the right call. Ever since Hugh Hefner died there's been a drastic shortage of virgins up there," I said, nodding up at the Heavens. "All those Muslim martyrs are in for a rude awakening. Ol' Hef is as insatiable as ever!"

Liz smiled at my lame joke. "At the end, Fred was on morphine and slipped into a drug-induced coma. He died peacefully early yesterday… Shortly after he passed, someone leaked it to the press along with my contact info, and within an hour, reporters were swarming all over the place. Fortunately, I had arranged to have his body taken over to a local funeral home as soon as he died. Per Fred's request, he'll be cremated. The death certificate will be filed with the authorities first thing on Monday. The funeral home told me I can pick up his ashes on Tuesday.

"I also drafted a short statement with the details of Fred's passing, thanking his fans for their support over the years, and ended it with his favorite quote from Yogi Berra, 'It's tough to make predictions, especially about the future.'

"Genius!"

"As a personal favor, the PR person at our bank disseminated it to all the press outlets, but I'm still getting harassed. I've gotten calls for interviews from newspapers, radio and TV stations, bloggers and crazy baseball fans from all over the country, but I have no intention of talking with anyone. There's actually a diehard ESPN reporter and some drunken Dodger fans holding a prayer vigil out in front of my condo right now. Too bad they all waited until he died to show up. A week ago, Fred would have regaled them for hours with stories about his career, and of course, his legendary exploits off the field."

"Well, I really enjoyed meeting him. I know you two had a rough relationship, but Fred was a legend."

"And thanks to you and your angel friend, he died with a smile on his face."

"We should all be so lucky," I said, raising my glass.

Wishful thinking—perhaps?

Liz sighed, "Soon, he'll just be dust in a jar. A very expensive jar, I should add. I spent over five hundred dollars for an official Dodgers urn. It's pretty fancy. He would have loved it."

"Is there going to be a service or memorial for him?"

"No. He was adamantly opposed to anything formal like that, but he wanted his ashes scattered on the mounds of every MLB park where he pitched."

Frowning, I said, "That's problematic. A lot of those old stadiums have been torn down and relocated. Not to mention, most of those teams despised your father, because he was their nemesis on the mound. Their rabid fans would never stand for such a thing."

"I think they hated him more than I did."

"He should have peed in a bunch of bottles like Howard Hughes. Then we could go to all those places and douse their mounds. Frosty would get a real kick out of *that!*"

For the first time ever, Liz actually giggled. And then she gave me a strange look. "What do you mean 'we' could go to all those places?"

"After I break down BoomerWorld over the next month, I'm going to have a lot of free time on my hands. That's all."

We sat in silence for a while, sipping our drinks.

"Actually, I've been thinking about doing something different with my life too. After five years at the bank, there's not much chance for any upward mobility," she said. "And besides, I'm bored. Now that Fred is gone, I really don't have much incentive for staying in Southern California."

"Do you have any other family?"

"Just a few distant relatives scattered around the country."

I said, "My parents are both gone. Besides Sarah, I've got a younger brother up in Jackson Hole. Ray's an artist. You'd like him. He's almost as charming as me."

"What kind of artist?"

"You know, the classics. Mostly clown paintings on velvet."

She laughed. "Do you ever stop with the jokes?"

"Actually, Ray's specialty is gigantic metal sculptures. He welds all kinds of animals, dinosaurs, and the occasional phallus. Needless to say, his work is quite eye-catching and controversial."

I tried to refill her glass, but she waved me off.

"I'd better not. Gotta drive home soon."

"Sure?"

She shrugged. "Well… maybe just a little."

I gave her a healthy pour.

"Can I ask you a personal question, P.T.?"

"Of course."

She paused. "What are your plans for the future?"

"I'm ready to start a new phase in my life: hibernation. I'd like to drive this trailer up the Coast, camp along the Pacific Ocean and have a long, long nap. And then play a little golf, go fishing and maybe do some more lizard catching. That's my true talent!"

She rolled her eyes. "Seriously… what do you want to do with the rest of your life?"

"Originally, I was planning to open the world's largest ant farm or maybe a chain of participation trophy stores up in Portland. They could both be gold mines! But then I came up with a truly brilliant idea."

"And what's that?"

"Snowflake Safety Pods! Picture this: Freestanding capsules about the size of an Orgasmatron, placed on college campuses across the fruited plain. Emotionally damaged students, who suffer panic attacks if their favorite Starbucks is closed or feel threatened by roving packs of Young Republicans, can seek shelter in these special safe places. The Pods would be solar-powered to save the planet, feature an ergonomic heated chair, and have a port to charge their smartphones so they can call their friends to whine about the latest micro-aggressions and the menace of 'toxic masculinity.' It'll cost five dollars for every fifteen minutes of solitude. Such a deal! I'll be rich!"

"You know, P.T., you're completely full of shit."

"That's the nicest thing you've ever said to me," I said. "Hey, wanna play 'Truth or Dare.'"

"No, I have a better idea." Liz placed her drink on the side table and stood. She lifted me to my feet, gave me a long, tender look and placed my hand on her left breast where I caught the pesky lizard. "Let's go to work on that technique."

And then she led me to the bedroom.

3:00 a.m.

"Bang a Gong"

Unable to sleep, I slipped out of bed, leaving Liz in a deep slumber. I walked outside and over to the side entrance to the museum to scan the interior. As I peered through the double doors, I could see old Gus, the worthless security guard, sitting in the driver's seat of the Batmobile. A small silver flask sat on the dashboard. Gus was passed out, his head lolling back with his mouth agape. I could hear his thunderous snoring through the glass.

Pissed off, I almost started to bang on the doors to wake him up like Dustin Hoffman at the chapel in The Graduate, but I decided to let it go. His job was to keep a close eye on the Batmobile, not sleep in it, but this was better than finding him curled up in the Black Light Room. If he didn't puke in the classic car, no one would ever know.

I went back to the trailer, spooned in behind Liz and fell fast asleep.

8:30 a.m.

"Strawberry Fields Forever"

As a gentleman, I won't go into any of the specifics about my romantic encounter with Liz. Suffice it to say, I think we set a few records for middle-aged acrobatics. And for the first time in years, I awoke with a smile and was at peace.

Apparently, having sex more than once in a decade can really improve one's mood.

At some point in the wee hours, Liz slipped out of my trailer. She left a note on the kitchen table: "Depending on what happens today, I hope to see you later this evening… Save the last dance for me."

Too bad she left so early 'cause I wanted to make her breakfast in bed. And then I remembered that unless she wanted to share a bowl of Gravy Train with Walter she was out of luck. Besides a half-eaten jar of peanut butter, a box of Pop Tarts in a cupboard, and a shriveled-up grapefruit in need of carbon-testing in the fridge, the kitchen was bare—except, of course, for the bottle of Stoli in the freezer.

Do I have a drinking problem?

Anyway, I was facing a long, daunting final day at BoomerWorld. Soon, my long shtick as the grand master of BoomerWorld would be over. Knowing I'd be entertaining the last daily visitors to the museum, I chose the ultimate hippie outfit that would turn a few heads and stimulate lots of conversations: a white embroidered dashiki shirt, bell bottom jeans, a psychedelic floral print vest adorned with fringed leather strips, some colorful love beads and leather water-buffalo sandals. I topped it off with granny glasses and a shoulder-length brown wig, held in place by a headband festooned with peace symbols. Standing in front of the mirror on the back of my bathroom door, I looked like a member of Foghat lost in a time warp.

Lastly, I filled my pockets with small packets of popular Boomer candies like Chuckles, Red Hots, Dots and JuJuBees to share with my guests. I flashed the biggest fake smile I could muster. "It's show time!"

9:45 a.m.

"Won't Get Fooled Again"

Courtney appeared, looking as perky as ever. She announced that she felt much better after getting a good night's sleep. I was surprised to see her carrying an SAT prep manual.

As she sat down in the ticket booth, I asked, "Are you taking the SAT?"

"Yes. My father promised to take me on a ski trip to St. Moritz over the Christmas holiday if I do well."

Fat chance.

"But I thought you wanted to study Astrology online."

“I do,” she chirped. “By the way, what’s your sign.?”

I grabbed a pen and a pad of Post-It Notes off the desk. On the top slip of paper, I wrote: “OUT OF ORDER.” I slapped the note on my forehead.

“What?” she asked with pure bewilderment. “I thought you might be an Aries.”

“It’s a joke, Courtney! It’s a sign. Get it?”

The blank look on her cherubic face said it all. Moving on, I removed the sticker and gestured at her SAT manual. “So, why are you even taking the test?”

“Because my father also wants me to apply to junior college.”

“But you don’t have to take the SAT to get into a JC.”

“I know! That’s the beauty of it! He thinks I do. Now, when I tell him I got accepted, he’ll buy me something extra special.”

I had to admit, she had her old man wrapped around her pretty little finger.

“You know, I’ve got a perfect score on the SAT,” I bragged.

“Really?!”

“Actually, I never took it. So technically, I still have a perfect score.”

Her brow furrowed as she pondered the ridiculous assertion.

I added, “Remember the old saying, ‘If you never try, you can’t fail.’”

Now, she looked completely bewildered. “But—”

“I’m kidding, Courtney. That’s *terrible* advice.”

For a rare, fleeting moment, I chose to act like a responsible adult and not a smart ass. “The truth is, life is all about trying and failing, setting tough goals and working hard to achieve them. You learn from those experiences and, over time, you evolve and grow as a person. Understand?”

She slowly nodded, but still looked confused.

“For instance, even though I’ve failed with BoomerWorld. I’ve learned some valuable lessons and met some fascinating people.”

I guess I was still on a high after last night's romantic encounter with Liz, because she immediately came to mind. Although I remained disillusioned about the last fifteen years, BoomerWorld had brought us together… Maybe there was hope.

Anyway, I told Courtney she could study for the SAT during the slow times throughout the long day ahead. Trying to be optimistic, I said, "You can do well on that test, if you really apply yourself."

She fanned through the thick SAT manual and let out a deep sigh. "I don't know… There's a lot of math."

"Don't worry. Statistics show that four out of three people struggle with math."

"Really?"

Man, I was too sober for this chat.

I said, "Here's a math question: Why is six afraid of seven?"

"That's easy. Because seven-eight-nine!"

"Brilliant! You're a natural!" I added. "By the way, remind me to tell you about Cliff Notes some time."

"That's okay, Mr. Apple. I'm afraid of heights."

10:00 a.m.

"L.A. Woman"

With Walter at my side, I opened the front doors to the public for the last daily museum tour. The line to get in was even longer than the previous day, which was a good omen; however, I was stressed out that only Courtney had showed up as scheduled. Rolling with it, I greeted each visitor, passed out BoomerWorld brochures and pushed the headset rentals.

After the first surge of patrons started wandering around, Mona rushed in, frantic and out of breath. I barely recognized her.

"You're late!"

"Sorry, the bus broke down again."

"Would that be the Merry Prankster's Magic Bus from the Summer of Love? It may need a tune-up."

"Are you trying to trigger me, Bob?"

"Come on, Mona! You know BoomerWorld is a safe place."

"No, it's an old place filled with old stuff and run by an old geezer."

"Touché!"

Instead of her usual dark Goth attire, she was wearing a brightly-colored dress. And she had braided her hair like Dorothy from *The Wizard of Oz*.

"You look like a totally different person. Did aliens abduct you—or what?"

"Since this whole Boomer thing is coming to an abrupt end. I figured it was time for a change—a new look."

One thing that hadn't changed was Mona's snarky comebacks, "You know, Bob, that outfit you're wearing is God awful. I totally get that the hippie is the iconic image of the Boomer era, but you look like a real dork."

"Maybe if you closed your eyes and clicked your heels twice, you could magically go back home."

"I would in a heartbeat, but remember, I live in Calabasas not Kansas."

I laughed, but inside I was fuming about Mick and his crew being late for the last big day.

For some odd reason, the soundtrack from 'Car 54, Where Are You?' echoed in my head.

"Where the hell are Mick and his bandmates?" I bitched, barely controlling my anger. "They promised they would be here early today."

Mona snickered, "Maybe they were carried away by a bunch of flying monkeys."

"Nice try, Dorothy."

For the next hour, while Mona manned the gift shop, I finished cleaning out the storage area. Then we restocked the racks and shelves with all the remaining BoomerWorld swag.

"Today we blow it all out, Mona. Sell everything for full price throughout the day. And when the party starts to wind down tonight, discount everything for a quick sale."

Mona sighed, "I hate to admit it, but it's sad to see all this stuff go. But don't worry, I'll tell everyone how much more valuable it will be once BoomerWorld shuts down."

"That's right! From this moment forward, everything will be a 'rare, collector's item,'" I announced with great authority. "By the way, in appreciation for your fine work over the last few years, if there's anything you want, just ask. Your cheery attitude and stellar work ethic have been inspirational."

"Yeah, up yours, Bob."

"That's my Mona!"

"You know, that security guard who works during the day has been hitting on me."

"You mean 'Dudley Do-Right'?"

After only one day on the job, the son of the owner of Dudley Security was already a punchline around BoomerWorld, particularly with the boys in the band who called him "The Dud." But those slackers could take a few pointers from the squared-away guard. He was polite and courteous, in top physical shape and his uniform was immaculate, topped off with a ridiculous Royal Canadian Mountie hat.

"He definitely takes his job very seriously. Maybe he sees you as a damsel in distress and—"

I heard some commotion outside the gift shop. Mick and the boys had finally arrived.

11:15 a.m.

"Shattered"

"Hey, look what Walter dragged in," Mona said.

Mick looked very flustered. "Whoa! Sorry we're late, boss!"

All the guys looked fried and were still wearing their same clothes from the night before.

Trying not to be too pissed off, I said, "Well?"

"You can't believe the shit we've been through," Mick said as the guys all hung their heads. "Last night, after work here, we got a call to do a set up in West Hollywood. Some big music producer was supposed to be there. We loaded up the van with all our gear and drove up there—ready to rock."

"It was going to be epic," said Keith.

"Yeah, we were stoked," said Ronnie.

Charlie added, "Locked and loaded."

"And?" I asked, knowing it could only be bad news.

"Well, while we were inside introducing ourselves, some low life ripped off the van with all our stuff in it!" Mick said. "We called the cops and then spent all night driving around in a friend's car looking for the van… It's gone, man."

"I'm truly sorry, guys."

"Toe Jam is finished. Stubbed out!" Keith said wistfully. "We're victims of grand theft auto."

"Hey, don't be so fatalistic," I said. "Equipment can always be replaced. It's just stuff."

"But it was *all* our stuff," replied Ronnie.

"Every last drumstick," bemoaned Charlie, the distraught drummer.

Depressed and overwhelmed, the guys hunched their shoulders and stared off into space. It was clear they were too burned out to work the day shift. Knowing I could get by without them, I said, "Look, guys.

You've had a long, upsetting night. Why don't you just go home, get some rest and come back at six o'clock to work the final party."

"Thanks, boss," said Mick. And the band members all shuffled off—a soft parade of cosmic dejection.

"I'm not going to miss their annoying music, but that really sucks," said Mona, who looked genuinely sad. Then she let out a little laugh. "All is not lost. Mick will always have his air guitar."

"Well, it looks like I'll be spending most of the day in the café," I said, resigning myself to making caffeine speedballs and selling snacks to visitors for the next seven hours.

1:00 p.m.

"I Can See for Miles"

The café is a small, pleasant place where visitors can sit and relax. You enter via the front hallway near the main entrance or on the east side of the building near the doors leading out to the parking area. Signs hang on the exterior walls next to all the entrances: "No shirt. No shoes. No problem." There are some comfy couches, tables and chairs clustered around a large coffee bar, where visitors get amped up on caffeine before another lap around the museum.

The walls are covered with more classic movie posters like *Sunset Blvd., Dr. Zhivago, The Sound of Music, Stalag 17, Patton, The Godfather, Forest Gump,* and *Plan 9 from Outer Space* among others.

After working for a few hours as the designated baristo, I took a brief break. Sitting in a corner of the empty café, I stared up at the playbill promoting the classic movie, *The Caine Mutiny*. I reached over into the cash register and removed two small steel Baoding Balls—a gift from my sister to help me deal with stress. As I rolled the balls around in my right hand, I channeled Humphrey Bogart in his role as Captain Queeg…

Mick and the band's story about being ripped off to explain their tardiness were lies. All lies! They were trying to pull a fast one on me. Well, I had no intention of being made a fool of... I recalled an incident the last time they worked at BoomerWorld when some strawberry-flavored popsicles disappeared from the freezer in the gift shop. When I confronted them, they laughed at me behind my back and made jokes. They were all misguided and disloyal, scoffing at me at every turn, and spreading wild rumors about the working conditions in the museum. Of course, I was to blame for Mick's incompetence and poor leadership. He was the perfect boss—not me... Ahhh, but the missing strawberry popsicles! That's where I had them!! I proved beyond the shadow of a doubt, with mathematical logic, that a duplicate key to the icebox in the BoomerWorld gift shop did exist! I would have produced that key, but they all ran off to some rock'n'roll gig with their shirt tails hanging out and—

Finally, I snapped out of it—realizing that I was totally paranoid!

Throughout the day, there was a steady flow of people in and out of the café. My hippie outfit inspired many comments from visitors. It's amusing how Boomers like to refer to "the good old days" when life was simpler, change came slower and America was the greatest country on Earth. Boomers tend to remember the good things while conveniently forgetting the gross stuff like tofu and leisure suits.

The conversations touched on many diverse topics: soap box derbies, Twister parties, drive-in movies, feeding nickels into tableside juke boxes in greasy-spoon diners, building model cars and planes, reading Playboys stashed in treehouses, "pulling all-nighters" to write term papers and cram for finals, flashback dreams about not wearing pants, and stupid pranks like phone booth stuffing and flushing M-80s down school toilets.

One old guy, who sat at the coffee bar knocking back espressos, went on a long tirade about the lousy service we get these days. "Remember going into a service station back in the day? You'd pull in your car and some young guy would run out to greet you with a smile. You'd just say, 'Fill'er up' and he'd go to work. He'd check the oil, radiator water level, the pressure in each tire and wash the windows while you just sat back and listened to the radio. After he topped off the gas tank, you'd hand him money and he'd run inside to the cash register, then run back, and carefully count out your change. And then he'd hand you a bunch of Green Stamps that you could use to get all kinds of free things. Man, those were the days! 'Service' actually meant something. Nowadays, you've got to do it all yourself. Some stations even charge you to fill your tires. They're selling air now! Unbelievable!"

He blathered on. "Forget about getting any decent customer service these days. After you spend a fortune on some new computer, phone or TV and have a problem, you can only talk with somebody in the Philippines or India who can barely speak English. You're on the phone for hours, frustrated and fed up, and the problem usually remains unsolved. And then they ask you if you want to take a ten-minute survey about their crappy service!"

"Yeah. Poor service is one of the signs of the coming Apocalypse."

"What are the others?" he asked.

"Chia Pets, Carrot Top and ShamWow."

When no one was in the café, I put up a sign on the counter ("Back in 15 minutes!") and went to check on Courtney and Mona. Despite the large flow of visitors, everything ran smoothly throughout the day and we closed the doors at five o'clock.

The last regular day was over. Only the big final party remained.

5:30 p.m.

"Please, Please Me"

The Hey Judes, the Beatles tribute band, arrived on time and their roadies set-up the stage with all their equipment. I let them use my office for the evening to unwind after each set and change into their various costumes for the show. During their four-hour concert from 7:00-11:00 p.m., they would perform four 40-minute sets wearing different costumes to reflect the Beatles at the various stages of their evolution as a band: the *Meet The Beatles* years when they wore matching suits and ties; the casual clothes from the days of *Rubber Soul* and *Revolver;* the grand uniforms of the *Sgt. Pepper's Lonely Hearts Club Band;* and finally the psychedelic outfits from the *Magical Mystery Tour* and the *White Album*.

The band members really looked a lot like the original John, Paul, George and Ringo. They even faked British accents, keeping in character from the moment they arrived, and were quite funny, polite and professional. It was like being on the set of *A Hard Day's Night*.

Meanwhile, Carla's catering team was busy setting up the tables and bars, and preparing the dinner buffet.

Mick and his bandmates stumbled in around six o'clock. I had told them to wear their best clothes, but they still looked like they just had returned from Burning Man. I didn't care anymore. I assigned them their duties for the evening: manning the café, collecting any trash, and helping Carla and her staff as needed.

During the Hey Jude's sound check, Mick and his fellow band members stared jealously at the classic Rickenbacker and Epiphone guitars, Ludwig drums and Vox amplifiers on the stage. I felt bad they lost all their equipment, but I couldn't afford to help them.

I retired to my Airstream to shower and dress for the evening. I hadn't worn a tuxedo in years; however, I decided a formal look was appropriate for the last big event, so I'd rented a classic black Ralph

Lauren number. Back in front of the mirror, I adjusted my bow tie. I was ready for my final BoomerWorld performance.

Walter was still exhausted from the night before, so I left him in the trailer for the night.

6:45 p.m.

"Come Together"

I opened the doors to BoomerWorld and warmly greeted the guests. Many friends and acquaintances came to say goodbye. As the crowd began to swell, Booker and the twins arrived. From the looks of it, they had hit it off the night before. We headed to a bar outside for a drink.

Sipping a glass of champagne, one of the girls said, "You're a big liar, Bob! That was no magic trick you did last night. Booker told us it was all just a 'coincidence'."

I raised my hands. "Yeah! You got me."

Booker said, "Like my Mama always says, 'coincidence' is God's way of remaining anonymous.'"

"You know, Albert Einstein said the exact same thing," I said.

"Well, that's a coincidence!" laughed Booker.

We shared some small talk for a while until The Hey Judes took the stage and began their first set. It was like turning back time to 1964. Their first song "She Loves You" got the growing crowd in the swing of things. Couples began to hit the dance floor and the party cranked up. I walked around the party area, interacting with the guests as the band covered all the early Beatle's classics like "I Want to Hold Your Hand," "This Boy," "I Feel Fine" and "I'm a Loser."

That last song sounded like my autobiography.

When the band left the stage for a break and to change their outfits, I spotted Sarah and Julie. Thirsty from dancing through the entire first set, I got them some cold beers. They congratulated me on putting on such a great party and wanted to know if Liz was coming.

"Hopefully, she'll stop by later," I said.

After chatting briefly, I climbed the stairs to the stage and shook hands with the DJ, who was back for a second night to play background music between the Beatle sets and to run the auction.

I stepped up to the microphone. "Good evening everyone! I'm Bob Apple, the founder of BoomerWorld."

There was a respectful amount of clapping until the crowd fell silent.

"I want to thank you all for coming tonight." Although I'm rarely emotionally incontinent, I felt a wave of sentimentality welling up inside of me. I steadied myself and forged ahead. "Many of you probably don't know that my wife, Amy, was the inspiration for BoomerWorld… We were childhood friends, lovers and eventually, man and wife. Knowing we were living through some of the most amazing times in history, she always thought it would be cool to have a museum dedicated to the Baby Boom. And eighteen years ago, right before she passed away in 2002, I promised to make her dream a reality. It took a few years to get everything ready before I opened the doors… I've had the pleasure to meet thousands of interesting people from *every* generation. Hopefully, the museum has given visitors some insights into the unique times and experiences that shaped the Baby Boom Generation."

The applause became a little louder.

"This evening will mark the end of BoomerWorld. I've tried to find a new home for the museum, but it didn't work out. The property has been sold by the bank and, effective December 1, this incredible art deco building will be demolished for a new hotel." I shrugged as a hush fell over the crowd. "Like Jackson Browne sang, 'All good things gotta come to an end.'"

Prior to my little speech, I had made arrangements with Carla and her catering team to pass around flutes of champagne to everyone in the party area. One of the waitresses gave the DJ and me a glass of bubbly too. I lifted my glass to the Heavens and said, "And now, I'd like you all to raise your glasses to toast the Baby Boom Generation."

Everyone raised their flutes.

"What a long, strange trip it's been!'"

As the glasses were drained, I added, "Lastly, just a few quick announcements… I encourage all of you to take a final tour of the museum. Also, the band will be playing until eleven o'clock so dance the night away! And in a little while, we'll have an auction for a few classic Boomer items that I know you'll love. But now, the dinner buffet is officially open. Enjoy all the good food and drink, courtesy of Carla's Catering Company. Trust me, she's the best!"

I made brief eye contact with Carla down near the bustling buffet line, who gave me a big thumbs-up. "Thanks again, everyone! Have a great time!" I took another sip of champagne and raised my glass again. "Party on, Wayne!"

"Party on, Garth!" replied many in the crowd in unison.

As I walked off the stage, the DJ began to play some mellow cuts from the "British Invasion" before the band began their second set.

8:00 p.m.

"Go Your Own Way"

I left the stage to work the party. Since I had no appetite, I headed to the lobby to check on things. Mick, Ronnie and Charlie were busy in the café while Mona and Keith were swamped in the gift shop. I encouraged them. "Go, go, go! Sell it all!"

While I was checking in with Courtney at the front desk, Senator Whitehead, his wife Shirley, aide Monica Cummings and Nate Katz, the billionaire, arrived.

Everyone knew Katz. He was one of the richest real estate developers in the world. He owned skyscrapers in many major cities, enormous land holdings throughout the West—and also had plenty of bought-and-paid-for politicians in his pocket. Apparently, Senator Whitehead was his latest project.

Keeping up my façade as the gracious and loquacious host, I greeted the group with open arms and my usual hyperbole. "Welcome to BoomerWorld! I am Bob Apple, your humble curator and head docent."

I snapped my fingers at a nearby waiter to bring a round of champagne to the guests. After Ms. Cummings paid for their tickets with a check, I gave them all a museum brochure and offered to get them started on their tour.

The Senator and his wife wore expensive designer suits and did their best to project a regal air of power and success, while the mousy Ms. Cummings remained in the background in her role as the fawning assistant. Casually dressed in an elegant camel hair sports coat, black cashmere turtleneck and slacks, Nate Katz was a short, partially bald man with intelligent eyes and shrewd demeanor.

As we entered the main pavilion and turned left to proceed clockwise around the perimeter, I gave them a general overview of the museum and answered a few questions about its history and contents.

Nate Katz commented, "I saw the article about BoomerWorld in the *Times* last week. It's really a great concept and you've clearly put your heart and soul into every detail. Too bad you have to close the doors."

"Yes, it truly is a stunning cultural achievement!" I bloviated for the last time. "It would have been nice to keep it all intact, but that's life."

Katz gave me a wry little smile.

We continued the slow tour through the pavilion. When we reached the beginning of the 60s section, I excused myself and promised to meet them later at the outside party.

"Help!"

Thinking I should check on Walter and freshen up for the final few hours, I walked back to my trailer. As I entered the party area, The Hey Judes were playing "Run For Your Life" from the *Rubber Soul* album, which seemed particularly prescient when I saw Matt sitting in a chair inside the picket fence right in front of my trailer.

I froze...

Matt was staring straight ahead at the party scene. Disheveled and unshaven, he was wearing the same clothes from the last time I saw him four days ago. I noticed he had his lighter in his left hand and a beat-up shoebox sitting on his lap.

Cautiously, I walked up to the gate and called out in a friendly manner, "Hey, Matt!"

Sloth-like, he slowly turned to face me. "Hello, Bob."

I walked through the gate. "Nice to see you again," I said, watching as he flipped open his lighter with the familiar "click" and then snapped it shut.

There was another chair next to him. "Mind if I join you?"

"Sure... This where you live, right?"

"Yeah." I wondered how he knew that, but decided to let it go. "I'm glad you came tonight, Matt. Enjoying the music?"

The band began to play "Rain." We listened to the first verse. As usual, Matt seemed distant and lost in his own thoughts—kinda like Jack Torrance staring at his typewriter in *The Shining*.

"Did you get something to eat?"

"Not hungry."

"Well, can I buy you a drink?"

"Nah, I'm good."

Trying to keep him engaged and the mood light, I pointed at the Batmobile. "Did you check out the Batmobile? Pretty cool, eh?"

Matt didn't respond, making me even more nervous. Finally, he asked, "Is Stu here yet?"

"As a matter of fact, the Senator just arrived. He's inside with his wife, taking a tour. Want to go say hello?"

"No… I'll wait."

Wait for what?

He casually lifted the lid on the old shoebox. Peering inside, I could see a collection of items he had saved from the Vietnam War: Army angled-head flashlight, K-Bar knife in a leather sheath, dog tags, some valor medals including a Purple Heart, a B&W photo—and a scuffed-up Colt .45 caliber semi-automatic handgun.

Avoiding the gun, I pointed at the photograph. "Hey, is that you in 'Nam?"

Matt removed the faded snapshot from the box. "Yeah. That's me and my mentor 'Frankie The Ferret,' the Aussie I told you about who was killed in the tunnels." Pointing at the third GI, he said, "That's another Army rat named Jamie Bates. He committed suicide shortly after he was discharged. He couldn't handle the demons."

"That's terrible, but I'm glad you're okay."

Again, he flipped open the lighter and snapped it close. "Am I really 'okay,' Bob?"

Then, he reached into the box and removed the handgun, cradling the scary-looking weapon in his hand. I took a deep breath, frantically trying to figure out what to say and do. Finally, I asked, "Is… is that the gun you used in the tunnels?"

He nodded. "It was loud but lethal. Always did the trick."

I've never felt comfortable around guns. And this one looked particularly ominous.

"I haven't touched it since I came home from the war. It's been sitting in this shoebox out in my mother's garage for decades."

I recalled my conversation with his vet buddies at the church meeting on Thursday night. They said Matt met his wife after being homeless for ten years, when he was probably dealing with PTSD. She got him off the streets, they fell in love and enjoyed a long period of stability and happiness together. But after she died a few months ago, he abruptly quit his job, sold his house, and disappeared. I was no shrink, but I was betting he had some kind of breakdown and was now fixated on his old friend, the Senator… Perhaps Matt had been staying with his mother. After all my paranoid nightmares about him, I envisioned his mother in a rocking chair down in a fruit cellar.

"So, uhh… Are you living at your mom's house?"

"For the time being. She lives in Culver City. Ninety years old with mild dementia."

He stared down calmly at the gun, almost like he was in a trance.

"Yesterday, I took this gun apart," he said. "There was still clay and grime from the tunnels in all the nooks and crannies. It took hours to clean it and get it working again."

He dropped the lighter into his pocket and transferred the gun into his left hand. In a quick, fluid motion, he racked the slide on the top of the gun. Grinning, he turned to me and said, "Nice and smooth, huh?"

Now, my head was reeling. For a few seconds, I couldn't focus or think straight…

Measuring my words carefully, I said, "I know you've been through a lot of dark times in your life, Matt. Your experiences in Vietnam were horrific and incomprehensible to most people, but you proved yourself to be true hero. I'm in awe of your service to our country."

I could tell my words had little impact on him. He just stared at the party scene where people were dancing and having fun. There was no real malice or hatred in his eyes—just pain.

"I should never have gone to 'Nam. If I had a rich father like Stu to pull strings with the local draft board, I could've gotten a deferment, too, and finished college. It would have changed my entire life…"

Suddenly, Senator Whitehead and his entourage appeared near the Batmobile. Matt saw him too.

We sat there watching the Senator laugh and banter with the crowd. More people recognized him and walked over to shake his hand. Tank, who was standing nearby, offered to take some group photos. I was glad the big guard was hovering close to the Senator in case Matt went off the rails.

As Matt narrowed his gaze on Whitehead, he wrapped his fingers around the gun's hand grip and squeezed it tight.

I sucked it up and asked, "You're not going to do anything crazy, are you Matt?"

After what seemed like an eternity, Matt turned to face me. His horribly scarred right check twitched as he asked, "Crazy?"

"Ahhh…" I stammered, looking down at the gun. "You know… like maybe shoot your old friend."

Without saying a word, he glanced back over to the Batmobile where the Senator was swarmed by a small crowd. And then something amazing happened: Matt's veteran buddies from the church in Inglewood arrived. The old, dapper Korean vet was accompanied by a twenty-something woman who was probably a grandchild. The wheelchair-bound Vietnam vet was being pushed along by his wife. And the young Marine vet from tours in the Middle East was accompanied by a hot date. I was glad they decided to use the free tickets I gave them—yet terrified they could possibly end up in the line of fire.

With a puzzled look on his face, Matt asked "What are they doing here?"

"Well, I… I met them the other night. Great guys! We played poker for a while. Lost my shirt."

"What? You came looking for me?" He looked genuinely perplexed. "Why?"

I figured now was the time to lay all my cards on the table. Maybe I could convince him to put the gun away and save the day. "To tell you the truth, Matt, after we met and you told me about your bad blood with Whitehead, I was afraid you might try to harm him… I went to the vet group meeting, hoping to talk to you again." I paused. "And… I've had a series of disturbing dreams about you."

"Dreams about *me*? That's pretty weird."

"What's even more weird is that I dreamt about you *before* I even met you. You were throwing gigantic lawn darts at me."

"Lawn darts?" For the first time since I met him, Matt laughed out loud. "You need help, Bob."

I stared down at the gun in his hand. "You're probably right. But can you please put the gun away? It's making me nervous."

Matt looked over at the Senator again who was surrounded by an even bigger crowd. After a long beat, he turned back to me. "Relax, Bob. It's not loaded."

He thumbed the release on the side of the semi-automatic and the clip popped out. He showed it to me. No bullets.

I exhaled hard. "Man, I'm so sorry. I feel like an idiot."

"No worries." He slid the clip back into the gun grip and de-cocked it. Then he placed the gun back in the shoebox. "By the way, this is for you," he said, handing me the box.

I was incredulous. "What? I don't understand."

"I really liked your Vietnam exhibit inside. I thought that maybe you could display this stuff too. Maybe set-up a little display case near where that Viet Cong was peeking out of the tunnel hole. People could learn about what some of us had to endure during the war."

I was moved by his gift. "That is very considerate of you, Matt, but as you know, this is the last day of BoomerWorld. It's over."

"Is it?... You know, every time I went down into those holes, I didn't expect to come out—but I always did." He smiled for only the second time. "Trust me. There's always light at the end of the tunnel."

"Well, it looks bleak for BoomerWorld. I've exhausted every option and—"

"You gotta have faith, Bob."

He pulled his old lighter out of his pocket and dropped it into the box. "You might as well have this too. I don't want it anymore. Besides, playing with it annoys my mother. Taking care of her is my priority now. You know, 'the circle of life' thing."

As he placed the lid on the box, I said, "Your vet buddies told me you lost your wife a few months ago. I'm sorry."

"She was a good woman. Saved me from myself."

"I lost my wife too."

"Yeah, I heard your speech."

Matt and I sat for a while watching the party scene. Finally, he rose to his feet and buttoned up his old jacket. "Well, I guess I should go say 'Hi' to Stu. It's about time."

I was dumbfounded. How could I have been so wrong about Matt? I felt like such a paranoid jerk-off for imagining anything sinister would ever happen. Clearly, Matt was saner than me.

We shook hands. I watched him walk out my gate and over to the group. As Matt greeted his vet buddies, Senator Whitehead saw him. He abruptly stopped talking with the people soliciting photos and walked over to his old friend. They stood face-to-face for a few moments. Whitehead said something and they hugged.

And that's when the bomb went off!!!

Nah. Just messin' with ya…

9:00 p.m.

"Getting Better"

I sat alone in front of my Airstream for a while trying to get my act together… It became more and more clear to me that I misjudged Matt as a disturbed psycho to avoid confronting my own fears and life-long guilt about Vietnam. Perhaps he was some kind of spirit guide—an angel of sorts. Ultimately, Matt showed me that life is too short to let friendships fade away and, most importantly—to be grateful.

The band ended their set with "Taxman" from the *Revolver* album. I'd always liked that song, but tonight it just reminded me of my financial problems. After the stress of dealing with Matt, I desperately needed a stiff drink. I put the shoebox under my arm and cut through the crowd over to a bar to the left of the stage. The Beatle who looked like Paul McCartney announced that they'd be back for their popular Sgt. Pepper Band segment after a short break.

I surveyed the party area. Although I hadn't had anything to eat, most of the guests had already hit the buffets and were now getting well-lubed on booze, waiting for the final two sets of Beatles music.

I had pre-arranged with the D.J. to auction off three unique items: an original *Casper "The Friendly Ghost"* Jack-in-the-Box, a replica *Get Smart* Shoe Phone, and a vintage *Star Trek* Lunch Box. These items were duplicates of mint condition units I had on display inside the museum. To hype the auction, I gave the DJ some index cards loaded with info about each item.

The DJ deftly handled the auction, engaging the audience with a combination of facts and humor. He managed to sell the Jack-in-the-Box and Shoe Phone for three times their actual values. I knew the final item would generate the biggest interest because every Trekkie in the crowd would love to own that original lunch box.

"And now ladies and gentlemen, we have a very special item you *Star Trek* fans can cherish forever," he teased. Holding up the vintage metallic lunch box with a stunning color illustration of Captain Kirk, Spock and the Enterprise in space, he said, "We all grew up watching *Star Trek*, right? Well, this is your chance to own a rare piece of history. Plus, you'll 'live long and prosper.' Guaranteed!"

I only spent fifty bucks for the lunch box so I expected a hefty payday. The DJ read off a few facts from the index card I gave him: "Back during the show's original run from 1966 to 1969, *Star Trek* only licensed a handful of companies to create products using their popular name and images. Although 250,000 of these lunch boxes were made in 1968, the vast majority have been lost or are too damaged to be worth much; however, they are still sought after by collectors around the world. In recent auctions, mint condition sets have sold for as much as

$1,500." He opened the lunch box and pulled out the matching Thermos to show the audience. "This particular set is in excellent condition. Anyone interested in bidding on it, can come forward to examine it now. Bidding will start at five hundred dollars."

As a small throng of potential buyers surged forward, I heard a voice behind me, "Excuse me, Bob." I turned around to see Nate Katz, the billionaire, standing there with a fresh glass of champagne in his hand.

"Hello, Mr. Katz. Are you enjoying the evening?"

"Very much so. You know, I had one of those lunch boxes when I was a kid. Loved it." He sipped his drink. "Can I ask you question?"

"Sure."

"How much?"

Visions of hundred-dollar bills danced in my head!

I looked over at the group ogling the *Star Trek* Lunch Box. "We'll, since you're one of the richest guys on the planet, I'd just wait for the auction to almost end and then add on a few thousand bucks. It'll be yours!"

"I think I know how to bid on things, Bob" he chuckled. "No, I meant how much for everything? I want to buy BoomerWorld."

"SHAZAM!!!" For the second time in a half-hour, I had been blindsided by the Gods. After what happened with Matt, I was getting punch drunk on serendipity.

"I… I don't know what to say, Mr. Katz."

"Call me Nate. And I'm serious. I really enjoyed my tour of the museum. You've done a great job here and it would be a tragedy to see it all just fade away. Besides, I just may have a solution that can benefit both of us." He glanced around. "Is there some place we can talk privately?"

"Absolutely."

I escorted Nate back into the museum and through the lobby. As we turned down the front hallway, the band emerged from my office dressed in their Sgt. Pepper's uniforms on their way back to the stage.

"You gents are doing a great job!" I said.

They nodded politely.

Nate chimed in with a decent British accent, "Break a leg for Liverpool!"

Since my office was cluttered with the band's clothes, musical equipment and a couple of half-smashed roadies, I ushered my new billionaire buddy down to the Rare Collections room at the end of the hallway. This small space is where I kept some very expensive artifacts on consignment from wealthy donors who did not want them on public display. The room was heavily secured and not open to the public, unless special arrangements were made for private viewings.

As we walked along together, I inquired, "Are you good friends with Senator Whitehead?"

"Not really. I need his help to get some major federal financing for a large commercial development I'm doing to help revitalize part of downtown L.A. I just put on a fundraiser for him in Trousdale this afternoon. To be blunt, most politicians are just part of a long conga line of useful idiots who will jump through hoops to get big bucks for their next campaign. It's the age-old ritual of mutual back-scratching. Business as usual."

I entered the password on the keypad, which automatically unlocked the dead-bolted door. We went inside the private room and I locked the door behind us.

Luckily for me, a special endowment from one of the wealthy collectors covered the extra security for this special area. Secured glass display cases, filled with rare books, magazines, historical documents and memorabilia, wrapped around the perimeter of the room. The walls were covered with one-of-a-kind posters and paintings by famous rock stars and other celebrities. Video cameras were mounted in all four corners.

I placed Matt's box on top of a display case, which was filled with many rare books that impacted Boomer psyches and imaginations. Max carefully scanned the complete collections of *Tom Swift, Hardy Boys* and *Nancy Drew* mysteries, and the first editions of *Where the Wild Things Are, Charlotte's Web, Animal Farm, Nineteen Eighty-Four, Catcher in the Rye, In Cold Blood, Funk & Wagnall's Encyclopedia* and *The Alice B. Toklas Cookbook* among others.

Pointing, Nate asked, "Can I please see Dr. Spock's book?"

I unlocked the case, removed the hard cover and handed it to him.

Dr. Benjamin Spock's *The Common Sense Book of Baby and Child Care* (1946), the second best-selling book in history at over fifty million copies, changed the way Boomers were raised. Instead of the traditional one-size-fits-all child rearing approach where kids were put on regular schedules and trained to be conformists in a harsh world, Spock encouraged parents to trust their instincts and treat their offspring more as "individuals," allowing them to make their own rules and timelines.

As he fanned through the pages, Nate said, "This book had a big impact on our generation. Millions of parents followed Spock's recommendations."

"It unleashed a tsunami of spoiled, self-obsessed little brats."

Nate said, "Yes, but my parents didn't buy into it. They were old school. Loving and supportive, but strict disciplinarians."

"Maybe that's why you're so successful in business."

"Being 'successful' means nothing. It's all about creating value. That's accomplished by dreaming big, working hard, learning from your mistakes, and of course, a little luck."

As I replaced the book inside the case, Nate said, "I'm curious. What's in the box?"

"Actually, it's an amazing donation I just received from a veteran who was an Army tunnel rat in Vietnam."

"Man, those guys had balls."

"Actually, he's an old friend of Senator Whitehead."

"A real rat!" laughed Nate. His wicked sense of humor was starting to win me over.

I removed the lid and showed him all the contents.

He said, “These are truly remarkable artifacts. They deserve their own display. A salute to a great American warrior.”

For the next ten minutes, I showed him some of the other rare collectibles in the room.

“These are all on consignment from collectors around the country and only occasionally displayed in the most secure displays out in the main museum or for special charity events.”

Nate was impressed but was anxious to move onto business. “As I mentioned before, perhaps we can help each other. Are you familiar with the Silver Shores development in Arizona?”

“Yes. It’s a giant new retirement community near Sun City in Phoenix.”

“It’s one of my premiere real estate projects,” Nate boasted. “A massive twenty-billion-dollar, multi-phase, thirty-square-mile community, located up the Aqua Fria River near the Lake Pleasant Regional Park. A beautiful setting! The infrastructure plan is state-of-the-art, replete with the smartest new technologies, sustainable energy systems, driverless vehicles, and on and on. Ultimately, there will be tens of thousands of homes, condos and townhouses nestled among man-made waterfalls, lakes, streams and parks. Plus, shopping centers, a hospital and medical clinics, sports facilities and seven designer golf courses—one for every day of the week.”

“Sounds like Mecca for blue hairs.”

“It is! And lots of Boomers are already moving in,” he said. “The centerpiece is a million-square-foot senior center with every imaginable amenity: a concert hall, art galleries, antique car museum, IMAX movie theater, restaurants, a continuing education complex, arts and crafts area, huge bowling alley, Olympic swim center, etc.”

I said, “As a matter of fact, I sent a letter to your Project Manager at Silver Shores about nine months ago. I also contacted some other large retirement communities around the country in hopes that one of you had room for BoomerWorld, but I never heard back from anyone. I figured it was a lost cause.”

Nate smiled. "You know, young people today don't understand the power of letters. They think everything from thank you notes and birthday wishes to important business correspondence can be handled with a quick text or email. Hardly anyone takes the time to write letters anymore. What they don't realize is that such old-fashioned correspondence has a profound impact on the recipients, especially in this age. It stands out in a sea of fleeting digital communications."

He was right. Too bad my letter got lost in the shuffle.

I glanced around the room and said, "Somewhere around here I have a letter from Bill Clinton to Monica Lewinsky. It says something to the effect: "Sorry about your blue dress. I'm enclosing $100 for dry cleaning. Keep the change. Best, Bill. PS: And next time, hold the anchovies!"

"Good one!" laughed Nate.

"You know, Clinton never apologized to that young intern," I said. "Maybe he should have written her a nice note. Things could have turned out a lot better for both of them—and our country."

Nate reached into the breast pocket of his sports coat and pulled out a folded piece of paper and handed it to me. "You're right. A good letter is often kept and sometimes, it can change lives."

I opened it. Surprisingly, it was my earlier correspondence to Silver Shores. "Amazing! So—it was *your* idea to come here tonight, not the Senator's."

"Yes," said Nate. "BoomerWorld has been on my radar ever since we got your letter. Knowing I was scheduled to be here this week, I wanted to meet you and check out your facility—so I got Whitehead's assistant to set it up. And that article in the *Times* last week confirmed my instincts."

He looked me squarely in the eye. "I have an empty thirty-thousand-square-foot space that I think would be a fabulous new home for BoomerWorld."

I was flabbergasted. All seemed to be lost and now, suddenly, I was in the catbird seat.

"So, what do you say?" asked Nate.

I gulped hard. "Obviously, I'm intrigued, but to tell you the truth, after over fifteen years, I'm pretty burned out on the whole Boomer thing. It's been a long slog."

"Forget the past, Bob."

"I live in the past. It's my job."

"Believe me, I'll make it worth your while." Nate stroked his chin. "The fact is, BoomerWorld meshes perfectly with my target demographic for Silver Shores. It's a great fit and you're the right guy to take it to the next level. It could be a 'win-win' for both of us."

That old Clash song "Should I Stay or Should I Go" started to cycle through my head. Little did Nate know that I was about as sober and solvent as Otis from *The Andy Griffith Show*.

Deciding to play a little hard-to-get in order to drive up his offer, I said, "I don't know, Nate. I was actually looking forward to just liquidating the assets and riding off into the sunset."

"Sunset? No, no, no. It's the dawn of a new day for you—and BoomerWorld! But first, I have a few questions."

"Hit me with your best shot!"

"I understand most of these artifacts are on consignment to you, correct?"

I nodded.

"Do you think you can convince the owners to extend their agreements if the museum is moved to my new venue in Arizona?"

"Probably. I have good relationships with most of them. I also know other collectors who would like get involved. Since there is limited space here I had to turn them away."

"Great! The goal would be to keep the basic museum intact, but there will be a lot more room to expand the collections and add more architectural and design flourishes to give visitors an even better experience… Another question: Do you have the digital files for the giant mural and paperwork for all the licensed and copyrighted images?"

"Yes, all the designs are on hard drives. And I have all the agreements and contracts in my office."

"Okay, let's cut to the chase: You agree to sell me the name BoomerWorld, all the existing graphics and any other intellectual property you've developed, plus all the Boomer items you personally own. Starting tomorrow, you will commit to a one-year contract to work with my people to immediately break down and move everything to Silver Shores. Working with my attorneys, you will extend the current consignment contracts and make sure all legal matters are in order. You'll coordinate with my design teams, lighting experts, etc. to expand the entire exhibit to make it a jaw-dropping attraction. We'll build new displays, cases and graphics."

Nate paused. "Also, we need even more Boomer memorabilia. I want you to buy every mint-condition Boomer-era artifact available. Since music and media are such an integral part of the Baby Boom narrative, let's display more music-related items, classsic TV and movie costumes and props. Anything and everything! And I don't care what it costs. For instance, we should be having this conversation under the original Cone of Silence!"

"Yeah, but we wouldn't be able to understand anything we were saying. We'd just be yelling at each other."

"Good point," he laughed. "Find it! Buy it!"

No wonder this guy was a billionaire. He had a laser-like ability to drill down on facts quickly, confidence in his decisions, and of course, the big money to get anything done. I was starting to get genuinely excited at the prospect of BoomerWorld becoming a premiere museum.

"When everything is in place, we'll throw a huge grand opening party!"

"Hey, maybe we can bring back The Hey Judes for an encore performance," I said.

Nate frowned. "Forget that. We'll get the *real* Beatles to put on a concert for us—Paul McCartney and Ringo Starr. I know them. That will really boost the publicity for Silver Shores!"

Nate cut to the chase. "Here's the deal: You do everything I just outlined and I'll give you an immediate hundred-thousand-dollar signing bonus and pay you $10,000 per month in salary for the next year. And if things go smoothly and I'm happy with the finished, new-and-improved BoomerWorld, I'll give you another hundred-thousand-dollar bonus. Plus, you can live rent-free in one of my luxury homes at Silver Shores. After that, we can discuss a longer term deal if you want, or you can 'ride off into the sunset.' It's your choice… That's a damn good offer, Bob, and a great opportunity to make Boomerworld a world-class venue. What do you say?"

Somebody pinch me! Half an hour ago, I was a dead man walking—believing I was about to either die in a hail of gunfire or a bomb blast, courtesy of Mad Matt, the unhinged tunnel rat. Plus, I've been depressed for months, believing I'd spend the rest of my life dumpster-diving in some obscure trailer park.

I had no choice but to accept, right?

Of course, my money problems would be over, but what about my budding relationship with Liz? How would she react? But first, I still had to confess my deceit regarding the insurance hoax. She could easily kick me to the curb and walk out of my life forever…

Then it hit me: If I had to choose—I'd rather be broke and in love.

"It's an incredibily generous offer, Nate. And I want to accept; however, I need to discuss it with someone before I can make a decision. It's complicated."

"I completely understand."

"However, if I'm able to work things out, there are a couple of things I need."

"Name it."

"First, I'll transfer every Boomer item I personally own, except for one."

"And what's that?"

"An autographed baseball from 'Fastball Frost.'"

"Yes, I saw it out there in one of the display cases in the Sports section."

"Fred gave the ball to me as a gift, right before he passed away. However, it really belongs in the Baseball Hall of Fame. That would mean a lot to his daughter."

"Sure. By the way, I have a large collection of expensive baseball memorabilia too, which we'll put on display." He shook his head. "You know, when I went away to college my Mom threw out my entire baseball card collection."

"Bummer!"

"That really pissed me off! I vowed to make a ton of money so one day I could buy whatever I wanted. A few years ago, I paid a fortune for a primo Mickey Mantle rookie card. It's one of my most cherished possessions. Next, I want that famous T-206 Honus Wagner card."

"I guess sometimes fate has to kick you in the ass." Adjusting my bow tie, I continued, "I have one more request. Do you still own that national chain of retail stores called Guitar Galaxy?"

"Yes. We sell more guitars, drums, keyboards, mixers, mics and amplifers than anyone. Why?"

"Well, some of my current staff, four guys in a punk rock band called Toe Jam, got all their stuff stolen last night. They're devastated."

"Well, if you're asking me if I'll replace their instruments and equipment, it's no problem." He made a quick note on his smartphone. "I'll have one of my people contact the manager of our store in Santa Monica tomorrow and set it up."

"I appreciate it."

Nate added, "Actually, I was in a heavy metal band in college. We called ourselves *Hell Hole*. Essentially, it was a tribute band for every metal group at the time: *Black Sabbath, Judas Priest, Iron Maiden, The Scorpions,* you name it. Of course, it was all about getting laid."

"Still is."

As we exited the room into the hallway, Nate handed me a plain white business card. No name, title or address, just a telephone number and email address. "If it's a go, this is how to reach me."

We shook hands. "I'll contact you tomorrow."

In the distance, we could hear the band cranking out "Lucy in the Sky with Diamonds."

I shook my head. "You know, this is all so bizarre. I feel like a real hypocrite. Here I am holding a wake for BoomerWorld while we're talking about relaunching the venue a year from now."

Nate contemplated the situation. "Let's keep everything under wraps until we get all the pieces in place. Then my public relations firm will work their magic… Here's a suggestion: Save the contact information for everyone here tonight. We'll invite them all to the grand opening—free of charge. We might even entice some of them to move to Silver Shores, too!"

The guy was already thinking a year ahead. No wonder he was fabulously wealthy.

"Well, I should go find the Senator and hit the road," said Nate. "Let's talk soon."

10:15 p.m.

"Peaceful Easy Feeling"

Still stunned from my interaction with Nate Katz, I walked out the front door of the museum to get some fresh air. Standing at the top of the steps, I watched the parking attendants that worked for Carla's Catering Company scurry around, retrieving the cars for a small line of guests waiting on the sidewalk.

I walked over to my VW van parked near the bottom of the staircase. The double-side doors were still open to reveal the staged hippie setting within. The velvet rope strung between the doors as a barrier was in place, but of course, the bag of oregano I left on the small table near the giant glued-down bong was long gone. I closed the van's doors, crawled into the driver's seat and shut off the music tape.

For a few minutes, I sat there in the dark. As I tried to mentally process everything that happened over the long evening, I saw a black stretch limo pull up to the curb. Senator Whitehead, his wife, Ms. Cummings, and Nate Katz emerged from the museum and walked to the waiting car. They all seemed to be in good spirits, talking and laughing among themselves. After Nate handed a hundred-dollar bill to the parking attendant, they were whisked off into the night.

I locked up the van, went back inside and made another loop through the museum, touching base with each member of my staff. I reminded them to meet me in my office at 11:30 for a quick, final meeting.

Out in the party area, The Hey Judes were playing their last set—songs from *Abbey Road* and *Let It Be*. The crowd had thinned out. I looked around for Booker and his dates, The Three Stooges, Sarah and Julie, and good 'ol Matt, but they were all gone. They probably left while I was talking with Nate.

As I walked over near the stage, I saw the DJ mingling with a few partygoers. He saw me and casually broke off the conversation. Since the decibel level was rather high as the band belted out "Get Back," we walked behind the stage to talk.

"So how did the rest of the auction go?" I asked.

"Fabulous! Had a blast!" he said, pulling a wad of cash from his pocket. He handed it to me. "There's two grand there."

"Good job, my man!" I peeled off two hundred dollars and handed it to him. "Here's your ten-percent cut as agreed. And thanks again for your work the last two nights. Carla will be paying you."

"The pleasure is all mine," he said as he pocketed the bills. "Well, I guess I'll pack up all my equipment and split. Good luck!"

Circling back to the front of the stage, The Hey Judes segued into playing "Here Comes the Sun." I was familiar with the band's playlist and knew they closed their final set with some other mellow songs like "Across the Universe," and finally the encore, "Imagine."

I ordered a Scotch from the bartender. Carla came over, removing her headset. "How are you, Bob?"

"Actually, things are going very, very well."

She motioned to the bartender to pour her a glass of white wine. "This must be bittersweet for you," she said, her eyes moving over the party scene. "You know, the final minutes of BoomerWorld."

Per my agreement with Nate Katz, I didn't want to say anything about the museum rising from the ashes like the great Phoenix (ironically, just outside of Phoenix). Instead, I said, "It's all good. And as usual, you and your crew did an excellent job."

I held up my drink to salute her. We clinked glasses. "Cheers!"

"When do you want to settle up?" I asked.

"How about tomorrow? My people will pack up all the tables, chairs, bars, stage, etc. in the morning so let's meet in your office around noon. I'll have the final accounting ready," she said. "And you'll be pleased to know the bars have generated more cash than we expected."

I had to admit it was getting better, a little better all the time.

10:50 p.m.

"All Right Now"

The only thing missing from this truly remarkable evening was Liz. I was hoping she would have arrived by now since I was looking forward to having that "last dance" with her.

Circling the periphery of the dance floor, I saw many Boomer couples swaying to the final Beatles' songs. but she was nowhere to be seen. And then 'I saw her standing there,' knocking at my trailer door.

"Glad you could make it," I said, opening the gate.

She turned to face me. "Sorry. I wanted to come earlier, but it's been another long, long day."

"Well, you look great." She was wearing a tailored black pants suit that accentuated her figure in all the right ways. "And you're right on time for the last dance."

The Hey Judes finished their last song together and the crowd clapped politely. All the band members left the stage, except for the John Lennon lookalike. He sat down at the electric piano and began to play "Imagine."

I held out my hand to Liz. "Pretty please."

She smiled. "You really are a piece of work, P.T."

"I think you mean 'pièce de résistance,'" I said with a French accent.

She rolled her eyes. "You're incorrigible, but like black mold, you're growing on me."

"How sweet," I said as I led her out onto the dance floor.

As we slow danced cheek-to-cheek, her hair smelled like lavender, her body was warm and inviting.

"After tonight, I guess I can't call you 'P.T.' anymore now that BoomerWorld is past tense," she whispered in my ear.

"Not so fast, my dear! I have some big news to share with you later."

"Can you give me a hint now?"

"Are you still thinking about quitting your job?"

"Yes. I decided today that I'm giving notice tomorrow. I'm ready for a big change in my life."

"How do you feel about Arizona?"

"Why? I thought your dream was to drive up the coast with your Airstream."

"Yeah, but something else just came up."

"Sounds interesting."

"There are a few other things we need to talk about. Can you hang out in my trailer while I meet with the staff and lock up?"

"Sure. I wouldn't mind laying down for a while. I'm exhausted."

We danced slowly, enjoying the final melodic strains of the classic Lennon song. Then the rest of The Hey Judes came out for a group bow as the remaining crowd warmly applauded.

The lights dimmed and the party was officially over.

"Money"

As Carla's catering team and my staff scrambled to close up, I escorted Liz back to my trailer and then headed to the lobby to send the remaining partygoers on their way. Several of my friends from town lingered near the front door, wanting to wish me well. I graciously thanked them and promised to be in touch.

After all the remaining guests were herded out, I popped into the gift shop to check in with Mona. The room was practically stripped bare. The leftover swag could fit in a couple boxes. Mona was behind the cash register counting up the day's proceeds.

"You did a superb job, Mona!"

"Thanks, Bob." She slid the stacks of bills into the cash bag and handed it to me. "Today we brought in $6,295. That makes the two-day total just shy of $12,000."

"Excellent! Right on budget!"

At 11:30, Mona and I walked through the lobby towards my office. We bid farewell to Carla and the rest of her crew and locked the front door behind them. Since I had already cut a check to The Hey Judes before the gig, they had quickly packed up and left too. Courtney, Mick and the rest of the guys were waiting for our final meeting. Everyone looked fatigued and ready to go home.

I decided to keep it short and sweet. After depositing the cash bag from the gift shop in the safe beside my desk, I faced them all. "I know the hours were extra-long and you had to work late the last few days, but you all did a great job. Your checks will be ready to be picked up tomorrow afternoon around four o'clock." I reached into my pocket and pulled out the wad of cash from the auction. "And as promised, here's a little bonus." Since my financial woes were now a thing of the past, I was feeling very magnanimous. I handed $250 to everyone. They were all grateful but the mood was still glum.

"Thanks, boss," said Mick. "This will help us get some new equipment for the band."

The other guys nodded.

"Oh, there's one more thing. Did you guys happen to see the gentleman who was here tonight with Senator Whitehead."

"You mean the short dude in the expensive threads?" asked Keith.

"His name is Nate Katz."

No one in the room had a clue who he was.

"That guy was passing out huge tips like crazy," said Ronnie. "He gave one of the waiters a C-note just for bringing him a glass of champagne."

Charlie shook his head. "Rich fucker!"

"But a very *nice* rich fucker," I said, pausing to get their full attention. "Are you guys familiar with Guitar Galaxy?"

They all nodded.

"Well, Mr. Katz owns it and when I told him about the theft, he agreed to replace everything you lost. Free of charge."

"No, frickin' way!" screamed Mick, grabbing his shaggy head in disbelief.

An exuberant Keith shouted, "You 'The Man'!"

After I slapped hands with the entire band, Toe Jam came together for a group hug. Even Mona couldn't suppress a small smile.

"Drive My Car"

After everyone filed out the front door, I locked up and made a quick sweep through the museum. Everything seemed to be in order. As I approached the side double doors, I saw Tank inside the velvet ropes shining the Batmobile with a special buffing cloth the owner's handlers had left to keep the car spiffy and dust free.

"Hey, Tank! How's it goin'?"

"Good evening, Mr. Apple! Things are going great," he replied, polishing one of the chrome engine exhaust pipes sticking up behind the car seats. "Just giving Batman's ride a little tender loving care."

"Looks good."

"The TV series was pretty corny, but I love this car."

"Corny?! It was a masterpiece!" I declared in a last blast of Boomer pomposity. "The witty dialogue, colorful characters and brilliant choreography were breathtaking, especially the fight scenes! The Dynamic Duo smashing balsa wood chairs over the heads of the evil henchmen of The Joker, The Penguin and Catwoman—punctuated by those big graphic explosions: 'Kapow! Zap! Crack! Crunch! Bonk!' It was a comic book brought to life."

Tank shook his head. "I prefer *The Dark Knight*. It's a lot more realistic."

"Trust me: 'Realism' is overrated," I said.

In our early years, Boomers lived in a world where innocence reigned, wholesome values prevailed and the good guys always won. Who wants realism when you can live in a fantasy world, right?

"Thanks for doing a good job the last few nights, Tank. You were one of my key ambassadors—keeping a close eye on the Batmobile, interacting well with the guests, and watching the Senator's back as he worked the crowd earlier this evening."

"It's been a fun gig."

I reached into my pocket and pulled out the remaining three-hundred dollars from the auction proceeds. Handing it all to Tank, I said, “There’s a two-hundred-dollar tip for you and one hundred for Dudley DoRight on the day shift. Pass it on. But Old Gus doesn’t get a dime ‘cause I caught him sleeping on the job last night.”

“Sorry, sir,” said Tank. “You should have smashed one of those balsa wood chairs over his head.”

“I doubt it would’ve woken him up.”

I checked my watch: 11:55pm. Old Gus would show up at any second and I really didn’t want to interact with him.

“Anyway, I gotta run.” I said.

We shook hands and I walked back to my trailer.

Midnight

“Two Tickets to Paradise”

Liz was asleep on the couch, but the creaking metallic front door woke her.

“Sorry.”

“Just dozing,” she said wearily, sitting up, adjusting her hair and clothes. “How are you?”

“I feel pretty damn good!”

She rubbed the sleep from her eyes. “Really. That’s a big change… Does it have to do with that mysterious ‘big news’ you mentioned on the dancefloor?”

I nodded and sat down beside her. Walter was sound asleep next to the couch, snoring loudly with his legs sticking up in the air.

“Well, what’s the big news?”

I nervously tapped my knees with my palms. “Before we get to that, we need to have a little chat about something else.”

“Sounds ominous,” she said, sipping a water bottle.

Gently, I placed my hand on her arm. “I want you to know that last night was wonderful. I have been thinking about you all day and want to spend more time with you but, umm… first, I have a confession to make."

She sat up, folded her arms and waited.

"There's no good way to say it—I lied to you… The whole insurance thing was a sham. I know it's a violation of my lease with the bank, but to tell you the truth, I haven't been able to afford comprehensive liability insurance for years. And when you kept pressuring me to see the paperwork, I tried to stall until after this weekend was over," I said, hanging my head in shame. "I got an old friend named Pete Pendergast to pose as my insurance agent… I'm so, so sorry to have deceived you."

She sat there in silence, letting me slowly twist in the wind.

"I was wrong and I hope you'll forgive me."

Liz continued to give me the silent treatment as I ramped up my mea culpa, with more pleading and groveling. After a few minutes, she let a small smile slip cross her lips. "I knew it was totally contrived."

"What?!"

"While doing my due diligence, I called your so-called 'agent.' We spoke briefly and he assured me that you were fully insured."

"Yeah, old Pete can be very persuasive," I said. "He told me the conversation went well."

"Actually," she sighed, "there was one problem."

"Really?"

"Initially, he seemed legit, but there was something about his voice that bothered me."

"He does have some amazing pipes."

"Precisely. After we hung up, I remembered that voice from radio and TV commercials for a large bank I used to work for." She gave me a dubious look. "And given your advertising background, I smelled a big, fat rat."

I wanted to crawl into a hole.

"Consequently, I called the national office of your alleged

insurance carrier to find out if the policy was still valid. They confirmed it had been cancelled a long time ago."

"Again, I'm truly sorry, Liz. Back when this all started, I didn't know you as a person. You were just a faceless banker that I only talked to on the phone. You saw all my financial statements. Clearly, I've been on the verge of insolvency for years and I was scrambling to stay afloat… Still, that's no excuse. I crossed the line and I'm ashamed of myself."

Struggling to lighten the mood, I turned my palms up and said, "Looks like I've entered the pantheon of the Biggest Liars of All Time: Benedict Arnold, Bill Clinton, Jon Lovitz."

Liz leaned back into the couch and gave me a long, stony stare. "Yeah, *that's* the ticket."

As I mumbled my deepest regrets and begged for forgiveness, I realized that short of someone hotwiring the Batmobile for a joy ride late tonight, there had been no injuries, damages, potential claims or threatened lawsuits. "Anyway, in the final analysis, it looks like I didn't need the coverage after all."

"Perhaps not," Liz said. "However, the bank can't take any risks with liability. After clearing it with my boss, we placed the property under our corporate insurance umbrella to play it safe."

I bowed my head. "Thank you."

She continued, "You know, if you had told me the truth from the beginning, we could have easily resolved this matter without all the shenanigans."

"You're right. I feel like a real schmuck."

"And you also should know that if you hadn't told me about your deceit, I was going to walk out of here tonight and never see you again."

She sipped her water bottle again. "I've cut you a lot of slack, P.T., because you were kind to my father and, after seeing you interact with Sarah and Julie, I could tell that you weren't a complete asshole."

Asshole? ... Moi? ... Well, maybe she does have a point.

I cleared my throat. "Do you accept my apology?"

At long last, she relented. "Okay, okay. You're forgiven. Now, tell me what's going on."

She listened carefully to my animated recap of the meeting with Nate Katz. After I finished, she said, "That's incredible! Did you accept?"

"It seemed like an offer I couldn't refuse. And let's face it, it's a helluva lot better than finding Walter's head in my bed. But no, I didn't accept. I wanted to talk to you first. That's why I asked you how you felt about Arizona. Now that you're leaving the bank, I want you to come with me. It can be a new start for both of us."

Looking away, I could tell she wasn't convinced yet. I didn't blame her. I was hardly Prince Valiant, just an impulsive douche bag who just won the lottery. Still, I wasn't about to give up.

"Remember that TV show called *Queen for a Day?*"

"Yes. My mother watched it when I was a little girl."

"The host, Jack Bailey, would always say 'all women should be queens every single day.' Well, you can be a queen for an entire year! You deserve a break from the drudgery of the banking world. I'll be making plenty of money and we'll have a beautiful, free place to live. When you're not sunbathing, you can take up some new hobbies like golf, yoga, and welcoming me home every day after work, dressed in a negligee and holding a tray of martinis."

"That's your fantasy, not mine," she replied. "I have always supported myself and have no intention of playing the role of some hausfrau."

As usual, I was acting like a selfish jerk, fixating on my good fortune while Liz was still coping with her father's death, worried about her future professional life, and probably wondering how she could kick me to the curb.

While Liz contemplated things, I counted my blessings. If Nate Katz hadn't made me such an incredible offer, I could easily have ended up drinking Night Train under a freeway overpass. And the biggest irony of all: I built BoomerWorld as a tribute to my late wife.

Over the last fifteen years, I never believed I would meet anyone to replace Amy. And then Elizabeth Frost walked into my life.

Down deep, I knew we were meant to be together. I needed to show her I could be sensitive, caring, and supportive. I took her hands in mine and looked into her eyes. "I know this is all very sudden, but the truth is, I think… uhh… I'm falling in love with you."

She smiled.

Bungling along, I squeezed her hands tighter. "Look, I know it's not the right time to bring this all up. You probably need more time and space to think about things. But if you want to take our relationship to the next level, I'll do anything you want, including blowing off the Silver Shores deal, and—"

Liz pulled me close and said, "I guess I can still call you P.T. after all."

Then she gave me a long, deep kiss.

And yes… We lived happily ever after…

“Runnin’ Down a Dream”

July 30, 2021

Dear Boomers,

Hey, we all want a "happy-ending" right? All those old black and white TV shows we watched as kids always ended on a positive note—so why not this book?... As the TV credits began to roll, the world was in total harmony. A perfect, well-adjusted family sat on the couch together, smiling at the camera. Even dogs and cats coexisted, happy and well-fed. And it was all followed up with a big sloppy kiss from the sponsors.

As originally conceived, this memoir was meant to be an entertaining overview of the Baby Boom. Instead, it degenerated into a petty, self-serving narrative—a barely coherent collection of crazy characters and rants that should be relegated to a buried bookcase in the far back corner of some hoarder's basement. Using yet another feeble analogy: you may have expected *Citizen Kane*, but ended up getting *Howard The Duck*.

"Sorry about that, Chief!"

Unfortunately for you, my dear readers, I still have a few things to get off my chest; hence, this glorious screed has one final curtain call:

First, a lot has happened over the last eighteen months. After I accepted Nate Katz's offer to relocate BoomerWorld, Liz and I packed up and moved to the Silver Shores retirement community in Arizona in late November 2019. We took up residence in a beautiful rent-free home and began a new life. We felt like the lucky recipients of a big check from John Beresford Tipton on that classic 1950s TV show, *The Millionaire*.

While I worked on the new and improved museum, Liz got a nice gig as the manager of a local community bank. Everything was going great, that is until Chairman Xi and his conniving ChiComs allowed a lethal virus to spread across the globe. COVID-19 was cooked up in a state-controlled research lab—not some wet market where bats and pangolins are the daily specials. It completely screwed up the world: killing millions of people, destroying our economy and causing the U.S.

National Debt Clock to spin faster than a stoned flower child at a Grateful Dead concert. ($30,000,000,000,000 and counting!)

As the pandemic got worse and our country was shut down, BoomerWorld's planned relaunch (originally set for January 1, 2021) was put on hold indefinitely.

Meanwhile, after the 2016 "Election from Hell," we were treated to another five-alarm dumpster fire on November 3, 2020. Rehashing all the specifics of that election boondoggle is about as appealing as shaking hands with Jeffrey Toobin—so I won't be commenting... However, after having four Boomers elected president (Clinton, Bush, Obama and Trump), how the hell did we end up with old Joe Biden? "C'mon, man!" The butter slid off his pancake a long time ago. Plus, the guy is older than the Baby Boom itself! Even 'Corn Pop' is scratching his head in disbelief. *(BTW: Where's that Kraken?)*

Anyway, as our freckles turn into liver spots, we obsess about the weather, sit on our overstuffed couches and watch the steady decline of America on our giant flat screen TVs. And what a spectacle it is! Our politics are marinated in tribalism, intersectionality, gender-fluid sexuality, virtue signaling and something called "covfefe." Everyone is yelling at each other and the din is deafening. Generally, there continues to be a lack of basic civility and thoughtful conversation in our political discourse. The erosion of our First Amendment rights by the progressive social media authoritarians and the emergence of "cancel culture" are very troubling. Plus, we've got wide open borders, a massive crime wave, poorly educated K-12 students, trillions of dollars in new bureaucratic spending, and more lying and incompetence in Washington D.C. than ever. The comparisons between America and the fall of the Roman Empire are undeniable. The only things missing are the lead goblets. Meanwhile, the usual suspects like Putin, Assad, the Taliban, the mullahs in Iran and "Dr. Evil" lurch around on the bloody international stage—while China quietly takes over the world.

As Boomers slowly relinquish the reins of power and slip into retirement, we have plenty of time to pop open a bottle of Blue Nun and reminisce. So many of the fond memories that defined our generation have slipped away: Watching cartoons on Saturday morning and westerns all afternoon. Vacationing at the original Magic Kingdom. Eating grilled cheese sandwiches and tomato soup on chilly winter days. Comparing our smallpox vaccination scars. Gazing at astronauts hitting golf balls on the moon. Leatherface chasing around teenagers with a bloody chainsaw. *It was magic!*

Yes, Boomers love to romanticize the past. So many of the things we grew up with are being phased out and forgotten. No one will really miss elevator operators, home milk deliveries, soap-on-a-rope, phone books and clip-on ties, or the inevitable demise of land-line telephones and the post office.

Nostalgia is the ultimate drug for us, but things change. Remember Candy Stripers? Lots of our mothers and sisters used to dress in pink-and-white striped pinafores and volunteer at local hospitals to cheer up patients and help the staff. It was such a wholesome enterprise—but now, *Candy Stripers* is better known as an X-rated movie. And it doesn't stop there: The Fuller Brush Man knocked up the Avon Lady and moved into a double-wide in Rio Linda. Mister Rogers' Neighborhood has become a haven for MS-13 gang bangers. Dirty Harry is "feelin' lucky" at tonight's bingo game at the rest home. And most disturbing of all: Elon Musk and Mark Zuckerberg don't even wear pocket protectors? *It's all very suspicious...*

Of course, there are countless analogies and jokes about getting old and senile, but I can only remember a few. The brains of Boomers are slow, because we know so much. It's science... Just like a computer freezes when the hard drive gets full or there are too many apps open, it takes us longer to process information and understand complicated technology like quantum physics, smartphones or how to open jars. It's time to face facts: We're all starting to lose it. Exactly how ancient are we? Well, iGens think Millennials are old.

"First you forget names, then you forget faces, then you forget to pull your zipper up, then you forget to pull your zipper down."
– Leo Rosenberg

At our advanced age, dementia is our new wingman. Walking into a bathroom and remembering why you're there is a minor miracle. Experiencing "nocturnal emissions" now means drooling on your pillow. And if some government bureaucrat tells you "It's time for your nap"—grab your walker and move towards the light. *Your number is up, babe.*

To get a better idea of the status of Boomers from a purely Darwinian perspective—consider the wildebeest. You've seen those wildlife shows on TV hosted by Marlin Perkins: the giant herds of animals roaming the sunbaked African Serengeti as danger and death encroaches from all sides. The younger, stronger wildebeests (or Millennials and iGens for this comparison) are concentrated in the safe center of the pack while the slightly older animals (Gen Xers) push the elderly, diseased and injured creatures (Boomers) to the periphery – where ravenous lions, jackals and hyenas patiently wait for lunch. *It doesn't end well.*

Freed from the youthful scourge of acne, school, curfew, and fear of pregnancy, now we can focus on what really counts: our failing health, injuring ourselves while sleeping, trying to reach down and tie our shoes, and affixing a fresh set of tennis balls onto the back legs of our walkers. *(Personally, I prefer using Wilson Tennis Balls but you may prefer the Penn Championship brand. It's really a "toss-up.")* Yet, despite all the aches and pains, diabetes and obesity, erectile dysfunction, diminished mental acuity and chronic diaper rash, getting older is still a privilege. Life should be enjoyed as much as possible. Like Maurice Chevalier said, *"Old age isn't so bad when you consider the alternative."*

On the bright side, Boomers are the most active and physically fit generation ever—and we're living longer. Most of us have plenty of time to post our latest colonoscopy video on Facebook, learn how to open an email attachment or spend the day restocking our pill boxes with all the essentials like blood pressure, cholesterol, incontinence and anti-anxiety tablets – plus, a double dosage of memory meds. We used to play with marbles, but now we're obsessed with keeping them.

The reality is: no one really cares what seniors do or say. We're practically invisible. Our tolerance for stupidity and ignorance decreases with age. Every time some idiot says or does something stupid or cruel, we say whatever we want. No one is really listening anyway... And we're not going to live forever, so why waste time standing in lines, lamenting what could have been or worrying about what will be. Once people start calling you "ma'am" or "sir," you're over the hill. Just try to enjoy the trip—singing along to "American Pie" as you waddle toward the Great Void.

As the world devolves into a super-sized shitshow, young people are getting more depressed about the future, retreating deeper into their 5G-powered fantasy worlds. Let's hope they won't blame Boomers for the entire mess, because they'll be taking care of us during our twilight years at the old folk's home. While you're lying on the cold bathroom floor, screaming "I've fallen and can't get up," don't be surprised if your young "caregiver" can't even hear you. Sitting right outside the door with their expensive earbuds paired with their smartphones, they'll be floating in The Cloud—streaming music, playing games, and sexting their friends.

Look, I'm not an expert about anything, but I've learned a few important life lessons from fellow Boomers. Here are a few key things to "try" to remember:

1. What to Tell Your Children About Your Past: Beware! If you have kids or grandkids, particularly young teenagers, they'll surprise you with questions about your own past when you're lecturing them to save their money, the evils of drug and alcohol consumption, and sexual activity. Remind them that you've lived an exemplary life worthy of sainthood and then quickly change the subject. (And the last thing you want to discuss is your brief stay at the Spahn Ranch in L.A. back in the late 1960s.) If pressed for any details, act like every politician caught in a lie: *"Deny, deny, deny—until you die."*

2. <u>A Short Guide to School Reunions</u>: Don't go! Unless you're wealthy and look fabulous, it's going to be a disaster... After so many years, time has taken a toll on your old friends and acquaintances—physically, mentally and emotionally. The once god-like captain of the football team and prom king is now a washed-up, alcoholic, ex-construction worker with bad knees. That buxom head cheerleader you used to dream about can now play soccer with her boobs and can't remember the names of her grandchildren... You'll also hear sad stories about old classmates who are disabled, dying or dead, can't remember their Social Security number or still live under their parent's sink... So—avoid reunions at all costs or you'll be depressed for months.

3. <u>Dating Tips for Boomers</u>: First, lower your expectations! Face facts: You're old and your new significant other will probably be old too. That is, unless you are rich enough to afford a young gigolo or trophy wife—or both. Second, there's a high probability you'll have to rely on one of those online dating sites to find anyone crazy enough to hang out with you. Sand is slipping rapidly through the hour glass so don't waste precious time. Tell the truth on your personal profile and post a photo of the real you <u>now</u>, not some glamour shot from twenty years ago. Third, understand that dating can be a frustrating experience. After decades in the trenches of life, our bullshit detectors are set on high. Boomers' tolerance levels for idle chitchat and superficiality are low. If there's an immediate attraction or connection to someone on any level—go for it. If not, be ready with some clever excuse like: "Sorry, gotta run! I don't want that fresh corpse to spoil." Lastly, the odds of finding someone (anyone) are good. Boomers continue to divorce more than any other age group so there's a big pool of seniors looking for companionship. However, if you do find a new mate, don't be in any rush to co-mingle your finances—unless you're a deadbeat and your new partner just won MegaMillions... And if you are married, you can always go for a "Silver Separation"—the latest lifestyle idea for Boomers. You get to keep all of your toys and save face at family gatherings, but you live separately, making it easier to snore, burp and fart without your spouse scolding you.

4. Giving Back: Boomers are very generous—creating and funding thousands of charities, NGOs and nonprofit organizations to combat disease, poverty, disabilities, save animals and the environment. Raising money for good causes takes many forms. From the tame ('The Ice Bucket Challenge' and 'Date a Famous Actor') to the lame ('Donate a Toy – Get a Lap Dance' and 'Be a Dear and Donate a Brassiere'), Boomers will do some wild'n'crazy things for charity. Crowdfunding sites like Kickstarter and GoFundMe feature many reputable causes, but in this shameful digital age, there are plenty of stupid scams to lighten your wallet, like sponsoring the World's Largest Jockstrap, Anti-Zombie Soap, Help Me Fix My Yacht, and the timeless Nigerian Prince email hustle. If you want to change lives for the better—get involved and work hard to make a difference. Remember: You can change the world! Well, probably not, but it's more gratifying than watching reruns of *Manimal, The P.T.L. Club* or *Celebrity Boxing.*

5. Boomer Book Clubs: The thrill of reading books about Boomers and how they have made the world a better place is a national sensation! *(Just ask any Boomer.)* As thousands of these book clubs spring up across the country, it would be wise to purchase multiple copies of *BoomerWorld* for friends, family and yes, even younger generations who thirst for brilliant prose, profound insights and revisionist history... While the men cluster around the BBQ, drinking heavily and telling lame jokes, the women (who actually read books) can discuss, debate and praise *BoomerWorlds'* deep historical and philosophical narratives.

6. "Less cowbell!"

Well, that's about it. I'm happy and grateful for everything I have...

My best bud Booker is visiting for a few days. In fact, we went to a Diamondbacks/Dodgers' game today. I found myself thinking about the late, great "Fastball" Frost. I'm sure he was smiling down from above—but the Dodgers lost anyway...

Walter and Big Al are passed out on the floor... And Liz is floating in the pool. She needs another Mai Tai so I should sign off.

Oh, I almost forgot: I'm now living on the cutting edge of high tech! As you know, I've always been a luddite, but after my ancient flip phone finally broke, I upgraded to a Jitterbug. It's pretty complicated for my shriveled Boomer brain, but I'll eventually figure it out.

Sincerely,

Bob Apple

Acknowledgements

Heartfelt thanks to my family, friends and fellow Boomers who have supported me as this novel evolved over the last few years.

There are countless articles, websites, PDFs, blogs and videos floating around on the Internet about the Baby Boom. Much of that content can be terrifying for younger generations—so please handle with care…

Before you email or text a funny meme that mocks a Millennial, iGen or Labradoodle, remember that virtually everything you think is interesting or humorous can be an insensitive microaggression on some whippersnapper's fragile ego.

"Okay, Boomer?"

About The Author

Robert Q. Apple III was born in Los Angeles in 1952. In high school, Apple was an average student but excelled in extra-curricular activities, serving as President of the Checkers Club as well as organizing many weekend kegger parties. *(Note: Apple claims to have invented the Beer Bong, but the USPTO has no record of it.)* When he was rejected by Harvard, Yale and West Covina Junior College, he decided to enter the work force. His father pulled a few strings and Apple landed a coveted job at Grayson Moorhead Securities, where he was briefly in charge of "The List"—that is, until he misplaced it and was abruptly fired. In 1980, after flunking out of McDonalds' Hamburger University in Oak Brook, IL, Apple started to sell used cars in Burbank. Within three short years, he mastered the art of placing classified ads and eventually opened his own business, Apple Advertising, specializing in retail automotive clients, funeral homes and nail salons. Over the next fifteen years, his creative skills and media buying expertise became legendary throughout the ad community of Southern California. In 1998, Apple Advertising was recognized as one of the "Top 500 Agencies" by *AutoTrader Times*. He retired from advertising in 2000 to care for his ailing wife. From 2004-2019, Apple managed BoomerWorld in Venice Beach, CA, before it was relocated to the Silver Shores Retirement Community in Arizona.

Email: RobertApple1952@yahoo.com

Made in the USA
Las Vegas, NV
29 October 2021